Love
&
Vengeance

The Gladiators, Book 1

Gina Danna

Copyright © 2015 Gina Danna

Love & Vengeance
Media > Books > Fiction > Historical Romance
Category/Tags: Historical Fiction, Ancient Rome, Gladiators, Slave

Cover design and Interior format by The Killion Group

All rights reserved. The unauthorized reproduction or distribution of this copyrighted work, in whole or part, by any electronic, mechanical, or other means, is illegal and forbidden.

This is a work of fiction. Characters, settings, names, and occurrences are a product of the author's imagination and bear no resemblance to any actual person, living or dead, places or settings, and/or occurrences. Any incidences of resemblance are purely coincidental.

DEDICATION

To my Champion of the Arena, Rich, the Celt who stands Gaul as well, the one who holds my heart and showed how the proper path can set one to purpose. Gratitude, my love.

CHAPTER ONE

Rome 108 CE

A menacing growl followed by an earth-shattering scream bellowed above the rafters. The roar of the crowd snapped her out of the numbness. The applause echoed through the chambers as particles of sand rained through the wood slats in the ceiling.

She was filthy, covered in sweat, blood and grime. What damage could more dirt do? Toes on the dirt floor wiggled as she stared at them. Her hair hung around her face like a curtain, matted with dried blood. Inadvertently, she lifted her hand to tuck one side behind her ear but jerked to a halt, restrained by the iron cuffs around her wrists, bound together with a chain. The same chain connected to the metal collar around her neck. How had she forgotten its weight resting so heavily on her shoulders?

Another scream and the sound of flesh ripping, laughter and clapping became louder above. Fear snaked down her spine and she shuddered.

Gustina sat on the stone ledge, chained with the other miscreants, waiting to be forced up the ramp to the carnage above. If she could just return to the numbness again, where nothing mattered any more. The place she'd escaped to before she'd heard the animals attacking the condemned out there. But she couldn't silence the roar of the crowds enjoying the executions as their noontime entertainment. Trembling, she pulled her sluggish legs up, wrapping her joined hands over them, and buried her face in her knees.

In the hallway outside the chamber, Marcus stood, flexing his muscles, his arm extended with the metal disk in his hand.

It equaled the weight of his sword—a weapon he would not have until it was his turn in the arena. Besides, there was no room in the corridor to swing it, to loosen his arms in preparations for the next fight.

Christians and convicts. What a surly lot. But it was an easy way to feed the vast array of beasts the Empire kept to compete in the games. Did he ever feel sad for the poor souls about to perish by their claws? No. Nor did he mourn the loss of life at the end of his sword.

He was one of the rare attractions people paid to see. He was *gladiator*. And he soon would be victor of all he opposed on the sands. Marcus' victories gave him the privileges and money he wanted—as long as it remained wine and women. But not his freedom. Not what he had lost to the Romans. No, the only way to gain that came by victory in the arena and in front of the Emperor. And to earn that opportunity, he'd kill whomever they placed before him.

He closed his eyes as the screams filtered downward. His soul heard them and his body tingled with the smell of blood and dirt. Breathing in the welcoming atmosphere, he exhaled and opened his lids to look straight into the captives' chamber.

He found her. Sitting, hunched on the small ledge, draped in chains and metal bands, her head down. But when she looked up, through all the muck and grime, her pale blue eyes shone, sparkling and bright. Her unmarred face was a rarity among captives dragged to this place, usually after rough treatment. He noticed her high cheekbones, a small nose, narrow chin but ripe mouth. Her eyes locked on him and his mouth went dry. When her tongue licked her lips, his body tightened.

He had to have her. Period. Regardless if she was a convict, runaway or Christian, he wanted her.

A guard butted past him into the room and yanked the chain, pulling all the captives up. Many moaned, some pleaded. She didn't. She stood straight, pushing her shoulders back, waiting at the end of the line. Her eyes locked on his until the guard turned, chain in hand, to lead them out.

Marcus stepped back. Instantly, his hand went to his stomach guard and pulled the narrow pick-knife out of its hidden sheath. As the captives stumbled past him, he extended his foot, causing her to trip. She fell into his grasp. His free hand placed the knife into the lock and twisted it open. His hand covered it to deaden the noise as his other arm encircled her tiny waist and pulled her against him.

"Not a sound," he whispered. He shoved her to the wall, his massive body hiding hers as he flexed his limbs. The guard stopped at the sound of the loose chain but didn't look far when he saw the gladiator's well-muscled body. Marcus glanced at him over his shoulder and gave the man a nod. His status as a victorious gladiator allowed some privilege. The guard shrugged and moved on. The frightened woman gasped for air and shook with fear.

Quickly he lifted her. She was light, seemingly lighter than his sword, but he knew that couldn't be. In a swift move, he turned. Next to the doorway was a covered alcove. He dropped her in it.

"You'll be safe here." He looked her over. Her wide eyes, full of fear and mistrust, returned his gaze but she said nothing. He heard the gong of his master calling him, reminding him he fought next, after the final execution. "Remain here. I will be back for you." He touched her cheek, his bulky hand swallowing half her face. Her skin was soft, like silk. Back in the days when he wore silk... He banked the anger. With a final nod to her, he left. He knew she'd be there when he returned.

To leave meant death.

CHAPTER TWO

Marcus stood at the gated door to the arena. The roar of the crowd increased as more Romans arrived for the games. After the morning of the lesser-known fighters and the noontime executions, the better gladiators fought. An audience favorite, he knew they'd cheer when he walked out onto the sand. Through the bars, he saw the slaves in the arena. The group of five pulled wooden rakes in an attempt to cleanse the sands of the blood and carnal remains of the executions. He laughed at them. How ludicrous, to clean the grounds only for him to litter it again with the body and blood of his opponent?

As he watched the slaves rotate around the arena floor, the vibrations of the crowds moving in the stands seeped into him, their voices loud. Marcus' mind wandered back to the young woman he saved from death. He frowned. Why had he done it? Despite her filth, she was attractive. But she didn't have that pitying look most Christians wore waiting for their death. If anything, she looked defiant. It made him question the real reason for her being there.

The trumpets blew the music he loved to hear, summoning all for the next round of spectacles. He closed his eyes and inhaled the fumes of dirt and blood with a scent of death. His inner beast danced at the smell. *Kill. And kill again.* The demon inside him rose, snarling with anticipation. Marcus welcomed it as the blood raced furiously through his veins. He vaguely heard the announcer from the perch above ramble about some battle to be recreated next. It was a joke. Marcus slayed his opponents, and his inner demon looked for more. His arms tensed, and his grip on his swords tightened.

The gate opposite him flew open and his prey arrived. Some fool from the provinces, Marcus guessed. The man stood the same height as him. He held the spear and shield of the murmillo style of gladiator. He Marcus snorted. The spear appeared to man a longer arm and beneath the shield, he gripped a gladius sword. As if he'd get the chance to use it. A bronze helmet with a facemask covered the man's head. Thick cloth, covered with a greave of metal on his left shin, wrapped around his leg. A leather casing protected the man's spear arm from a blade while his other hand held a round shield that covered the bare arm and chest.

His demon laughed. Murmillos were easy to kill but he'd toy with this one today and incite the crowd.

In comparison, Marcus preferred the style of dimachaerus. Legs covered with strapped on greaves over battered cloth, his right arm and shoulder were encased in the leather sleeve. Like his opponent, he wore a balteus, a wide tooled-grain belt, around his stomach. Only clothed in a linen subligaculum, or loin cloth, his chest and back exposed to an attack. He had no shield, helmet or facemask. He held a gladius in each hand, the standard swords used by the Legions. Fast and furious, he sought no protection from a blow to his head. In fact, if he died in the arena, that suited him well. But the thought irritated his demon's desire for blood. He flexed his muscles, waiting for the doors to open.

The gates before him swung wide and he stepped into the arena to the roar of the crowd. Marcus flipped the swords in his hands and held them straight above him, revealing a forced grin for the stands. He hated this preening to them but winning the adoration of the crowd would serve its purpose. If he wanted to win a rudis, the wooden sword designating his freedom, he needed to have them cheer for him. And the people did love him. Actually, they loved his demon.

Tingles of excitement raced down his spine as he eyed his opponent. The damn facemask hid the sucker well. He met the man close in the center of the arena and they both turned toward the podium, the seat of the higher officials and guests.

Marcus tuned out the announcer and the magistrate who stood on the podium to signify the fight's start. The volume from the crowd became a low buzz in his head as his grip tightened on the hilt of his weapons. He bowed his head to the dignitary standing above. The crowd silenced.

With a gag, Marcus barely suppressed the urge to laugh. He had been a member of the crowd once, even sat in the podium, placing bets on who'd win the fight and drinking wine with the others as they watched. Later, he stood on the sands, before the same set of seats, sentenced to *damnatus ad gladium*, death by sword, the crowd cheering for his demise. Now they cried his name upon victory in the games. And they would do so today. The standing puppet of Rome gave a hand gesture to commence and Marcus's demon roared.

Gustina stood in the shadows of the alcove, rapidly breathing in gasps of air. Her hands clenched as the corridor emptied. Her heart thudded loudly in fear. She was safe—for the moment. That tall gladiator, the one who freed her from the chain, loomed large before her. She remembered he had sable brown hair, already damp from the heat. His dark walnut colored eyes seemed to see deep into her and that frightened her. He was massive, a wall of muscle and leather. The softness in his voice contradicted his appearance of a feared fighter, his promise to return for her even soothing her frayed nerves.

She shuddered. Back for her? Why?

The silence broke as the mob in the Colosseum yelled. Dirt drifted down from above and the walls of her sanctuary vibrated. Fear snaked down her spine and she shook uncontrollably.

Terror clouded her eyes as scenes from the last five days collected and showed her condemned to this place. *Blood. Blood everywhere. The other house slaves screamed. Gustina held her dead domina, the woman's mouth agape, the poisoned wine spewing out of its corners, her eyes wide open in shock. It didn't matter that she had found the woman already dead—the woman's husband found Gustina holding her and the clay cup of wine in her hand.*

The evidence of that simple gesture, holding the dead woman with no one else around, the reek of death and rotting wine in the air, sealed Gustina's guilt. The dominus claimed she killed his wife, her owner, and sent her with the rest of the house slaves to be executed *damnatus ad bestias*, torn to pieces by animals. The sentence Christians received.

But Gustina suspected her master was the guilty party. Terpio's loss of his senate seat sank the family fortune and his wife, who despised him, turned her vile verbal attacks on him. Without the prestige of being in the Senate, Terpio would lose his purse and his mistress to be stuck with a vindictive wife.

And her body slave, Gustina, was the one who'd found her.

Terpio had grinned at her. Her presence, holding his poisoned wife, cleared any suspicion of him killing her. Only the gods would be this cruel to Gustina, to condemn her prayers to end the nights he called her to his chamber with a death sentence. The nights he used her for his own delight. The sinister gleam in his eyes frightened her down to her bones. It was as if he had planned the entire event and its outcome.

Of course, she couldn't accuse him of killing his wife. No one listened to a slave. As the magistrate gave the verdict, she went numb. Freedom would be hers, but not in the way she prayed for. The end of her life also meant no more slavery and no more submission to a sexually decadent tyrant.

More sand rained on her, returning her to the present. She was free, in the bowels of the Colosseum. The stench of blood and death permeated the air around her, more strongly as each second passed. If they found her, they'd kill her. The yells from the crowd above her rang in the echoes of her memory of fellow slaves, screaming as she held her mistress. They all knew they'd die. The law was simple. One slave kills an owner, all the slaves in the house died. And they all did—except for her.

Her heart raced. That gladiator told her to wait, but how could he save her? He was also a slave. She had to run.

"Hello there."

Squinting through the dust-filled haze, Gustina swallowed. Who was that? Was he talking to her? She leaned farther out and found a man, a slave, standing before her. He was not tall, not even quite her height but he wasn't absurdly short. He was waspishly thin, his head bald and his eyes too big for his gaunt face. He had a devious curve to his lips that frightened her. She had little room but still tried to dart away.

"Whoa, there," the man's hand grabbed her wrist. His

fingers clamped onto her bruised skin and she winced. "I'm here to help you. Marcus sent me."

She frowned. Marcus?

The stranger's eyebrows furrowed. "You must be from the provinces if you don't know Marcus," he said, his tone one of disgust. "He is the man who saved your dirty ass." His gaze roved over her. His face revealed just how bad she must look, covered in grime and blood. "Only the gods know why." He shook his head.

Gustina glared at him. Her wrist throbbed under his pressure and she tried to move it out of his grasp. "Who are you?"

He smiled. It was a genuine smile, as if no one ever gave the ugly creature any attention. "I'm Tevis. Marcus' friend."

She eyed him. His pleasure at the question gave her the opening she needed. The corridor filled with dust and the air held the sound of the spectators. The clash of metal rang overhead. The fight must be right above them. With her heart pounding as she heard a moan come through the ceiling with the sound of impaled flesh, she wrenched herself free of Tevis. She sped down the corridor, looking for a stream of light. There had to be a way out of this hell.

Behind her, she heard Tevis call for her, his voice clear. Fearing he'd overtake her, she turned down another hallway and saw light. His voice was overwhelmed by the crowd above, their demands for death heard clearly through the ceiling above her. Then the whistles and yells escalated beyond all levels and Gustina screamed, willing to do anything to escape.

She turned once more and found the doorway to freedom. With a sprint, she leaped out only to hit a wall of flesh. Big hands, strong hands, clasped her upper arms.

All she felt was solid muscles and leather. Her hands were splayed across a man's bare chest. A chest warm and slick with sweat and blood. Her hands were covered in it. Her eyes widened as she gazed up. It was that gladiator and he looked like a demon. Her mouth fell open as she gasped for air.

※

Marcus won against the murmillo. Whether the crowd begged life or death for the grounded gladiator, Marcus' demon didn't care. His swords held little blood and craved to be drenched. And since the man actually stabbed at Marcus, the gladius slicing his chest, his demon screamed vengeance. In one swift move, Marcus rolled across the sand and retrieved one of his swords. Turning to the murmillo, he plunged the blade into his chest. The man stumbled, dropping his weapons. Prostrate on the sand, he held up the two fingers for missio, to end the fight, but Marcus' creature smiled. He grabbed the two fingers and waited. He wanted death. Vaguely, he saw the crowd's hands, their thumbs pointed up, the sign for death. The demon waited no longer and buried the blade into the man's throat. With a gurgle, blood poured from the wound as the spectators roared their approval.

The magistrate nodded at the win but said nothing more. Guards opened the door for the slaves to haul the dead gladiator through and the opposite side opened for Marcus to leave. Fists tight around the hilts of his swords, his demon demanded they use them and swath their way clear in blood. With deep breaths, Marcus fought for control. He would not die today. There was the Christian or slave girl he promised to return to. He told Tevis, a fellow slave and friend, to check on her.

Into the cavern of the Colosseum, he breathed deep, the smell of blood and victory kept his own surging through his veins. Tonight, he'd get his reward of wine and whores—that is, after any paying patrons were through with him. It was an odd side of the coin, to be sought after by the highest paying patrons, women who wanted a victorious killer to fuck them. Though he'd known of this practice before his descent to slavery, it remained the strangest aspect of his life.

Barely had he stepped into the shadows when someone ran straight into him. A fan already desiring him? Her breasts smashed against his bare chest and it hardened him. He grabbed her arms and held her as he waited for his eyes to adjust to the darkness. The creature trembled in his grasp. Within seconds, he could see and he looked down as he heard her whimper with shock.

The woman he left in the alcove.

The guards heard the commotion and were at his sides. This wasn't good. He needed to protect her but how? Where was Tevis?

The manager for the complex, Clodius, walked up to the scene, shaking his head. "What do we have here?"

Marcus tensed. The man was a serpent, the only type to manage a circus this large. He ruled as long as the Emperor approved of the games and he did anything required to keep it so.

He wouldn't release her. Not that she tried to flee. He felt her stiffen under his hands, as if straightening her spine against a new enemy.

Clodius sauntered up to the gladiator and woman, a crooked smile on his lips. "Marcus, keep your whores for later." His fingers went under her chin and turned her head toward him. "Ah, Gustina, we missed you earlier today."

Marcus watched her nostrils flare as she lifted her head higher, off Clodius' fingers. He felt her tense under his hands and her lips puckered as she spat at the man. The gladiator bit the inside of his lip to keep from laughing.

The man wasn't amused. "Take her," he ordered.

Marcus pulled her closer. They had taken his swords the moment he stepped through the gated door so he had no weapons to protect her. "Mine," he stated possessively.

Clodius' eyebrows rose. "Really? A murderer for a murderer. Interesting." He eyed the woman again. "After all the clean patrons who pay for you, you'd rather have a dirty slave?" With a sigh, he looked Marcus in the eye. "Fine. You need to go to the baths. Your services are already desired." He shook his head with disgust. "As for your new *friend*, I'll hold her until Gaius arrives and then we shall see if she lives or dies." He laughed.

As the laughter echoed down the hall, Marcus looked at her. The guard took her arm to lead her away. She stared at him, her eyes questioning, pleading with him until the guard yanked on the chain still dangling from her neck. With a last glance at him, she flipped her hair defiantly, grabbing the chain out of the guard's hand in one fast move as she walked ahead of him.

Marcus smiled. *Gustina*. A murderer? That made them perfect for each other. Even more so, her defiance stood against Roman authority, despite the odds. It made him wonder why.

CHAPTER THREE

Aulus lay back on his cushioned bench and opened his mouth for another grape. His slaves popped one in and he hummed in gratitude when it spurted juice between his teeth. He closed his eyes and savored the ripe, sugary taste. Another slave, the pretty little brunette he sampled last night—new thing, he couldn't remember her name—brought him a cup of wine. He smiled as he took the goblet, watching the blush come to her cheeks as she struggled to maintain a stoic face. Ah, yes, she has such a tight ass. He hardened at the memory.

The curtains to the salon parted and one of his guards entered, followed by the champion of Aulus' house, Marcus. Aulus sat up, balancing his wine, taking in the view of his fierce gladiator. The man had been to the medicus after the battle, to have the slice in his chest attended. Bathed and oiled, his body shone in the sunlight streaming through the open roof of the villa.

"Ah, Marcus," Aulus began, swirling the wine in his goblet. "Another victory in the Arena. You make me richer every day." He finished his wine, handing the cup to his personal body slave as he walked to his champion.

Marcus' face didn't reflect the congratulations. He stood still, his wrists and ankles cuffed and chained together. The man's violent tendencies ruled in the fights but containing them here, so quickly afterwards, was questionable without the irons.

"Dominus." His voice was level.

Aulus inspected the stitching on the puckered wound and looked up into the gladiator's eyes. "You've been summoned because your services are required."

"I've been told," the warrior said, sounding bored with the demands his winnings brought.

Aulus squinted at him, his eyes roving over the man. Cleaned and scented, Marcus wore a simple white linen tucked around his waist and nothing else but the chains. In the ludus, the man's chamber was with the other gladiators. One would think being sought afterwards by Rome's wealthy ladies for sexual pleasures would be sufficient reward for slaying his opponent. But of course, the beast wanted more.

With a deep sigh, Aulus stepped back. "What else is it now, champion? Hm? I've given you ample rewards for your victories. After you're through with the lady, you'll have access to enough wine tonight to forget your own name."

The gladiator didn't move.

Frustrated, Aulus twisted his lips. "What is this I hear from Gaius? That I have a new slave, at your demand? What say you on that?"

The man's cheek ticked and his eyes flickered. He looked at his dominus. "She is mine."

"Yours? A gladiator's? Have you been hit in the head, Marcus?" He waited for the response that didn't come. But he saw the man's upper arm muscles clench. Ah, what muscles, Aulus sighed. What he wouldn't give to...he shook his head. The female slave, yes, back to that.

The gladiator glared at him. "I want her as my reward for winning."

"Truly? You want me to acquire a slave, sentenced to die in the arena for killing her domina, just for your amusement? Is this a jest?"

The gladiator's jaw tensed but he looked straight ahead. Aulus was glad the man was in chains, for this woman and his demand for her were different from any of his other requests. Frankly, Aulus himself wished to fuck many of the women who paid highly for Marcus' cock. The man attracted the better half of Rome's female patrons, but he wanted some lowly slave?

He sighed. The coin the man brought to Aulus house added considerably to his wealth and standing in the community. What was one more slave?

"Go see to your admirer. I will acquire this slave. But, if I suspect for one moment that she is a danger, I will kill her. Do you understand me, slave?"

The second Aulus' words came that he'd take the girl, the gladiator's stiff shoulders relaxed. The man gave Aulus a nod.

"Dominus."

Aulus dismissed him with a wave. He sunk onto his cushions and exhaled a frustrated groan. His champion won at the Villa too. Now Aulus had a murderer in his house. Damn!

⸻

Marcus' temper flared at each turn in the villa's lower level. The guard yanked his chain, forcing him to miss a step. With his muscles twisting, pain radiated in his chest. His demon seethed deep inside him. *Kill him!* Marcus gritted his teeth, biting back the appearance of pain or anger. The one guard leading him was a nuisance but there was also the one following him. Both armed.

His frustrated demon stilled.

The chamber in the lower section had been carved out of the ground and lined with rock. Tallow candles hung from the ceiling, giving pale light to the room. Marcus tensed as he was pulled into the chamber and taken to the far side. The chain on his ankles was released and his wrists independently anchored to the wall mounts. A cot, pinned to the floor so he couldn't kick it away or move it during rough play, sat next to him. He had enough room to maneuver, so he could service his patron. But only just.

As the guards left and their stench of sweat and leather faded, he picked up the sweet scent of vanilla and honey that wafted his way. The door opened to let her through and then locked behind her.

That scent, not uncommon for Roman women, had another layer to it. One he recognized. His skin prickled. No, not her. Damn it all!

His demon stirred, deep in his loins. His cock twitched.

The cloaked woman came carrying a cup, sipping from it as she sauntered in. Wine. Always with her it was wine. He grimaced.

She placed the cup on the small table on the far side of the cot. With a haughty laugh, she threw the hood of her cloak back. "Marcus, my love." A sadistic grin on her face, she presented the back of her hand for him to kiss.

He didn't move. Anger flashed over him. "Lucilla."

She laughed again, pleased at his discomfort. She parted the cloak, revealing her naked body beneath.

He tried not to run his gaze over her. He knew her contours well. Even now, her plump breasts bobbed, her rose-colored nipples hard. Her flat stomach quivered. She had round hips, the type a man loved to grasp during intercourse, and long slim legs beneath. At the apex of her thighs, blonde curls hid a cunt he knew was already wet. Those curls were so soft, the lips hidden in them inviting.

His cock hardened at the memory, tenting the linen cloth. To the gods, he hated himself.

"I had to come and see my favorite gladiator," she cooed as her fingertips trailed down his chest, over the muscles that flinched under her touch.

He clenched his fists and closed his eyes. Lucilla was a beautiful woman. Her blond hair fell in ringlets around her shoulders. It smelled sweet, like vanilla and honey. And her. The touch of it hitting his chest when he pulled her on top of him, his cock deep inside her. The echoes of her mewing and begging him to fuck her. Oh yes, he knew her.

His wife. The bitch.

He wouldn't look at her but couldn't help it. His head bent, watching her fingers run over his body and he heard her sigh. When she reached under his linen cover, her hand cupped his bollocks and squeezed. His cock throbbed painfully.

She looked up at his eyes. "Oh, yes, I know what you like," she murmured and pulled the cloth away.

It took every ounce of energy he had to stay still. To not throw her on the cot. *No.*

"I will not fuck you," he said, his voice angry.

Her hand clutched his cock and she looked up at him with a crooked smile. "No?" Her hand slid up and down his shaft, her fingers tightened at the hood around the head.

Damn her! She knew his cock well. A shudder traveled through him as her hand squeezed again. He refused to look at her and instead stared at the door.

She ran her thumb over the slit in the head and she sighed. She released him and looked up at him, suckling the thumb.

He couldn't stop the groan the sight brought forth.

With a wicked grin, she bent over, closing her lips around his cock, suckling him as her hand squeezed it up and down.

He bit the inside of his mouth, trying not to feel her. It was impossible, the memory of her seduction too strong. When her mouth took him all the way in, the pressure built, and he wanted to explode his seed in her mouth. It required everything he had to fight it. He grabbed her head and pulled her off him.

His cock twitched painfully. "No, Lucilla."

She broke into laughter. "I paid a pretty coin for your services, slave."

"I'm sure the senator, *your husband*, would be so proud to know that," he spat.

Lucilla reached inside her cloak and took a knife out, pointing it at his sewn wound. "Marcus, maybe you failed to understand this. You are a slave. If I want you to fuck me, you will do so," she threatened, poking the corner of his wound.

A pinch of pain radiated as she slid the blade in deeper. Warm blood seeped from it. Madness flared inside him but he could do nothing. She was right. Though killing her sounded better every second, the urge growing stronger as her twinkling eyes smirked at his. He could strangle her and bring his own death—and freedom.

But what of the girl? Gustina? Damn.

Lucilla withdrew the blade and licked the sides of it, cleaning it of his blood. Then she grabbed her wine cup, pressing it into the wound, collecting blood into it.

He watched her as she took the cup to her mouth, the blood on the rim colored her lips deep shiny red. He grimaced. She grinned and downed the wine and blood in one swallow. Her tongue licked her lips afterwards.

"What the hell, Lucilla? Drinking my blood? The man you condemned?"

She laughed as she turned to pull her hood over her head and close the wrap. It was an evil laugh. He remembered it well. The night the praetorians dragged him from their bed.

But his memory was cut short as she turned, pressing the blade at the side of his neck.

"Yes, gladiator blood is known to cure all illnesses and I need the blood of a champion."

"Whatever for?" For the love of Jupiter, he hated her.

Her lips pursed and her eyes hardened. "Very well, since I'll probably be back for more. I want a child, slave. You will give me one."

A slice of pain went through his heart. "I gave you one, long ago, and you rid yourself of it. An inconvenience, you told me, to carry the child of a bastard. And now, I'm to submit to you? What of your pristine senator you had to get rid of me to have?"

She flinched but caught herself from an outright shudder. "You despicable man! You were nothing then except for your cock." Her eyes washed over him. "And in so many ways, you still are nothing, *slave*. But if your blood doesn't help bring me a child, I will pay for your seed and you will deliver it, do I make myself clear?"

Every nerve in his body pulsed. The demon flared, roaring within. Marcus gritted his teeth. He'd pray fervently to the gods to give her a child so he'd never have to lay with her again. It would drive him mad.

Lucilla harrumphed as she stormed to the door and pounded for the guard. The door closed behind her and Marcus slid to the floor. He felt coated in slime from her touch. Blood dripped down his chest and neck. The pain of her knife still stung in the corner of the wound and the incision on his neck.

The demon muted inside him as another voice struggled to be heard.

Gustina.

She waited for him upstairs, in the villa proper. Marcus promised he'd protect her. His hand fisted and he slammed the wall behind him. Pain raced up his arm. More blood. But he felt nothing.

He would get free soon. Or die trying.

CHAPTER FOUR

Gustina halted behind the thin, scrawny slave. He'd led her from the baths into the villa and up to a tablinum. Sun streamed through the rafters, reflecting off the decorative pool in the atrium behind them. In front of them, as a barrier to the peristylium, stood decorative slatted wooden screens. Scents of basil and lilacs filled the air from the walled garden. The warmth of the room brought a peace of sorts to her battered soul, but her wariness of the place still remained. Where was she?

Slaves milled around the villa. Her guide brought her to an older female slave, who stared at her with stern brown eyes that roved over her ill-clad, filthy body. The woman's nose crinkled in disgust. With a shake of her head, the matronly slave ordered her taken to the baths. Gustina couldn't help but marvel at the fortune of this house to have its own baths. Even Terpio's house held no such convenience. People attended the public baths daily. There, the citizens enjoyed the company of their friends while bathing and playing games. Plenty of political scandals as well as alliances formed there. But to have private facilities meant money. And opportunities…

Unfortunately, from the scolding she got, Gustina took too long soaking. But she hadn't bathed in a sennight. It took an eternity to wash away all the filth and grime from the Colosseum. The oil laden water soothed her frayed nerves, washing away the stench, but not the memories. She pushed them back, locking them away. Here, she could begin again in a large house and not be singled out.

Now she waited impatiently, her toes curling on the tiled

floor, for the Roman lounging on the cushions to notice her. She tugged at the cotton of her pale wheat-colored tunic. It tied behind her neck, baring her back with only her breasts covered, and the overlaid wrap hanging to her knees. New iron ankle bands snaked around her legs, above her feet, their curved shape worn and smooth, not marring her skin. But their weight made her feet feel anchored to the floor.

The man on the lounge scribbled onto the book before him and handed it to the slave, ordering him away with a flip of his hand. His eyes roamed to her and fear mingled with disgust rolled through her.

"Ah, so you're the one." He swung his feet to the floor and stood in a fluid, graceful movement. His gaze roved her body as he padded closer to her, his lips curling in a predatory way. When his finger touched her bare shoulder, it took the strength of years of training to remain still and not flinch. He stood a head taller than her but not as tall as that gladiator, nor did he have the muscles. But he wasn't soft-looking. No paunch to his belly, at least not now. His white toga, trimmed in a blue silk band with silver designs, gleamed in the sunlight. The man's dark hair, almost black in color, shone.

"I am your new dominus," he stated, his finger tracing her bare shoulder blades as he circled around her. "Aulus." He stopped behind her. His finger lowered to her waistband and from there, both of his hands glided over her ass, lifting the back of the skirt.

She clenched her hands for a second when she heard him sigh at the sight of her bare buttocks and one hand caressed them. The noise of a slip of his tongue, the slosh of saliva echoed in her ears. The masque slid into place, shielding her from the revulsion when his wet finger traced between her legs, at the folds of her sex. She knew this type, so when he invaded her core, she stood quietly. His finger entered and withdrew and fucked her again. Out of years of forced submission, her hips swung back a notch toward him, giving him freer access though she'd rather retch instead. She bit her tongue when he sighed at her stance and the slick noise of enticed sex sounded. She shut her eyes, revolted at her body responding to him.

"Ah, yes. You will do." He shoved his finger in hard and deep.

A painful sob uttered from her mouth at the harshness. He heard her and chuckled.

The tunic fell into place as he circled in front of her, sucking his finger. "Fuck, I'd lay coin your ass is tight," he said, a devilish grin spreading.

She shuddered.

"Ah, Dominus," a male voice from the corner, near the lounge, interrupted. "Your champion claims her."

Aulus rolled his eyes and sighed with disgust. "Of course, how could I possibly forget?" He returned to the cushioned seat and plopped down.

The voice became being as he stepped closer to his master. Tevia. She recognized him as the slave who'd retrieved her from those wretched bowels of death. For Marcus, he'd claimed. Gustina fought every twitching nerve to school her face into the docile and dim-witted slave they expected. Head up, she tightened her shoulders, throwing them back a bit, to appear strong and uninterested in this decadent master.

Tevia glared at her for a moment before turning to Aulus. "Dominus, may I make a suggestion?"

Aulus grabbed his wine goblet from the ground and gave a quick nod.

"Perhaps this is one you'll send down to him now, as payment for his winning, considering…"

"Considering what?"

"The patron who bought his services."

"Yes."

"Dominus, do you know who it was?" She noticed Tevia looked a bit agitated, as if he were afraid. Strange, for he seemed to have the Roman's attention, as if he were a favored slave. "Lucilla Vibenia."

He frowned. "Senator Vibenius wife?"

"Yes, sire." His voice dropped as he added, "and Marcus' former."

Aulus threw his head back and moaned. "How in the name of Jupiter did she get in?"

"Cernia."

Gustina caught the intense emotions flicker across her new master's face. Whoever Cernia was, Aulus looked as if he'd kill her.

Aulus leapt off the cushions, storming past his new slave, motioning Tevia to bring her. He led them through the house to another bathing chamber. Unlike the one below that serviced the slaves and gladiators, this bath in the villa was strictly for a proper Roman. And thanks to Marcus, Aulus could afford to have it instead of trekking into the city for the amenity. Granted, he went anyway. Good business could be conducted there, but he preferred the sweet, soothing smells of his private baths.

But if Cernia were still there, any quiet comfort and tranquility here would be gone after he was through. His wife knew better than to have done this.

He entered the room and stood on the side of the large bath, his hands fisted as he glared at her.

Cernia sat with a slave at her side, rubbing her bare arms with sponges. The scented vanilla oil, mixed with peach from the leaves that floated on the top of the water, filled the air. The combination clung to her skin and made his mouth water. His gaze devoured the vision of her creamy skin, her bare breasts bobbing at the water's surface. Her black hair coiled above her shoulders and tendrils curled around her face. If it weren't for the necessity to chastise her, he'd gladly join her and let his cock scrub her from the inside.

She looked at him, annoyed. "Aulus, where did she come from?"

Ah, yes, Gustina. Another subject. "We just acquired her."

"Really, dull of the others already?" Her tone conveyed boredom. So she was still angry over him screwing the new stable lad. Really, she needed to forget that....

"Not the point I've come to discuss," he stated firmly. "What I'd like to know is why you arranged for Lucilla Vibenia to buy time with our champion?"

Her eyes crinkled as her mouth twisted in disgust. "Truly? That is what you so rudely came here for? To barrage me with nonsense? Aulus—"

"Do you like your silks? Or your slaves?" His voice dropped. "And what of the jewels? The Falernian wines of late?"

Her lips pursed. "You know I love it all."

"Are you sure?"

"Of course, why would you say such a thing?"

His voice turned vicious. "Because arranging him time with her will only make our champion angry, the man whose victories in the Arena allow you those indulgences. To piss in the pot you bath in! We do not need his anger at us, Cernia." He stood, running his hand through his hair.

"She paid double the rate."

"Never again, do you hear me?"

Her lips eased into a lopsided grin. *Damn, she knew she had him.*

"Of course."

He rocked back on his heels. His gaze landed on the new slave. The girl looked too luscious for only his champion. She tasted divine, apparently not a virgin but that was good. He hated all that screaming and whatnot. The curve of her hips, the round ass....*Oh, yes, he'd be of a mind to take her but then again...shit.*

"What of her, Aulus?"

Yes, what of her? His mind tossed ideas around, but the solution remained the same, thanks to his wife and her friends. He ran his hand through his hair again and looked up at the heavens. *Jupiter, please give me the strength.*

The slave stared straight ahead, her face devoid of any emotion. Obedient. Like good slaves should be. Except for her eyes. Those pale blue pools flickered, like she was anything but compliant. For the love of the gods, taking a murdering slave under his roof was a disastrous move and against Roman law, but Marcus did lay his winnings down for her. And as a champion, brought fortune to this house. No, Aulus knew better than to deny him. What was another slave? He'd get her to kneel before him...and so much more. As to Marcus, she could service him too. But that was all. Despite his coin, Marcus didn't really own her.

With a deep sigh, Aulus made his decision. He walked over to the girl and took her hand as he turned to his wife. "Your new slave, my dear."

"Her! You can't be serious, Aulus," Cernia loudly protested. "She murdered her last domina. I will not have her!"

Aulus caught the tick in the slave's face at the mention of

the death. Her cheeks seemed to pale. She swallowed hard, and he watched the motion of her throat. Built to suck Jupiter's cock. He hardened.

"Yes, dear wife, you will. Or you can service Marcus but considering what you did, I doubt you'd last."

"How dare you," she snarled. For the love of the gods, how he loved her so enraged.

With a wave of his hand, he motioned all the slaves away as his hand slid under his toga and threw it over his head to the floor.

"No, no, I will not have her," Cernia continued but her eyes were glued on his movements. "Aulus, do not think…"

He smiled as he stepped into the bath. "No, right now, I have only one thought, and it has nothing to do with slaves." He pulled her into his arms as his mouth claimed hers.

Marcus seethed as he fell to the floor of his cell. His demon roared for Aulus' death but he squelched the longing as he downed the cup of wine. No, if Aulus valued his life, he'd make sure Gustina came here, right here, in front of him, now.

Tevia poured him another cup, his eyes skittish as he handed it to the gladiator. "You should have the medicus look at that."

Marcus glared but took the cup anyway. The puncture of his newly-sewn wound by Lucilla gaped open held Tevia's attention. Marcus ignored him. The blood left a trickle down his chest but the throbbing stopped. Thankfully he had enough wine to no longer feel it. Bitch.

He'd returned to his cell, his heart racing still from having her in front of him, begging for a child. His stomach turned at the thought. They'd married young and without consent though his parents and hers knew they were matched. The thrill of their vows taken that way hung for several months, making them take all sorts of risks. They fucked at the baths, in the Forum, at the theaters, during gladiatorial games, during social events—particularly dinner parties. And the drinking and other indulgences. Opium. Ah, the taste of it in wine, on grapes, sprinkled on olives and the places it took him were truly memorable.

Then, Hades opened on him….

He shook his head. Sprawled on the floor, his bare legs stretched out before him, the hard wall behind his naked back. All he remained wearing was his subligaculum. His chest hurt now from the knife cutting the stitches and driving a little deeper. Others asked for his blood. Disgusting thought. Drink from the champion and have whatever ailment cured. But to have *her* do it to cure her supposedly perfect husband's imperfection galled him. Anger flared again and the demon screamed *kill her!*

He felt the blood trickle down his chest.

Pressing the cup to his lips, Marcus downed the entire contents. In one swallow it was gone and he shoved the cup back at Tevia. The gangly slave took it and poured more. Marcus watched his friend, the only slave here who had the guts to actually talk to him, thus freeing Marcus from his lonely, silent life. Tevia knew many of his secrets but not all. Not Lucilla.

Now, though, the man looked terrified. Maybe it was his Syrian upbringing. Gods, the Syrians were worthless creatures. He took the cup, but he felt suddenly as if he had drunk the entire ludus' wine supply. With a sip, he knew instantly—at least as quickly as his now-sluggish mind would let him.

"Tev," he called muddily. "What is in here?"

Tevia shuffled for a moment and let a slow smile come to him. "Also from our Dominus. To ease the pain."

Opium. The bastard put opium in the wine. Fuck.

"And more," Tevia continued as he stepped back. Marcus could barely hear him, but a flash of light-colored cloth breezed before him. He blinked, trying to focus as the slippery feeling of the drug-laced wine seeped through his veins.

Against the dark stone floor, small bare feet shifted. His eyes wandered up. Cleaned and smelling like almonds, the girl from the Colosseum. Gustina.

He slanted his head, fighting to clear his vision. Shit, he'd forgotten how wine and indulgences screwed with his head. Fuck. He could kill Tevia, without his demon's aid.

Gustina stood silently, her gaze on the wall above him. Damn, she carried that slave demeanor before him. Fuck. But his eyes devoured. He'd almost not recognized her without the muck and mud. Laughter came to his mouth, but he pressed the cup to his lips to silence himself.

Her light brown hair shone even in the torchlight. Her crystal blue eyes glowed, still defiant, but something else too. Damn, if he didn't have that shit in his body, he might figure it out. His eyes fell, taking in her full breasts that begged for his attention. Her hips rounded, giving her narrow waist the perfect size to grip. Long slender legs emerged from under her tunic. The snaked iron anklets appeared more as jewelry than shackles. She curled her toes under his gaze. Gods, how he'd prayed to know if they did that from desire as his cock fucked her.

"Gustina," he slurred, tilting his head against the rock wall.

Her gaze fell to his. Her eyes sparkled. Tears? Damn, he couldn't tell. She stepped closer and knelt before him.

"Why?" she asked.

He frowned. "I need you." Jupiter, he sounded like a fool. Perhaps he was. Weren't women just demons dressed in seduction? Had he learned nothing?

Her brows knitted. Slowly she reached out to his chest. "You're bleeding."

"It's nothing."

She tore part of her tunic hem and dipped it into his cup. He opened his mouth to say something but when she got closer, his tongue dried. As she touched his wound with the cloth, her hand warm on his chest burned down to where his heart would have been. The ache inside twisted, but the pain of his wound lessened as the opium numbed him, inside and out.

He remembered days, years ago, of this state of being. Colors appeared, bright and loud, but to look at her, all was calm. Soothing. He covered her hand with his.

"Marcus, she's here for the hour. No more, according to our dominus."

Tevia was still here? The demon stirred.

Marcus' eyes couldn't leave hers. She licked her lips. Desire shot down to his groin. He pulled her into his arms.

"Get out," he growled.

"Champion."

"Now. And tell Aulus she stays here. With me tonight," he said coldly. When her eyes flickered, he felt a shiver in her arms. No, he wasn't letting her go now.

He vaguely heard Tevia mutter something but he didn't care. The cell door shut and he groaned. She stayed rock still. As he pulled her closer, the impact of the opium and wine hit him full force, and the world before him swirled and turned black.

CHAPTER FIVE

Pain stabbed like a sharp lance to his temple. Damn, how he hated this. Part of the reason he no longer missed indulgences like last night. Wine was good, wonderful. But from the other, he didn't want to move, let alone open his eyes. Marcus reached out with his hand, searching next to him. All he found was empty space.

Shit.

He fought through the splitting in his head and cracked open his eyes. The shaft of morning sun shone through the narrow window above the door to his cell. It burned, sending a dagger of torture into his head, but he refused to retreat. He'd seen a flash of something lighter in the far corner. Dragging his body upright, he sat on the edge of his cot.

With his eyes slit open, he scanned the small room, blinded by that brilliant beam and cursing it. He found her. Sitting on the stone floor, her legs bent and arms wrapped around them, her eyes fixed on him. Those light blue gems glowed in the sunlight, both mesmerizing and burning.

He remembered, vaguely, pulling her into his arms. Sitting on the floor, wine in his hand. And then nothing. How had he made it onto the raised pallet? And more importantly, why had she left him?

Gustina's back ached, scrunched as she was against the wall. The small room reeked of dirt and male. Aside from the narrow wood-framed cot, there stood a small table and from the ceiling, a round oil lamp hung. Stone floor, solid cemented walls with a wood door and above it, a narrow window, covered with metal lattice. Just the perfect hole for a gladiator. A gladiator who saved her from death. Who claimed her. She shivered at the realization.

Now the goliath was awake, sitting and staring at her, like a little boy whose dog ran away. And she was the dog. As he stretched, flexing his shoulders and back, she couldn't take her eyes off him. He looked like Hercules or one of the gods, Apollo perhaps.

His black hair was short and mussed with sleep. The sunlight highlighted his angular cheekbones and square jaw. His nose had a bump, as if broken on several occasions. He had a thick neck and broad shoulders defined by muscles and tendons, rolling with each move. His bare chest and abs displayed corded lines, defined by years of physical labor, tapering to a narrow waist. As he cocked his head, the crack in his neck echoed loudly in the room.

This was a man, a gladiator, considered a champion by this house and most of Rome. Oh yes, she had heard of him and several others. Had been in the market with her Domina and seen the trinkets that were for sale—pictures of him and others on plaques, adornments, supposedly dipped in their blood and sweat, sold to give good luck and many more things.

He watched her, his gaze intense. She felt the pressure on her body but his eyes were dark, foreboding. Then he stood. The coarse blanket fell to the pallet, exposing his nude body. He was a god. She couldn't shake her vision from him at first. Muscled thighs and calves flexed as he came upright and his cock jutted, rigid and hard, thick with arousal. Desire filled her and she swallowed the lump in her throat, trying to regain control over her senses. When his lips curved wickedly, anger flared through her. How dare he enjoy her attraction to his body! She whipped her head toward the door and stood.

She stepped over to the transom, looking upward into the warmth of the incoming rays.

∞

Marcus' smile remained, pleased at her blush when she saw him naked. He partly expected her quick denial of her reaction, but why he wasn't sure. Just as he didn't remember how he'd gotten into his bed or when he removed his subligaculum. Rubbing the sleep from his eyes, he studied her as he reached for the cloth and wrapped it around his waist, binding the ends through his legs over the front.

She looked at him. Her fingers made a movement at her forehead and lowered as she closed her eyes and bent her head. Praying like those pathetic creatures... gods, she was a Christian. The idea irritated him. Last thing he wanted to do was to put up with her ramblings like those others he heard spouting in the market as they got closer to the Colosseum.

With a disgusted breath, he grabbed the batting and wound it around his calf. "What are you doing?"

He saw her gulp. Damn, the arch in her slender neck, the movement of her throat, sent desire coiling down his spine. Violently, he pulled the ties to the leather casing over the batting. Last thing he needed was to fuck a Christian. Jupiter laughed at his arrogance.

She turned her head, and her eyes sparkled in the sunlight. Blue. Crystal and sharp. Damn, he wondered how they'd look satiated by his cock.

"I pray to the gods, seeking their guidance."

He scoffed. "Do they answer you?"

Her gaze narrowed. "Perhaps. If I wasn't interrupted."

He chuckled as he tied the second legging on. Outside, the loud snap of a whip filled the air.

"Gladiators!"

Doctore's yell, calling all Aulus' gladiators for training. He'd be late. Shit. He slid his feet into his sandals.

Confusion at Doctore's command made Gustina's brows crease. He waited, slipping the leather belt over his waist.

"Doctore calls." He pulled the batting over his right arm. "Time to train."

"Train to kill?" Amusement rang on her tongue.

He frowned. Women paid to be with him, to have him fuck them even. His popularity was high enough that women fawned all over him. But she looked as if she'd start laughing. He shook the anger off.

He strode to the door. She didn't move out of his way. Lifting her and moving her to the side, he reached for the handle only to find her again next to him. His brow twitched as he turned toward her.

"You expect me to remain here?"

He released his grip on the latch. "Yes."

She laughed scornfully. "You cannot truly expect me to wait here for you, like a servant or, or..."

Of course he expected her to stay. He'd paid for her. He couldn't stop the wicked smile curving his lips at the thought of her lying nude in his bed when he returned from training. His message got to her but not how he expected. She paled.

Her expression went bland, like a statue. A mask of submission. A damn slave façade. Without a response, she turned, offering him her back, and bent over.

He gulped. She offered him her body in that manner? When the skirt flipped over her hips, his cock throbbed. The round, creamy buttocks presented before him, her feet parted and he saw the hint of her slit. His body reacted violently with desire. A feeling he instantly squelched despite the fact he did want to fuck her. But not now, not this way. Such a crude way to offer herself, like he was no better than her master demanding her body. He'd saved her from being attacked and mauled to death by lions, bears and whatever carnivore stood in the arena. Surely she might be grateful. But this, this hit him wrong. He blinked, his head pounding. Had to be the opium and wine affecting him.

"That's the best you can do?" he snapped.

She stood instantly, her hands rapidly straightening the skirt and hugging her waist. He could see her tremble.

"For love of the gods," he muttered, amazed. The fear in her eyes, a new look for her and one he didn't like, explained it all. She'd only been taken and never given. Hades, he doubted she'd ever been kissed. Fuck.

He ran his fingers through his hair then stepped to her, grasping her arms and placing her on the bed's edge. "Stay here. I'll be back."

She shook her head rapidly. "I can't stay here. Domina will call for me and I can't be late."

His eyebrows knitted. "Domina?"

"Yes, Dominus gave me to her."

He turned and spat. Figured Aulus would do this. Arrogant swine. His thoughts twisted. "Did he touch you?" The words left his mouth more like an accusation at her instead of the perverted beast in the Villa. Harsh and strained.

Her eyes widened for a split second as the blood drained from her face. "No, no," she muttered.

Marcus snorted. He knew she was lying.

The pounding in his head increased. Jupiter's cock, he'd kill Tevia. He turned to the door and grabbed the handle.

"Gustina, stay. Sleep. You look tired and since I woke without you lying next to me, I take it you haven't slept. I'll tell Dominus you'll be up later." He waited for her to nod and when she did, he left the cell, closing the door behind him. *Shit.*

Out in the training square, Marcus stormed to the group of gladiators. Anger rolled off him and he gladly took the wooden swords from the slave boy. He wanted to strike someone, anything. To kill would be better.

"Marcus, stop."

He came up short. Automatically, he halted at the husky tone of Ludo, Doctore of Aulus' stable. Marcus eyed the tall, heavy, scarred-face Cicilian standing before him. The man was a titan in his fighting days, and even now, whip in hand, he commanded a stable of twenty gladiators. The man hadn't gone lax in his days outside of the Arena, his muscular form up to par with Marcus and any of the other men. He commanded respect, and it was well-earned. And maybe the only man to waylay Marcus' desire to slice another of his brotherhood to shreds.

Breathing heavily, Marcus complied. He'd seek an audience with Aulus later and solve the issue of Gustina. He'd paid for the girl. But he didn't doubt she told him the truth and that Aulus, in his demented thinking, took her in his own household. What a cock, that man!

"Pair off!" Ludo's whip snapped the air.

The sleep-weary fighters sectioned themselves off in the usual pairings, wooden replicas of their weapons in their hands. One did not use the real weapon to practice skills but the wooden version. Wood meant they'd all live, something Marcus' demon despised. Paired off against Iduma, the only fighter in this ludus that gave him competition, Marcus swung quickly and accurately. Iduma, a Brit—short, wiry and angry—glared at him.

"What in Hades is wrong with you?"

Marcus narrowed his vision. "Nothing."

Iduma ducked against his next blow. "Why is it that I do not believe you?" His blade swung mid-section and fast. A lopsided grin etched his mouth. "What, she didn't suck your cock long enough, huh? Lost your touch with a slave?"

The vision of Gustina submitting to Aulus, bent over like she did for him, made Marcus' insides roil with madness bordering on insanity. His demon roared. He could see Aulus grabbing her naked hips as he....

His thoughts turned red like blood, distracting his attention so that he failed to block Iduma's jab at his chest.

Marcus grunted at the strike. "Fuck off, Brit."

Iduma laughed. "Never, Roman." And he jabbed the wooden gladius into Marcus side above the balteus laced around his waist.

Marcus groaned, swerving out of the man's next swing, and belted the Brit in his side, causing him to fall to one knee. Iduma's wooden shield dropped and Marcus flipped his gladius, holding the edge of the wooden sword at the Brit's neck, pressuring hard. Iduma's eyes narrowed as he exhaled from the fall and the position now cutting into his breathing.

Marcus stood like a true gladiator, not releasing his stand.

Snap! The whip swirled behind him. "Marcus, Iduma," Ludo ordered.

Marcus heard, unwilling to back down. But either he did so or faced being whipped. He gritted his teeth and dropped his sword arm, extending his hand to Iduma. The fellow gladiator took it.

"Jupiter's balls," Iduma swore quietly as he came to his feet. "Next time, fuck her before coming out here."

Marcus grunted. Why hadn't he? Only the gods knew. And only they would save Aulus if he found his Dominus had fucked her.

CHAPTER SIX

Lucilla stretched. The sunlight bounced off the tile floor, illuminating the bedroom chamber. Her nude body soaked in the heat.

"Feeling better, my love?"

She grinned at her lover. Terpio bent, tugging her extended nipple with his teeth. The sting came instantly and she hissed. His tongue laved the pain away as he suckled. She arched her back in response. Her hand wandered down his bare chest and stomach, noting how the texture was smooth, not rippling with muscles like Marcus. What a shame, she thought. Terpio's brother had quite the body—hard, solid and oh-so-exquisite. She sighed as her hand wrapped around his arousal. The man wasn't lacking here, though. She loved his cock, thick and so hard, filling her to the point of pain. Stroking his silky skin, her fingers slid up from his balls to the mushroomed head, one finger tracing across the slit. A pearl of pre-cum greeted her and she squeezed the shaft in response.

He groaned. "I want you to suck me dry."

With a wicked grin, she shook her head. "You know what the priestess said. I am to lay here and be filled with seed." She stroked again. "So fill me."

Within an instant, he opened her legs and rested his cock on her moistened slit. He moved forward slightly, rubbing her erect swollen nub. She mewled as her hips widened.

"You think you can take all of me?" He nipped at her neck.

She shuddered, moving her neck away. "Don't mar my beautiful skin, Terpio. I can't have any signs of you here."

He snorted. "Oh, my dear, but you will. I will fill you to

the rim so you'll drip my seed for the next day. That old man you call husband will just have to thank me for you appearing so aroused. I will leave you begging for me to fill your cunt, not his shriveled cock," he claimed. He pulled off her and sat up.

Her brows furrowed. He looked like a Roman statue—stately like the senator he was—but unlike the marble pieces, there was one difference. His hard cock, red from strain, the vein pulsing on the side, thrust out, like a horn on one of those exotic animals imported for the games. She bit her lower lip in anticipation.

"As a good Roman senator, I raise my attention to you." He smiled devilishly at her.

Her mouth became too dry to speak. He chuckled as his hands grasped her nude hips, raising her up.

"Terpio, I'm supposed to lay," she gasped loudly as he pulled her over his lap, spreading her legs, opening her to his throbbing erection.

"I think to give you the best seat in the house," he murmured, his hands lowering her hips as he thrust his hardened shaft deep inside her.

He filled her to his hilt. A strangled moan echoed in the room and it took her a minute to realize it was her voice. His thick cock pulsed inside her, overpowering her. He slid her up and down the length of his shaft and she gave in to his control.

"Oh, Jupiter!" He twisted, still buried deep inside her, throwing her back on the bed.

Her hips rolled back as he plunged inside her over and over again. Wrapping her legs up over his shoulders, she uttered primal groans. She felt him touching her womb and rejoiced.

She had called the goddess Juno's priestess to her home, to give her fertility. Her husband, Lucius Vibenius, failed in getting her with child. The priestess blamed him after Lucilla confessed an earlier pregnancy—well actually two—so the cause wasn't her but him. The fact Lucilla aborted both pregnancies remained unspoken. The priestess made a vile tasting concoction, spoke an incantation to Juno over it and told Lucilla to drink the blood from a champion gladiator with this potion and her wish would be granted. The look on Marcus' face was worth the price she had to pay to put up with the beast. One of the best champions in the Empire. And if his brother Terpio couldn't get her with child, she shuddered at the remaining consequence. Either she'd have to tell her husband she was barren, hence he'd no doubt divorce her, or go to Marcus and submit to his rutting. That thought appalled her. To think she once willingly spread her thighs for him made her retch. Well, he did make her squeal but she also thought it took a lot of wine and other indulgences to get over sleeping with a cast-off.

Terpio moved faster, lifting her hips off the bed, a groan of her name on his lips. Falling into the rhythm with him, they mated faster and faster. He angled her buttocks so his cock hit the spot deep inside her. She loved this about him. He knew how to hit that point and the universe exploded inside her head as her body shattered underneath him. He convulsed, embedded deeply in her, with a loud yell, "Yes! Oh, dear gods, for you, my love!"

She felt him showering her womb with his seed. He fell on top of her, damp with sweat. He stank and the whole area smelled musky and dirty. Disgusted, she lay still, but she so wanted him off her. She got what she wanted, she hoped. She closed her eyes.

Please Juno, bless me with a child.

Gustina's heart skipped a beat. The sounds of men groaning, panting, yelling filled the air around her along with the noise of their weapons clanking against others, the whirl of air from a net being thrown. Cries of victory and the sound of defeat. The sounds grew louder, more boisterous as the echo of feet on the sands multiplied. Her mind slipped back into the Arena, the air rippling with death and blood. She opened her mouth to scream and….

A bug flew right in. Its buzzing and the fluttering of its wings made her gasp and spit, waking her up out of a frightful nightmare. She saw the dead pest on the ground and she coughed up more saliva, spewing it on the floor, as bile rose in her throat. Vaguely, she heard the sounds from her dream but they were muted by what she imagined. Looking straight ahead off the gladiator's bed, she noticed the door to his cell was propped open and the sun poured into the room with its stifling heat. She wiped her forehead with her hand and discovered it was wet from sweat and that nightmare.

Slowly, she stood, her legs wobbly from the heat, the fright and the lack of food. But the scene outside the door caught her attention.

In the courtyard, she saw a couple of dozen men, gladiators, practicing their skills against each other, against a wooden pole or carrying heavy lumber. These men moved with cat-like grace, even in spilling to the ground under attack, to roll and leap up again, their weapon poised for attack. Their bodies were a mass of rippling flesh, muscles that flexed and bulged in their swinging of the wooden swords or the raising of flat wooden shields. They grunted when hit or knocked down, their bodies glistening under the stress and the sun reflecting off the sweat as it darkened their skin. The gods at play, she thought whimsically.

It didn't take her more than a second to find her gladiator. Marcus. He fought with an intensity that scared and amazed her. His opponent was also built to move though he was thinner and more milk-colored than Marcus, with reddish hair and skin mottled with specks of brown dots. He swung at Marcus and the dark-haired champion's feet stumbled though he didn't fall. The red-haired man laughed at him as he prodded him again. Marcus brought his swords under, flipping his wrists as he brought them back up and crossed, landing at the red's neck, a decadent smile creeping across his face. Both men fell into laughter and wandered to the side where she noticed a barrel standing.

"Ah, so you're up. Good. Bet you're hungry."

She blinked and tried to refocus on the slave standing before her. Tevia. The scrawny, thin-haired man stood straight, trying to display his height as intimating but it only displayed how slender and defenseless he was as each bone on his chest and collarbone showed. Her nose wrinkled at him. He smelt of beeswax and honey, as if he was too sweet to ignore. A truly repulsive smell, especially when mixed with dust and male musk and sweat. It took considerable effort not to puke.

He cocked his head, his brows raised, waiting for a response. Her stomach growled loudly and he smiled. "Come."

She followed him out of the room, across the dirt training ground to the Villa. The gladiators on the edge stopped, their gaze on her as she walked. Dust from the dirt filled the air and the dry ground, pummeled from their feet, actually felt soft to her soles, her toes digging into the rubble. She tried to not look for him but couldn't help it when she felt the pressure of his glare hit her directly. Gustina glanced and found him, in a half crouched position, swords raised, stilled by the sight of her. Their eyes locked. His dark ones bore into her, reaching her soul until she could feel it. Slowly he stood, never breaking his stare.

Why was he so intensely involved with her? She knew he attracted half of Rome's women, the highly perfect women, and she was only a lowly slave. A condemned slave.

He looked angered, of course he would. She left his room. How could she not? Infuriated that he'd think he controlled her, or could *own* her, she stood straighter as she whipped her head forward to follow Tevia until they reached the stairs to the house.

Inside the house, she felt dirty, her dirt-covered feet marring the floor.

Tevia took her back to the kitchen where the fat cook, the one with slanted eyes, shoved a bowl full of gruel and a torn piece of bread at her. Nodding her gratitude, she sat at the large table and ate, watching her escort talking to the cook in a language she'd never heard. The gruel's granular texture tasted of wheat and barley with a hint of honey. The grained bread definitely held a nutty flavor. Some of the best food she'd had in a long time. But by the time she realized how wonderful it was, she'd devoured most of it. Stuffed, she looked for Tevia, lost as to what to expect next.

"Through already?" Tevia chuckled. A tinny noise that grated on her nerves. "Knew you'd be starved. Marcus never thinks beyond his own needs. Apologies." He tilted his head.

She frowned.

He gave her a smile. "Follow me. Domina is expecting you."

He took her further back into the house, past the main floor's decorative pools and garden to a back sun-lit room. A bedroom, but larger than any she'd ever seen. It had a window with sheered drapes blowing from the breeze with the voices of the gladiators' training seeping through them. Two other female slaves worked in the room, picking up clothing and changing water in the washing bowls.

Domina stood in the center of the room with a slave woman pinning the brilliant blue stola at her shoulder. Gustina was fascinated. The pin glittered gold with the sparkle of emeralds and diamonds.

"Ah, so there you are," the woman greeted her in a dismal tone. Gustina flinched. "Well, come here so I can see you."

She stepped closer, lowering her gaze. No point in aggravating the woman just yet.

The woman came to her, tipping Gustina's chin up. Her Domina's brown gaze narrowed as she eyed her. With a look of disgust, she withdrew her hand. "You're Gustina?"

"Yes, Domina."

"I am Cernia. Your Domina. You will help Tamera with whatever I desire, do you understand me?" Her tone was harsh, like she expected Gustina to fight her. It rubbed her wrong but she could only nod. When Cernia's mouth thinned, Gustina corrected her reply.

"Yes, Domina."

"I know who you are." The woman lifted her wine cup off the table next to her. "You killed your last domina...."

"No, Domina."

The woman waved her off. "No matter. But do understand me well. If I catch even so much as one glimmer out of you, that you are a danger to this Villa, I will kill you without any chance Marcus could save you."

"Yes, Domina," she muttered. She hated this Roman.

Cernia sniffed, her lips curling in disgust as she gazed at Gustina. And just as quickly, she turned the look to indifference as she reached for her bangles to adorn her wrists. "Frankly, I fail to see what about you attracted our champion. He can have any Roman woman but no, he desires you. A slave. A murderer. And a rather," she sniffed again, "dirty slave."

Gustina's anger flared. It took every ounce of energy to curtail the look of hatred but her blood still boiled.

"Tamera."

"Yes, Domina?"

"Take Gustina and get her cleaned." She turned to Gustina

and her lips snarled. "As to staying with Marcus, you will not be there. You will stay here in the Villa, with the house slaves."

Her breathing hitched. As unusual as it seemed for him to want her, Gustina felt a measure of comfort with him. He refused to take her. In fact, had resisted her body. Oh, he wanted her, she'd seen his eyes and the response of his cock. And he seemed overly possessive of her, though why escaped her. But to be told she'd be held here, away from him, made her angry, upset and longing for him, all those emotions wrapped around her fraying nerves.

The Roman woman before her eyed her with contempt, as if daring Gustina to protest. To do so was rebellion. She'd get a lashing—or worse—for disobedience. Death, her welcomed companion, leered at her from the side but not floating any closer because she no longer hoped for it. There was something about this gladiator, a tug within her to stay alive and see him again, even if only at a distance. Shaking off the woman's disdain, Gustina tightened her shoulders and fought to keep her hands from clenching. With a nod to her new Domina, she gladly left the loathsome woman to follow the mousy brown-haired slave to the baths.

What would Marcus do now?

CHAPTER SEVEN

Marcus' head turned toward the opened door of his cell, his gaze scanning for a glimpse of the girl but he caught no sight of her. Tension wired him. Where the shit was she? His hand gripped the piece of bread in his hands, ripping and crumbling it through his clenched fingers.

"If you didn't want it, I would've relieved you of it."

The voice shattered his black thoughts. He blinked and looked across the wooden table at Iduma. The red-haired Brit's lips twitched and mischief danced in his eyes. Marcus looked at his fist and saw his portion of noon meal wadded in his grasp. With a growl, he dumped the remains in his bowl of stew.

Iduma laughed. "You'll regret not eating that."

Marcus scowled. "I can't see her."

"Who? The girl in your cell? Have you lost your head?" He snorted. "Tevia retrieved her hours ago."

"What?" His voice bellowed. Out of the corner of his eye, he saw the other gladiators in the covered room look up from their meals. "Why didn't you tell me?" he asked, his voice lowered.

"And have your gladius hit me? Not fucking likely," the man guffawed.

Marcus pushed his bowl away and stood. Anger flowed through his veins. Iduma had seen her, why hadn't he? He snarled, knowing he'd been to wrapped in the practice, so sure she was safe in his cell, he missed it entirely. Aulus took her, or maybe that cunt who stood as his Domina did. How dare they infuriate him so! He turned, determined to head back into the bowels of the Villa, past the gates and up the stairs to the building to find her.

"You'd be better to dampen those fires," his friend cautioned, his hand gripping Marcus' forearm.

The demon inside him roared, wanting vengeance. It was a desire, one yet to be satisfied but one day he would fulfill it with the death of Lucilla and his brother. And added to the list – his Dominus and Domina for stealing his woman. But without knowing exactly where Gustina was, he knew by the gods, he'd do more damage by storming off.

With a deep breath, he squelched the fire in his blood. The pounding in his ears from his racing heart cleared, and he heard the buzz of the other warriors talking as he felt their eyes burning into his black soul. Only Iduma stood at his side, nodding his head at Marcus' acceptance of delay.

"Do not worry about your pet now," Ludo stated loudly into his ear. "You have an afternoon of work before any pleasures."

Training. More fucking training. As champion, what the hell did he need more work on? He spat on the floor. Jupiter, forgive him, but he still wanted to kill....

"For love of the gods, Roman," Iduma slapped him on the shoulder. "Her cunt may be tight and yours, but there's nothing you can do about it without getting through doctore."

Slash. The sound of the whip sliced into the air. "Gladiators!"

The stable of slaves pulled away from their food, half laughing, the others slugging their way back to the compound where the younger slave boy waited to give them their wooden practice arms and shields.

"Marcus, Iduma, the posts," Luda ordered.

Marcus glared. Picking up the heavy, man-sized wooden beams to lug around the grounds as a means of strengtheing their upper bodies remained a grueling and demeaning task for a champion. But he knew the rules. As a slave, he must do as commanded or face punishment. And this time, that might mean no more Gustina.

"Damn," Iduma muttered low. "Remind me to leave you to yourself so I'm not called to ground with you."

Marcus couldn't help but laugh. He bent before the heavy squared beam, putting his hands through the leather straps nailed onto the side and yanked it up in the air. Uttering a grunt, he heaved it over his head and rested it on his shoulders, his arms wrapped around it to square it on his body. The weight of the beam and its splintered corners dug into his skin, making him adjust his movements to lessen the sting. The hot sun bore down on him, and combined with the dirt beneath his feet, the air felt thick and heavy.

As they walked the perimeter inside the walls of the training ground, he glanced into his cell with each pass, veering closer every time, praying she was there. By the sixth time around, his feet faltered when he stepped closer to his door. It was a mistake. The rapid stinging pain struck his naked back and the air electrified with a snap as the whip lashed down on him.

His flesh stung as the leather strap cut a fine line and he arched his back, losing hold of the beam, and it crashed to the ground behind him. Everyone around him stopped and stared. Even Iduma, several paces before him, turned toward him.

"Champion, remain focused on your task!" the Cicilian bellowed.

Marcus heaved in heavy gulps of air, trying to remain standing. The flinch backward brought a pinch of pain to his chest and without taking a peek, he knew the wound on his chest had opened. The sweat running down his face and neck hit the gashes and he gritted his teeth against the agony.

The slave boy, Marcus didn't remember his name, appeared at his side, handing him a hollowed out gourd full of water to drink. He downed the contents, the cool liquid soothing to his parched mouth. Swallowing all, he handed it back to the boy and glanced up. Ludo stood, arms akimbo, his legs planted firmly. He looked like a statue, domineering and in charge. The whip coiled in his right hand, ready to flick out at the next infraction. Marcus knew better than to push the man. He'd been whipped into submission when he first arrived—a painful experience, one well remembered with just the single lash across his back now.

Ludo's lips thinned. "Go to the medicus. Your wound needs attending."

Only then did the gladiator look down. He'd felt the pinch and the searing pain when his sweat hit it, the salt of his skin biting into it. But it streamed blood down his chest and stomach. His ears buzzed from the pain, heat and heavy lifting and a light-headedness from not enough food. He bent his head. "Doctore." And left for the medicus' infirmary, unable to stifle the hope Gustina might be there.

※

Lucius Vibenius Paterculus walked through the doors to his house, his long white toga trimmed in red scraping across his mosaic-tiled floors as he headed for his study. Halfway through the villa, he heard the feminine laughter from the atrium and the rippling of water. He paused. Did he hear a male voice as well?

With a deep breath, Lucius jostled the three scrolls he carried before he continued to his study. Dumping the papers on his table, he stood, pinching the bridge of his nose. A dull throb began when he walked into his own house and it made him so aggravated. Only his Lucilla could cause that ache. His beautiful wife, a woman he married without thinking. Idiot he was, thinking she'd been the answer to his prayers. Prayers he'd given offerings to Jupiter for. He needed a young, vivacious wife and Lucilla appeared to be all of that plus more. Her family, an established old Roman family, was of good standing. There had been rumors about her previous husband. The man apparently was not even part of the Flavus blood, his infant body thrown to the dregs outside the city, where many unwanted babies lay dumped. Lucius shuddered at the thought that she and her brother-in-law, Terpio Rufus Flavus, had been deceived by Terpio's father into believing that the man was of the family. Simply never done. How Terpio had rid the family of the rogue, Lucius couldn't remember but her marriage had ended and she'd been available again.

He heard her chiming giggles again, the trill of them sent a hum down his spine, pooling in his loins. Thoughts of her, clad only in her long tunic, a fine cotton from the southern sections of the Empire, made his cock harden. Today he intended to lay with her and hope the gods blessed them with a child. His age, though ahead of her by ten years, should have no bearing on his fertility but she claimed it did.

The male voice echoed after her ripple of laughter.

She told him the priestess of Juno told her to wait another

week, when her womb would be ripe for his seed to take hold. The male laughter, with hers, sent a jealous streak down his spine.

She wouldn't. Not in his own house. His mind plummeted at the thought.

A slave girl entered, carrying a cup and bottle of wine. His mind was so distracted at thoughts of his beautiful wife fucking another man, he almost missed her. Lucilla wanted all their slaves to be silent, so they slithered through the house, quiet as snakes in their bare feet. It unnerved him.

"Ethia, who is with your Domina?" He had to know before he stormed in and made some embarrassing scene. A senator like him should have a serene house, with no situations out of his control....unlike this house.

"Terpio Flavus, Dominus." Her head bowed, he couldn't see her eyes. Eyes told the truth.

Terpio. The man no longer her brother-in-law. Frankly, it wouldn't surprise him if she'd slept with the man before Lucius married her, but not now. He heard the chatter echoing down the halls and it grated his nerves. With a jolt of energy, his lethargic feeling cleared. Time to find out just what they were doing, alone here when normally he'd be at the Senate, as Terpio should be. He snorted and waved the girl off.

Treading out of his study to the atrium, Lucius heard muffled voices, hidden by the statue of Venus in flowing robes, pouring water into the pool in the center of the atrium. The scent of lilacs and eucalyptus with jasmine mingled with the smell of fresh soil from the planters. Ivy cascaded from hanging baskets and various statues surrounding the water. Tranquility filtered in the air, its peace making him feel almost outrageous for barging in on her.

Then he saw her, lounging on a cushioned frame next to the pool, her guest also reclining at an adjoining piece. Two female slaves and one male stood in attendance, filling their wine cups and feeding them grapes and figs. Lucilla's head tipped back at something he said, laughing. Lucius watched that swan throat of hers, graceful and elegant, adorned with sapphires paid for by his own purse. Gold and opals hung from her ears. She wore a vibrant blue stola, the cloth clinging to her like a second skin, revealing her curved hips and narrow waist, and draped scathingly over her ample breasts. With gold and silver rings, connected to armbands in fine metal chain as well as decorative pins at her shoulders and hair, Lucilla looked like a goddess.

His cock twitched, wanting to sink into her silken slit.

Terpio's loud laugh interrupted Lucius' dream. Narrowing his gaze and pasting a smile to his lips, he continued to his wife.

Lucilla saw him and smiled warmly. So perhaps he was wrong about her. She left small hints of her indiscretion, flippant remarks, poor timing on schedules, a piece of cloth here and there, making him wonder if she fucked others. But that smile now made him feel like a fool for such unspoken accusations.

"Dearest," she began, sitting upright. "My former brother-in-law stopped in to visit." She raised and kissed him on the mouth, her tongue nudging at his lips.

"Senator Vibenius," Terpio stood.

"Terpio Rufus, I am surprised to see you here," Lucius stated, dropping his smile but fighting to remain mild. He noticed the bronze and blue striped toga hung off Terpio's body, as if hastily put on. At least the man had the grace to turn red at being here.

"I came to see you, Senator," he quickly replied.

Lucius raised his brows. Lucilla touched his arm, adding, "Yes, he came to see you about aid to return to the Senate."

"Truly?"

"Oh yes." Terpio looked at him carefully. "As you know, I lost my seat as consul in the last election but the usurper who stole it has recently taken to foot."

"So I have heard." Lucius eyed him, knowing the man before him was of little good in the Senate. But he did little damage wandering the halls and, with him off the streets of free time, he wouldn't be here to meddle in a marriage he wasn't part of.

Terpio frowned, surprise passing from his face. "Good, so I was hoping to get your word, perhaps patronage, to return."

Lucius gave a forced smile, one that he made grow bigger as he eyed his wife's hopeful look. Women and politics were a bad mix. "Let me see what I can do."

"Thank you, Senator, I won't disappoint."

But he already had. Lucius thought the man's despicable

behavior damaged any position he might hold, but wrestling his position out of Senate nigh impossible, being a hereditary position. The man's father, if memory served correctly, served admirably. But his son? If it would rid his house of the vermin now by claiming support, then he'd do so. "Let me get back to you. For now, if you'll excuse us?"

It took the imbecile a moment to understand he'd just been kicked out. "Of course, please excuse me." He nodded to Lucius and turned to Lucilla, taking her hand to kiss its backside. "Thank you for keeping me company."

Lucius noticed her blush. His anger re-kindled. He glared at the man as he walked away.

"I'm so glad—"

"What were you doing with him?" He turned to her, his tone harsh. "I thought you were to rest for the next week."

Her eyes flared and he saw a tick in her jawline. "Rest but not expire."

He watched her school her thoughts. She truly was a naïve. He smiled at her this time, a true smile. Until she opened her mouth.

"He came by to talk to you but I told him you were gone today," she said, playing with the fold of his toga. With a nonchalant shrug, she added, "So, we were preparing to head to the races."

"Chariots?"

She laughed. "What other type is here? You know I love a good race."

"And gladitorial?"

Her lip curled before she stopped it. "They're very entertaining but none are in session today."

"Good," he patted her arm. "Let us make use of our time alone." He smiled broadly as his cock hardened. He took her hitch in step as one of excitement. He glanced quickly at her with expectation only to see her face pale.

※

Marcus sat on the table before the medicus. The man made him want to run. Aulus' medicus was a slight man with a limp in his step and a permanent bend in his arm, like he was born with it curved. Baldheaded, his beady dark eyes roved over the gladiator's body, as if he was no better than an average slave or swine even, for sale. And he stunk of honey and onion, only to have that awful odor magnified in the heat.

The man hummed as he prodded Marcus' chest, poking at the wound. Marcus grimaced at the pain. He'd blame Lucilla for it since she dug at it.

The medicus grabbed a wet cloth and a jar of golden honey. "This might hurt."

Really? The word was on his tongue when the wet cloth pressed against his chest. Pain shot through the muscle, radiating down his side and up to his shoulder. *What in the name of Jupiter?* His whole body clenched under the fire.

Just as he thought he'd never move again, relief flooded through him as the medicus removed the rag.

"Poison." He dampened the cloth again. "Almost got it out," he stated, pushing the rag hard against Marcus' skin.

This time, it didn't hurt as bad and he only tensed, not that tightening, readying to fly feeling. Another cloth after the second felt cool, not filled with lightning bolts to fire into his body. It also didn't stink of rotten wine and eggs like the last two had. The medicus took the needle and thread to stitch his torn flesh together again. His skin felt numb from the applications of the vile concoction placed on it, therefore no pain came from the needle just the pulling of the gutted thread lacing through his wound, binding it.

Cutting the end of the thread close to the skin, the man in charge of the gladiators' health piled honey over the cut and topped it with mud. The smell of honey and soil made a heady scent. A thin cotton strip looped around his chest and tied tightly.

"How is our champion?" The deep, authoritative voice of the Dominus filled the air.

"He'll be fine, tomorrow, after sleeping tonight." The medicus' squeaky voice drove his demon to cringe deep, hands over ears. "It needs to be wrapped tonight. Tomorrow, I will remove the cloth and take closer inspection." The man picked up his foul-smelling bowl and sponge, needles and supplies, to walk away.

Aulus smiled. "You must rest the rest of the day."

The pain in his chest ebbed but not the anger over Gustina. "Where is she?" he ground out.

Aulus' brows rose. "Who? That young slave girl? She's in the Villa, where she needs to be."

"She. Is. Mine." Damn, he sounded like an irate fool but he wanted her with him. Needed her with him.

Aulus snorted.

"I paid for her." His demon struggled to be free and kill the fool.

"She can come visit but not tonight," the Dominus stated, walking to the door to look at the gladiators still training on the square. "Perhaps in three days hence."

Marcus snarled. Obviously, the man didn't hear him correctly. And if he wanted to keep his champion happy, to continue winning, he'd better listen. "She's mine, Dominus. I paid for her."

Aulus spun, his eyes lit in fury. "I am your Dominus, slave. Do not push me or you will not have her at all."

Marcus' demon roared and the man fought to subdue the beast. As much as he hated to admit it, the fucker was right. He could sell Gustina if he wanted.

Aulus' anger diminished. "You paid to get her here and had her last night. That is all for now." He turned to leave.

Marcus stepped forward. The guards at the door bristled.

"You knew I wasn't in any condition for her last night. You made sure of that," he accused.

Aulus brows fretted, then a look of understanding spread across his face, like a cat stretching in the sun. "So that's what Terpio took." He guffawed. "Rest, recover from your wound, continue training and we'll see."

"Do not touch her."

Aulus stared at him, his mouth twitching. "You are not in the place to threaten me, slave."

"If you want me not to kill you or die in the Arena, making you lose your wealth, you'll leave her for me alone." His nostrils flared, the heat in his face fueled by anger.

"Recover, train hard, and win. But threaten me again, and I'll have her crucified or let the guards have her for the night."

Marcus heart skipped a beat. The swine could do that—or worse. Schooling his features as best he could, he nodded. "Dominus."

Even with his gaze lowered in submission, his demon raged from within. He'd recover, train and win his freedom.

And then, he'd kill not only his traitorous wife and lying brother but Aulus, the ass-fucker, as well.

CHAPTER EIGHT

The pebbled glass pieces in the mosaic-tiled floor dug into Gustina's knees and toes. She'd beg for a cloth to kneel on, but to ask might show weakness and in this house, she'd learned, weakness meant more pain and suffering. Anger mixed with the pinching of her skin increased as she rocked back and plunged the brush into the bucket next to her. Polishing the atrium's floor shouldn't have been a hard job, since the pools took the bulk of the space. She hadn't considered the pebbled floor when assigned the job. To walk across it, even barefoot, felt good but to put knees over glass beads was not.

A painful sigh escaped her lips as she knelt, brush to floor, and pushed forward.

Next to her, a low giggle interrupted her thoughts. Farina, the almond-skinned slave, also on her knees scrubbing, always bubbled. Gustina liked the girl. Close to the same age, they got along well in likes and dislikes in this house—a common belief was that Cernia was a self-centered Domina whom the gods threw in their path to test them. Gustina, though, was tired of the test.

"I fail to see how pain can be so humorous."

Farina laughed again. "How can you not?" She threw a rag at her. "Try this."

Gustina took the cloth, placed it under her knees and the pain diminished. "You've had this all the while? What type of friend are you?"

Farina smiled broadly. "A close one," she murmured.

Gustina frowned as she stroked forward, her brush hitting

a pair of sandaled feet. A woman's feet. Ones that did not move. Slowly she looked up and met glaring eyes. Verenia, Cernia's body slave. The tall, dark-haired woman's lips pursed.

"You ignorant cunt," she hissed. "Finish the tiles. Domina wants you two bathed and oiled for tonight's events." She stepped closer with her dirt-covered sandals, marring the cleaned floor, and kicked Gustina's bucket, sending the water splashing over the floor.

Gustina bit inside her mouth, holding back the scathing remark she wanted to make. The water splashed her and the rag she knelt on.

"She is such a bitch," Farina snarled.

"Why does she hate me so?" Gustina barely knew the slave's name but the woman hated her from the moment she'd been brought before the Domina.

"Because you're Marcus' favorite," Farina stated. "The bitch's licked after him since he arrived two years ago. Offered herself after one of his wins. Can't recall if he fucked her or not but he lost interest in her. In every slave and whore he's had. She just won't give up. And then he *bought* you." She shrugged.

With a sigh, Gustina rose, grabbing the bucket's handle. "What celebrations?"

Farina's mouth thinned. "Dominus is having a gathering of his supporters, some of the area's richest cocks, to aid him in his election to remain aedile."

Glancing down at her sodden tunic, she shook her head. "So we must attend and serve?"

She gazed at her friend and saw the girl's jaw clench before she continued scrubbing. Her movements were vicious against the floor, comical if it weren't for the anger on her face.

"Yes. Forgive me. I forget you haven't been here long enough for this." Farina pulled up and leaned back on her heels. "We're to wait on them, from food to wine to anything else they desire."

Fear snaked down Gustina's back. "What do they desire?"

Her friend snorted. When she opened her mouth, she shut it immediately.

"I see we've decided not to finish?" Cernia glared at her.

Gustina lifted the empty bucket. "Need more water, Domina."

"Then be quick. Guests will be arriving shortly."

"Yes, Domina," both slaves answered as one.

Gustina quickly went to the stairs, flying down them in haste to the water reservoir. The guard watching her made her jumpy. He walked up to her and she tensed, biting her lip. Dressed in his tooled leathers, the strips hanging from his waist flapped over his tunic as he took her pail and dipped it in the water for her.

"Gratitude," she murmured when he handed it to her and backed a step. The guards rarely spoke to her but he gave her a look of respect. She couldn't figure out why. This one seemed tame enough to ask but as she looked at him, she caught a glimpse of the movements behind him. She heard bodies moving, masculine grunts and groans echoing in the lower chamber. She moved past the guard to the woven metal gate and looked out.

Before her, in the open square past the chained wall, the gladiators trained. Numerous glistening bodies, muscular, defined by practice and exercise, swung practice swords and shields as they fought their brothers. Captivated, she stood. The afternoon sun baked the warriors' bodies, the sheen on them made them look bronze with a couple of ebony-skinned ones. She smelled the masculine scent, pungent with sweat and mixed with the smell of dirt kicked up during their training. A couple partners laughed. Others grumbled.

Her gaze roved the herd before her, looking for him. She hadn't seen him in five and a half days. Not since Tevia retrieved her that morning. Marcus. Her gladiator.

The guard approached. She felt his presence. He'd push her back to the stairs but if she could have but a moment more, till she found him. Instead, the man stood just behind her. His hand came over her shoulder and pointed to the right of the field.

Her gaze followed. There he stood, panting from sparring with a redheaded partner. Gods, he stretched, his muscles flexing in the sun. Apollo. Her heart skipped. His dark hair shone in the sun, slick with sweat. He laughed when his partner countered his move and in that split second, dimples danced on his cheeks. She saw the line of stitch marks on his chest from his wound. Had he suffered in her absence? The gods knew she had, missing his comfort. Yet why, she couldn't answer. She prayed constantly for the gods' advice, and they still remained quiet.

She swallowed, knowing she had to return to the atrium though she didn't want to leave. If he'd only look her way...

The gods must have heard her and granted this request for the tall gladiator's eyes suddenly caught her gaze and locked on. Her mouth dried and she licked her lips, wishing she could say something to him, but the distance was too great. She saw a slave boy hand him a gourd and, without breaking their gaze, he took the offering and downed the water, spilling half of it down his neck and chest. Venus knew she wanted to lick every last drop.

"You need to return to the Villa proper. Domina is calling."

The guard's words startled her and she broke her lock on Marcus' eyes, glaring at the man. But he was right. She picked up the bucket and cast one last glance out on the field. Marcus was gone.

∞

Aulus watched another magistrate finish the fourth pitcher of Flauvian wine and inwardly groaned. It wasn't even time for dinner and they'd drink him out of his supplies. Damn the lot of them, surly, snippy little goats.

An arm snaked into his and hugged. "I'd wipe that snarl off your brow, my dear," Cernia warned softly into his ear.

"The cock-suckers will drink us dry at this rate." Fuck, she was right. He schooled his features and pasted a smile on his face.

She laughed quietly, bowing her head at the next political magnate that passed them. "That's why I put six back for the festivities."

He glanced at his wife. She saved his ass in more ways than he cared to recall. Gods knew he loved her. He bent and kissed her temple. "You know I love you."

"Yes, I know," she answered with a quirky smile.

He sighed. Political dinners could be such a bore, especially when his invitation included these ancients and their matronly wives. The evening would send him to the afterlife with the dullness. He'd bet half of these men knew Julius Caesar, the way they droned on and on.

"I see that look in your eye." Cernia nudged his side. "Let us break the melancholy." Aulus' lip curled. The night might be saved, in the only way he could. His display would be the likes these stuffy Romans rarely saw. "Proceed."

She swept her hand to the right and the curtain behind them opened. Behind it stood their ten best gladiators, dressed for the Colosseum minus even their practice weapons.

Aulus grinned. His stable's outfits had been cleaned—no easy task for clothes that were exposed to blood and entails smashed against them—and their leather shone from oiling. Each man stood as champion, stoic yet strong. Ah Jupiter, he was blessed.

"Gentlemen and ladies, may I present to you my best men for your examination. Come, see them up close, and grade their worthiness for your next venture in coin at the Arena. Touch. They will not bite, unless you ask them to." His announcement raised a few laughs as his guests came closer to his men.

Aulus motioned to Tevia and the slave filtered among the guests and gladiators. He stood ready to take any orders or demands.

"I say, Aulus, fine showing."

He turned to the voice. "Consul Aculeo, I'm so pleased you've joined us."

The rotund magistrate bellowed. "Who would turn down the invitation to meet Marcus?"

Aulus flinched and bit his tongue as Cernia pinched his arm.

"Of course," she intercepted. "He is a champion in many forms."

Aculeo's eyes widened. "Truly?"

"At the sands, yes," Aulus said, gauging the potential supporter. *Shit*, Marcus would not accept any man's cock up his ass, not without being ordered. It wasn't something Aulus would impose on his champion, not even for this fat patron.

The magistrate's eyes narrowed. "Well, perhaps that is so and such a shame to be so one-sided. Too bad…"

"We do have other indulgences here that might appease you," Cernia offered.

The man laughed. Aulus cringed as he witnessed the rippling of fat wiggle at the motion. It was disgusting.

"Then I shall consider it," he said, waving his cup in the air and walking away.

"Cernia," he warned.

"If he wants to fuck a house slave, what does it matter, if it gets you his support?"

Because what if he wanted the slave only to find him or her ruined by that man's fat cock penetrating over and over? For the love of the Jupiter! "No, of course. It does not matter at all. But not my gladiators. I need them in fighting order."

She winked at him and sauntered off. His gaze fixated on her swaying hips. Damn, his wife was a seductive nymph, and he so wanted her. He downed his cup with a moan.

~

Marcus stood, feet planted firmly to the floor. He hated these damn parties. Show off the gladiators, touch them. He swore to the gods if one of these drunken asses grabbed his cock, he'd kill him. His demon prowled below the surface, eyeing the room for weapons and advantages.

That's when he saw her. Gustina. It'd been a week. His wound was virtually gone and still Aulus kept her from him. His hands clenched.

She looked radiant, wearing a strip of white sheer cotton, folded many times to hint at her nipples and her mound below. The tunic clung to her, displaying the curve of her hips as well. One pull at the tab around her neck and the outfit would fall at her feet. He gulped.

In her hands was a wine carafe and she floated through the guests, refilling their cups. Jupiter, he hardened instantly.

"I'd try to get your mind off the girl if I were you," Iduma warned softly. "You might attract other attentions you'd want to avoid."

He flinched. The damn Brit was so right. Gritting his teeth, he tore his eyes away from Gustina and focused on the wall instead. Guests filtered through the line, many women's hands traced the muscles on his chest and back, giggling and sighing, asking to see his cock. For love of the gods, he wanted to puke. The demon snarled.

Apparently, the men knew better than to caress him. None

touched him and for that, he was thankful.

Aulus gathered the guests for dinner.

After a few minutes, with them still standing, Iduma muttered, "So we are the decorations for tonight."

"Apparently."

"Gladiators," Ludo ordered loudly to them.

The guests lounged on cushions with the slaves feeding them, filling their wine and whatever else was needed. Marcus felt a ripple of resentment go down his spine. He remembered times like this. Drunken orgies often followed. Opium, wine and sex, from the very cushions the Romans sat on now. He recalled attending many and mostly not remembering the whole night. Often he woke with some naked woman at his side or some slave licking his cock. His gut twisted.

"What the fuck is this all for?" Iduma grumbled.

"Dominus is selling himself to remain aeidle," Marcus replied, his eyes on the guests. He saw Gustina with other slaves serving. One of the supposedly *honored* guests took a swipe at her ass. The hair on his neck bristled. He'd warned Aulus what he'd do if he touched her. The suck-ass knew it applied to anyone else.

Why did he care for her? He searched for the draw to her. Even prayed to the fickle gods about it with no answer in return. Ever since the Colosseum, he desired her, wanted her, the core of his being demanded her. But why? She was pretty to a point. High cheekbones, narrow, small nose, vibrant blue eyes he wanted to see darken underneath his touch. Her body was slender, but curvy in all the right places. He watched her bend, her ass facing him, and he felt his cock twitch. Damn! He shifted his feet. She stood and he found her breasts. They were small—not tiny, but the right size for his palms. The light brown hair, partially braided now off her face, shone by the oil lamps. And he remembered her defiant attitude toward the Romans, a look that said she'd take them down and he loved that. His demon even acquiesced to that.

"Thought he had office," the voice next to him said.

He shook his mind. "This is his attempt to keep it." His voice was rough, rough with desire that wound tight inside him.

"Fucking Romans," another gladiator cursed.

⚭

Cernia sipped her wine, eyeing her guests. With a motion to Tamera, the plates disappeared, replaced with the slaves offering grapes and nuts with more wine. She ordered the reserved vats of wine opened to serve. With a nod from her husband, she knew she'd done well.

Around her, political talk, war discussions and the Republic echoed loudly. She didn't give a shit about any of it. No, being the proper hostess required her to keep a watchful eye on her slaves and guests. They were getting fairly drunk and that pleased her. One of the men grabbed the slave boy offering grapes. In one fell swoop, he lifted the boy's tunic and smiled. The man peered around the slave to her, a questioning look in his eye. She nodded. As the man grinned, stumbling up and taking the boy's wrist, she smirked. That slave was the one Aulus fucked so she took an innate pleasure out of this. Aulus liked his toys as his, particularly the boys, but she tired of him doing so.

Another jar of wine was depleted and her guests wallowed on the cushions as the conversation eased. Half the guests had left. The six remaining, she knew, wanted to play. Aulus smiled at her. Oh yes, tonight had been a success.

The new slave girl, that murderer, flittered around them, offering more drink. One of the men, a large, bulky magistrate from Ostia, dragged her into his lap, and her pitcher of wine crashed to the floor.

"I've been watching you all night," the man said into her ear. Cernia laughed inside. He probably thought he was whispering. Drunken fool.

The slave, Gustina, sat still, appearing to know her place. Cernia's gaze narrowed. How the girl submitted or not would answer Cernia's question about her. She hadn't trusted her, not really. She gave her the menial jobs, anything to keep her hands constantly busy—too busy to contemplate trying to kill her Domina.

Cernia didn't see her breathing hard, but she did notice the bland expression that slid across Gustina's face. Good, good. She'd been taken before. Then she'd submit. Relief flooded her and she cozied into her cushions as the man's hand disappeared under the slave's tunic. He must have fingered her cunt as her jaw tightened and she rose in his lap.

"Ah, you're tight and slick," the man slurred.

A roar heralded from the side of the atrium. From the line of gladiators. Everyone's attention turned. Cernia felt the blood drain from her face. That animal, their champion, strained against the hold of four gladiators who held him back. Ludo's whip snapped in the air.

"Brutus," Aulus stated calmly. "Why don't you let that slave go? She'd not do well for any type of fucking now." He waggled his brows, indicated she wasn't well. "Here, she's perfect for you," he pushed Farina at him.

With a grunt, the drunkard let go of Gustina, shoving her off him with a force that made her stumble as he swayed to his unsteady feet. He picked Farina up, his grunt louder than her wail as he knocked the air out of her lungs. "Gratitude, Aulus."

Cernia's husband smiled and waved the fat man to follow the boy slave into the bedrooms. She stared at him shocked. When he turned to Gustina and told her to go to the baths, she wanted to yell. "What do you think you're doing?"

Aulus brows fretted as he stared at the gladiators. She too had noticed how Marcus had stopped fighting once the girl was released. But this made no sense. Why did her husband not allow their guests to choose whom they fucked?

Her husband glanced at her but failed to answer. Instead, he continued his discussions as if the matter hadn't happened. She fumed. They'd be the talk of the town if word got out that they curtailed to the whims of a slave.

Frustrated, she stood, glaring at Aulus. The man ignored her. She wanted to scream. He had no idea the damage he'd done tonight. To his family, his political life and the stability of his slaves. For it was painfully clear to see—that arrogant champion, a slave himself, controlled her husband, a true Roman, all over an insignificant slave girl.

"Tamera," she ordered, snagging a pitcher of wine off the table and heading to her own baths. She had filth, the dirt of nagging, demanding slaves to cleanse from her body.

Tonight she'd pray to the gods for their help because she needed to rid this house of that murdering bitch before someone died at her hands.

Marcus' demon roared blood when that arrogant ass took Gustina and finger-fucked her before him. Iduma grabbed him fast. "You can't kill him," he warned harshly. "They'll kill her and then crucify you for killing a Roman."

As if he gave a fuck. After three years of groveling before these people, his people, he didn't care. He fought to throw his friend off only to have three other gladiators wrestle him to be still. If he'd had weapons, he would have killed them all.

He caught Aulus' eye and saw his Dominus' flicker through the heady wine he'd drunk, slowly remembering what he'd told him about the girl. The man's quick action saved everyone, including Gustina from that fuck who thought to rape her.

The moment she'd left the room, Ludo hauled the gladiators back to the ludus. The guards threw Marcus into his cell. He smashed the back wall face first before he knew it. Pain shot down his injured chest and arm but he didn't care. It only reminded him he was still alive. Damn it!

"What seized your brain?" Ludo asked, his voice strained.

Wiping the blood from the corner of his mouth, Marcus glared. "I told Dominus not to touch her."

"You have lost all sense. She is but a slave. You may have pushed for her purchase but Dominus owns her and you," the doctore spat. "He could've ordered your death, all over a little piece of ass?"

"She's mine." He'd claim every right to her. Aulus knew that.

Ludo stormed up to him. The doctore stood half a head taller than Marcus, and he was just as strong but it didn't intimidate Marcus. And the man knew it as he went a step further and poked the virtually sealed wound with the end of his whip. Marcus felt the pinch against the puckered scab. The streak of agony dug deeper in his muscles.

"Worth your life?" The man glared at him, quiet for a moment. "Shit." And he left.

Marcus sank to the bed, breathing heavily. The demon growled inside, wanting life. He closed his eyes to tame the beast. It was not the time....

The door opened to his cell and closed. He heard nothing.

Slowly, he opened his eyes.

Standing before him, her hair still damp from the baths and dressed in a normal, sky-blue tunic, stood Gustina. Chin up, shoulders back, she stood, challenging him.

Despite the pain, the scrapes from hitting the rough wall, his body tightened. His mouth went dry.

Gustina.

CHAPTER NINE

Gustina stood before him, terrified, angry and numb. As the door shut behind her, fear coiled down her back but she refused to acknowledge it. He was just another man. Like the rest. No better and no worse.

Ah, but he's so much better looking, her mind teased. Still dressed in the pure white linen cloth, the folds placed so precisely over his cock, his skin weathered from hours spent outside in the sun, muscles rippling over his chest and stomach, he was a god. Apollo or maybe even Hercules. His bare feet rested on the dirt floor, corded tendons and contours ran up his legs. She couldn't tear her gaze from him. He knew it, just sat and drank her in.

The puckered seam stood out on his chest and the scrape above it. His lower lip puffed slightly, as if he'd been beaten, but it was hard to tell when his square jaw ticked. Those brown eyes, dark, desire brewing at the surface.

The pull to him came from deep within. Her heart skipped a beat, the air in the cell became heavy and she couldn't breathe. She tried to swallow but her mouth was too dry. Heat spiraled inside her, deep, pooling in her lower stomach. A small voice inside her screamed and fought for control—a control she could no longer maintain.

He exhaled, and she realized his tension matched her own. Strange, for this gladiator, this champion of death, to be tight because of her. That realization gave her strength to struggle from this quagmire of desire. Until he stood and took a step closer.

"I was sent to pleasure you," she stated as brusquely as she could. Even she heard her voice hitch.

He smiled. Warm and intoxicating, with dimples. She felt like she was drowning.

"Truly?" he asked, his voice rich, deep and smooth like good wine.

"Yes," she whispered. "Dominus said I am to see you satisfied."

He laughed. Her toes curled at the heat rolling off him, covering her. "And what do you want?" His seductive voice broke her defenses and lulled her into his arms. He bent his head to kiss her.

Marcus opened his eyes to find the woman of his dreams standing before him. She smelled of lemons, and her skin glistened from the oil in her bath. Her hair, still partially tied in braids hung loose, draped over her back and shoulders. He longed to run his fingers through it, to grasp the silken threads. Desire filled his body, his cock twitched and hardened with each second.

Saying she was here to pleasure him released his inner monster, his need to bury his shaft deep inside her burned him. She seemed so small and frail in his arms, but he'd seen her strength. For once, he didn't know how to act. Slowly, he lowered his his lips to touch hers. Gently. She stood, accepting them but nothing more. And she trembled against him. Fear gripped him. The man whose whole world had been destroyed, the man who'd been thrown into the pit of the arena, to fight for his life, who now stood as champion of Rome experienced a terror larger than the rest rolled into one.

She'd never been kissed without a backlash, without forced submission. He'd seen this result before. Never by his hand had he forced any woman. Not the wealthy matrons who bought his cock or the whores sent to appease him.

But her lips were soft and warm. She submitted, splitting them open for him, but she shivered again. He couldn't, damn it all. The demon in him slammed into his chest, protesting loudly, but he pulled back from her mouth, his gaze on her face.

Her brow knitted as she slowly opened her eyes. He caught the flash of fear, and saw the color drain from her face. A curse echoed in his head as he let her go and returned to his bed.

"You do not want me?" Her voice quivered.

He snorted. "I do. I have wanted you in my bed ever since I saved you. But not if you do not want it." Gods, he sounded like a spoiled Roman. Well, he remembered being that—once. Got him here for being so. His gut clenched.

He watched her swallow hard, her eyes glistening with tears. Her hands fisted at her sides.

"Has anyone else touched you? At the Villa?"

She looked up under the fringe of her dark lashes. How had he missed those before? Pulling her lips in nervously, she shook her head once. He gritted his teeth.

"Not even Dominus?"

"No." Her voice broke on that one word. She swallowed. "Not since that first..."

Damn, how he hated that man.

"Not to worry. He *tests* all the female slaves," she muttered.

He wanted to gag. Disgusting brute.

"They've left me alone," she whispered.

He frowned. His huntress, the woman of iron, melted here before him. What in Hades happened? He tilted his head, trying to get her to tell him without saying the words. Something happened because she inhaled deeply, standing straight, like the pole that stood on the training grounds, ready to be swung at.

"I was told to pleasure you. If I don't, they'll punish me."

Fuck. That bitch of a domina, no doubt, threatened her. *Cunt.* He bit back the curses and stood again. "Gustina, how long have you been a slave?"

She raised her chin defiantly. "My whole life."

He sighed. "And you were given to another to lie with? Ordered to do so?"

Her jaw tightened but she didn't answer. Nor did she back down. In fact, her eyes pierced his. "And haven't you, as Champion, been ordered to do the same?"

He laughed. "Yes, but for me, it is different." He had Rome's finest wanting him. She, though, had been stuck with the dregs, no doubt. He walked up to her and felt pleased she didn't move. "Have you ever been kissed? Really kissed?"

Her eyes turned troubled, and her tongue snuck out to lick her lips. A faint shake of her head told him what he wanted to know.

Desire swirled inside him again, fast and hard, like a storm at sea. As much as his cock throbbed, he would not take her, but he so wanted to kiss her.

"Gustina," he murmured, taking her hands and pulling her against him. He took her lips, pressing against the soft flesh, his tongue gently prodding her to open. He licked the corner of her mouth before he tried again. She parted hers and he invaded her mouth, not lightly but with a driving force that grew once his tongue tangled with hers. She tasted of sweet figs and almonds and her. His arm encircled her back and she molded to his bare chest, her breasts against his. He moaned. *She was his.*

༺☙༻

Gustina's world flipped when he kissed her. She'd never been kissed. Slobbered on, yes. Licked, assuredly. But to have him seduce her mouth undid her. It was sensual, sending a lightning bolt down to her belly, igniting a fire in her loins she never knew existed. No man had ever made her feel this way. His arms embraced her, hugged her, smashed her body against his rock solid chest and abs, each line defining his muscles shaping around her thin form. His hands held her, gently but firmly. This was a gladiator? The man who beat most of Rome's best?

Her breasts tingled against his chest. His erection pushed against her belly and the pool forming between her legs. A shiver simmered through her, one of excitement and expectation, a longing she'd never felt.

He stopped, looking down at her, his face questioning.

"I'm not hurting you, am I?"

She swallowed hard, unable to find her voice. "No, no. I've just never...." How does one admit she's never experienced gentleness? Or desire?

He pulled away from her.

She wanted to scream.

"I wouldn't hurt you," he whispered.

This gladiator, this rugged, hard man, was seduction and favor wrapped together for her. The gods had heard her prayers—to feel needed, loved, even if only for a second. Something she'd never truly knew in her life. Her last Domina cared for her, tried to protect her but couldn't prevent the Dominus from taking her. She swore she'd never be able to truly give herself to another man, not when her whole being had been struck in the hardest way. One could not refuse their master. But she'd longed to feel something, other than the numb shield she put on in those times, making her feel dead inside. A feeling that only amplified after her Domina's death. But this man, this gladiator, saved her. Why? Only the gods knew and maybe, just maybe, this was their reply. To let her taste a moment, however short or long, of true love, even if it wore the casing of desire.

She stepped to him and reached for his cheek. Standing on her bare toes, she tried to touch his lips again. With a growl, he met her. His gentleness was gone, replaced with hunger, and she found her own matched his.

"Gustina," he fiercely whispered again, his fingers nimbly undoing the tie at her neck with one pull. The top fell, exposing her breasts. His hand skimmed her body and cupped one mound, his thumb rubbing over the hardened nipple. She sucked in her breath at the sensation. Men had rudely gripped her there, pinched and bit, but not grazed for their desire or hers. The difference made her knees buckle.

He lowered his head, nibbling at her neck and down over her collarbone to her breast. His tongue lavished the nub, swirling and then his teeth nipped it. The sting was immediate but soothed by his tongue. The sensation sent a tempest roaring inside her. She arched her back toward him, her hands gripping his upper arms. A cool breeze kissed the skin of her backside as her dress slipped down her body. He'd released the belt at her waist without her feeling a thing.

The muscles in his arm flexed as his hands settled on her hips, lifting her gently and easing her on his bed. He slid in next to her, his fingers tracing down her stomach to her hip and skating over her outer leg.

His gaze found hers. "Tell me to stop, and I will."

Tension buzzed in his voice and showed in the tick in his jaw. He didn't want to. The dark pool of desire in his eyes told her everything. He wanted her, desired her, and would make her his if she said yes.

Nervously, she rolled her bottom lip into her mouth but never took her eyes off his. Her lips curved up on one side. "Yes."

∞

Her reply was so light he barely heard her. Gods, she had a body. He melted at her lips. He'd be a puddle before long. And her eyes—they appeared deep blue with desire, like the lapis in Venus' temple. The taste of her skin on his tongue remained, a fragrance of lemons and her. His cock hurt, hard as a rock.

Her hand fell to it and gave it a stroke.

He moaned. "One more and you'll be wearing me," he swore, gently removing himself from her fingers. He liked it but wanted to be inside her.

Her body stiffened. Something happened, something that made her feel like a bird ready for flight, but he was lost as to why. He gazed into her eyes and saw it, for a second, the flash of pain before they went dull, unfocused, and her mask of submission slid into place. What in Jupiter happened? His mouth opened but before he could speak, she twisted on the pallet, presenting him with her backside, her legs parted.

Everything tightened inside him as his arousal dissipated and the demon squealed unmercifully inside his head. This was what she knew of pleasure? If he could find the ass that did this, he'd kill him five times over!

With every ounce of energy inside him, he tamed the wild beast so he could show her better. His finger drew a line up her back to her shoulder and slightly nudged her backward.

"No," he murmured. He tipped her up, his lips catching hers as his thigh manuevered under her hip. As his tongue plunged into her mouth, he pulled her closer to him, on her side and maneuvered so she lay on her back with him over her. He lifted his head and smiled at her fearful eyes. "You have a beautiful ass, but I want more. Let me show you pleasure. I want you to feel the heat of me, like rays of the sun on your face."

She gulped. "To feel its warmth is a good thing."

His lips curved broader. "Yes."

His hand traced down her stomach to the inside of her thigh, his fingers brushing the curls at her apex as he plunged her mouth again. With a finger, he grazed the slit between her legs and rejoiced at the dampness. A gentle swipe of the finger and her legs parted for him. His cock pushed her hip.

His lips still kissing her deeply, his finger slipped inside her slick channel. He could hear her juices as he slid in and out, adding another. She felt so wet, tight and ready. When she groaned in his mouth, he nearly exploded. Raising his hips, he settled between her thighs, his cock nestled against her fold.

"Are you sure?" *Why in Jupiter's name did he ask her?*

She smiled at him seductively as she wiggled her hips under him, opening up. His eyes widened for a second, and he smiled as his shaft entered her. Buried to the hilt, he looked at her. Her mouth closed tight, like a thin line. Damn, he took her too fast. Despite his body's urge to plunder, he waited for her to adjust to him. Her lips softened as he moved inside her. He could wait no longer and withdrew, to thrust into her, over and over and over again. She matched his rhythm, meeting him, her body pulsing around him.

A groan slipped from her, or maybe it was him. Harder and harder he pushed. Her legs wrapped around his as she bucked beneath him. Faintly he heard, though it was difficult as his blood pounded in his ears, her call his name. Her channel clutched his arousal, squeezing and it set off the explosion, the stars burst in his head as his seed poured into her body. At the same moment, he cried, "Mine!"

⁂

Lucilla sat on the cushion, her cup almost empty. "Ethia."

The dark-haired slave with her olive skin appeared silently at her side, a carafe of wine in her hands. She watched her fill the cup, emptying the container. Lucilla grunted. The girl was so thick in the head. "Get more wine."

"Yes, Domina," she bowed and fled.

Lucius glanced up at her from his scrolls, a grimace on his face. "The girl had barely finished before you started throwing curses at her," he admonished.

Her lips curled in disgust. Setting her cup down, she slow rose. Gods knew, she practiced daily how to move sleekly like the panthers the Emperor imported. She grinned at his expression of appreciation. Oh, yes, she knew how to entice her husband—she'd better after all this time. She glided over to him, the veils of her stola floating around her. He licked his lips. It made her want to jump. He still desired her. *What a shame she couldn't care less about him.*

At his side, her face turned pouty. "You don't plan to spend all day over these parchments?"

Before him lay many texts from the Senate's meeting and the upcoming gathering.

"Lucilla, my balls are in the Senate's ass," he brushed a faint kiss on her cheek. "Let me get ready for this, and then I am yours."

Her heart skipped a beat, not in expectation but more of trepidation. If only she could delay him. "But I so wanted to go to the Portico of Octavia." She knew he liked the Grecian marble statues of the gods. Her fingers skittered along the front folds of his toga. The soft feel of the white wool, the edging of the red border and the smell of it and the oil lamp actually made her hot. Her husband, an up and coming senator. A consul, no less. Power and prestige upon his house and his family. On her. But that also required something in return. A child. According to the priestess, Lucilla needed her husband's cock, or any cock, inside her within the next day, before the sixth hour.

Lucius wasn't an old man nor was he young. His hair retained a brown color with only a trace of grey. He was a man who enjoyed life, particularly if it involved politics, which in turn left little time with her. She'd married him for his prestige and the coin he possessed. Riches to equal Crassus. No matter how much Lucilla loved Terpio to fuck her, she'd do it again in a heartbeat to be the wife of this strong and powerful man.

Just that issue with a child. If she didn't produce one, he'd divorce her for some young whore who'd take his cock. Or he'd adopt a child. But that was just as bad, for that left her with no position if he died and the child had a mind of its own.

His brown eyes sparkled as his lips curled. Bile rose in her throat and she swallowed, the acid taste, mixed with wine, burning. When his hand caressed her cheek, she feared he'd try to divert her with bed and she couldn't, not yet, despite what the Juno priestess claimed. It would take more wine, a lot more, before she could spread her legs for him. Not that he was loathsome, just boring. Dull and boring, like the Senate and all those dinner parties and festivities. But the denariis he made off this political status paid nicely for her loyalty. She hiccupped and quickly covered her mouth, trying not to giggle. Loyalty. Till Terpio was around…

"All right, we'll go to see the statues again," he stated. She jumped with anticipation. "And in return," he continued, his hand on hers, raising it to his lips. "I will bed you like a proper Roman woman."

Somehow, she continued to smile but her insides wanted to retch. Might as well give in and pray to Juno it worked. Otherwise, her only remaining option was to fool him, using Marcus' cock as the instrument to her wealth and happiness. His seed had grown inside her once. And this time, that gladiator would have no choice but to get her with child again. She grinned.

CHAPTER TEN

Marcus, for the first time in longer than he could remember, felt complete. Curled next to him, Gustina dozed. He should also, but he refused to close his eyes to slumber. Instead, he tried to capture her forever in his memory, the feel of her skin, the warmth of her body, the color of her hair, *everything*. His fingers travelled down over her shoulder blade, the ridges of her spine, and the rise of her hips. Soft, luxurious to him, so much he feared marking her with his callused fingertips. He'd taken her twice more, showing her the heights of the heavens with his touch, beneath him, over him, his cock deep inside her. When she cried his name in ecstasy, he relished the sound, roaring in triumph.

He'd exhausted her, and she trusted him enough to rest in his arms. The gods answer keenly felt. But the night would end, and life would return to normal. Him training, and she back in the Villa. Together, but apart. No, his path lay clear before him—he must win his freedom. Until then, protecting her would be difficult. Tension racked his body. If Aulus got close to her…

Gustina stirred next to him. Damn, his fears woke her.

She turned her head toward him, attempting to blow the stray hairs from her forehead and failing. He brushed them aside and smiled. She blinked. The sated blue sparkle in her eyes warmed him deeply. Her lips curved happily to him even more so. The gods blessed him.

"I wake to find you staring at me," she teased, shifting so she faced him. "I thought you were tired."

He chuckled. "I've rested." He nudged her nose with his

finger.

Her nose crinkled as her grin turned lopsided. "Stop."

Laughter filled the air. "I can't stop. My cock has a mind of its own."

"I'm too sore to consider such entertainment."

Inside, he winced. He should have known she'd never been exposed to passion. She melted under his touch. How could he leave her be? "Apologies."

"Don't be," she murmured, reaching over and kissing him.

He growled and pulled her tight.

"Champion," she said, her hand on his chest. "I cannot stay." She rolled out of his grasp and stood, stepping into her tunic, tugging the ties up around her neck.

Fucking Romans. No, as a slave, his right to have her all night evaporated into the air. At the sign of dawn, Ludo's whip would snap, and another day of training would begin. Her duties required her at the Villa, to attend whatever her Domina required. He wanted to spit. He threw his legs over the side of the bed and sat and watched her struggle to get the ties underneath her mass of hair that he had tangled with his fingers. With a deep sigh, he stood and helped her.

"So, I can report you are satisfied?" she teased but the slight tremor in her voice belied her humor.

His arm snaked around her waist, and his mouth plundered hers. Her body molded against his, as if made for him. He finally broke the kiss but didn't let her go. "Yes. But I want more."

Gustina laughed. Color filled her cheeks. It made her look so alive, how could he ever let her go? But he didn't stop her as she headed to the door. With a nod and a smile, she opened it and left him.

He fell back onto his pallet. Her smell remained in the wool blanket and he just lay there inhaling it. *Gustina*.

⁂

Terpio leaned against the chair, feeling the pinch of brass edge against his jaw. Esha, his body slave, excelled at the use of the blade and never nicked his face as he scraped Terpio's stubble. A painful procedure, even with water and the drop of oil over the blade, he ignored the raw attack on his skin, his mind adrift.

He hadn't heard from Lucilla in a week. Anger flared, and he quelled it for fear it would overwhelm him. Esha's skills might fail for him flinching. Holding his breath, he concentrated on the statue to Lares, the domestic spirits that protected his family. He laughed inwardly. What family? His father and wife dead, and his brother was indeed not his brother. A low chuckle echoed forth before he could stop it, but Esha stopped the stroke of the blade in time. He should praise the man for being so attuned to his movements, but he was a slave. In a good house. Terpio reassured himself this was a good house. Right. House of Flavus. This branch, though, was filled with lies and deceit. Fuck. He gritted his teeth, praying to the gods Esha would finish already.

Esha rubbed the spiced bay oil across his face, the tingling sensation caused a stinging and soothing feeling simultaneously. Terpio shook his head and yanked the cotton rag from his neck, shoving it into his slave's hands.

"Go."

Esha bowed, grabbed his tools and left. With a deep sigh, Terpio walked out to his veranda, overlooking his garden. The perfect yard, green with grass and various flowering bushes, looked as if Jupiter himself had pissed on it from the heavens. He rubbed his eyes. Damn inconvenience, not having total freedom. His father's funds remained tied up in some Forum chamber until....

"Dominus, Gaius Paetus."

Terpio nodded. Gaius better have brought the news he wanted. Adjusting the folds on his toga, he walked into his house and to his desk.

Gaius Paetus stood rigidly, his blue tunic and russet toga stained with dirt. The man's grizzly face and greasy brown locks made Terpio cringe but remain. Gaius was one of the best to find unique items. Hopefully, he'd discovered Terpio's.

Terpio squinted. The man didn't say a word. Squeezing his lids for a moment, Terpio went to the side table and poured a cup of wine. He shoved it into the man's hands. "What did you find?"

"Can't find her," he muttered and downed the contents of his cup. Threads of wine dripping down his grizzly beard. "It's like she didn't exist."

"You truly do not believe I will pay for that type of news?

Surely records are kept." Terpio did not think for one moment Gustina could've escaped her execution.

"Yes, of course, but she was only a slave. Why does it concern you now, a month after the fact, to verify her death?" Gaius pushed his cup for more wine.

The man was Terpio's only friend, if he could be counted as that. Swallowing the knot of dread down his throat, he splashed more wine into the beggar's cup.

"Truly, Rome keeps records of each execution."

"Of course, but I found no record of her being admitted in the first place."

Terpio's thoughts scattered. His worst nightmare unfolded before him. The gods came to him during his sleep and told him she still lived. A disaster for him. She remained the only witness to his his wife's murder. She didn't see him pour the potion into his wife's cup nor did she see him anywhere near the scene, but she did know how his contemptuous wife hated him and all he stood for, or perhaps, didn't stand for. Still, he knew the girl blamed him for this. But he believed the gods came to his aid in the deed by having Gustina discover the body and, by all appearances, be the one to kill her.

Alive, she could destroy him.

Dead would be far better.

But alive and returned to him answered his prayers. Strangely, he missed her. Her soft skin, the curve of her body, the taste of her mouth and the tight cunt. Oh, yes, he adored her body. And he'd trained her so well. It had taken him several times of beating her, forcing her to submit and frankly, he'd been disappointed when she finally succumbed to him.

But there was always a thread of an emotion, deeper than carnal pleasures, that ran through him when it came to her. And he hated the premonition the gods gave him—that he cared for her. His gut twisted. After everything that had happened to his family, to his feeling of self, a level of comfort resided when it came to Gustina. He knew it went further than the feel of her body. Perhaps it was more than the satisfaction of knowing she was here for him, anytime, and could never deny him, never abuse him. He sipped his wine and grimaced as it turned sour in his mouth.

Gaius stared at him, a blank look, as if expecting something. What? Had the imbecile been talking and he missed it?

Gaius harrumphed and set his cup down. "I shall leave you then."

"No, wait. Continue the search. I know she was taken to the arena. She killed my wife. Clemency for her actions doesn't exist. I refuse to let my wife's murderer escape her sentence."

Gaius snorted. "Terpio, how long do you think that will stand?"

"Have you found any indication in your search that would advise me otherwise?"

"No, no, but your ill-tempered marriage wasn't hidden from higher ups in Rome."

Terpio slammed his cup down on the table, wine splashing all around the tabletop. He fumed, wanting to strangle the man, but considering his situation, it was not a wise decision. Instead, he went the more indirect route. "Find what I need to clear this issue, and I will make sure your pockets carry enough to free you of such pursuits in the future."

The reward caught the man's attention. With his brows shooting upward in surprise at the hefty price, he curved his lips as he bowed out the door.

Terpio heard his faint footsteps going down the hall. The fireball of anger rose quickly inside him, and he threw his clay cup at the wall, wine splashing everywhere as the cup fell, breaking into many pieces. He feared his message from the gods was true, and Gustina still breathed. He must either take her…or kill her.

※

Whoosh. The sound of the wooden gladius slicing through the air wasn't loud but the pain of the sword's edge radiated through Marcus' arm, reaching upward, into his shoulders and chest. He growled, his gaze focused on the man who hit him. Spurnicus, the blasted Thracian, grinned, his sword ready to strike again.

Uttering a loud noise, he pounced on the man, his two gladius arcing, coming down in a cross angle as Marcus struck the bastard on his collarbone.

Spurnicus groaned and stepped back at the attack, his feet stumbled, and he almost fell. Stumbling to a knee, he raised his own shield as the champion leapt toward him, swords in air.

The Doctore's whip snapped in the air. "Gladiators, rest and eat. We'll resume after midday sun."

Spurnicus, still on his knees, glared at Marcus' raised weapon.

The champion breathed hard. He hated Thracians.

Iduma nudged his side with his own gladius. "Marcus."

Gulping down the fear, Marcus lowered his weapon. "Till we meet again," he said to Spurnicus. The man's hard look didn't alter, and it took him a minute to rise. The Thracian spat at the ground, near his feet and stormed off to the tables. Marcus clenched his fists around his weapons.

A chuckle cracked the air behind him. "Thracians are a nuisance, like the Gauls, but you haven't been in the fight all morning. Your cock too tired to let you think?"

The tension drained from him at once. Only Iduma knew him enough to make such bold assumptions, and he needed the man to bring him back from the edge of a dream. But she hadn't left his mind all day. He drifted asleep after she left him in the pre-dawn hours. When Ludo's whip cracked at dawn, he'd woken disoriented and confused. Had he lain with her last night? Her fragrance, the smell of lemons and her, remained on the bed, enough so that he didn't want to rise.

His arm hurt from his fragmented attention. He snorted, his lips curled upward. "Hardly a question I care to answer."

The man laughed and slapped him on the back. "That, my dear Roman, tells me all."

Marcus glanced toward the Villa. If only he could catch a glimpse of Gustina. As if the gods heard him, he saw her and the other girl, Farina, carrying something on the side of the home. His grin widened. Did he see a spring in her step? A happy stride because of him? When her head turned his direction, he caught his breath with a hope. He couldn't see her expression but did notice the tilt in her head.

"For all the gods, man!" Iduma laughed. "If you don't get your mind off her, I might even get a chance to beat the latest champion of Rome!"

Marcus' lips tightened. "Pull your cock out of your ass," he sneered. "I will beat you after noon sun." He picked up a bowl of gruel and lump of bread from the cook.

Iduma continued laughing as he grabbed his own.

<hr>

When Gustina's step hitched and they almost dropped the large water jug, Farina glanced down on the training area, the Ludus. She saw Marcus, the Champion of Aulus, standing in the middle of the sand, staring up at them. A quick glance at Gustina showed her what she expected. The girl was enamored with the man. Not a good thing in a Ludus. A mistake, actually, because it'd become another way to control her. Cernia need only find the most minor of offenses, blame Gustina and threaten to sell her or, at least, keep her from the man. To break her friend's gaze, she kicked a few loose rocks at her feet.

"Gustina," she said loudly. The girl didn't budge. She shook her hands, knocking the jar, the liquid sloshing out.

Startled, Gustina tightened her grip. "What?"

Farina's jaw clenched. The pang of jealousy rattled through her as she glared at her fellow slave. Gustina was no better than she. She knew it. So why had she been given to that fat slug? He'd chosen Gustina, not her!

The girl must have seen the accusation in Farina's eyes, because she frowned at her.

"Farina," she started. "I didn't mean to...."

"Don't," Farina cut her off. "Not now. It happened. But don't think you'll always be safe. That you won't be forced to...." Her voice cracked. Her eyes blurred.

"I know," she whispered back. "I know." She sighed. "I know I'm just a, a new body for him. He'll tire of me, and I'll be left to whatever."

Farina stopped, infuriated. "No, no, you think you're just like me or any other slave girl here? Oh, yes, Marcus has had most of us. We've been his *reward* for his wins. Anything to satisfy the Champion." She inhaled, trying to steady her breath. Gustina needed to know the truth. Farina tried to laugh at the absurd idea filtering through her mind. "He's possessed, you know. A demon, or so I've heard. The only thing that drives him to win. To annihilate whoever they place before him. No woman has ever made him happy, or at least, not for long." Her mouth quirked as sadness flooded her. Gustina's face was too blank to read. "Gustina?"

Gustina shivered at her friend's words. Farina was right. Her savior from that fat Roman cow was Marcus. She knew her role all too well. Slaves being used in every possible way, including coupling, by their master's whims, be it with another slave, a guest or the owner. Her position meant she could never marry, never have a normal family life. The slaves in a house formed their own union of sorts, a friendship in a way. And those relationships were often tested, as hers with Farina's was last night.

If it hadn't been for Marcus, she would have been forced to submit to the fat bovine who shoved his fingers inside her, drooling spit on her neck at how she'd be so good for him. As in the past, bile rose in her throat at what else he'd stick inside her. When his fingering lifted her off him, her mind cleared as her nerves went dull, the pain from the intrusion, the fact that she was a slave and pain was part of her life. In that moment, the welcoming numbness slid into place, so whatever the bastard did, she'd feel nothing.

Even after the Champion stopped her subjection to the Roman, the fact she was sent to Marcus came from her Dominus' command, not of her own free will. But unlike Farina and her own past sexual liaisons, last night the gladiator took her into a type of happiness she'd never felt before. He'd shown her that being with a man, with him, could be pleasure and not pain. The numbness was not needed to protect herself.

But now, from the look in Farina's eyes and her harsh words, Gustina knew her time with Marcus needed to be kept in her heart, memories to relive in quiet moments and not ones to be experienced again.

"Farina," she started again as they reached the door to the Villa. "You are right. I should not let a few fleeting memories stop my duties. My apologies."

Her friend gave her a weak smile. "I say it only to protect you. Domina will not be happy if you have airs of importance about you, of being protected from her orders. I'd hate to see you punished for being sent to do Dominus' bidding of satisfying the Champion. She'd dislike seeing you smile so absently as you have been this morning." Her voice dropped. "And for yawning."

Gustina couldn't help but giggle. Her tiredness plagued her and when she recalled the reasons for it, she smiled. Trying to school her face now, she bit her lip and the sharp attack by her teeth stopped the grin. "I will remember. Gratitude."

Farina nodded at her, and they both broke into laughter.

Despite all the warnings, Gustina's gaze turned left, trying to glimpse into the ludus, and she secretly prayed to the gods that Marcus didn't tire of her too quickly, because her heart was falling for him.

CHAPTER ELEVEN

Aulus stood at his desk, the scroll before him. He reached for his cup of wine, sipping the bitter dregs, the acid tearing at his throat. "Tevia!"

The gaunt, pasty-skinned man appeared before him. Damn, his stealth could unnerve even the gods.

"Dominus," the slave's shallow voice barely discernible as he bowed his head.

Aulus snorted, his lips twisted. "Is this all the wine I've got remaining?"

"Yes." Tevia shuffled his feet. "Domina's slave has been absent this morn. Sent to market, I believe."

Verenia. Yes, now he recalled. The cunt was swallowing his cock when Cernia walked in and took offense to it. Perhaps her justification had merit. He awakened to find himself in a state of arousal and his wife absent so he called for Verenia, who said her Domina went to check on the kitchen staff. The woman dealt with house slaves instead of being there, with him. Granted, he might have been aggravated at Cernia for her abrupt departure from last night's festivities after he gave that fat cow Farina instead of Gustina, but for the wealth of his house, it was the better choice. If the woman couldn't reconcile herself to his decision…out of pure frustration, he'd grabbed Verenia and pulled the tab at her neck, causing her tunic to fall off her body. The fact that Verenia dropped to her knees and wrapped her lips around his cock demonstrated what a well-trained girl she was.

Then Cernia walked in, right as he felt the rushing need to explode. But he held back, withdrew from the slave, tipped his wife over, lifting her skirts, and plunged in. Within three strokes, he roared, his seed splashing against her womb. He felt so much better, the tension drained from him as he pulled out. What a surprise when she turned and slapped him hard across the cheek.

"Cernia!" The sting of her palm burned his skin. "What in Apollo's name?"

"Do not swear at me after you took me like that!" Her face was inflamed with rage. "As if I was a common slave! For the love of Jupiter, do not ever try that again!"

Damn, she infused his arousal again. A smile slithered across his lips. "I love it when you blaspheme so." He snaked his arms around her middle, dragging her against him and she fought him every inch of the way—a mistake really, because he knew she enjoyed their rough play as much as he did.

So in retaliation, she took the slave to the market and the keys to the wine cellars with her. Damn. He poured the rest of the swill into his cup and downed it. Bitter to the last drop, he thought, wiping his mouth with his hand.

"Doctore requested your presence."

Aulus' lip curled as he tried to concentrate on his scroll. "Whatever for? A gladiator got his tongue in someone else's ass?"

Tevia shrugged, his face bland. Aulus snorted. Tevia's services were unequalled. Smart, dutiful and ever quiet, he reminded Aulus of a panther at night, eying his prey before he pounced. But he truly wondered if the slave ever had any inclination to "pounce" on his own? For his own gain? The man didn't flinch under his owner's watchful eye.

"Fucking balls," he muttered, throwing the writing stick down on the desk and closing his scribe book. He stormed off to the training grounds, his blood boiling.

Down the stairs, across the alcove, he walked to the edge of the overhang along the side of the training sands. Before him, twenty fighting men lunged, blocked and recoiled with wooden gladius and battered plank shields. Only the retiarius' net held true, swinging into the air and landing on the opponent, wrapping around him, a strangle hold. The air held the stench of sweat, blood and grime. Aulus' eyes strained to see through the dust cloud the men's sandaled feet made, maneuvering on the ground.

"Doctore," he called above the sounds of grunts and groans, the smack of wood upon wood.

Across the arena, Ludo glanced up at the sound of the call. Aulus waited while the man walked toward him, somehow avoiding being struck by the gladiators as the whole grounds was constantly moving, arms flying, bodies leaping. Aulus' hands heeled his eyelids, trying to rid them of the grit forming out of the dirt. Combined with the sour wine, he'd have a roaring headache and then some.

"Dominus."

"You wanted to see me?"

"Yes. You requested me to update you on the men, with the games to begin within a week."

Aulus felt the energy drain from him. That was all this was about? Position of men for the games? He swallowed the knot in this throat. "Certainly. Who gains favor in training?"

"Iduma should stand well. His training with the champion has aided his skills."

"Quiet a compliment from your lips for the Brit you figured dead, the moment he arrived."

The trainer chuckled. "The same response uttered from you upon Marcus' arrival."

"Truer words could not be said. Well, then place the Brit higher in the standing and we shall watch his abilities bear fruit or wither, equally as well." The slave of Britannia's cost was staggering at the time but Ludo assured him he saw the man's true colors under the filth and blood. Aulus didn't like wasting coin for nothing but trusted the old gladiator's advice.

As Ludo continued with his report, Aulus saw on the other side of the grounds, at the gate barred in the back, the return of his wife's transport and Verenia. His cock twitched as he saw the slave girl glance his way and her lips curve slightly. A dangerous girl, he thought, but one he'd gladly reprimand for taking her attention away from her Domina. That is, after he got the key to the wine racks back.

"And Marcus appears more on the mark," the doctore continued.

Aulus barely heard a word the doctore had said, his mind envisioning Verenia's mouth stroking his cock again. He shook his thoughts clear at the name of his money-making gladiator, the one who brought wealth and honor to his house.

"What of our Champion?"

The man glared at him. "At first, I wasn't thrilled you allowed that girl to service him, but I've pissed in the wind, doubting your judgment in the matter. Her attention to his cock seems to have worked. He isn't on a bend to kill anyone here in his path, solely out of his own torment."

"And his possession by whatever evil spirit?" Aulus knew the rumors. Marcus acted as a man possessed by demons from the Afterlife, ones that drove him to succeed at the arena and earn the wealth around Aulus' family, but it also haunted him, making him difficult to train and appease. The Brit's companionship had whittled away some of the cold, murderous gladiator here at the ludus. When the man demanded Gustina, paid his own coin to have her here, Aulus feared he acted out of other madness, since she, too, was a killer. But, apparently, she calmed him. She just better not tame him too much.

"The demon struggles to surface still," Ludo stated. "I see it in his eyes. Let her swallow his cock some more, and he should become more refined as a winner."

Aulus smiled. That he could do, because he didn't want her mouth around his cock. No, she looked innocent enough, but he wouldn't trust his body to her, especially her teeth. But that could give Marcus what he needed and if so, the house of aedile Aulus would soar to the gods in favor. *Yes.*

※

Lucilla threw the ball into the air and pummeled it with her hand, sending it across the netting to the opposing team. The duo gauged its arc and the man plunged, the palm of his hand nailing the leather ball squarely and returning it back over the net. Cernia dived but missed it and the thud of the ball hitting the sand resounded dully as it sat, immobile.

"Come here. We'll get them to drop as hard next time." Lucilla extended her hand to her friend.

With an aggravated sigh, Cernia reached up and grabbed her. Standing, she brushed the sand off her legs and stomach.

Lucilla laughed. "Don't forget your ass."

Her friend smirked at her but quickly ran her hand over her backside.

Trajan's Baths now called all Romans in the afternoon

hours, after the markets closed and lunch was devoured. A magnificent gathering spot, even those with baths in their Villas, like Cernia, still came here to mingle with friends, play sports and bathe. For Lucilla, a senator's wife, the Baths stood high on her social calendar. The place for her to appear, show herself and promote Lucius. She smiled. No, more the place to be seen and look over the male populace of Rome, in their athletic skills, to see who might make it to her bed.

Today's heat, though, climbed higher and the ballgame made her perspire more, her body wrapped in a loin cloth and her breasts wrapped securely in a long piece of linen, crossing her chest and tying behind her neck. A drip of sweat rolled down her chest between her breasts and further over her flat belly. Her blond hair, twisted and pinned off her neck, the ends loose and bathed in perspiration, added to her presentation of herself as Athena. Or she hoped it did. Cernia was attired the same, but her dive into the sand to reach the fallen ball had coated her bare skin and hair with sand. She definitely failed at the goddess look—something Lucilla strove not to ruin for herself. This also forfeited them the ball because she had a taller frame and longer arms than her friend and could have reached the ball. And in doing so, be coated in the grit. No, she wanted to remain goddesslike to the end, for the men they played against were quite young, handsome, and stood drooling over her. Her lips curved up on one side, and she blinked at them. It was hard not to laugh at the dark-haired Adonis whose mouth dropped open, his lust for her written in his eyes.

"Stop it," Cernia hissed, wiping the grit off her hands. To their opponents, her tongue turned to honey as she soothed, "Gentlemen, if you'll excuse us." She grabbed Lucilla's hand and turned to the water baths behind them.

Lucilla's jaw tightened. But of course, Cernia didn't want a male lover. For their opponents' view, as they walked away to the baths, Lucilla swayed her hips slightly and then turned her head.

Cernia giggled. "Showing them your best asset?"

Lucilla's anger at her friend dissipated. "No, what they're missing out on if they don't follow us."

"Lucilla, you can't fuck them in the baths."

"Why ever not? You're not naïve enough to believe

everyone is just talking in the baths, are you?"

She saw her friend's cheeks turn red. "No, I suppose not. But I'm not looking for a lover." Cernia looked at her. "Of any type."

"Oh, I see, and Aulus is quite the tiger, is he?"

"Lucilla, please," her friend begged.

"You used to be more open, Cernia. What has he done to you?"

They sat at the side of the pool. A rather large basin, filled with hot water that sent steam rising into the air, making it difficult to see clearly. Lucilla glanced back to the ball field. The two men were gone. *Damn!*

Both women slipped into the heated waters. The luxury of the hot water, the slight rolling of it as others moved, sending ripples and waves, made Lucilla want to lay back and forget her problems. Cernia, though, wasn't going to allow her that peace.

"So how goes the baby problem?"

The water lost its effect on Lucilla as a chill crept up her spine. A baby. She closed her eyes and prayed silently to Juno for aid. Swallowing the knot in her throat, she knew she had to answer because Cernia wouldn't let the subject drop.

"It's progressing." There, that was an answer.

"And you're with child?"

She breathed deep, forcing her body to relax. "We are still practicing."

Cernia laughed loudly. "Fucking will get you there. I asked if you were now with child but apparently not."

"The goddess said it might take a cycle or two."

"For what?" Cernia's voice sounded shaky. "What potions are they forcing down you?"

"No one is forcing me to do anything," she seethed. "I'm taking a drop of tonic, blessed by Juno herself. You know the goddess herself had problems at one time with Jupiter's seed."

"Yes, and as I recall, it meant she had to share him in bed because he strayed. Is that what you want? Lucius loves you."

Yes, she thought he did, too. But men were so frail when their cocks were involved. And if she didn't turn up carrying soon, she'd have more to worry about than his shaft penetrating another cunt. "Of course he does. And I him. I'm sure this time will work, and once a child is planted, then I can play with any man I want." She bent forward, her voice dropping to a whisper. "Like that black-haired stud who banked that ball."

"Lucilla!"

She shrugged.

"And if it doesn't? Will you do one of those treatments?"

Cernia's look of concern was warranted. The thoughts sent a shudder through Lucilla. Some women submitted to the worst degradations to get pregnant, but she refused to lay there, her legs spread for them to pour seed and other stuff into her. Bile rose in her throat at the image in her head. But she needed to produce a child or find herself divorced and abandoned. To have that happen from her senator husband would mar her forever, alone and destitute. Fear slithered through her.

"No, of course I won't. I will get with child," she said, smiling tightly. One way, or another, even if it meant submitting herself to Marcus' rutting again. *Holy Juno, please hear my prayer!*

⮠

Marcus sat at the side of the bathing pool in the lower chambers of the Villa. The other gladiators also there, dipped into the pool of oil and took the strigil, a long, slightly curved, flat-edged tool, to scrape the grit and oil off their nude bodies. The task masked their low existence, not to have water but just oil. It took Marcus weeks, once subjected to his role of slave and gladiator to become accustomed to this. Memories of going to Trajan's Baths and many other delicacies was just a fading dream of a life long since dead.

His hand slipped. The sharp edge sliced into his skin. He hissed.

Iduma chuckled. "Keep your thoughts here or you might find yourself at the medicus tonight instead of your bunk."

He snorted with a nod. Thoughts of Gustina filtered into his mind. A snarl rose inside him. She'd better be waiting for him. He saw Aulus talking to Ludo earlier, saw their gaze fall in his direction. If they thought once about removing her, he'd kill them all.

"I can hear your growls," his friend's voice was low but tense. "Cease all thoughts of violence. If I can hear you, don't think the others can't."

"I saw Dominus with Doctore," he hissed.

"So? They speak. All the time. Nothing worth slaughtering over."

"If they touch Gustina...."

"Jupiter's cock," Iduma laughed. "One night with her and she's got your balls in her ass? You can't think?"

Marcus glared at him. His friend didn't know these people like he did. Pain and suffering was an easy gift to the slaves. Meted out daily, hourly.

"Dominus won't deny you this," Iduma continued. "You are his champion, his bread. You earn his fortune just by being alive and fighting. He'd not risk losing any of it over some mere slave."

With one final sweep, the excess oil was off and Marcus threw the tool to the floor and stood. "For his sake, you'd best be right, Brit."

Iduma snorted. "You know it better than I, Roman."

Marcus grabbed his subligaculum, wrapping it around him as he grinned at his friend. The Brit, so wiry and savage when he'd arrived a year ago, had filled out under the training. His wildness tamed, his body toned to fight to the death if called for, *sine missione.* But in comparison to Marcus, he remained more wiry and light on his feet—a way to best a stronger, bulkier man—and an excellent training partner, unwilling to fold before the Champion. He grinned and left.

The guard stood next to Marcus' cell door. The room, built out of a wall of rooms for those who won enough to get singular quarters, remained a cell regardless of title of its occupant. The night was warm but he felt a chill sweep over him, as if warning him he'd be alone tonight. The guard's face was blank revealing nothing of what waited inside for the gladiator. Inhaling deeply, he steeled himself for the emptiness of the room and the jug of wine he knew awaited him.

He walked into the dark cell and heard the door close behind him, the latch clicking into place. Eyes closed, he allowed the spectre of loneliness to pass over him. But in that second, he smelled something. Not dirt. Not wool. No, sweet, like almonds. He opened his eyes.

"Hello," Gustina said. She lay on his bed, lounging in a simple blue tunic. Her belt off, the slit on the side parted, showing her thigh. Long, light brown curls hung loose around her shoulders and down her back. Her pink lips pursed, as if holding back a smile and waiting for his lips. He tightened, his cock twitched. When she swung her bare legs over the edge of the bed, his insides clenched with anticipation.

She stood and pulled the fabric tie at her neck. "I've been waiting for you." The tunic fell to the floor, leaving her nude body for his appraisal. Her nipples hardened, her body bare of any hair.

His mouth dried, and he stood breathless for a second. His wish was granted. In one step, he had her in his arms, his lips on hers, parting them as his tongue plunged in. She returned his kiss heatedly, her arms around his neck and as he lifted her, her legs wrapped his bare waist.

Yes, no killing tonight. No, the gods heard him well.

Lowering her onto his bunk, he realized he'd already torn the subligaculum aside, and her hand was on his cock, guiding him to her opening. He stopped her and looked into her blue eyes. They sparkled, like sapphires in the moonlight. "Gustina," he whispered.

"Yes, Marcus."

At the sound of his name rolling off her tongue, seductive and low, he slipped into her and forgot his world.

CHAPTER TWELVE

Terpio hated crowds. Especially crowds of Romans. The type that lingered around the Forums as if they had all the time in the world, oblivious to the needs of others to get to appointments – or even better yet, the time between them, to catch a senator's attention. Groveling he didn't like to do but if he didn't, Lucius might wave him off as if he were nothing more than a slave, or worse yet, a bug.

The Roman Forum stood, brilliant and blindingly white between the blue sky and pale packed dirt and brick road. The piazza itself was overwhelming to newcomers, the type Terpio ran into, because they came to a stuttering halt and marveled over the complex site. Long porticos lined the space with freestanding columns sprinkled in the middle. Statue masterpieces at the top depicted the gods and the Caesars. Noonday sun beat mercilessly down on the people milling about, their mouths flapping uncontrollably with nonsense, or so it sounded to him. He passed one of the many temples that lined the piazza, like sentries on guard. Perhaps he should find a deity that could aid him, if only he'd taken the time to make an offering and pray. Except he had nothing to offer and the gods frowned on those promising to pay later. No, he had to continue on, past the temple of Jupiter and Juno, beyond the crowd at Castor and Pollux, with the cacophony of people bickering over the exchange rates posted there. Bankers, moneychangers and fathers loitered—the fathers not so much for money but to register the birth of a child, as common Roman law demanded.

With a mutter of disgust, he shouldered his way through

the masses to the Senate building. Walking through its pillared hallways, he found Lucius' chambers. He stopped, adjusting his blue toga, making sure the bronze-colored striped trim lay just right. Shoulders straight, his arm bent to carry the toga tail appropriately, Terpio inhaled and took a step into the room.

Lucius wasn't alone. Terpio faltered, his sandaled feet scuffing the tiled floor.

Lucilla's husband looked up from the scrolls on his desk. With a tight smile, he said, "Terpio, what a surprise."

"Yes, well I'd hoped to catch a moment of your time, Senator Vibenius." That sounded steady to his own ears.

The senator grunted. Nodding his head to his right, he kept his forced smile. "Senator Decimus Porcius Scaurus, may I introduce—"

"Terpio Rufus Flavus," the man said, his eyes squinting at Terpio. "Yes, I believe I recall you from the court hearings. When was that? Three years prior?"

He ground his teeth, forcing his lips to curve. Of course, the bastard remembered the judgment against his imposter of a brother. As big as Rome was, surely that story would have been buried by now. "Senator Decimus, how nice to see you again. It has been ages."

The man's nostrils flared, like a disgusted sow at a bucket full of shit. He did give a small nod, finished the drink in his cup, placed it on the desk. "Lucius, do let your wife know I will miss her company tonight, but I've matters I cannot avoid."

"I'll tell her you'll grace her presence upon your return."

Decimus nodded and left.

"And what can I do for you?" Lucius bent over his papers again, as if Terpio was nothing more than a slave. It was an insult he'd not let slide—after he got his position back.

"I wanted to thank you for your support."

Lucius sighed, glancing up at him. Terpio so wanted to hate the man. He'd stolen Lucilla from Terpio's grasp. But, truth be told, he couldn't blame him. She was gorgeous, willing, soft and so fuckable. And she was like him, taking whatever opportunity presented itself to make it in this life, despite what the gods did to make one fail. She just hadn't waited for his wife to pass. Pity.

"I aided you at the request of Lucilla. While I'm aware of

LOVE & VENGEANCE 89

your acquaintance through your brother, I do hope for your sake, it is simply an old circumstance."

Terpio got the warning. So Lucilla hadn't been able to pull the wool over the man's eyes about her indiscretions. He smiled and winked at the senator. While he might admire the man's assumptions, it wouldn't stop Terpio from screwing her to insanity next time he touched her.

"I have no brother, as it was clearly stated. The man was an imposter."

"Don't you mean *is*? He fights in the Arena as champion gladiator."

Terpio guffawed. "Perhaps. But one knows, gladiators don't live long. Not that I'd do anything so crass as to forward him to the Afterlife." Outside of taking his wife from him and condemning him as a criminal for impersonating a Roman in a respectable house.

The rebuff made Lucius' face soften, as if he struggled to refrain from laughing. Terpio watched the knot in the senator's throat slowly fall as the man swallowed. "Truly, for I'd lay coin you bet on his wins."

Terpio shrugged.

Lucius laughed and poured more wine, shoving a cup into Terpio's hands. "I believe you'll do fine back in some position. I believe I can have you placed as a quaestor."

An investigator? Over financial issues? Sounded better to him all the time. That, along with the bribes he could inspire on certain issues. Played right, he could win Lucilla back. The gods definitely showed him their love. He smiled.

※

Gustina sighed in utter contentment, stretching her nude body over Marcus' as he lay on his bed. Resting her cheek on his bare chest, she let her finger slowly swirl around his nipple, her nail scraping the hard nub once then twice. He twitched beneath her and she smiled. His fingers threaded through her hair and tugged gently as they combed through her locks.

"I wish it could be like this forever," she whispered, fearful that saying the words would end this time of happiness.

His fingers stopped mid-stroke in her hair. The interruption to his caress made her look up into his eyes as she tried to figure out his thoughts. He remained quiet for a minute.

"Why should it end?" His voice was gentle, soothing in a way. Rather disconcerting considering he fought on the sands to survive.

She frowned. "Because we are slaves. We're not allowed to be happy."

He chuckled.

"It is nothing to laugh at," she said, annoyed he'd thrown her fear aside as if she were but a child. Propping her head up at him, she glared at him.

He cupped her cheek. "How long have you been a slave, Gustina?"

"All my life."

His lips curved. His hands grasped her shoulders, pulled her up to his face and, in one swift move, turned her beneath him. She loved the feel of his flesh next to hers. The oiled baths he took made his sculpted torso and thighs smooth like marble but soft and warm from the summer evening. She quivered and anticipation ignited the fire in her belly, the length of his arousal pressing against her abdomen.

"And you?"

With a growl, he bent and took her lips. Soft, inviting, his tongue nudged her mouth open. His hand cradled her skull as he plundered her mouth, his tongue seeking hers. His kisses were like honeyed figs, sweet, luxurious and addicting. Her hands slid around his neck as one of his snaked around her back. His other hand scooped under her thigh, lifting it right as he raised them up, her resting against him as he steadied on his knees, without breaking the kiss. With one leg up, she felt open and vulnerable. The tip of his cock pushed against the wet, swollen lips of her core and then slipped inside her, hard and fast. She sat on his lap, pinned by his cock and his arm holding her. Pistoning in and out of her, his arm lowered some, allowing her to bend back, arching toward him. His mouth latched onto her nipple, his teeth grazing the hardened nub. The sting of his teeth shot right through her just as his tongue laved away the pain. It made her insides tighten, the river of desire flowed through her groin as she moved in sync with him, her hips rising at his thrust.

"Gustina." His voice was husky, raw, painful.

Her mouth was too dry to answer, but her body responded

to him, driving her hips faster to his plundering of her wet slit. Another move and he hit her womb. Stars exploded in her mind and she shattered in his arms as he groaned. Inside her, his cock trembled as it filled her. He breathed heavily, never releasing his grip. Which was good, because she didn't have the strength to hold herself.

Slowly, he lowered them to the pallet, still intertwined as one. His shaft diminished and she wrapped her legs around him as if she could keep him inside her forever.

He buried his head into her neck and hair, nuzzling her.

"You didn't answer my question," she stated finally. He groaned, the sound vibrating against her skin. "You don't act like a slave. You're too forward, too demanding."

The ripple of his breath fell on her as his chuckled.

"You do," she stated adamantly. "Very demanding. And you have a look…."

The last few words made him look up, his eyes gazing inquisitively into hers. But he said nothing. She dragged her bottom lip between her teeth, studying him. His dark brown hair was tousled, the faint lines at the corner of his eyes visible, his square jaw firmly set. *But his nose.* It had the look of the aquiline Roman form with a hitch, no doubt from sparring in the Arena. She frowned.

"You look Roman." She stated it as a fact. That got a response out of him. She saw the flash in his eyes and the tick in his jaw. "That's it. You're Roman. Not born a slave." His lips tightened to a thin line. She'd hit it right. Still he refused to say a word. She snorted. "How did you become a slave?"

Four years ago….

Marcus lay on the cushions of his bed, plopped another almond into his mouth and grinned.

"Truly, consider it."

He shook his head and held his wine cup out for more. The slave girl quickly filled it and backed away to the wall. The frightened look on her face he chose to ignore. Easy to forget when before him stood his wife, nude and luscious. He licked his lips as he fixated on her breasts, large, firm and their tips ruby red, the nipples erect from his suckling them. Her long blond hair hung loose from the pins and ribbon that made it stand up on her head in a style he saw so many Roman women wearing. He hated that look. No, running his fingers through those silken strands was what he desired and he did, despite her protests.

"Marcus, you're not listening to me."

No, he wasn't and had no intention to, not as long as she stood before him, naked and so desirable. Her ivory skin glistened from their lovemaking. His gaze roved down her body. The indent of her waist, the curve of her hips, the long shapely legs and the slight bulge of her stomach with his child. *Oh, how the gods had blessed him.*

With a sip of wine, he answered, "No, I am not willing. You are carrying my child and now you want to play? Not even with slaves but to bring Terpio in?"

She smiled devilishly and crawled back up to him. "It might be amusing."

"To be in bed with my wife and my brother? Somehow I think not."

Lucilla huffed and jumped out of bed. *Damn, out of his reach!*

"I ask for a little excitement and you, you shut it down without consideration!"

"Lucilla," he said, the words slurred. Strange. He hadn't drunk enough yet. "I can't stand the thought of watching another man fuck you. Why do you wan' that? Why...Terp...Terp...my brother?" What in Jupiter's name was happening to him?

She sighed loudly and picked up her wrapper. "I knew you'd do this. There might have been a chance but, like most things, you'd send it to the piss-barrel before any rational thought crossed your mind." Uttering a disgusted huff, she whirled and left the chamber, the frightened slave girl following closely behind.

He lay there, confused, not even noticing his hold on his wine cup had slipped. When it dribbled on his chest, he looked down, his mind muddled. What just happened? In his own Villa? He and Lucilla enjoyed a rather wild sex life—they fucked wherever and whenever they wanted. And now that she carried a babe, she wanted variety? With his brother, for Jupiter's sake!

Maybe, though, sex was the only thing they had to hold them together. His thoughts stumbled. His father, the stern and domineering Tiberius Didius Flavus, threatened to disown Marcus for marrying her but didn't. No, instead the old goat went on to the Afterlife, leaving Marcus to enjoy his wife and home.

After only four months, now she wanted them to invite his brother to their bed. A shudder passed through him. What if she hadn't waited to ask? What if she'd already fucked Terpio? Pregnant, she wouldn't be 'caught.' His stomach roiled.

"Dominus," Cadmus said softly, into Marcus' ear. He didn't hear his body slave approach and he started, spilling the rest of his cup. The slave pursed his lips, taking the cup and handing Marcus his clothes. "Praetorians."

Praetorians?

Now he could hear their marching feet. And the noise grew closer. For the love of the gods, what was this all about? Shrugging the tunic on, he grabbed his toga, wrapping it shoulder to waist and back to his opposite arm right as the Roman guard entered.

"We are here to take Marcus Sextus Flavus for treason."

⸺

The memory of that day haunted him for months. It disappeared when they gave him over to the ludus—the Emperor's training fields—to see if he could fight. Even with practice gladius, he felt free. What had replaced that nightmare? Justice? No, but it would come. What replaced it was the sands, the bloody fights and his inner demon, coiling with the desire to kill.

He blinked hard, banning those memories. The weight of Gustina grew heavier as his mind returned to the present.

"How did I become a slave?" He repeated her question. A hollow laugh escaped his mouth before he could shut it. Gently pushing her off him, he reached for the wine jug, poured himself a large amount and downed it with a gulp. "Yes, I am Roman—or so I thought."

She swallowed. He could hear it. "Arrested?" she asked. He heard her voice falter. "For debt? You sold your freedom?"

If it could have been that easy. Some did that by choice,

others because the creditors sold them for payment. Low, despicable position. But not in his case. "No, I was accused of falsifying who I was. Apparently they had papers, of my father, that declared I was a deserted child, cast off as a babe, and he claimed me. Later, my brother was born, to my parents. Therefore, with them dead and me taking the home, I *stole* from my brother. A thief, a liar and a traitor to the family." The bitterness seeped back into his blood. The demon prowled.

He walked away from her. Could not bring himself to see her face.

The silence was thick. He could've cut it, if he had a gladius. Hades, they'd never allow him to keep such a thing.

"They kill those accused of such." Her whisper hung in the air, like a noose to strangle him.

He shook his head, squaring his shoulders. "True. But I wasn't going down without a fight." He turned, looking out the small barred window above the door. The early evening sun gave off pink rays, bathing his face in its warmth. The bars reminded him of what he was. A slave and nothing more.

Oh yes, he remembered, standing there, in the Basilica Julia, before that pompous judge and all the crowd. Yes, the trial made the talk spread. The famous house of Flavus, burning in the flames of a false son pretending to be real, so he could claim it all. And Marcus only added to the show, appearing before the judge with his right eye swollen shut, his lips torn and still bleeding, his left arm bandaged. The guards behind him not much better, bandaged and puffy from the battle he waged for being held for trumped up accusations.

"Therefore, my verdict was guilty, but I didn't get sentenced to die by animals or the sword. No, I'd fought my guards and anyone who'd tried to get in my way. It took several of them to keep me under lock and key." He laughed bitterly. "So the ass who ruled over the case, sentenced me *damnatus ad ludum*." Sentenced to be a gladiator. And he knew the man hoped he died in the Arena.

Bile rose in his throat as all the sour memories hit him in full force. He closed his eyes, dampening the hatred that burned deep. No, not now. Gustina was here. If he didn't stand before the closed door, he'd have thought she'd slipped out, it was so quiet behind him. As if she had deserted him. Just like

Lucilla had.

Clamping his mouth shut, forcing the vomit back down his throat, he turned. Before him, she sat on the edge of his bed, the color washed from her face.

His demon roared.

CHAPTER THIRTEEN

Five days. Five nights. Alone. Anger and remorse loomed at the last edges of sanity. Instead of dwelling in the abyss of loneliness, Marcus focused on the inner demon, the monster that lurked beneath the surface, delivering another crushing blow against his opponent. However, the man who stood before him, the man who suffered the strength of madness behind his swing, was a brother in this ludus of gladiators.

The thud of Ahaz's knees hitting the hard ground, his wooden shield and sword shattering soon after with his grunt, caught Ludo's notice and his whip lashed the air.

"Marcus!"

Marcus snarled, but he lowered his wooden swords, switching them to one hand as he offered Ahaz his other. The Syrian panted in pain but with a seething breath, ignored the champion's assistance and pushed himself up, using his own weapons to aid him. He stood, glowered at Marcus and limped off to the water barrel.

"What's crawled up your ass?" Iduma stood next to him, watching their fellow gladiator hobble away.

Marcus inhaled deeply, glancing at his friend. Only the Brit had the guts to come close to him when he was in a fit of rage. Either the man was immensely stupid or wise beyond his years. Marcus frankly didn't care, for the anger subsided for a second.

Rubbing his forehead, Marcus answered, "Five days. It's been five days."

Iduma laughed. "Five days since…?"

Marcus growled. The Brit laughed.

"Five days since you've fucked? So Ahaz is to pay for it? Granted, he's a shit-eating Syrian, can't trust the lot, but since when did you switch to men?"

"Fuck off, Brit."

"No, no," he continued laughing. "I get it now. It's not that. You mean your slave. Gustina." He chuckled loudly. "You, boy, are a gladiator. Not some coddled Roman. Or had you forgotten your status? Kill or be killed? For the honor of this house?"

"I am well aware of my status," he spat. "But I did pay for her...."

"You paid to keep her from the beasts. Nothing more. If anything, you forced Dominus' hand in this."

Marcus' anger flared. How dare they keep her from him! His demon danced, begging them to continue, fanning the gladiator's madness.

Iduma's gladius blocked his friend from going toward the Villa. "Five days is nothing. You've gone longer, you know. Perhaps not that long without wine, granted, but without cunt, yes." His voice lowered. "Keep up this arrogance and Aulus might rid himself of the problem."

Marcus stopped. "He wouldn't sell her."

"If his champion kills his fellow brothers, why would he keep her? She'll be considered too big a distraction to you."

Inside, he knew the Brit was right. He clenched his fists, fighting for control. The demon whimpered. "I think I might've driven her from me."

The Brit snorted. "If your bedside in any way resembles your aggression on the sands, I might agree. But I've seen you driven to possess other cunts, whores even, with more lenience than a blood-thirsty gladiator. So I doubt you've made her run...."

"I told her about what happened." Marcus' words fell from his mouth before he could stop them. Even he could hear the anguish in every syllable.

Iduma's eyebrows shot up. "Truly? Why?"

The whip snapped. "Gladiators! Resume!"

The Brit turned to face him, still waiting for his answer.

Marcus exhaled as he placed his feet into position for the first thrust. "Because she figured out I was a Roman." His arms came up, wooden blades poised.

"That isn't a secret here, you know." The Brit took his stance, the shield and gladius in position. "What drove you?"

Eyebrows knitted in frustration, Marcus shrugged. Why had he? Because he again wanted to share his life with another? Or had that demonic being inside him, which ate at his soul, pushed him to drive her away? Reasons didn't matter at the moment. What did matter was how he could get her back.

※

Aulus rummaged through the papers, frustration rising. He could have sworn it was here. Where the fuck did he place it? All that coin and nothing when he wanted it. He uttered a moan.

"My, what has you in such a temper?"

He glanced up from his desk to find Cernia standing before him, her body slave Verenia behind her. A smile began to slowly curl on his lips when he realized it was the slave he gazed at, not his wife. *Shit.* He dampened the grin.

"Papers, my dear. Important papers."

Her mouth pursed. "I suggest you put that aside. You have a guest."

The impatience in her voice caught his attention. No more fucking her slave—for a while. "Who has graced us so?"

"Quintus Verus Agrippa."

"The Magistrate Verus?"

She nodded.

This could mean great news. Or the worst. Verus was not one to stop by for social calls. Not at this Villa. "Have the best wines out and—"

Bitter laughter spilled from her mouth. "I do believe I know how to greet our guests." Her eyes were cold. He'd have to make it up to her later, and stay away from Verenia. "He awaits you in the atrium."

Aulus stood straight, his fingers lightly threading over the folds of his toga, but he found none disarrayed. Squaring his shoulders, he walked past Cernia and her voluptuous slave, who winked at him. *Maybe later.*

Verus stood in the center of the Atrium, at the edge of the indoor pool, watching the colorful flower petals floating on the surface.

"Magistrate Verus, to what do I owe this momentous visit?" Aulus walked up to the man, extending his hand in welcome.

Verus' brows shot up for a second and, after a moment of hesitation, he grabbed his host's hand.

"News from the Senate." He took the proffered seat.

Cernia took a chair to the side. As Aulus sat, he saw out of the corner of his eye his adoring wife giving simple gestures to the slaves around them. He so enjoyed her ability to direct them with vague orders given by her seemingly vague hand movements, barely noticeable to the naked eye of their guest.

Farina appeared along with Gustina, carrying a wine jug and metal cups, followed by a boy slave lugging a tray full of olives, grapes and figs. They settled the food and wine on the tables. Farina poured, Gustina offered the cups and the boy—what was his name? Esdras, yes that was it—took the bowl of almonds around.

Verus, lounging on the cushions, took a handful and dumped them into his mouth. Aulus appreciated the hum of pleasure from the man and caught his eyes following Esdras. Information Aulus would pocket away for the future.

"So, what is so vital at the Senate to prompt a visit? Unless you have other interests worth requiring?" Aulus feigned, gauging Verus reaction.

The older Roman smiled. "News of Trajan's win over the Dacians."

"Finally!" Aulus exclaimed, raising his wine cup in the air.

"Yes, how truly exciting," Cernia added, a sly grin on her face to her husband.

Verus nodded, his face flush with excitement and the Falernian wine he swallowed. "Yes, so a hundred days of games are to be offered in celebration."

Aulus' anticipation leapt. "One hundred days?"

"Yes, within two weeks time. Trajan will be returning, and we want the crowd's enthusiasm high."

"Surely, that will be no problem."

"No, we'll start with chariot races until we gain more beasts for the Arena and get the outer gladiators in."

"True, with that many days, many will be needed…"

"Which brings me to my visit," Verus turned to Aulus. "Though I am curious. Why do you not have a lanista for your ludus? As aeidle, surely your time is busy...."

"With no doubt," he interrupted. He waited before continuing. All too familiar with this argument, for Cernia had badgered him for months after his first election to the post. But it was *his* ludus, they were *his* gladiators and with Marcus, he didn't care to make any changes. "After my last lanista died, it was best for me to run it. When I got it from my father, after his passing to the Afterlife, I worked to get it to the winning stock it has. With an excellent doctore, I have no need not to keep a hand in it. A minor hobby, so to speak."

"Well, with champions like you have, I can see you have an easy time," Verus laughed. His eyes, though, roved the room, back to Esdras. And then they wandered to Farina and Gustina. Aulus noted it.

Cernia sat back, watching her husband so easily slip into the role of host. The man was born to lead. With her help, Verus stayed, drinking wine and talking. Frankly, she found herself bored by the whole thing. But the magistrate's connections helped her husband and she had to remain, like the dutiful wife she was.

Her watchful eye kept an accounting of food and wine available. She sent Verenia for more and caught her husband's gaze following the slave. That'd have to be stopped. The fact he owned the girl and all the rest meant he could order any of them to suck his cock whenever and however he wanted, but for her to walk in and see him plowing into her body slave and then into her was too much. Let him have his orgy, but she would never come after a slave.

Arguing in her head about this incident, Cernia nearly missed Verus' hand snake under that new slave's tunic and slap her ass. The girl stopped and didn't move, the wine jug gripped firmly in her grip. Verus' hands skated up the girl's legs and under the skirt again. At the same moment, his gaze slid over to Verenia.

Over her shoulder, she whispered to Verenia to get more wine. The slave gave her a slow, sadistic smile and disappeared. Cernia grinned at her husband and guest as if nothing had happened.

"Because of the numerous games, I suggest we have your

men spaced, in the beginning, middle and end. So they can rest and get ready, of course," Verus stated.

"Of course, that sounds right." Aulus noted in a wax tablet Esdras brought for him.

Verus brought Gustina closer, facing him. He took the wine jug out of her hands and set it on the table next to him. "Come, my dear."

Cernia smiled.

Verenia ran down the steps to the storage, key in her hand. Behind her, the metal-barred door to the ludus stood. She could hear the muted noises of the men still practicing their fighting styles and the lash of Doctore's whip. She stood between the two doors, twisting the metal key in her hands, debating with herself. Her domina sent her for more wine. It would be dinner hour soon, and they had a guest. Only one half-empty jug remained upstairs. Three new ones would definitely see them through the meal, but she couldn't carry three. Two might work but three meant....

She toyed with the idea in her mind, wrangling the thought and liking the outcome. It would require Ludo's aid. Adjusting the strap around her waist so the skirt of her tunic was held open at the slit up her thigh, she turned to the gated door to the ludus.

With a simple twist, she unlocked it and opened the gate to the Afterlife for that bitch upstairs, Gustina.

Verenia's lips curled sadistically as she slipped through the doors. Marcus would be hers.

Gustina poured another cup of wine and gave it to her dominus. Her skin crawled as she felt the eyes of their guest lingering on her. Farina frowned at her from the side, still pouring another helping into their domina's cup.

"Gustina."

It was a whisper, but she heard it. She gazed up and found Aulus watching her. "Dominus."

"If our guest requests you," he said quietly. "You will gladly submit."

She swallowed hard. The protection Marcus' rank of champion placed over her evaporated as did the morning fog hit by the sun over Tiber River. Dread filled her bones. She nodded and backed away to the side table.

Aulus, Cernia and Verus laughed over something they were discussing, not noticing Gustina clenching her fists, or the tremor passing over her. Farina grabbed her wrist.

"Gustina, are you well?" her friend asked, her voice barely audible. Gustina nodded, afraid to talk. Once more, she felt the lustful gaze of the men in the room. Farina's hand tightened on her. "They are all whoresons. No one passes without notice by them." Her voice was tight, threaded with hate. "Let it pass, or you'll bring too much attention upon yourself." She brought Gustina closer to whisper into her ear. "Some of them like to force those who are the most fearful. Surely you know this."

Oh, yes, she did. Strangely enough, she had gotten off lightly at her old house. Her domina was very protective of her and the other women who served the Villa. But her dominus, Terpio...she shuddered at the memory. He'd forced her to do disgusting things and if she refused or was slow, he'd slap her hard, making her do what he wanted. That was when she found the escape—to turn numb. He still took her, always from behind, always pulling her hair, hurting her, but she'd shut down her feelings and survived.

Marcus had changed that. He taught her the beauty of sex, made her feel desirable, made her feel her own passion surface, bringing her joy. To have him take her, face to face, kissing her, nipping seductively, making Mount Vesuvius erupt stars in her head as he brought her to full fervor, screaming his name killed the numbness inside her.

Now, she'd have to find that pathway to feeling nothing again. A couple of times, she'd felt other hands on her and that way seemed to appear, but this man behind her, his eyes full of lust, she wasn't sure if she could not feel it if he fucked her.

And what of Marcus? Surely, he'd understand. She was a slave, just as he was. A being to be used by the Romans, with no remorse for the degradations and abuse. And if that meant lying there, allowing some Roman to slake his lust into her, she had absolutely no control over that. But he'd hate her for it. For having another plow into her.

She hadn't seen him in five days. Not by desire to stay from him. Her flow arrived and with it, pain. It took every ounce of strength to keep up with her tasks, let alone see him.

No man wanted to lie with a bleeding woman. But it ended last night, and she'd hoped her domina would allow her to visit him. Glancing up at Cernia and the feral look on the woman's face as she licked the drop of wine from the corner of her mouth, the odds stacked against her.

Two more guests arrived. She'd never seen them before and didn't care. But she poured the last cups of wine out of the jug to the couple that now lounged on the cushions next to Aulus. The woman was a blonde, strikingly pretty for a Roman, and had a loud voice. Her companion was a young, dark-haired man, who acted unsure about arriving at the drinking fest before him.

The older man, the magistrate, still drank, eying Gustina. She shuddered at the thought of this paunchy, balding man, with his lustful eyes fucking her.

"Get rid of that look, like you might faint," Farina warned her. "The old goat has been staring at Esdras, too, so you might get out of sucking his cock."

Yes, she'd seen his gaze wander to the lad. Esdras' face looked bland, his eyes vacant. He'd found that place. Why couldn't she?

Farina shoved the bowl of dates into her hand. With a nod, she returned to the den of vipers behind her and offered them the sweet. When she got to the old man, he was seated upright, at the edge of the lounge, legs open. Her legs moved sluggishly toward him. When he grinned at her, licking his lips, she wanted to retch. Biting her bottom lip, she held the bowl for him to grab a date. Stubby fingers picked up two and promptly dropped them, one onto his lap, the other onto the tile floor.

He stared at her, his head cocked, indicating he wanted her to pick them up. A chill raced up her spine, her knees bent, trying to keep a distance between them. Reaching down to pick up the one on the floor, Gustina's ears buzzed and she felt lightheaded as the others laughed—over what she had no clue, maybe her clumsiness as she stumbled.

Verus wasn't laughing though. His eyes turned dark with desire, and she saw the date on his lap move slightly. She closed her eyes. It moved as his cock thickened beneath it.

"Come, my lovely." He grabbed her wrists. Her eyes shot open. She'd given him such easy access to her, and she blamed her own stupidity. "Pick it up with your lips," he murmured.

The heat from everyone else in the dinner party bore into her, and their laughter ceased the closer her lips got to his lap. He still had her wrists and he pulled her to him. "Oh, look. Clean that up, too."

The date had stained the cream-colored wool toga.

Laughter started again, though she did notice one male voice absent. Aulus. *How strange he didn't participate.* When her lips brushed the fruit, she found the pathway again. The swine twitched his cock and the date jostled a smidgen to the right for her. She moved and wrapped her lips around it, her chin rubbing the fabric lightly. Verus groaned low. Inside, she winced. She'd rubbed not just the cloth but his shaft as well.

Verus didn't release her wrists. She knew he wouldn't. So she had no choice but to swallow the fruit. Staring at his chest, refusing to look into his eyes, she inhaled the date and quickly forced it down her throat, gagging.

"Oh, Venus," Verus moaned. *Damn, the man watched her movements and of course, carnal thoughts came to him.* "Now, lick my stain away," his voice growled.

No more emotion, outside of utter disgust, washed through her as her head lowered. At least, there was a layer of wool between him and her. Cold seeped into her bones as she bent above his lap. At the obvious sign of her acquiescence, the old man let go of her wrists, which fell to the cushions on either side of his legs. Her mind shut down as her tongue took the first swipe.

∞

Marcus drudged up the stairs, unable to believe his dinner was postponed until he acted as a common house slave, carrying more wine for the Romans. He, the champion of this house, doing drudge labor. He should have known better when he saw Verenia on the landing, asking for Doctore. Ludo assigned both him and Iduma to carry two jugs of wine. The doctore must have seen the anger flare in Marcus' eyes, because he trailed behind them, his whip in hand.

"Stop that glaring," the Brit muttered at the foot of the stairs. "Perhaps you'll see your woman and find out why she's been vacant from your bed. Or, at the very least, we might get wine tonight to drown your sorrows."

He growled but nodded.

Verenia had a shit-eating grin on her face that he couldn't ignore. It was like she planned for his help, not that Dominus had sent her for it. Something wasn't right, but he couldn't figure out what it was. The hair on the back of his neck bristled. As they got closer to the Atrium, his demon prowled near the surface.

They rounded the corner, and Marcus barely held the two jugs at the sight before him. Romans, lounging on the furniture, laughing, the smell of wine in the air along with almonds, sweets and...sex. Among his owners sat three guests, the two men he didn't recognize but the long-haired blonde he'd never forget. That bitch of cunt, Lucilla—his wife. The sight of her alone clenched his muscles. The demon yelled to kill her, but he stamped it back. Not here, not now, he promised it. But soon....

Verenia took one of his jugs, and he balanced the other, concentrating on the scene before him.

He tore his eyes from Lucilla as the group fell silent. It was strange for them to quiet when but a moment ago they'd been boisterous. It lasted only a second and then applause filled the air with the sounds of amusement. They all seemed focused on one spot. It took a second, but he zeroed in on the elder man, magistrate robes on him, looking down at his lap, his mouth in a sated grin as his head fell back and he groaned.

"For the love of the gods...." Iduma swore.

Marcus found Gustina. His woman. The one who controlled his demon, his dreams, his hopes and desires, bent over the crotch of the magistrate. The man's bare knees, the fabric pulled up, the back of her head bobbing, and the man's moan undid the gladiator.

The wine jug slipped from his hands, shattering on the tile floor.

His hands clenched and his blood boiled. His demon roared for blood.

Kill them all!

CHAPTER FOURTEEN

Aulus couldn't believe the pile of shit he just swam through to recover the disaster upstairs in the Atrium. His own blood still raced through him, causing his head to ache. That bitch Verenia was trouble and he knew it. Cernia begged him not to beat the girl, that she was only doing her job of getting more wine for their guests. It still galled him that his wife was so quick to protect that little cunt but berate him for fucking her. *Damn, Jupiter's balls!*

He paced the cell floor, dust in the air from his sandals stirring it up as he turned in the tight space. No wonder his head hurt. He stopped, ran his hand through his hair and stared at his champion who sat on the floor, his wrists bound in iron cuffs chained to the wall behind him.

"What in Jupiter's name were you thinking?" He spat at the man. Marcus' head was bowed but he slowly raised it and stared back at him. Aulus winced. The gladiator's left cheek was cut and swollen, turning greyish-blue, and his lip dripped blood from the corner. The guards along with Iduma and Ludo grabbed for him as he roared madly from the side of the room and crouched to attack the guests, particularly Verus.

Though he looked at him, Marcus didn't answer.

"It takes fingers up the right asses to stay in power, to get you and the other men positioned in the games and you try to throw it all away over that girl?" He groaned contempt. "Thanks to the gods, the others stopped you. Fuck!"

"She's mine," Marcus stated flatly. "Not to be used for base sport."

Fury rolled through Aulus as he spun, grabbed the knife

from the guard at the door and stomped close to the gladiator, pressing the blade against the man's crotch. "Base sport? She'll do whatever I command her to do," he hissed.

"Yes, dominus." The gladiator's head fell in submission. He never gave in that quickly.

Aulus pulled the blade back and yelled, "What the fuck is it with you over her?"

Marcus shook his head. "I won the coin. And instead of wine and whores, I want her. And I don't want to share her."

This man, this champion, made no sense to him. All over some little cunt who may have killed her last domina. Shit, that was half his problem with Cernia in dealing with the girl. He saw his wife's crooked grin at Marcus' shocked and angry face when he saw Gustina over Verus. Only Cernia would find a sadistic sense of humor over this, though she had hidden it quickly as she moved to help him recover the room. Gods, the twit's tongue only touched the magistrate's toga. Granted, the piece over his cock, but still....

"You do not tell me what can or cannot happen with my property. You are property, you shit-eating slave!" He paced again. But at the corner of his mind, Verus' news of upcoming games echoed. Fuck! He'd need his champion in rare form—as a fighter, not a rebel. He glanced down at the chained man and sighed. "We have fights coming. I'll expect my best. Reward will be the girl and all the wine you can drink. But, if I send her to another for satisfaction, you will learn your place without pissing in the wind." *Definitely forceful but not encouraging. Shit.* "Or I will deal with her myself."

"Yes, dominus." His voice was tight but his head bowed in submission.

Aulus was through with him tonight and left his champion to sit, shackled to the wall, so he knew his place.

☙

Gustina still felt herself shake and stopped moving, trying to calm her erratic nerves.

"Gustina, take this," Farina said quietly, shoving a bucket filled with broken jug into her hands.

She grabbed it, staring vacantly at the shards of the wine container. The one Marcus dropped because he saw her bent over that Roman's lap. She squeezed her eyes shut as her gut twisted. Her savior, her champion, thought she was sucking the cock of another man. Her trembling came again, this time making the pottery pieces jiggle, like a broken chime.

"Stop it," her friend warned her, her voice low. "You are not responsible for this. You had no other choice but to do as the man told you. Because you are a slave. Just like Marcus." Farina placed another piece into Gustina's bucket. Her free hand lay on her arm and squeezed it with a tiny smile of encouragement on her face. Gustina nodded slightly.

"Besides, if anyone should be blamed, it's that bitch, Verenia," she snarled, looking across the Atrium.

Gustina looked up and saw the other slave standing behind their Domina as the woman talked to the guests. The look on the slave's face when she glanced their direction told Gustina the truth. Verenia must have known the older man wanted amusement and since she herself was protected by Cernia, and the man had toyed with Gustina, the bitch knew he'd press her into it.

"Yes, look like you won, stupid whore," Farina seethed. "But he still won't fuck you."

Gustina appreciated her friend's hatred of their domina's body slave but it didn't change what happened. Her vision blurred as the anger and sadness filled her. "No, but then, he won't want me, either." A tear escaped and fell among the broken pieces.

"Gustina," her friend whispered. "You've done nothing wrong."

She swallowed the fear in her throat. The only man who given her any sort of kindness, who taught her intimacy that brought joy and not pain or suffering, found her servicing another. Her skin crawled, like she'd been sent into the mines, miring through shit and grime. She balanced the bucket on her hip to wipe at her mouth again. The taste of the fig on wool wouldn't disappear, no matter how many times she spit or tried to drown it with water. The warmth of the material, the bulge underneath, the one that vibrated under her mouth, made her want to vomit. Thank the gods she didn't have to actually inhale his cock.

But Marcus didn't know that. He'd think she sucked the man dry. Why would he want her? Her mind twisted the scene, making her feel light-headed. Her disgusting mouth was so dry but she wanted nothing in it. Fear gripped her and she gasped.

Farina made some type of noise, one she didn't hear clearly because her ears began to buzz. The bucket disappeared from her hands and she felt someone, Farina probably, directing her to the stone bench, near the pool.

"Stop this," her friend warned her directly in her ears. She forced Gustina's mouth to open and poured water down her throat. The liquid squelched her dryness, and despite the first response to gag, she let it slide past her tongue. Her eyes shut, trying to bury the pain and loss but the hole inside her, one she didn't have before, grew.

∞

Marcus sat on the floor, the concrete wall behind him scraping into his back but he didn't care. The world before him shifted and he came to the conclusion death would be his only way out of this hole in Hades.

His face ached from being pummeled into submission. To move his lips brought a sharp stab of pain as the split opened again. His right shoulder was sore to move and his knees still felt the deadening pain of being slammed down onto the tiled floor. But his vision couldn't break the scene before him— Gustina, forced to swallow that Roman's cock for pleasure, none of which was hers. And there was nothing he could do to help her. The pain wrenched his gut, stabbing through his heart. No one should be submitted to that.

And yet, hadn't he, as a freed Roman, had slaves do just that very thing? He so wanted to deny it but a voice inside him screamed he had. The demon, restless, angered and frustrated, prowled below the surface, snarling to kill, for death. A place he wouldn't get to easily. One he refused to submit to without freeing Gustina of the torment her life was.

Outside the wall of his cell, he heard the shuffling of the guard. He could take the man, strangle him within seconds if he weren't chained to the wall. Inwardly, he laughed. That was exactly why he was chained. No, no point in looking up. Nothing would change tonight. Aulus left him here to consider his actions again and know that next time, he'd be punished by whipping or even crucifixion. But he doubted anything would've stopped him. He knew she'd been ordered to suck that man's cock. But she belonged to him, Marcus, not the Dominus and the rage still rolled through him, despite his bodily pains now.

He saw her doing as ordered and he broke. Dropped the blasted wine jug, a snarl hurling from his lungs as he launched to her, only to have four men descend on him at once. Ludo, with his whip wrapping around his arm, gave him the lacerations that still burned now. Iduma grabbed his other arm with two guards at his chest, barricading him. He'd struggled, broke free of his friend but not of the whip, which only dug deeper. Twisting, he got past one guard when the other's fist hit him in the nose, throwing his balance off. The Roman guard struck again at his jaw, the ring on his finger scraping Marcus' lip and chin, just as the lasso yanked his arm back and he crashed to the tile floor. *Bastards, all of them,* the demon screamed.

The only winning part of him being detained was that it interrupted her sucking. The old man got up, as did the other guests. He'd shoved Gustina to the floor, her body splayed on the tiles. Marcus' last vision of her was the look of surprise that turned dark as she stared at him, horrified, perhaps? He could handle that. But when her hand wiped her lips, he roared again as a sharp pain radiated the back of his head and blackness took him.

And then he woke up here, bloody, chained, defeated. For he was alone, without her.

Fucking Romans.

"Outstanding display tonight. Dominus truly enjoyed watching you erupt like Vesuvius over her."

Marcus closed his eyes. "I already know his opinion," he muttered, pulling at the chains with his good arm. The anger surfaced but he tamped it back. Tevia couldn't do anything for him except....

"That other arm is in bad form."

He didn't look up at the body slave. Instead, he guffawed. The arm torn by Ludo's whip looked worse than it felt. It still bled and if he moved it too fast, it shot shards of pain up his arm. But he'd been hurt before. Nothing yet seemed to kill him—not his brother, not his wife, not any sot they stuck before him on the sands.

He heard the key enter the lock on the door and the

tumbler fell. "When Dominus thinks my mind is set to purpose and frees me, I'll see the medicus. But for now, leave me be."

"I brought you something to ease the pain," the slave said, but his voice wasn't in front of Marcus. It still lingered to the side, where he stood before the opened door. The gladiator frowned and looked up.

Before him, Gustina stood, barefoot. No wonder he didn't hear her enter.

"Gustina," he whispered, struggling to stand, his gaze drinking her in.

She raced to him, her arms encircling his bare waist, but he winced as her wrist hit his side. Quickly, she stepped back, a worried look on her face. "I'm sorry."

He gave her a smile as his good hand reached for her. The chain had barely any slack to get her but he did manage to get a hold on her and pulled her to him. Snaking the arm around her, he buried his head in her hair and neck, inhaling her sweet almond and lemon scent. He felt her tremble, pressed against his naked chest.

"I'm so sorry," she whispered softly, her lips brushing his skin. The scent that was her, simply her, filled his pores down to his bones.

"Don't be," he returned, moving his hand up her back. Damn cuff and chain stopped him from totally engulfing her and the other hand was useless now. As he twisted to get her closer, he knocked the injured arm and flinched.

She stilled and then pushed back. With a glance at the injured arm, she shot a look at him. "You need that attended."

"I will. Dominus will not let it be."

"Tevia," she called over her shoulder. Marcus didn't like the horrified look on her face.

"Gustina...."

"Here," Tevia said, placing a dish of water and a rag at her feet.

She bent and wet the rag. The first wipe nearly undid him. The wound burned as she slowly, methodically cleaned it, without uttering a word. He stood, mesmerized by her motions. She looked like a nymph, quietly taking care of him. Afraid to even blink for fear she'd be gone, he planted his feet to not move, even if the rock under them stabbed his soles.

The pain subsided as she finished. She wrapped the damp

rag around his arm, splitting the ends to tie it. He noticed she hadn't looked up at him and it puzzled him. Her shoulders straightened and her head raised as she turned, taking a step back.

He frowned. Why wasn't she next to him? He opened his mouth but she cut him off with a glare.

"You almost were killed because of me. What a foolish thought, that you could *save* me. We are slaves, you and me. There is no freedom for the likes of us. No denial of demands, regardless how distasteful they are." She spat the words at him, lashing him like Ludo's whip. He felt it deeply, the bitterness of her tone turned his blood sour. "You do not own me. *Buying me* with coin only stopped them from ending my life that day. But I've been dying for years. Slavery is just that, dying, more and more, each and every day. The only way the gods will set us free. Dominus can order me to suck the cocks of any man he wants and I cannot, ever, say no. You know this." The strong woman he first met at the Colosseum, the one who steeled herself against impending doom, had returned.

Unfortunately, she was correct. Slaves were expendable. Workers and playthings. A life with no meaning. Damn, but he knew another life. He had tasted freedom, squandered it, only to have it removed. And yes, placed in the same position as her, Tevia, Farina, Iduma and all the rest. At the command of their masters. As if Romans were really any better than they, any more chosen by the gods to reign supreme. To speak those words could also condemn him but that had never mattered to him, not in the last three years. Nor, really, before then when he was a stupid man, thinking everything was his for the taking.

"Gustina," he started but her hand raised to silence him.

"They might've killed you for what you did. I could not live with that. As it stands, I'm here only because Tevia snuck me past the guards. I pray to the gods we might return to before, so I ask, no, beg of you, to remember our place. As slaves."

He saw the corner of her mouth quiver and moved toward her. Shaking her head, she stepped back and the chains kept him from reaching her. "You will remember and not risk your life for me?"

How could he do that? Even the demon inside whimpered. He sighed with resignation, inside admitting defeat and he didn't like it. For her, his head fell in admission. Instantly, her hands took his wrists and she turned the key in the locks, freeing him. As the metal crashed back against the wall, he went to touch her but she twisted out of his grasp and flipped her head, the wild mane of brown locks swung to the side and she marched out of the cell, never turning back.

CHAPTER FIFTEEN

Marcus walked out on the sandy training ground, feeling the heat boring down from the mid-morning sun. Three days had passed since he'd been freed, since he'd seen the medicus. Three days since he'd seen her. Three days kept abed, waiting for the lash marks to mend. His orders originally said five days. He agreed to stay inside if he got out of the saniarum, away from the slimy-fingered, shifty-eyed medicus and his nasty-smelling herbs and potions. But alone, in his cell, brought him to the brink of madness.

The fourth hour sun warmed his limbs that felt too tight from sleep. He stretched, his muscles flexing, snapping them into place like a well-oiled machine. Even his forearm, of course, his right arm, the dominant one, burned some as the honeyed marks, wrapped in linen, protested at the fire the sun put on them. He splayed his injured arm's hand, gripping the air and outward, testing the movement.

"Marcus," Ludo called.

He squinted at the Doctore, standing still, legs spread, feet firmly placed. He dared Ludo to send him back to his cell. He needed to be moving, to cast his loss, his fears of no more Gustina, to the winds. The demon, lurking in the back of his head, even called for him to exercise his torment.

"To the palus," he replied.

Ludo nodded. The young aid ran to him and offered the champion two wooden gladius. Marcus' injured limb rejected the grip but he took the other and moved to the freestanding pillar that stood, like a wooden man, for practice work.

Marcus swung the gladius with his left arm, wielding it in

swiping arcs. Being dominantly right-handed, he was used to the feel, but the twist in his torso moved the injured arm. Pain tried radiating upward but he fought it, turning the agony inward, swallowing it in the hole that formed when she stomped away from him after forcing him to accept her independence. He snorted. Freedom from him. From his protection—which proved to be worthless, as she sucked that Roman's cock in front of everyone and he could do nothing to stop it. He hit the palus hard, the vibrations racing upward, into his shoulder, down his spine. Angered at himself, he swung back and whacked again.

He'd get back onto the sands and prove he was champion, win his freedom and truly free her. And once liberated, he'd kill his brother and Lucilla.

The demon smiled.

Ludo stood on the sidelines, watching his gladiators. He trained them, taught them all he knew, on how to survive and win. Their wins reflected well on him. They were all brothers, fellow gladiators. Except, perhaps, for Marcus. Hades drove the Roman. As he watched the man at the wooden pillar, he tilted his head, analyzing. Fuck. The man had an inner demon that pushed him, but now there was someone else fighting that demon for possession and he knew who she was. Gustina.

Double fuck.

"How is he doing?"

Jupiter's cock. Ludo exhaled. Tevia. Dominus' spy...the slave also befriended their champion. How the fuck had that happened?

"He stands before you, swinging a sword."

Tevia twisted his lips. "Dominus is in need of his fighting ability."

Ludo exhaled loudly. "He'll be ready."

"For the first round?"

Ludo turned, his eyebrows furrowed. "He'd put our champion against the rabble?"

Tevia's eyes stayed straight, not moving. Damn the man. Skinny, scrawny even, he didn't give in under pressure. No wonder he was Dominus' and Marcus' favorite.

"No, no, but if he has to, he will. Can he?" Tevia inquired.

Ludo stared hard at Marcus. He still moved stiffly, his body stilted in the swings. The Doctore knew his gladiator, his champion, and knew the man really wasn't there. He needed something. Damn, he recognized it. Hated it. But if he got him back to form, he'd save both their necks.

He turned to the questioning slave. "Yes, if...."

※

Cernia inhaled, throwing her shoulders back and shaking her head, letting the mass of curls fall just a little more from the pins struggling to keep them off her shoulders. Her hands grasped the folds of the sheer silk wrap that hung loosely around her neck, draping over her breasts. The feel of the cloth as she pulled the front tighter scraped against her bare nipples and she felt them harden, sending sensations through her, pooling in her lower stomach. The fabric barely covered her backside and its translucent design made her look like a siren, sent from the gods, as an offering to her husband. She smiled.

Barefoot, she made no sound, as she got closer to their bedchambers. She wanted to surprise him, but as she turned the corner she stopped.

Aulus stood, his back to the wall, wearing nothing but his toga. His head tipped against the wall, his eyes closed for a minute and a silent moan escaped his lips. Slowly opening his eyes, he glanced down, and grinned as his hand weeded through the red-haired slave kneeling before him. Her lips swallowed his cock and his hand guided her movements as she inhaled it fully only to slide back and then swallow again.

Cernia twisted her lips in disgust as she leaned against the doorframe. He must have heard her because he looked up, but he didn't stop the girl from sucking him.

"My beautiful wife," he said slowly, like a hum.

His seductive tones would not work this time. With a huff, she threw herself on the bed, leaning on her side, sending him daggered looks. She'd bathed in milk to soften her skin, oiled herself afterwards with jasmine, became aroused at the thought of him seducing her only to find him with a slave. Again.

He gave her a lopsided grin that turned to a groan as the girl sucked faster. With a motion of his hand, Esdras stepped forward from the corner and bent next to the lounger Cernia lay on. Without a sound, he parted the folds of her wrap and he moved closer, his hands parting her thighs as his tongue darted to the folds of her sex. She felt his hands gently holding her legs open, his mouth caressed her slit, back and forth.

"I made myself for you," she muttered. Damn, the slave's tongue laved between her folds and her body liked it. Her breathing hitched but her eyes remained focused on Aulus. Thank the gods, he returned her gaze, his eyes dark.

"I know." He pulled the slave off his cock. Cernia couldn't help but notice it glistening in the oil-light, still hard and red with need.

Her mouth dried. She never glanced down at Esdras, just stared straight ahead at her husband as he took a step closer. His eyes roved her body, just as the lad's tongue fucked her and she reacted, feeling her juices surging at his skill. She also noticed that her husband's cock flinched. One more step....

Instantly, he was at the bed, his hand pulled Esdras away and the cool air struck her swollen lower lips. She gasped at the loss and condemned herself in the same moment. This wasn't the first time Aulus had done this to her—have a slave get her wet so he could walk up to her and plunge in. So degrading, but her body betrayed her and begged her to take his thick cock and guide it inside her.

Aulus smiled seductively at her as he climbed on the bedding, towering over her. His hand flicked her right knee back and with no reluctance, her legs parted. He growled as he gazed down. "I love what I see. You're so wet for me and those lips...I adore those."

Her jaw clenched, ready to retort she was soaked not by him but by a slave boy, when he set the head of his cock at her slit and plunged in. She bit her lower lip, trying to remain silent but the burn of him inside her always surprised her. He withdrew and thrust deeper, pulling her up to meet him. Silence broke and she groaned.

"Yes, that's what I like to hear," he mumbled and plunged again.

Once he got her going, it didn't stop. She continued to moan at his thrusts, getting louder, deeper, more primal. The wild look in his eyes took control as he buried himself, nudging her womb. She felt the pressure from deep within her. Her body responded naturally and her anger fled as passion ruled. Another thrust and….

Her eyes shut as her thoughts shattered and she felt her body convulse around his cock. He yelled her name with the last thrust and stayed, buried inside her. She swore she could feel his seed filling her…and maybe, gods willing, giving her a child.

He collapsed on top of her, his head nuzzling against her neck, into her hair. Despite it all, she smiled, sated. She opened her eyes, ready to push him off her, but what she saw made her lungs suddenly fill with anger.

Aulus' ear felt like it exploded as his wife screamed hellfire into it. He pulled off her and turned.

Verenia stood there, the blank stare vanishing instantly. He saw the flicker in her eye as she glanced at him. Inwardly, he groaned. The slave was too forward.

"Dominus," she muttered and quickly stepped back.

Aulus pulled his toga wrap over him as he stood, blocking the sight of his nude wife as Tevia entered.

"What was so damn urgent now, Tev?"

The slave was truly odd. He never flinched enough to be noticed. Not even when his dominus yelled at him. The job he'd given him was simple enough. Find out the status of his champion. Aulus needed him to fight in the upcoming games. Whatever he discovered couldn't have been good if it caused him to interrupt him and his wife.

"The champion, dominus." The slave finally looked chagrined. Perhaps it was his tone that made the man whimper, for now the man failed to continue.

"Speak." *For love of the gods, he now had to order the man?*

Tevia's nervous swallow clearly showed. "He is improving."

"Excellent," Aulus said in a dull voice. His hand waved him on, for surely the man had more.

He cleared his throat. "Doctore believes he'd recover faster if the slave girl returned to him at night."

"What?" Cernia blurted.

Aulus' jaw clenched. He also noticed Verenia flinch. *Jupiter! That girl wanted the gladiator as well. Shit, shit, shit.*

"Tell Ludo I'll have her come visit him but I want a report tomorrow and every day after."

Tevia bowed. "Dominus." And he left.

Cernia sat up, tugging the sheer cloth around her. Aulus frowned. He'd like to return to bed, with her naked in his arms but the look on her face clearly showed that wasn't likely to happen.

"All this," she spat, "for a fucking gladiator?"

"Cernia," he began.

"No, he is a slave. Do you understand me? A slave. You'd risk everything over him?"

Her irritation colored every syllable. He sighed. Something about Marcus brought strong emotions to whoever knew him. He was well aware Cernia's body slave Verenia craved being fucked by him. Lucilla had been married to him and even bought his services after his last win. And perhaps little Gustina liked his cock as well. Fuck.

"I do not waste time over him," he replied. "Why do you hate the man so? Did you want to fuck him as well and he refused you?"

She gasped, her faced took on a look of mottled pain, as if he killed her last puppy and served it for dinner.

"How dare you! I have no need to stand in the queue for that slave."

He chuckled and sat next to her. "Oh, but you would, my dear, if he withheld your fancy wine or apricots or silk." He took her hand, rubbing it gently. "It is an easy thing to grant him and if it makes him better, then the gods favor us. If he doesn't improve, than I shall sell her and that will be the end of that. Will it suit you?"

She blinked, a look of surprise on her face. "You'd do that?"

"Yes."

"All right." Aulus smiled as he pulled her into his arms, falling back to the bed top.

He saw Verenia's lips also curl upward as she stood to the side. He'd ignore her for now. Cernia's attention was back on him. He smiled at her as his cock entered her.

Marcus sat, propped against the wall, on his sleeping

pallet. The wine slid down his throat, its bitter taste actually welcomed by his tormented soul. Another swallow and perhaps he'd feel it distract his thoughts from Gustina. Gods knew, Iduma sitting on the floor in front of him wasn't doing it.

"Come," the Britannica slave muttered, bottle in hand. Marcus put his cup out to be filled with the red liquid.

"How'd you get this?"

Iduma laughed. "You think you're the only one here who can manage drink at a simple request?"

Marcus frowned. What had his only true friend been doing while he'd been sulking in self-made pity?

The man fell over, his golden head on the dirt floor as fits of laughter rolled off his tongue. Apparently, the wine was more agreeable to deadening his pain than the champion's. *Fucking not right....*

"Aren't we such the simple fucks?" He sat back upright. His blue eyes sparkled with mirth over this.

Marcus glared. His right arm was injured but the left fist worked....

"Farina."

The champion's eyes widened. Farina? When the fuck had that happened? He snorted, raising his cup. "Good."

"Good? That's it? I get a girl you haven't fucked so it's only good?"

He chuckled. The Brit always teased him, even if it seemed unwise. "How do you know I haven't?"

Iduma slapped Marcus' foot, almost falling on his side. "Cuz she said so."

Marcus smiled. His friend's voice slurred. Oh, how the gods must hate him, not allowing him to find escape in drink tonight. Shit, he'd more to drink than Iduma.

The door to his cell opened. Into the room stepped Gustina.

They both went quiet. Iduma still kept a smile on his face. Marcus stared unbelievably.

"I thought you'd be alone," she stated softly, glancing at Iduma.

"I'm leaving." The man clumsily righted himself. "And you asked me about gifts?" He laughed and left the room.

Gustina stood, her lips curved slowly. "Hi."

He gazed over her and noticed her bare toes curled on the dirt floor. With a smirk, he returned, "hi."

Every nerve in his body tingled at her presence. She was here. In his cell. And it was night, long after the final meal. He wanted to get up but found he had no control and it wasn't all wine-induced. There was no need to bother. She came and sat down next to him.

His mouth dried. His insides tightened. And for once, the demon was silent. He felt the creature hovering, as if crouched and waiting. Last time, she stormed away from him.

She reached for his hand on the injured arm. Lifting it gently, she untucked the ends and unraveled the linen, exposing the wound. He watched, as if in a trance, as she turned it slightly, humming. A small pot he hadn't seen her bring in was at her side. She popped the corked lid off and dipped her fingers in it, pulling them out covered in golden gel—honey.

"Tell me if I hurt you," she said quietly, gently covering the healing lash marks with the stuff. Her touch was warm. It didn't hurt except for the longing that burned deep within him. With every one of her strokes, he felt his cock stiffening, hard and painful, but he wouldn't tell her. Fear she'd flee from him kept him quiet.

She tied the ends of the new binding and slowly gazed up at him. He wondered if she noticed his tented subligaculum. Every muscle tensed, expecting if she looked into his eyes, she would run. Because he couldn't hide his desire to feel her body next to him, his cock buried inside her, his tongue tasting her mouth. It was a fever, one he hoped she had too. He shivered at her touch. As he watched the knot she swallowed, so elegantly the muscles in her neck worked, he was almost undone.

"Marcus," she whispered.

He felt the raw, primal urge sweep through him. To claim her again. Make her his again. But he didn't move.

"I. Want. You." Gods, his tone was so husky and deep, it didn't sound like him.

Her cheek ticked as her teeth tugged her lower lip between them. She nodded.

His body understood that language. Without another word, he pulled her into his arms, his mouth covering hers. Her arms snaked around his neck as she smashed herself against him. His tongue traced the seam to her lips, barely a touch but they fell open to his invasion and he moaned loudly.

They were on his bedding, arms embracing, legs intertwined, and tongues dancing in a hunger older than the gods. He turned her underneath him and broke the kiss. Her face was flushed, her breath deep and hard like his. He grinned as his hand pulled at the tie on her tunic. It separated and he quickly snagged the cloth from her. *Damn, she was beautiful.* As he bent to kiss her, she spread her legs, her hips shifting below his hardened cock, begging him. With a growl, he took her mouth as his arousal slid into her.

The demon purred.

CHAPTER SIXTEEN

Lucilla sat on the seat, the cushion the slave provided squishing underneath her as she fidgeted. The crowd around her roared at the spectacle happening on the sands below. It was the tenth day of the one hundred dedicated to the celebration of Emperor Trajan's victory over the Dacians. One hundred days of spectacles in the Arena. She sat near the podium, the special balcony seat of the Emperor and his guests. Terpio invited her to accompany him and since her darling husband sat with the Senators, a place not for women, she accepted.

The sun reached the high point for the noon hour. It was lunchtime, but even in the heat, no one planned to leave, particularly the vulgar crowd in the higher seats. They'd lose their prime perch, the spot they'd fought for in the early morning hours, after the gates opened. And if they didn't leave, neither did most of the upper Romans. She squirmed. Even with the cushion, the white marble bench seats were uncomfortable, despite the shade to keep them out of the sun.

No, she admitted only to herself, her discomfort came from one thing. Her body cramped with the coming flow and she cursed the gods for ignoring her pleas.

Terpio turned to her and smiled. He sat two rows in front of her, as was proper for this location—women, except those fucking Vestal Virgins in their own box seats, never sat close. But she forced a smile on her face and nodded back. Her lower back twisted in torment and she bit her lower lip. She drank the rest of her wine and thrust her cup out for the slave to refill.

Without a child, the timeline Lucius gave her closed in tighter. One more cycle. One month. What was she going to do? Her husband's seed failed to take root. Terpio's hadn't yet but then again, she'd been denying him after the last ritual by Juno's priestess.

The stadium seats sounded yells of ecstasy as the lion pounced on the woman's arm and flipped her, screaming and yelling to the ground. The impact silenced her. The animal's jaws gripped tightly around his victim.

Lucilla turned away. Her mind needed to clear if she was to figure this out. She closed her ears to the sounds of the ravaging and the hoots and hollers of the crowd, looking at the phallic statue, one of many, that jetted up on the landings. What an interesting thing to catch her attention now. While they displayed the might of Priaspus and the male ego, they also slowed the exits into the vomitoriums. She shut her eyes, trying to calm her frantic nerves.

She'd arrange another visit to the Temple of Juno. And then work her charms on Cernia and her uptight husband to get to Marcus. She'd need several times with his cock dumping his seed inside her so she had to find a way to make sure she'd get those times. But what?

With all the screaming and hooting in the Arena, no one could think rationally. She frowned, watching the antics in the stands. It was truly appalling to see the vulgarity of some people puking, some half naked, a couple two sections down fucking. The woman was on his lap, bouncing. She smiled. Was that truly any different than years ago with Marcus, after they'd seen some matches, drinking through them, intoxicated enough to throw caution to the wind? Only they fornicated in the walkways or niches.

Her scan of the crowd brought her to Aulus and Cernia. They sat in a section behind her and to the left. An area for minor politicians and their wives and mistresses. And slaves. She watched with morbid fascination as that girl, what was her name? Gustina? Yes, the one that was sucking Verus' cock that night when Marcus made such a scene. She smiled. He must have affections for her. Her fingers tapped her wine cup, totally lost in the thought. That slave was her ticket to his seed. Her smile grew broader.

Oh yes, she'd have her baby. Marcus would father another.

Despite his refusal, this time Lucilla had the key that would make him beg to fuck her.

※

"Total shit is what it is!" Iduma rolled in laughter as he sat on the floor to Marcus' cell, a jug of wine between his legs.

Marcus smiled and raised his cup. "It is time, brother, to see you positioned so."

The Brit's grin was infectious. He leaned toward his fellow gladiator's leg and punched it. "Would not have been without your aid."

"Sick fuck, to grant more skill to die with." But he still chuckled, raising his cup to his lips. He almost gagged, laughing while swallowing, but it didn't upset him. His arm had healed and he could fight again. Iduma showed he could be placed higher in the rankings. Though not as good as Marcus, the man's ability increased even in practice and his air of confidence soared to where he no longer proved a minor pawn but a true gladiator.

While Marcus was pleased for his friend that he'd moved up, the champion knew his skills would never get him to be victor—not as long as Marcus breathed. To be where he was came at a price: kill everyone. Easy. Easy because if someone actually had the gall to beat him, it'd better be to the death. And what they never understood was Marcus longed for death, would embrace Hades' arrival through the Arena's Gate of Death. The Underworld would give him the peace he couldn't have here, until his wife and brother were dead. Revenge drove him. Whereas Iduma had been stolen from his native land. A loser in a war his people could never win, the man's only desire was to do well on the sands as a gladiator.

"Perhaps I, too, will be champion." Iduma interrupted Marcus' thoughts.

Marcus snorted. "Over my dead body."

Iduma's eyes sparkled from the wine. He raised his cup high. "Amen, brother."

Marcus' greeted his and the clank was loud, as well as their laughter.

Gustina sat next to Marcus, her legs curled up beneath her, close to him. She peered over her cup and squinted at them. "Iduma, you would kill your brother?"

The Brit chuckled. "Yes, just as he would me, if a chance was so presented." He looked at her. "Who do you think is the better victor?"

She glared. "Marcus."

"Oh, for the love of the gods, save us!" The Brit fell against the wall, mirth sounding off the dirt walls. "You get her for numerous nights, your *aid* to recovery, and get us spited for our own abilities."

She nuzzled closer to him. Marcus felt every nerve in his body register her presence. Her scent, mixed with almonds and lemons, sent his senses to madness. He glanced at her and felt the warmth of her smile. For all her arguing against the Brit, he knew she liked the man. With himself, well, the last five nights proved how deep her feelings for him went.

Every night, she came to him. They made mad, passionate love, a type that built on the precipice of disaster. Tomorrow Allus' house fought. If the gods finally heard his prayer, and he died tomorrow....It made him wonder if they'd accept a retrieval of his prayer—at least until after he'd won, set himself free, killed Terpio and that bitch Lucilla, and bought Gustina's freedom. The demon inside him snarled. His jaw tightened. Not likely. The gods were a fickle sort.

"I've no doubt you will be victorious tomorrow," Marcus stated. "But perhaps, you'd fair better without...."

The Brit snorted. "Without the wine. Perhaps." He stood. "Perhaps, my portion of the winnings will be more than wine."

Marcus felt Gustina tighten. He nudged her cheek with his hand. "Not you. I think he has another in mind."

She frowned and turned. "Who?"

The Brit stood silent, his bare foot scuffing the floor.

"A slave?" She pressured. Still the man remained silent. Frustrated, she turned and slammed her fist into Marcus shoulder. "Who?"

"Ouch!" He winced. The strike hadn't hurt, but to hit him seemed unreasonable. It wasn't as if *he* wanted anyone else.

Iduma laughed. "If she's gone to striking, I'd change topic. Good night." He opened the door and the guard outside pulled it shut. The latch slid into place, followed by the click of the lock.

Marcus turned to her. "So, you want to injure me? Make it so I can't win tomorrow?"

Her eyebrows furrowed. "You've barely healed. Why would he waste your life so early in these games? We all know this is too soon, that there are many more...."

His mouth curled in a grin as his arm snaked around her waist, pulling her to him, reclining her back on the pallet. She gasped.

"So you'd have me refuse?" He nuzzled her neck. He inhaled her fragrance as his tongue lightly traced up to her ear. She was more intoxicating than the wine and he'd never get enough.

He's demon stomped inside him, angry that he'd dare think of anything other than killing.

"I wish that you could," she whispered faintly.

He hovered over her, kissing her lips lightly as he pulled the tab of her tunic. His fingers pushed the material off her shoulders. Her chest inhaled sharply as he nipped at her taunt nub and laved the injured flesh with his tongue. Undoing the strap about her waist, he flipped the material open, his lips kissing down her bare stomach.

When he got to her hips, she stilled. He felt her tremble beneath his touch and it rocked him. He'd never taken this liberty with her. As a Roman man, his pride too high to consider it, he never kissed a woman below. But right now, all he cared about was pleasuring her, and getting her mind off the fight tomorrow. He didn't think he could manage it if he knew she worried about him.

The demon prowled, still mad, spitting blood, demanding it in return. To answer that darkness, he needed to be focused tomorrow.

And if the gods decided to answer his wish for the afterlife, then he wanted one more night in the luxury of her arms. To hear her sighs, her moans and groans, as he took her to ecstasy. His last thought before life escapes him.

When he kissed her inner thigh, close to the apex of her legs, she put her hand down there, trying to stop him.

"You don't have to," she said, her voice quivering.

He glanced at her, not moving, a slow smile spreading across his lips. Without a word, he put his hands underneath her buttocks and lifted her, knocking her hand away. He settled her body before him, flat on the pallet, no restrictions.

The smell of her essence, only a fraction away from his

mouth, nearly sent him to madness. Iced with almond and lemon, the real her was overpowering. Lowering his head, he kissed her. Her body trembled. Stifling a chuckle at her innocence, he placed his hand on her lower belly to hold her down and he leaned back in, his tongue tracing up her lower lips. She gasped. This time, his swiped up gently to her nub at the top, circled and caressed it before he tugged with his mouth. Her hips responded, relaxing in his hands.

Marcus took the hand from under her as he traced his tongue again between her legs. This time, though, he parted the folds of her sex, dipping into her core before moving on. He did it again before he got the response he wanted—a groan from her lips. But the next time, he didn't use his mouth, he inserted a finger, then two, moving them in and out of her core. They slid in so easily. She was wet, ready for him.

His cock twitched. Hard, the aroused shaft hurt, forced into the pallet. And the muskiness in the air nearly pushed him beyond his limit. Despite his inner agony, he thrust his fingers again, felt the walls of her silken canal tightening. She was so close, he could hear her pants, her hips moving toward to greet him. And then she shattered, quivering beneath him. Inside, she clenched his fingers, pulsing. Then he felt it—all of her juices flowed, fast, covering his fingers. Quickly he withdrew them and inserted his tongue. She moaned louder and he coaxed her to flow. He suckled from her sex, breathing her in, drinking her, but his own body couldn't take it anymore and insisted for her to call him.

"Marcus." Her voice sounded anxious, demanding, almost mad.

He was up, hovering over her, smiling at her. Her hands reached for his face, her palms cupped his cheeks and brought his lips to meet hers. And as he lowered, his strained cock found its haven, sliding right into her. The pulsation of her earlier climax gripped him. He kissed her deeply as he found purchase inside, stroking her, felt it in her mouth as her body tightened again. His own insides clutched, trying to keep back his seed until she came again but he was losing hold. Faster and faster he moved, her hips meeting his every thrust. He broke free of her mouth, unable to kiss and breathe at the same time. Gulping in air, he opened his eyes to see her darkened ones, half hooded. Her hands on his shoulders squeezed and then he lost everything. One final push deep into her and he felt it. Felt her grab hold of his cock, pulsing rapidly, draining him of everything he had as his seed splattered against her womb. He didn't move, couldn't. His body demanded he stay inside, letting her milk him of everything he had.

Her hands didn't release him any faster than her channel. He collapsed, his head buried against her neck, her hair silky next to his damp face, soaking in the exertion his climax brought. He felt her hands clasp around him, hugging him, just like her legs were wrapped around his thighs. Intertwined as one, he didn't want to leave, just wanted to hold her next to him.

He was lost.

The demon snarled with rage.

The next day, Marcus stood in the corridor near the gates to the sands. Adjusting his greave's binding on his leg, he hardly paid attention to the noise around him. Frankly, it was music to his ears—the roar of the crowd, the sound of the sand being smashed by bodies, the lower noise of the guards circling. He heard it but didn't. The only thing that mattered was his fight. It was later, the *primus*, the final fight of the day. His position warranted such a position and he relished it.

He stretched. The feel of the leather and batting next to his flesh brought comfort, a meaning to his life. Except today, it was missing something. What, specifically, he didn't know and it sent a fluttering inside him that didn't diminish. Even the demon paced with trepidation.

The roar beyond the metal barred gate screamed at a fevered pitch, one that made him look up and find the cause of the yelling. On the sands, trees were scattered around, propped upright in a makeshift forest for the next execution. Events he didn't care about. Most of these people deserved their death. A favor verses living under the sentence he had as a gladiator. And he was one that refused to be killed, despite an inner longing. No, that wasn't correct. Once the demon possessed him, he couldn't lose. It made his fate worse than death at the hands of the sword. So he adjusted his goal. If death eluded him, he'd take those who condemned him. Easy. Said. Set.

Gustina.

The thought of her flitted through his thoughts and he banished it. *Not now.*

Another squeal, though, caught his attention again. He looked beyond the bars. Amongst the trees stood a man, dressed in a filthy subligaculum, strapped spread-eagle between two of them. He looked terrified, his head turning rapidly back and forth, knowing his death was imminent.

Slowly, the sand doors flipped up and open as pulleys brought the platform carrying an animal cage and two slaves, animal handlers, stood, spears in hand. The animal inside the cage humped, its black fur ruffled as its mouth opened, exposing its sharp teeth, the fangs glistening in the sun. The roar coming from its mouth sent terror to the condemned and excitement to the crowd.

A black bear. Large, rotund and angry. The platform raised to ground floor. Within seconds, the door to its cage opened but the animal only roared. The two men at the rear corners of the cage poked at it with their spears, agitating it further, and got it to leave.

The bear's paws scampered across the sands. He was disoriented with the movements of the crowd in the stands above him, their voices demanding his kill. The animal stood, his nose pointed upward, sniffing, searching.

Marcus squinted, caught in the moment. The animal finally sensed the man, no doubt because he'd been fighting his irons and actually found freedom. He darted away from his trees, but his movements only caught the bear's attention. The man darted, ducked and ran, managing to avoid the creature's paws. He ran to the walls. The flat surface an impediment to his escape. Fascinated, the gladiator watched as the convicted leapt upwards, finding a crevice to cling to as he reached for the top. The bear stood below, snarling, swiping paws into empty air.

The man got to the top, despite the resounding disapproval of the crowd. He'd reached the top, and he needed to grasp the round, rotating bar but it moved with his grasp. The crowd laughed openly, half of it demanding satisfaction. The top ivory bar, an African elephant tusk sent in brackets, made to turn as a method to stop any escape, scraped as the man continued trying to hold on.

Marcus had never viewed sentences like this. As a free

man, he was too drunk at this point to care. His only desire was to fuck Lucilla. And for the days here as gladiator, he never cared. He fought worthy opponents. Gladiators. A strange brotherhood of men, fighting violently, one-on-one to live or die, honored as brothers, a true death. Who cared about convicts and their bestial sentences?

But this terrified him. It hit him hard, slamming into him like a gladius broadside, painful and reverberating. This had been Gustina's sentence. To die *damnatio ad bestias.*

Marcus swallowed hard as an archer's arrow struck the convict's back but still he held on. Two more arrows and he lost his hold. Falling to the sands, the bear leapt on him.

Marcus turned his head, unable to witness the carnage. His heart skipped a beat as the realization hit him. A wave of weakness washed over him and he gripped the barred door, trying to gain his bearing.

The demon inside him whimpered, cringing.

Iduma appeared at his side, his head tilted. "Are you well?"

Marcus shook his head, schooling his expression. "Fine. Fine." He looked at his friend. The Brit, dressed as a murmillo, his long shield able to cover most of his body, grinned.

"I am brother." He grinned. "Position raised. First fight in the afternoon, but better than any morning."

Marcus chuckled. "Yes, at this rate, it will become but a competition between us as to who'll best the primus."

Iduma snorted as he took his free hand and slapped Marcus on the shoulder. "Sooner than you think."

Marcus grabbed his friend's wrist so their tattooed inner arms touched. "Do well. I've no wish to make sacrifices in your memory."

Iduma's grin widened. "Hardly. We shall drink wine tonight in celebration, with whores everywhere!"

On the other side of the gate, the trees were gone, the bear caged, and the cart picking up the remains vanished. The sands were tan, awaiting their next victims. The doors swung wide as the announcements rang for the next battle. Gladiators.

Iduma nodded to his friend and shoved his helmet on his head, the outrageous fish-design on its top making him another foot taller. He walked through the gates to his first afternoon fight.

∞

Marcus stood on the Arena's floor long after Iduma's win. He felt the sand shifting under his bare feet. He dug deeper, planting his stance for the fight. Both gladius crossed before him, ready, willing. The murmillo before him stood, ready for the attack. The helmet murmillos wore hid their facial expressions, always frustrating the Champion. It was his first priority to get his opponent to lose that protection.

At a gesture of the editor, the man directing the fights in Trajan's absence, the command came. Begin the fight.

Plaguing Marcus in the recesses of his mind stood the man, chained between the trees, to die by bear's attack. However, in his mind, it wasn't a man but Gustina. Though the trees were gone and the sands wiped clean of earlier carnage, the ghost of the execution lingered.

The murmillo swung. His sword slammed downward on the champion and he thrust his long shield before him.

Marcus, fighting with two swords and no shield, tried to fend off the blow but the distraction in his mind hung, clouding his thoughts. He returned the blow and the man sidestepped. In that moment, he felt something wrong. Another hit on his arm, his injured arm, sent him to the sand floor. The demon—he didn't feel it. No raging wrath inside, no demand for blood and death. Dumbfounded, he knelt, trying to find his bearings. Big mistake. His opponent turned his blade and swiped at Marcus' side, somehow missing.

Marcus jumped to his feet. He felt lightheaded, giddy. Blood dripped onto his foot. He hadn't avoided the last blow. There was blood. Pouring down his side. *Shit!*

His opponent was sluggish at first. Probably disbelieving that his mark, this champion, was losing. The murmillo gained composure, his confidence high as he swung again.

The devastation climbed. Marcus felt lost on the sands. The execution had unraveled him. He'd saved Gustina from a similar fate. And now, was she protected? Could he save her from that?

And the demon deserted him.

Blood drained down his face. He felt the sting in his side from the cut and his leg was soaked from the bleeding, but he couldn't stop. Numbness enveloped his right arm from high on his shoulder. A quick glance revealed the bare flesh ripped open, a river of blood descending over his fingers still gripping a sword he didn't feel. The murmillo saw this as his charged, sword high, to slice Marcus down and become champion.

Fuck you.

Marcus forced his arms upward, swords raised and countered the blow. It made the murmillo step back. Marcus glared, his lip curling. Unfortunately, the victory didn't last. His knees buckled and he slammed into the sands. Stunned, he shook the feeling and rose, unsteady on his feet, his ears buzzing.

Where was that demon? He spat onto the ground and saw blood mixed with the spittle. *Shit.* He'd never lost before.

Gathering every ounce of energy he had left, he knelt down in the sand again. This time, his opponent thought it was over and had raised his sword. In the background, as part of that noise he heard daily, the crowd began chanting for his death. Him. The Champion. He bit the inside of his lower lip. It'd take everything and then some to do this.

Suddenly, he was pinned to the ground. Marcus eyed the crowd first as the fucking murmillo stomped around him, yelling his victory through his mesh-fronted helmet. The reigning champion lay there, unable to move. He closed his eyes and prayed fervently to any of the gods that would listen.

As the roaring continued and the murmillo pranced, Marcus knew he had but seconds. *Missio* or be killed. His one sword, the murmillo took. The other was mangled in the fight Marcus didn't remember as his head pounded. No, there was only one recourse left to him and it ate at his craw.

Lying on the ground, he looked up at his opponent. The man obviously didn't know how to take a gift like this because winner looked at the editor, questioning. Kill or be set free. Marcus always chose his own and it would be kill. It was wrong, but without it, Gustina would be left alone in this world with only the gods to protect her.

They'd failed her last time.

The decision was made. He swallowed the knot in his

throat and raised his right hand, two fingers pointing upward. *Missio*. Surrender and live.

CHAPTER SEVENTEEN

Cernia's mouth dropped open. It took everything she had not to drop her wine cup.

"For love of the gods, Aulus, are you paying attention?"

Aulus broke off his conversation with the other lanista and focused on the scene below. *What in Jupiter's name?*

Marcus, his champion, the man who brought fame and fortune to his dominus' house, lay on the ground, covered in blood, his weapons no longer in his hands. And, in the air, he raised two fingers. *Missio.*

Aulus blinked. Surrender? Rage roiled through him. He'd never seen this man back down. Swords swinging, Marcus won repeatedly, despite significant odds against him. Even in the beginning, as a new gladiator fighting in the lesser matches, he proved he was a force to reckon with. But this murmillo he fought today was not that good…good enough to fight in a primus event for the earlier matches of this long celebration, but not for the finale.

At doctore's suggestion, he'd placed the recovering champion in the early round to let him flex, get his hand back into shape without any problems. Instead, the gladiator was prone, begging for his life from a crowd that loved his victories, celebrated his name. *Shit!* He ran his fingers through his hair, anger growing. What if the crowd actually turned on him? Asked the editor to end his life? *Fuck!*

The Roman next to him laughed. "Appears you have a problem with your champion, Aulus."

His jaw tightened, his hands clenched. Holding back every ounce of anger, he forced his lips to curve into a smile. "'Tis only the opening set of games. Marcus is simply feeding the frenzy of the lesser lanistas, to help them build their confidences. We have the bulk of the games yet to come. I would hate for any to feel poorly for being here."

The man slapped him on the back. "Well said. Interesting twist, if I do say so myself. Will look forward to his *return*, so to speak." And he turned away.

"What will you do about this, may I ask?" His wife's stern face irritated him. Cernia never understood men and their business.

He watched the crowd yelling for blood, but there was a ripple, one begging the editor, the man in charge, to let Marcus live. His heartbeat quickened. If their plea could just get louder and the gladiator survived, he'd make sure that if he thought he could repeat this performance, Aulus would open the Gates to Death for him.

The gods must have heard his prayer. The people's demand that the gladiator live amplified as they stomped their feet on the marble flooring, their hands clapping a steady beat. The editor in the podium turned his head, taking in the sight, his fist held out before him, ready to give the *pollice verso*, the thumb gesture up or down, for the decision. Aulus found he too watched the crowd, his stomach flipping as they decided Marcus' fate.

The verdict came. The gladiator lived. Hoorays and joyful screams filled the air as the murmillo lowered his sword, bowed to the podium and stepped back. Marcus dropped his hand and rose, his stance unsteady. Aulus frowned. The man was covered in blood and sand. He motioned to Tevia and the slave scampered away to get the gladiator to the medicus.

"So, what will you do with him now?"

Cernia's tongue sounded bitter. He couldn't figure out why she hated the man so. She claimed she hadn't faced refusal from the man over fucking. He thanked Jupiter for that, but how could he stop her if she did? The man was a slave. Nothing. Just a way to increase the riches in his house. Otherwise, he was expendable. Like any other form of low life. Still, the hatred seemed out of place. The man's wins enabled Aulus to keep his wife in the luxuries he knew she adored and depended on. He sighed.

"I suppose you have this figured out, so please enlighten

me."

She sighed and flipped her fan open. "You shouldn't have given him that cunt every night."

He frowned. "Why is that?"

"You gave him reward before he earned it." Her voice lowered as she leaned toward him. "What had he to fight for if you let him have his fuck every night?"

"You hate that slave still?"

"It is difficult to control her if I have no say. I mean, for whatever reason, women so want his cock inside them. I truly don't know why. He may be the champion but he's surly, battered looking, bulky to where he could crush you." She shivered.

Aulus wanted to laugh. She wanted him despite her denial. Oh, her open hatred of the man made it evident she'd never laid beneath him or over him. Good. Slaves sucking her cunt to satisfaction he could tolerate, but another dick inside her made him furious. And if Marcus disgusted her, so did all the other muscle-bound gladiators. Inside, he relaxed.

"So I should keep him apart from her, despite all the coin he paid. If she'd been a prostitute, he spent enough to keep her with him for the next year."

Her lips curled in disgust. "He survived today, only by the will of the gods. Let him have his wine tonight with all the other victors. But not her. Give her to another and show him how his lack of win, how his begging to live, made him unworthy of champion title."

Aulus listened. She did have a point. Tonight, when he sent victory wines and whores down, he'd have to send Gustina to another true winner. His skin prickled at the thought. Marcus' rage would either make him revert to his animalistic ways to win again or undo him. And if he pined for that girl in such a matter that it interfered with his fighting, then Aulus would be better off without him.

"I like your decisive nature, my darling. Remind me not to get on your bad side." He chuckled. "No, tonight, we will let the gods decide whether he lives or dies."

Cernia nodded, a sadistic smile on her face.

Verenia, standing along the back wall to the box of seats, smiled.

∞

Whoops and yells rolled off the walls in the baths when the gladiators returned to the ludus. The ones who didn't get to go on this expedition greeted those that did with accolades.

Ahaz slapped Iduma on the shoulders. "Great showing, brother!"

Iduma smiled. "Yes, and more to come."

Marcus grinned. He was pleased for the Brit. His higher position in the standings was now secured. But it did make Marcus wonder about his. Nothing had been said to him yet but he expected it.

As he stepped into the baths, the oiled pool enveloped him, soothing over his recent wounds. Neither his inner torment nor open, bleeding wounds were enough keep him from the games, but they still irked him. He knew better than his showing today. That murmillo wasn't worth the loss. But the memory of that execution haunted him. He'd seen those before, years ago granted, and not sober, but why did they affect him now?

And where the fuck was that demon?

Slipping further into the pool, he relaxed. He needed to concentrate. Without winning at the end, he'd be no better than the gods when they failed to protect Gustina.

Iduma slid next to him. "So brother, where did your skills flee to?"

He snorted and shook his head. "I do not know." He pulled himself out of the pool and sat on the wooden bench, picking up a strigil. He scraped the first layer of oil and dirt off, carefully avoiding his wounds.

Iduma wasn't far behind him and actually opened his mouth to speak when Tevia arrived.

"From Dominus," he announced loudly. Marcus always found it amusing that this diminutive man, frail in appearance, could boom his voice over the bawdy laughs and comments of gladiators. "Wine and cunt."

Applause sounded even though they all expected it. It was the same after every victorious game and, in this house, frequent. Wine awaited them in their cells. Doors in the ludus to the various bedchambers, a small hole in the wall, so to speak, remained open for them to drink together, relax, fuck,

LOVE & VENGEANCE

and gamble because no one fought tomorrow.

Marcus watched Tevia and saw the man flinch when he glanced at the champion. He frowned. Something was wrong.

"Come, let us drink to my victory, brother!"

The tug at his arm by Iduma distracted him as they headed to the dining area, but he couldn't shake the feeling that tonight wasn't right.

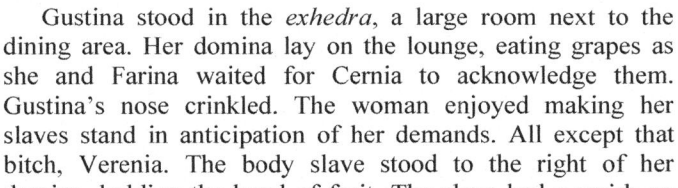

∽

Gustina stood in the *exhedra*, a large room next to the dining area. Her domina lay on the lounge, eating grapes as she and Farina waited for Cernia to acknowledge them. Gustina's nose crinkled. The woman enjoyed making her slaves stand in anticipation of her demands. All except that bitch, Verenia. The body slave stood to the right of her domina, holding the bowl of fruit. The slave had a smirk on her face and it unnerved Gustina.

What was this conniving little whore up to?

Cernia stood, straightening her stola, the multi-layered dress that hung from her bare shoulders. The yellow and rust colors were brilliant, making their domina's black hair gleam in the sunset streaming through the doorway.

"Gustina, Farina," she began, her nose high in the air to show her importance. Gustina wanted to laugh. The woman owned them. No need to show off airs to the slaves....

"I will have you two and Verenia," she continued, "go and help with the celebrations in the ludus."

Gustina frowned. She knew the gladiators had returned and many were victorious. But she spent her nights with Marcus. Her insides twisted. Unless something had changed. A sharp glance at the bitch next to her domina and the sneer in her eyes told Gustina everything.

But their domina failed to see Gustina pale as she feared what was ordered.

"We have a couple who have moved up in position and showed their worth," Cernia stated. "As reward, instead of the usual slop, we are giving you to them for the night. Farina," she turned to the girl.

Farina tried to keep her face stoic but she shifted on her feet. Inside, Gustina knew the girl hoped she'd get Iduma.

Cernia paced, wringing her hands. Gustina noticed.

Strange how this woman, who controlled them, acted as if she was frightened of them. Troubled by this oddity, Gustina had a very bad feeling about this. The metal collar around her neck suddenly felt heavier.

"Farina," the woman repeated. "You will go to Ahaz and Gustina, you are to go to Iduma."

Gustina's heart fell into her stomach as she heard her friend gasp. She reached for Farina's hand and clutched it tightly, trying to stop her from trying to protest. Cernia continued walking, paying them no attention.

"And Verenia, to our former champion."

Gustina gulped. Her domina's tone went cold on those last two words. Just like her heart did as her eyes darted to that bitch and saw the satisfaction in her eyes. She clenched her hands tight, hard enough even the distraught Farina gave a faint squeal.

Cernia turned, her hard steel grey eyes zeroing in on the two slave girls. "Do I hear a problem here?"

"No, domina," Gustina quickly asserted, schooling her thoughts and her tongue. It did no good to complain. These Romans could easily submit them to the entire group of gladiators and guards for physical pleasure—or worse.

"No, domina," Farina said, her voice barely above a whisper.

Cernia's mouth tightened. "Then go, get to their cells. When they've had enough wine, see them well satisfied."

"Yes, domina," the three chimed. Gustina noticed Verenia's voice was the highest pitched, almost happy. *Fucking whore.*

Cernia waved them away.

Verenia turned to them. "Off to the baths. We must make ourselves ready."

Gustina bit back a snort. Maybe she could drown the bitch in the oil....

≈

Iduma sat at the table, his hand wrapped around the cup of wine. The bitter taste of the liquid burned going down and left a bite in his mouth, but it was a victory. Stolen from home four years or so ago, gods knew when, the Romans carted him back to this god-forsaken capital of theirs as a slave, first selling him to the pits. Hauling rocks in mind-numbing repetition day after day took its toll. The physical activity built up his body, making him stronger, muscles building upon muscles that hadn't existed before. The strength gave him a false sense of invincibility, which surprised him. He wasn't free. The number of guards, their severe response to any infraction, but he didn't care. And along with his body increasing in mass, so did his anger and frustration. He lost control and started fights constantly. Finally, he was sold to a lanista. Aulus brought him here, into his ludus.

Here he proved himself worthy of the price. Being a gladiator gave him purpose. The roar of the crowd in the arena spurred him onward. To kill there, at the applause of the people in the stands, filled his blood with excitement.

He'd trained and fought for the last year, but his matches were in the morning, after the beasts, before the executions. Minor matches. Never spectacular, not name-worthy opponents. He'd go down in history as a nobody.

His wine-laden gaze glanced across the table to Marcus and he chuckled. This man, this gladiator and champion of the house, his friend, showed him the better methods. Quick slice to the left, clever with the right gladius handle, use of the shield as a weapon, and so many more. To be his training partner brought him more practice, more honing of his skill. And now he sat, a winner of the afternoon games.

"Gratitude," he mumbled, raising his cup as he stared at Marcus.

The gladiator's face had been set in a frown all evening. He drank some, but not much, and any attempt of being jovial was impossible. But at his friend's gesture, he gave Iduma a half-smile and raised his cup. "Just taught you how to save your ass."

Iduma laughed. He took another sip and made the mistake of closing his eyes. Big mistake. When they opened, the world tipped. "Oh, Jupiter's cock, I'm...."

Marcus snorted as he grabbed Iduma's arm when he lost balance trying to set his cup down. "Bed. I think you need sleep."

Iduma nodded. Bed. And hopefully, not alone. His smile turned crooked. "Perhaps I will take a whore with me." He eyed the room for the few women available. But most were busy at the moment.

Marcus shook his head. "No, with your victory, perhaps Dominus sent you that sweet thing you've been craving."

Farina. Yes, that sounded wonderful. "For my win today, he'd do that?"

Marcus finally smiled genuinely. "He's been known to, if it suits his purpose. And with more rounds to play in, rest assure, he will want your cock happy."

Planting both hands on the table, Iduma got to his feet. Standing wasn't much improvement but he managed, trying to gain his bearing. Still propped by the table, he gazed at his friend. "And what of you? What happened?"

Marcus shrugged. "My demon left." He sounded lost.

"Thought you said there was no demon."

The gladiator cocked an eyebrow at him. "My need to kill left. It took me a moment to accommodate...."

"Well, you did that rather poorly."

"Yes, I did." Marcus stood. "Come, let us see you to your comfort and I to mine."

They took two steps, Iduma leaning on the gladiator. "What if he doesn't send you Gustina?"

His friend squeezed his arm. "Then I'll have to sleep alone. And press the matter tomorrow." They got to the turn in the corridor with one branch heading down to semi-private cells and the other, to the door outside and the champion's room across the training field. Iduma nodded and left for the hallway as Marcus turned outside.

Iduma let his hand touch the side of the wall. He needed just a bit of wall to stabilize him. Wine. Cheap wine. *Shit.* He'd pay for this tomorrow...unless he had a willing wench in his room to help him work off the wine. His lips curved.

At the metal-barred door, a guard waited. Iduma tipped his head at the man, the signal he was home for the night. As he stepped into his cell, the door snapped shut behind him, the latch locking into place.

Across the room, he saw a female body on his bed. The one oil lamp, hanging precariously from the ceiling, threw some light into the darkness but it was pathetically bad. He couldn't see if it was Farina, but he bet it was. Ivory skin, rounded hips, long legs. Eyes sweeping upward, he found her round breasts, nude and waiting for suckling just as the apex of her thighs needed his cock. His shaft hardened and he felt his insides tightening as his mouth went dry.

Stepping forward, stripping his subligaculum off, he grinned.

∞

Marcus walked across the training ground to the portico on the other side. The guard stood near the door to his cell and a faint light issued out from it. He bit back a smile. Gustina. He needed to see her, to hold her. Perhaps, as he prayed to Jupiter himself, the feel of her in his arms would make this fear inside him cease.

He needed to win in the games. To be champion. To win his freedom. Only then could he get the vengeance his soul demanded from that greedy manipulative brother of his and power-hungry former wife. His spine still jolted with outrage that she had paid for him and the fear remained she'd do it again if she needed to. And the price tag? He gulped. Whatever it might be, it remained too high.

The jug of wine in his hand, he took a swig before he entered his cell. The burning bitter liquid burning down his throat actually felt good, a taste of reality, of how his day went. Still no demon.

He heard the door shut behind him, latching. The dim oil lamp, hanging above, barely lit the room and it took him a moment to adjust. He blinked several times. Finally, they focused again. His eyes went straight to his bed pallet as his mouth started to curl into a lopsided grin.

Before him, on the wool blanket, she lounged, wearing nothing. Her breasts, their tips already hardened with anticipation, on full display. The pale light illuminated porcelain skin indented at her waist, curved hips, long legs. She was beautiful and his. He took a step forward as she stood.

"Verenia," he snarled. "What in the name of Jupiter are you doing here?"

The dark-haired slave smiled wanly. "I was sent to pleasure you."

"You're nothing but a cunt wanting advancement," he spat, stepping away from her. He glanced back at the door.

"She isn't coming."

"Get out."

Her foot placed her a step closer. "I was ordered. What do you think they'll do to me if I don't?"

"I don't give a fuck what they do to you." The snarl was back. And the demon. It prowled below the surface. But Marcus' anger raged and he didn't notice it at first. "And where is Gustina?"

He couldn't believe it. The bitchy slave actually cringed. At his tone or where the girl was?

"She couldn't be here and I was sent."

"Do you think I lost my hearing? I heard your lies. Tell me!" He was in her face, grabbing her upper arms tightly, knowing he was hurting her but he didn't fucking care.

She winced. "Sent to pleasure Iduma."

Gustina's words hurled back at him. She knew her place as a slave. And he remembered when she visited him after he was hurt trying to protect her—the time he failed, just like now—when she said if they told her to suck the cocks of all here, she'd have to. She was a slave. His heart fell to his stomach. Hurt and anger became one. Even the snarling demon curled up, snapping its fangs.

He pushed the slave to the wall, heard her thud and slump to the floor, her eyes filled with terror. He threw his blanket at her, hoping she'd throw it over all of her so he didn't have to see her.

On the opposite wall, he sunk to the ground. He could do nothing. Nothing.

Despite all the wins, all the praises, all the fear he evoked, he was helpless. A slave. A slave who lost the woman he loved.

CHAPTER EIGHTEEN

The morning arrived too early. Marcus felt the sting of the sun's rays boring into his temples, making the pounding in his head go at a fierce rate. Pain reached down deep, internally felt in his heart. Slowly, he opened his eyes, unwillingly but with no choice. The door to his cell swung wide and banged off the wall.

"Gladiator." The guard stood, gladius in hand.

Fuck. If he didn't go, they'd drag his ass out onto the sands.

He glanced across his cell. The bitch Verenia wasn't there. Good. The cunt really thought he'd take her to bed if Gustina weren't here? He spat on the ground. But even the thought of her drove a blade into his belly and twisted it. He felt hollow, deprived. His life lost, bereft.

Iduma fucked her. His mind tried to wrap around that thought and it couldn't. The man was too drunk when he left the table, thus he probably didn't think past his cock last night. Only it wasn't a whore in his bed or Farina. Marcus closed his eyes again.

A bang at the door made him open them again. Shoving himself off the floor, he adjusted his subligaculum, and reached for his greaves and sandals. Every movement brought reality slamming into him with a severity he couldn't stop. Anger built upon madness screaming to unfurl, against his past, against life, against Aulus and, the ultimate, against Gustina. For her accepting her fate so easily. Furious, the leather tie broke in his hands.

It all meant nothing to him. The demon roared, flexing its

power, spreading throughout his body, demanding vengeance.

He strode out the door onto the training grounds. The pounding in his head increased with each step but it was insignificant in his lust to kill. He needed his freedom and then all that wronged him would pay.

Ludo stood next to the water barrel. The other men picked up wooden versions of their weapons. No one appeared remotely interested in his rampage onto the dirt. He grabbed his two gladius and flipped them around as he turned his wrists. Doctore's eyebrow raised but did nothing else. Marcus' demon snarled, just below the surface.

Snap.

The whip whizzed through the air, cracking at the end. All movement stopped, including Marcus.

"Gladiators, position one."

The men paired up. Marcus scanned them, looking for his partner, or this time, his victim. And then he found him, rubbing his eyes off to the side, as one hand held the gladius and shield. Marcus' eyes narrowed as what was left of rational thought fled. *Tired from fucking my woman all night?*

Without a word and his feet making little sound, Marcus charged the Brit. But Iduma wasn't that out of it and saw the champion coming at him, weapons raised. From months of training, to be ready to move at the split of a second because, on the sands, it may be all the time a gladiator had between life and death, the Brit's free hand grabbed the shield, thrusting it high to meet the blow with the other hand blocking the other sword. Iduma regained his feet and his stability. At the next attack, he threw himself at Marcus, sword and shield blocking the next strike.

The maneuver stopped Marcus from downing him but not the drive that pushed him stumbling backwards.

"Fuck, Marcus," Iduma sputtered, his arms locked in place to stop his friend.

The champion roared blood. He raised his arms again, his attack forward. Blood. He wanted blood. The Brit blocked it with the shield and wooden sword and spun, just out of the blow. Marcus roared again, renewing his attack. The wooden sword's aim made contact on the center of Iduma's back and the man bent from the pressure. Marcus repositioned himself, going again but his victim rolled, out of his reach, only enticing the demon's wrath further.

The whip cracked in the air. Everyone came to a stop except Marcus and Iduma.

"Marcus, Iduma."

The command couldn't be ignored. The champion dropped his arms, but the fire didn't leave him. Iduma spit blood.

"I didn't touch her," the Brit muttered, his voice low.

Marcus coughed. His breath caught. A small voice in his head, not the demon, but a sane one, told him that the Brit was telling the truth. The demon spat. No, Gustina's body would make any man desire her. Fury rose again.

"I might have been staggering but I knew who they gave me." The man took a step closer. Marcus tensed, the urge to strike high but he restrained it. The Brit was his friend at one time. "She was crying, you ass. She didn't want to be there anymore than you wanted her there."

The champion spat onto the dirt. "But you didn't kick her out."

"Like you did Verenia?" Iduma smirked and raised his arms to position to practice. "I know you did. Verenia being punished for that is her own damn fault. No, I didn't because I wouldn't see Gustina hurt. There was a reason they did this. I'd bet it was your ill performance yesterday. Concentrate, go back to winning, and she'll be returned. You know last night was a warning."

Marcus gripped his weapons, knowing the Brit was right but it ate at his gut that she slept in that cell. Once again, he'd failed at protecting her.

"Continue!"

The Brit gave him a lopsided grin. "Use that anger in the sands. Here, I'm ready for you."

Marcus wanted to believe him. Needed to. If he couldn't control the rage here, they could lock him away from the games or sell him, and then how would he get free? No, he needed to focus. Swallowing the torment that still blackened his thoughts, he charged again.

∞

Lucilla pulled her stola straighter, flattening the pleats just a little as she walked behind the slave to see Cernia. She could barely contain the smile on her face. Her flow stopped and she felt confident with her plan.

"Lucilla, what a surprise. To what do we owe the honor of your visit?" Cernia greeted her, taking her hands and giving her a gentle kiss on the mouth. Lucilla managed to maintain the curve of her lips. Cernia obviously loved her husband, but Lucilla often thought the woman wouldn't mind a dalliance with another woman. An issue she couldn't deal with. She struggled against repelling the woman. This mission Lucilla started needed Cernia's help.

"Why can't I just come to visit you?" She sat down on the lounge, accepting the cup of wine from the slave. The slave with brown hair. She crinkled her eyes, trying to remember her. The girl looked so familiar.

Cernia laughed. "Of course, you can. But Lucilla, I know you. Rarely these days is your mind on anything other than producing an heir." Her head tilted and Lucilla felt the heat of her gaze as it lowered to her stomach. "Unless you have news...."

She swallowed the knot that formed in her throat. "No." She cast a glance at the slave girl. Now memories returned. That slave Marcus favored. The grin returned and she quickly stared into her wine. "Perhaps I needed a distraction."

Cernia frowned. "What type of distraction?"

Lucilla felt a flutter of excitement course through her veins. Victory would be hers. "Your men are in the next round of games, are they not?"

With a sigh of disgust, Cernia's lips curled. "Yes."

"I'd so love to see them fight."

"But you have seats...."

"Only if Lucius goes." Her eyelids hid her gaze. "But to be with a lanista...."

"You want to sit with us? The vulgar crowd?"

Lucilla laughed. "Hardly. Your husband carries more title than lanista." She bent forward. "And those seats are closer to the Arena than the ones the Senate allows for us women. It would truly be a thrill to watch your men march out on the sands."

Cernia narrowed her gaze. "Or perhaps, one particular gladiator."

Lucilla shrugged.

"Fine, then by all means, we'd be honored to have you

with us."

A smile beamed across her face as she settled back along the lounge, sipping from her cup.

Gustina stood to the side, a jug of wine in her hands, her faced schooled into bland expression. Stilling trembling hands she found a bit harder to curtail. Inside, fear and anger twisted her stomach. This woman, she was bad news for Marcus. And as a slave, she knew she had no way to stop her.

The weapon sliced through the air, coming down with lightning speed, the roar of its holder echoing through the air. The impact sounded into the stands as metal hit metal. The gladiator fell to the ground, shield out of his grasp, and his sword on the ground. His attacker stood above him, his weapon raised again, aimed to finish the man off. But instead, he remained poised, ready, glancing up at the podium for the editor's decision.

The crowd's voices increased with their verdict—*kill!*

Marcus' nerves bordered on impatience. He had no problem making the decision. His demon danced inside, gleeful and blood-hungry. The champion glared at the man whose decision reigned in the end. He could see the Roman fuck's head turning as he scanned the crowd's mood.

Fuck their mood! Kill!

The man made his decision. Thumbs up.

Marcus growled as he thrust the instrument down, slicing through the man's armament, into his chest deep. His victim's gasp audible as he drowned in his own blood and his eyes dulled as he passed into the Afterlife.

The crowd roared. His demon purred. But he felt nothing. This fight was a victory, the primus this day, but still he was empty. What little was left of his humanity inside demanded the hole be filled. Gustina. But with the stands filled to capacity, even on this fifty-sixth day of the games, he knew he had to answer their bellowing. They were the answer to his freedom yet his insides twisted. Breathing deep, he turned to the podium, the grip of the swords still in his hands. He flipped them in a circle and raised them high above his head, matching their intensity with his yell for victory.

The applause increased two-fold. He was still champion.

But from the look in their screaming, jumping and flaying in the stands and the smile on the editor's face, he remained a slave. *Damn!*

The gates opened for him to return to the bowels of the Colosseum. With a heavy breath, he lowered the weapons and walked toward it. The Roman guard at the gate took his swords. Marcus wanted to laugh. As if that fop could really hold him back if he wanted to slice his way free or die trying. It was a fleeting image, one his demon longed for, one he had to deny if he was to save Gustina.

"Marcus."

He cleared his mind and focused on the slave in front of him. Tevia. "What?"

"You're to see yourself to the baths. Your presence has been requested."

"Jupiter's ass," he snarled. The price tag for his victories. "I'm too tired to consider...." his voice faded. The look on his friend's face was too placid. Tevia knew better than to interfere with any commands from Aulus. And honesty, neither could Marcus. "Fine." He stormed off to the baths.

∽

Oiled, the blood peeled off his skin, the few marks of the fight barely discernible, and with a new subligaculum on, Marcus walked behind the guards. The cuffs of his chains rubbed his wrists raw but he didn't notice. His mind was on one thing—to get through this request and return to the ludus and Gustina. His victory and return to champion status for Aulus meant she'd return to him tonight. It had been virtually a month. He'd seen her, on the perfidy of the ludus, her gaze darting to his only briefly. It plagued him, the fact she accepted her fate as slave. He knew she had a rebellious streak, had seen it. Where was it now?

Lost in thought, he barely felt the guards attach the chains from the walls to his wrists. The smirk on their faces irritated him.

"I don't get it, Maximus," one guard muttered, sliding the lock into place. "Why a good Roman woman wants a slave."

His friend laughed. "Because he has the blood blessed by the gods, or so they think. Leave him alone against us, and we would correct their short-sightedness." Both guards laughed.

"No, she wants to rut with him, she's no better than a whore."

They left him. He knew their comments were fueled by envy. He'd gladly let them pleasure whoever they brought him. Why they'd think he longed to fuck a Roman woman escaped him. Being a slave, he had no choice in the matter, damn them all. Bile rose to the back of his throat.

The door scraped open. He steeled himself. Easy. Quick. In and out of her cunt and then it'd be over. Think about Gustina as a reward, his mantra stated.

The hooded woman entered. He caught her scent. Vanilla and honey. *Fucking shit! No!*

The door closed and he heard the latch fall into place. She walked up to him, barely within his reach, and pushed the cover off her head.

"Hello, Marcus."

His teeth gritted but he refused to speak. Hands clenching, he knew he could get her closer and kill her now. The demon smiled. Blackness edged at the corner of his mind.

Her stola parted, revealing her nude body beneath. Her one weapon against him. And after a month with no relief, his own cock betrayed him. One thing about his former wife, she was built to pleasure a man. He gulped when her finger traced down his chest and inched under the edges of his loincloth. A wicked smile came to her lips as he felt his arousal twitch at her hint of her touch.

"No," he stated firmly.

She let her clothes fall to the floor. "Yes."

Every muscle in his body tensed. Her nipples were hard. Narrow waist, wide hips. The smell of her arousal filled the air, suffocating him with a cloak of lust.

"I will not fuck you." He looked at the wall behind her, concentrating on it, praying his cock lost interest. It didn't.

Her fingernails grazed down his erection, the tips of her fingers, the soft area, tracing around his crown. She gave him a seductive laugh as her hand wrapped around him and squeezed. Unable to stop her, he stood still, keeping his gaze on that nail near the door. When she bent and her tongue licked the slit of his cock with a hum on her lips, he felt his control sliding rapidly away.

"You still taste sweet," she murmured. Her hand still holding him, she glanced up, her lips curled. Her other hand dropped between her legs and he saw the flicker in her eyes when she inserted a finger into her, heard the slight groan. Damn, was that her or him?

She brought the glistening finger up to his lips and enticed him. He refused to accommodate her so she ran it across them, dampening them with her juices. The musky scent sent his blood racing. Damn her!

"Oh, you will fuck me," she said softly and stepped closer. Close enough to strangle. Buzzing in his ears from his heart pounding, desire unfurled inside him. When her pearled nipples grazed his chest, the rutting animal inside him grappled for control. "You will fuck me hard, like you used to do, and spill your seed inside me."

The last broke part of the hold on him. "Why?"

"I need a child."

"You have a fucking husband," he snarled, though his cock pulsed madly in her hand.

"I need the seed of a champion," she purred.

He gulped. But his hands were on her hips. To bring her closer or shove her away? The demon inside gnawed violently.

"I gave you one once," he spat. "You rid yourself of it."

"True. So I know you carry a virile cock. And I've paid for this. You will give this to me or I'll make sure you never see that little cunt again."

His breath hitched. What did she know about Gustina?

She caught his reaction and laughed. "Oh, darling, did you think I wouldn't remember when you went after her for sucking Verus? Yes, I saw and know you've been denied her for a while." She bit her bottom lip, as if she could barely contain herself. "You fuck me, I'll make sure you have her again. If you don't, maybe she'll be sold."

His eyes narrowed. "You have no—"

"I'm very close to your Domina," she whispered, her hand tightened around his shaft. He felt it leak again a pearl of his seed. Damn his body.

He wanted Gustina, needed her. If it meant taking this whore to secure it, he had no choice. Anger and lust rolled into one. His hands clenched her bare hips and swung her body around, onto the pallet behind him. Her legs spread wide. The apex of her thighs glistened with desire.

"Forgive me," he mentally begged Gustina as he bent over and filled Lucilla with his cock.

CHAPTER NINETEEN

Gustina lifted the bucket one more time, feeling every muscle, every tendon strain to keep steady. She knew she had overfilled them, but her nervous energy made her think she was stronger than she was. A few more paces until she set it down again and wiped her brow. If she weren't inside the posticum, the side entrance for slaves at the Villa, she'd splash some of it on the ground. Here, that would be a disaster. Water on the marble flooring would make even her bare feet slide, not to mention what would happen if her Domina returned to check on her and found it so.

She looked around, searching, and found no one around. Dragging her bottom lip between her teeth, the pain brought her back to reality. When the fights were over, and all returned, then she'd know if Marcus won or lost. The edginess of the moment, though, ate at her nerves. If he won, she hoped she'd see him. Since the night she'd been forced to Iduma's cell, she'd avoided the champion. Not that she was allowed to see the gladiator again, but any wayward glances or side passes to the ludus she avoided. How could she seek him out and know the truth—if he fucked Verenia or not? The slave's foul mood made Gustina think he shunned her, but the nagging question remained.

Nor did she want to answer to him about Iduma. He had no right. And neither did she. Anger filled her and she kicked the bucket, some of the water splashing over the sides.

"Gustina!"

She glanced up and saw Farina darting across the atrium.

"He won!" Farina laughed in excitement.

Gustina's heart missed a beat, like a startled rabbit. "What?"

"Marcus," her friend said, gulping for air. "The primus. He won."

Her tongue soothed the bottom lip she'd torn savagely at a minute ago, her mind racing. Would they allow her to see him tonight? Better yet, did he want to see her? The whore? The word tasted bitter in her mind. Whore. She was nothing more than a slave and did as commanded. What would a champion gladiator do with her anyway? All he'd really done so far was fuck her. *And save her from execution.*

Her gaze lifted and met Farina's. Her friend's mouth pursed and she snorted.

"You need to stop condemning yourself. I don't hate you."

"I know, but he will." She grasped the handle again. Just a few more feet to the domina's bedchamber.

Farina reached down and helped her. "I do not understand you. You act as if you miss him and within a flip of a coin, act as if he didn't exist. The two of you collide like birds in flight. You crash and fall apart only to take to each other in the air."

Gustina grimaced. It was a question that plagued her. He saved her, obviously desired her, but to what extent and why? And why did she care outside of gratitude for his salvation? She shook her head. Her heart called to him. There was comfort in his arms, a gentleness where others saw brutality and death. A man obsessed by a demon, a creature she never saw when they were alone. He taught her pleasure...and she betrayed him by lying with his friend.

"There is nothing outside base desire." Her voice was cold.

Farina's eyebrows rose. "Yes, well, his base desires have been at wits end without you. I was sent to see you washed for tonight." She giggled. "And perhaps, this time, I will get Iduma," she whispered. "Tell me, will he make me moan?"

Gustina snorted. Did she tell her friend the truth? She shuddered at memories of that night. "Of course," she lied. "Tell him your desire, and he shall see it filled, for as a Brit, he is very trusting."

Her friend giggled as they toted the bucket to the bedchambers without spilling any more. After they dumped it into the washstand, Farina grabbed her hand and dragged her out of the Villa to the baths.

So she'd have to face him and his condemnation of her. His bought and soiled goods. Her mind shifted back to Terpio and his rough ways. Would Marcus demand the same from the woman who serviced his friend? She prayed to Juno he wouldn't.

※

Lucilla walked into the atrium of her Villa, pulling the top of her wrap off her head, satisfied with today's events. In fact, she couldn't keep from smiling. The blessings of the gods descended around her. Every few steps, she still felt a slight weep between her legs, and her smile deepened. She carried the seed of the champion inside her. Now, with their continued blessing, she'd soon be....

"Where have you been?"

Startled, she stumbled. With a frown, she looked for the voice. Across the atrium's greenery, she saw the crimson and gold fabric, almost blending in with the flowers but too big to be a plant.

Terpio.

She sighed. What in the name of Jupiter did he want? As he cleared the foliage, she managed to school her features and give him a smile.

"Terpio, I didn't know you were coming to visit. I'm sure Lucius...."

"I'm not here to see him," he hissed. "I came to find you. With him gone, I figured you'd be here, waiting. What a surprise to find you absent."

"What do you want?" The man could be so aggravating. Throwing her stola to the nearest slave, she held out her hand for another to bring her wine.

He leaned closer. "You know what I want."

She breathed in and caught his scent. Sweet, young, enticing with a touch of myrtle berry. Terpio still held a certain fascination she'd never be rid of. But right now, he wasn't welcome. Oh yes, she knew what he wanted. For her plan to work, the gods told her in the dream very clearly to avoid the brother's cock. And that 'brother' had to be Terpio because the same spirits had directed her to Marcus.

The distraught look on his face ate at her. She sighed. "I went to the games with Cernia."

LOVE & VENGEANCE

His mouth thinned. "You went to see Marcus."

"Darling, you worry so," she said coyly and plopped a grape into her mouth. "She asked me to join her. What was I to say?"

"That you were busy."

She turned and cupped his cheek, a wary smile on her lips. "It is known my husband is absent. I cannot deny her company and be dallying with yours. You know this."

"I just missed you." He sank onto the lounge, a forlorn look on his face.

Sitting next to him, she offered him a grape, placing the fruit next to his lips. "I went to see the priestess today."

"What shit filled her mouth now?" he snorted.

Her jaw tightened. "None. It is good."

"So we go to bed now?"

She swallowed. "Not today, my dear. But soon."

Terpio's gaze narrowed. "I suppose you know what is best."

She nodded, trying to appear at ease. The man could unravel her whole world with just one word if he opened....

"Did you know that cunt I saw kill my wife still lives?" He stated, stealing another grape from her dish.

"No. How are you so sure? I thought she was killed with the other convicts in the Arena."

He shook his head. "No trace. No nothing. Just some ragged tale about a gladiator saving her."

She knew. Her grin widened. "Let us not worry about that now. We will find her and send her to the Afterlife."

He glanced down at her hand wrapped around his wrist. She saw the momentary flicker in his eyes, the type she'd seen before, if he thought she was fibbing. Well, this time, she wasn't. She knew exactly where the bitch was. Again, she smiled broadly. It was a good day after all.

 ⁂

Terpio smiled back at her, watching the satisfaction in her eyes.

She was lying.

Bitch.

Lucilla knew too much. And wasn't sharing. It took every ounce of energy not to flare up at her, accuse her of anything.

He swallowed. Only one way to find out.

Taking her hand into his, he turned it and kissed her wrist. Gently. He heard her sudden intake of breath. Her pulse beating frantically under his thumb. With the practice of a habitual lover, he nipped at the skin. She stifled a groan but not before he heard it. *Got her.* Except she also had him—her wrist smelled of thick oil. The type gladiators and slaves used.

So she'd finally done it. Crawled back to that shit-eater of her old husband. Desperate for an heir. He should have seen this coming. Closing his eyes, he fought the anger and hurt. He'd loved her all his life but knew her ambition outdid his own. Jupiter's balls, he'd lost her twice—once to Marcus and then because he married. Lucius wasn't the winner. No one was. No one could control Lucilla.

He glanced at her, trying to deceive his own feelings into forgetting his discovery.

"I want you."

She licked her lips. Oh, the hooded glaze in her eyes, the slightly parted mouth told him everything. She wanted him too. And would refuse him. Why?

"I said not today, Terpio." She pulled her hand from his grasp and stepped away.

He walked up behind her, pulling her hair off her neck and kissing below her ear.

"You better leave."

"I don't have to," he murmured and kissed the top of her shoulder. "At least, not without seeing the scroll."

She stiffened in his grasp. He couldn't help but relax, knowing in this game, she'd lose if he let her.

"I don't have it here. You know that," she hissed.

"Well, before you dally again, I'd like it." He kissed her cheek. "Good night, Lucilla, my love."

He heard her violently spewing some epitaph after him and he laughed.

※

"You, of all the slaves, should have known about this."

Gustina heard the hardness of her domina's voice on the other side of the fauna. She glanced over, trying to be nonchalant, setting a wine jug on the cart. An easy task, to get the wine for the gladiators' celebration, but she hadn't expected Cernia here. Through the green leaves, she saw the woman handing Verenia a small clay vial. For once, the slave looked recalcitrant.

"After tonight, I want you to watch over everything, you will take this and end such encumbrances."

"Yes, domina."

Gustina frowned. Whatever had the slave done?

"What are you doing?" Farina whispered next to her.

Her heart jumped but calmed when she saw her friend. She nodded toward the foliage.

Farina peered through and snorted softly.

"She was never very smart in that context," Farina muttered, standing back. "She'll be sick for days. Serves her right."

"She's with child?"

"Yes, and Domina doesn't want that here. And I'd bet neither does the bitch. Takes her out of seeking favors."

Gustina's hand went to her stomach as her insides clutched. A child to a slave was nothing more than bringing a young life into bondage. But to so savagely take it—she'd seen the effects of this drug and cringed.

"You aren't...." Farina whispered fearfully.

She shook her head. "No, but I've witnessed this after it was taken. At my old villa. Vile." It was one of the good aspects of her former Dominus taking her the way he did, as disgusting as that was, there'd be no chance of a child. She shuddered.

Farina's hand clamped around her wrist. "Forget her and think of better things." She grinned. "You'll get to see your champion tonight."

Gustina swallowed but managed a nod. She was so excited she felt every nerve inside her wanting to explode with anticipation, the need to see him so great that she grew fearful of it. Already her skin felt clammy, tingly, and her stomach flipped.

"Come," her friend tugged her hand. With a forceful nod, she grabbed the handle to the cart and they went to the ludus.

Would he want her? Or would he be angry over her being with Iduma? A choice she had no say in, but men were never rational creatures. She'd heard of the tempers flaring after the event and knew what Iduma must have said to placate the man for both were still alive. But could she hold her tongue if so pressed? Gripping the handle tighter, no longer hearing Farina's joyful banter, she descended into the gates of Hades and to the man she'd betrayed.

CHAPTER TWENTY

The air filled with the gladiators' whooping and hollering on the arrival of Marcus, Iduma and the others from the Colosseum. Today's wins marked the games as halfway through and with the arrival of Trajan tomorrow, the spectacles became grander, as if the first fifty days had been practice.

"Champion!"

Marcus turned at the yell and barely grabbed the wine jug thrust into his hands. Tevia, in one of his rare moments of breaking stoic face, grinned animatedly. Marcus tilted his head in the slave's direction, a solitary thanks. He knew Tevia was uncomfortable in the lower ludus, as the gladiators either belittled him as Aulus' toad or, if he was lucky, ignored him. Marcus was one of the few that treated him as another slave, not better or worse, though his position near Aulus placed him as the man to seek for favors or advice. The champion's knowledge from his prior slave days gave him the insight to Tevia's position and befriended the man early. But for him to be here now was a puzzle.

An even bigger puzzle was the flash of anger jetting through Iduma's eyes at the Domina's personal slave. Marcus frowned.

Tevia's shoulders straightened. "Marcus, all the wine you can drink. There's enough for everyone to get as much as they want."

Roars heralded throughout the chamber as the others heard this, doubling when the doors on the other side, leading from the Villa's storage, opened. In came two slaves pulling the wooden cart carrying the wine jugs. Marcus watched as he took another slug from the one he had.

Tevia bent closer. "Dominus made comment about special reward for you, later, in your cell."

Marcus' heart skipped a beat. Trying to maintain a plain, indifferent face, he downed more wine. *Gustina.* His eyes narrowed on the man, trying to pinpoint what he meant. Tevia just smiled and nodded. The confirmation made fire pore through his blood. He hadn't seen her in weeks and felt her absence strongly.

But even in his rush of excitement, he did notice the angry look on the Brit's face as he snorted and walked away. He turned to follow.

"Marcus," Tevia called. "Be wary of those you trust. Even the gods bend wills to make us do as they want."

"What is your purpose?" The house slave's statement sent a chill snaking down his spine. Odd, once more, the demon was absent. Inconsistent beast.

"Perhaps nothing," the man said with a shrug. "Be wary of Iduma. He now carries his own demon."

Marcus smirked. He knew they thought he was possessed. And maybe he was, though he now believed it was by the brown-haired beauty he stole from the Afterlife's grip. Something wasn't right. He could feel it, but after the day he'd had, sweltering on the sands, he just didn't care. He put the wine jug to his lips and gulped. When he looked down again, Tevia was gone.

He turned and hit an onslaught of his brothers, his fellow gladiators. Most had cups in their hands, slapping backs and joking. Even Iduma.

Time to solve the issue. Marcus walked up to the Brit. "Time to celebrate, brother." He poured into the man's cup.

Iduma smiled, raising the cup in thanks and downing it. Pushing the empty container back at him, Iduma's wayward grin was restored. "Yes, brother. And we championed with the luck of the gods."

Marcus guffawed. "Perhaps you needed their aid, but not I."

Iduma laughed and stepped back a space. "Surely, you jest. Or I will give safety a wider berth, in case they send a lightning bolt ripping through the ceiling."

Marcus laughed. "I am not their plaything. I need not worry."

Around them, the others downed wine and roared in satisfaction when the whores arrived. Marcus retrieved another jug, pulling the cork from its neck and flicking it across the room. One of the harlots caught it and ambled up to him, grinning.

"Champion, I have your attention," she said seductively, sauntering closer.

He smiled. Her hand came to his chest, lightly tracing a design as she continued talking to him, trying to entice him to take her. She wasn't bad looking, considering her profession, but his heart tugged for another. He opened his mouth to tell her no when beyond her, he saw his brother gladiators enjoying the night, drinking and fucking the other whores. Against the far wall, he caught a glimpse of Gustina, and he felt alive. Even the quiet demon purred.

It only lasted a moment. Just as he reached to take the whore's hand off him and go to Gustina, he saw Iduma step closer to his woman. Marcus' gaze narrowed. The Brit spoke to her and she nodded, her hand went to him, resting on his chest. Iduma's head bent closer.

Marcus' blood boiled. They looked too familiar with each other. As if they were lovers.... The demon prowled, snarling.

The whore slid away.

"Champion!"

He wouldn't have heard the call if he hadn't been hit in his bicep by the other gladiator. He whipped around, fury unfurling, to find Ludo, jug in hand. An unusual appearance. With a frown, he tilted his head, damping down the anger. "Doctore."

"Come, let us drink to the return of your prowess," the man's arm encircled Marcus' shoulders as he poured the wine into the empty cup.

Marcus snorted. He drank, wanting to look for her, but Ludo had turned them around. Though the man may be drinking with him, Marcus saw the whip was still attached to the doctore's waist. He took another sip, resigning himself for the moment. She would be with him soon and then, he'd find the truth.

She swallowed as she stared at the wooden door. What she wouldn't give not to go in. He'll kill her. Reject her. Either way, it didn't matter. He'd hate her. Jupiter, the tension emanated out the wooden slats before her.

Gustina inhaled deeply. Her hands flattened her tunic. She'd seen him earlier, at the gathering of gladiators. He looked totally intoxicated on the wine and men. She hadn't meant to talk to Iduma. He'd cornered her...like he had several times since that night. Eyes closed tight, breathing deep, she tried to calm her nerves. Her heart was in her throat. Sounds of the Colosseum flooded her head—death, applause, and blood. Did blood sound? Yes, to the victims, to the attackers, to the next in line to die....She heard her blood.

The guard in front of her, even with his helmet on, stared at her. The hesitation in her body must have glowed. How does one face the man of her dreams when she wasn't worthy him? Inhaling deeply, she tried to steady her nerves and nodded her head.

The door opened. Light of the oil lamp lit the chamber before her. Everything inside her clenched as she stepped forward.

He stood near the bed, facing the wall, arms crossed. Like a statue. Like stone. No warmth. No sympathy.

She was a slave. Sent to pleasure him. All emotions thrown aside. She felt nothing. Not allowed to. Then why did her heart cry? She'd been through this turmoil before and lived. Her heart kept a staccato beat, her toes curled, hands fisted. She was on the defense, and he hadn't even registered her presence. She forced herself to breathe, to unclench her hands and force her shoulders to relax.

"Champion." Three syllables. It flowed smoothly to her ears. Or was she lying even to herself?

He turned to her and smiled. "Gustina." His hand extended to her, open.

She forced herself to smile, wanting to believe he wanted her. Her palm rested on his, waiting. He wrapped around hers and pulled her to him. Breath escaped her when he crushed her to his body, his arms encircling her and holding her tight. His lips sealed hers, his tongue seeking her mouth, tempting, prodding, promising. She opened to his invasion.

He growled, picking her up in his arms. She laced her arms around his neck, kissing him back more desperately, hoping, praying to the gods he truly wanted her. Nimble fingers, almost an oddity coming from a man as big as him, trained to kill, worked on her tunic, unraveling the tie at her neck. Her exposed breasts tingled when his fingers skimmed down them, lowering the material. The leather belt around her waist smacked the stone floor, allowing the flaxen material to follow in a heap.

The air was thick, laden with the heat of summer, tension and lust, but a chill raced up her spine as his eyes roved her nude form.

"You are blessed by the gods," he whispered.

She swallowed hard. "You flatter when there is no need. I am yours."

His gaze returned to hers, questioning, probing, but no words came. She shuddered, needing to control her emotions before they undid her. Lowering her view, she noticed his nose looked slightly more bent, as if it'd been broken recently. He had a freshly stitched line on his chest and a couple other scabs from recent fights and practices. A voice deep down wondered if any wounds had been caused by her deception with Iduma. Quickly, she quelled that question. It served no good to seek the truth, only a path to further pain.

He grabbed her by her shoulders and brought her closer, tipping his head down as he raised her slightly up. He nibbled at her neck, her shoulder and down to her breast. Kissing and biting, he lowered to her nipple, already hardened with arousal. His tongue circled it before his lips engulfed it. She gasped as his teeth grazed it, his tongue then soothing. It was raw, primal, and awoke the sleeping need within her.

Decadent tingles spread within her, like mini lightning bolts, zeroing in on her womb, causing a pool of desire. She wanted him, needed him. Overcoming her fears of his refusal, she touched his sides, feeling the top of his subligaculum, tracing its edge. The bulge in the front, the heat of his arousal, made her find the tuck of the fabric and undo it. Like her tunic, it fell to the floor, unraveling itself. Her hand wrapped around his erection and squeezed lightly, amazed how he was made of finely chiseled muscles, skin darkened by the sun, rough from hard work and sweat, but his cock felt smooth, as if made of silk. Her touch made his breathing hitch and she smiled as he nipped her neck. When her thumb caressed the slit in his arousal's head, the wetness of his pre-release moistened it. The ripples of his growl vibrated off her breast as he pulled back, lifted her to his pallet.

Her back hit the wool blanket, her legs parted. Above her, Marcus knelt between her knees, his eyes hooded. Her mouth dried. His hand parted her legs farther and she moaned. The dampness between her thighs and the musky smell in the room fueled her desire. He gave her no more time to think as his hand placed the tip of his cock at her opening and drove into her.

Hard, carnal. Her body adjusted to his width as he invaded her. Back arching, forcing her hips lower, meeting his demands. He had his hands on either side of her head, still bent over her, tipping her at an angle, thrusting wildly into her. Eyes locked, she felt him shuddering, the vein in his cock pulsing madly inside her. Each invasion hit her clit, causing tiny eruptions that mounted, making her spread farther, so it touched him with each thrust.

This gladiator, this champion, demanded his prize. Nothing would stand in his way. Now. Here. Raw. Hard. A brutal attack in a sense, but she accepted it, longed for it, need matching need. Her legs locked around his hips. The aftermath not even a subject of consideration.

"Gustina." His voice tightened with possession. It echoed into her soul, causing inner quakes, building with each following word. "You. Are. Mine."

Her world shattered, stars exploding, blinding her as her slick canal tightened repeatedly over and over around him. He moaned deeply, one last thrust. His head hit her womb, shivering within as he stayed, his seed filling her.

She opened her eyes and found him, still deep in her, watching her, his own gaze dark. His arousal, depleted, diminished and as he naturally fell out of her, the gladiator collapsed next to her, pulling her into his arms.

"Shhh," he whispered into her ear. His thumb caressed her cheek and the wetness there surprised her. She was crying.

He held her tight, naked in his arms, cradled against him. He didn't say another word – not wanting an explanation, a denial from her of what happened or a forgiveness from him for her betrayal. It made her inwardly thank the gods for his silence.

Marcus took her two more times that night. Never speaking a word. He just aroused her body as she slept, waking her as he parted her legs and filled her with his cock. It wasn't right, not the way it should be if he felt for her anything other than a being for his sexual release, but she did nothing to stop him or ask anything from him. He wore her out. After the third time, she lay replete in his arms and fell deeply asleep.

In the morning, she awoke.

Alone.

CHAPTER TWENTY-ONE

"I want to fight in the next round of games."

Aulus glanced up from the wax tablet on his desk and found his champion standing before him, legs firmly planted, arms straight, hands clenched and his face determined. Sitting back on the stool, Aulus frowned.

"It is too soon since the last spectacle. I won't take the chance...."

"I will win." The set voice held defiance, almost daring Aulus to show disbelief in his abilities.

"So, with the will of the gods, to push precedent this quickly might—" he stopped. The fire in Marcus' eyes ignited. The man wasn't asking, he was demanding. Why? Was it the demon the man possessed that pushed him? Did he punish the gods for giving him such a champion? His head started to throb. "I will consider. Return to the ludus."

Marcus dipped his head slightly. "Dominus." And he left, a guard following.

That man never gave him deference like that. Something was up. "Care to explain, doctore?"

Ludo stepped forward from the corner he stood in during the request. "He's burning to go back to the sands and kill."

"I can see that. He did so yesterday, admirably well. He got his reward. That should keep him satisfied."

"Yes, apparently that is the problem," Ludo interrupted. "He drank ample wine but while the others jested and fucked the whores, he stood, with a look of fires burning, ones that wouldn't go out."

"Like Mount Vesuvius?" When Ludo nodded, Aulus'

brows furrowed. "Why? He got whatever-her-name-is back."

"Yes, and Gustina may be the reason for this fire."

Aulus sighed. He could guess but pushed. "You and I have virtually grown up here, fought each other as children. I placed you as doctore because your wins on the sands are legendary in their own right. You won against Dionysis, the Gaul demons and killed the undefeated Vestus before a standing crowd, cheering your name. Now, you teach the best in the Empire, outside of the Emperor's, and we both know Marcus should stand champion of all of Rome. So what is his problem with her?"

Ludo grasped his hands behind his back. "His problem is one you created." The man shook his head. "The night you sent her to Iduma. Whatever possessed such a thought? He obviously is enamored with her so you sending her to another has had him at wits' end. He almost killed the Brit when the man finally shows status on the sands."

"He can lust after another," Aulus stated angrily.

"Not likely the same. He paid for her, not like a whore, and you know that."

Aulus glared at his doctore, a slave he'd known for years and knew well enough to listen to but....

"The man was obsessed with her, like that demon that controls him. He'd lost on the sands, begged for missio, for Jupiter's sake! Not a champion to be rewarded with other than what he got."

"So you sent her to his friend and gave him that cunt? Oh yes, we all know of Verenia's lust for him. The position he'd give her. He refused her, you know."

Aulus snorted. He did. Almost laughed about it but the girl was good in lustful ways. Not his fault the fallen Roman didn't care for her. Shame, she knew how to suck cock well....

"It was done. I did what needed to be done. And it refocused his sights back to the sands."

Ludo shook his head. "The results are yet to be seen. Let him fight. I know it is unusual to resubmit him to the games so soon, but I'd prefer it versus losing many men to the medicus when he explodes on the training ground because he is denied."

Marcus' request was highly unusual. Most gladiators fought sparingly, honing their skills on the practice fields with wooden gladius. Over-fighting in competition meant wear and tear and loss of assets. Aulus closed his eyes. He'd seen the determination on the man's face, the coldness in his eyes, the voice that sounded demanding not requesting. The demon that held his soul must be havoc to the man and the only solution was to let him take blood on the sands and pray to Jupiter it was enough.

Aulus nodded.

"Dominus." Ludo backed away.

Shit, he needed wine. And a good fuck.

∾

The fifty-fifth day of games. Marcus flexed in the corridor before his match, his mind trying to focus on the upcoming fight, but thoughts of Gustina, writhing beneath him last night, her response to him matching his, and her tears, tore at his heart. Without a word, she confessed to fucking the Brit. Why did that ass deny it to him? He knew the man was too drunk that night not to follow his cock. And if she waited for him in his cell like Verenia had him, naked, willing, how could the man deny her?

Anger flared inside him. Why didn't she refuse to become his whore? He stopped in mid-motion of stretching, his arms extended, hands gripping the lead balls. Realization zeroed in. She didn't because she only knew how to be a slave – to answer the demands or be punished. And what good was he? To know all this and have had experience as a freed Roman, distributing punishment to stubborn slaves. The gods now sought pain from him. Physical pain he could manage. But the pain in the center of his chest, brought forth by a woman, hurt more than sword or poison.

He bought her to protect her and, in the end, failed.

The demon prowled, snarling beneath the cover of his skin. Eyes narrowed, mouth tight, his gut twisting, he wanted blood and wanted it now. To see Death and spit in its face.

The roar of the crowd escalated as the announcer named the upcoming opponents. He was to fight Titus now, a Gaul from some region, geared as a murmillo. Good. Gauls were asses in the first place. Being dressed as a fishman only added to the flavor.

Marcus stood at the gated door, his eyes closed in

concentration, feeling the demon surging through him. Blood. The taste for blood boiled inside. And the outrageous bellowing of the crowd only ignited his passion to kill.

⸻

Lucilla paced the box, anger and fear wanting to overpower her—and that she could not let happen. Around her, the crowd's chant for blood radiated through the stands. The stomping of their feet echoing their voices made her blood race faster.

"What in the name of the gods is wrong with you?"

Lucilla stopped and turned to face her friend. Cernia sat still, so pristine this afternoon, looking refreshed and cool, something that irked her that much more. It was blistering hot in the late afternoon sun. Even the wine burned her mouth.

Unable to contain herself, she stepped closer to Cernia. "How could you allow this? For him to fight again, so soon?"

Her friend's eyebrows arched. "He requested it."

"And you gave in to a slave?" Lucilla wanted to spit. "What if he loses? What if he dies? All that time and money."

"Whatever would it matter to you?"

Lucilla closed her eyes. It meant a great deal. They'd only fucked once. The priestess told her to consummate the act five or seven times a week for the next month to receive Juno's blessing. How could she if her stud died on the sands? He wasn't supposed to be here for another thirty plus days and today, she found the markings on the walls, of a surprise contestant in the primus. Marcus.

Cernia would never understand. She forced her lips to grin. "It's just so against the nature of things, to give in to a slave's desire."

Cernia exhaled loudly. "He is a gladiator. Beast more than a slave."

Now Lucilla's smile turned real. "Yes, they are beasts. Ravenous beasts." Her voice dropped. "Out of all those under your roof, have you never fucked one of them?"

Cernia's shudder was visible. "No, I have no desire to allow any man outside my husband, between my legs."

Lucilla snorted. She always suspected Cernia's leanings were for women so she turned, muttering, "I bet his odds barely fair better...."

"Marcus is now on the sands," Cernia said, pointing to the spectacle below. Lucilla thanked the gods silently her friend didn't hear her. But apparently, Cernia's thoughts hadn't strayed. "Why do you care so much? He is your former husband, reduced to beastly fights in the arena, as slave. Why do you want to rut with him? Is your husband so lacking in that regard?"

Lucilla's insides flipped. No one knew that Marcus had gotten her with child before the discovery of his birth and the aftermath. How could she explain that Lucius' seed found no ground in her? Neither had Terpio's. But where Marcus had succeeded, she needed him to again. *The curse of the gods for her ending the child's life.* Swallowing her pride, spreading her legs to him was an act of desperation, though, she had to admit, his skills in completing the task never lacked appeal. Her mind wandered to the sight of him, now all muscular, like Apollo's statues, and his erection always hard and big for her. Her womb fluttered. She shook her head, trying to dispel the image, feeling her cheeks becoming hot.

"The heat," she exclaimed, grabbing the fan from her slave and waving it quickly. She licked her lips. "The priestess told me I needed the seed of a champion for my husband's to gain the strength needed." That part was true. She felt better. "But if he's killed, I too may find myself wayward, without home."

Cernia laughed. "With your looks and body, I doubt that'd be long in the taking."

Lucilla forced a laugh. The woman had no idea. At her age, Lucilla wasn't the catch young Cernia was, and at this point, men came to her wanting an heir. She knew Lucius loved her, but he needed a son. He hadn't told her he'd dissolve their marriage but she knew the threat was there and real.

The fight started. The clanking of the gladius sounded through the Colosseum. The barefoot gladiators poised and thrust at each other. Titus swung and blood spewed in the air from Marcus' arm and he roared in protest. The murmillo carried a shield, but Marcus didn't so he could wield two gladius at once. Lucilla cringed. He had no defense other than to counter the other's attack.

Another loud grunt and Titus fell to one knee. Marcus' arms raised, weapons in the air, when the Gaul made an arc with his blade, hitting Marcus' greave, slicing through it. Blood dripped from the gladius as it was recalled and the victim roared, falling to his knees. It gave the Gaul the opportunity to rise and charge.

A gasp sounded next to her. Lucilla turned and found her friend pale as marble, her hand to her mouth.

"Are you well?" She'd never seen her like this. The woman sat at numerous games, never veering from view, no matter how bloody. This time, she gagged behind her hand. "Verenia!" Lucilla called.

Cernia's body slave appeared at her side. The girl also looked peaked. What was happening in Aulus' house?

Verenia took Cernia and steadied her. She looked up at Lucilla. "She is with child."

Lucilla thoughts fled her. The woman who didn't need to produce an heir right now, carried Lucilla's desire. *Damn!* She wanted to scream in rage to the gods.

Marcus stood on the sands, facing the podium, blood soaked arms and hands grasping crimson blades, dripping, above his head. The crowd roared with approval at his win. The Gaul, with all his pretense and fish helmet, lay on the sands dead, head severed. Blood oozed everywhere. The demon pranced, soaking it in. Marcus felt nothing. He wanted to kill more.

The emperor, Trajan, stared at him from the balcony box. Marcus waited. He'd broken the rules, killing the gladiator without the emperor's permission. Perhaps now he'd get his sought-after freedom in the Afterlife. But while part of him welcomed the thought, another voice struggled to be heard.

Gustina.

He'd fail her—again. Iduma could take her. His blood boiled. The damn Brit had. That realization, that she'd lain with him, his best friend, stoked the fire to be here on the sands today. But his inner turmoil couldn't throw her away. The woman had a hold on his heart. What little was left of the wretched thing.

Trajan smiled and nodded. The crowds cheered, many jumping up and down. Marcus heard them roar "Champion!" and "Marcus!" Many bare breasts showed from the rafters as women displayed their affections in curious ways.

He'd won another day to kill. His demon purred.

As he walked to the gates, hearing the dragging on the sands behind him as they drug the body of Titus to the Afterlife gates, he sought only the baths and wine. And Gustina

The guards took his swords immediately, and he wanted to laugh. As if he had the strength now to attack them. A slender slave boy, a young man really, led him to the baths, eyeing Marcus with fear and wonder. Of course, the way he swung his ass, the lad's subligaculum barely concealing his erection, let Marcus know he wanted to be fucked. He snorted. Never the type to take a man, either in his ass or mouth, he shook his head and the slave disappeared.

The oiled bath soothed his aching muscles. He took his time with the strigil, scraping the grime and blood away. The demon still prowled, picking up Marcus' thoughts about Gustina. He'd been cruel to her last night. Claimed her, took her repeatedly, never worrying about pleasing her just dumping his seed into her over and over and over. He'd left before daybreak, sickened with himself.

She'd done what she was told. Both for Iduma and now him. And he consumed her. *What a sick bastard he was.* The strigil slipped, slicing the inside of his forearm. "Damn."

"Gladiator."

He looked up at the guard. They'd sent two. With a sigh, he stood, tucking the corner into his subligaculm and went to them, leaving his balteus and greaves on the floor. He knew Tevia would retrieve them.

They led him down the familiar hall. Some bitch paid for him. Jupiter's cock, how tiresome this was. However, a faint thought flickered through his mind. Wasn't he doing what Gustina had done? Obeyed orders? Fucked another? Only he'd get some of the coin for this. His stomach twisted.

He walked into the cell and outstretched his arms as they anchored him with metal cuffs to chains on the wall. His eyes caught the pallet next to him. Bile rose in his throat as he stared at it, hearing the door close and the lock fall into place.

It was then he smelled her. Vanilla and honey. *For the love of Jupiter, no!*

Lucilla.

"I should be angry with you," she murmured, letting her stola fall to the stone floor. She pulled the tab at her shoulder and the gown opened, pooling at her bare feet. She stood before him, nude. And hairless below. Even in the dim light, he smelled her arousal, could see her lower lips swollen and parted.

No! But his cock didn't listen. Whatever it was about her that got him, he'd never understand. He was cursed by the gods....

"I need your seed," she whispered, leaning to his chest, her tongue tracing the slice in his breast. She bit and he felt the sting, knowing she'd done so to get the blood flowing again. She'd done her work well. The blood of a champion was always reported to cure all ailments. He wondered if it could, for she was an ailment to society and if his blood could kill her, then he'd know he truly was champion.

"Fuck off, Lucilla." Even saying her name made him ill.

When her hand wrapped around his arousal and stroked it, he wanted to die.

"Oh yes, I do want to fuck off," she said slowly, rolling over each word like a caress. "I want you deep inside me."

"No." Damn, one more stroke and he'd yank away, if he could. *And he was upset at Gustina for giving herself to Iduma.* At least he didn't think his friend was a demon like the bitch before him.

"Yes, for you see, if you don't, I'll take little Gustina away. I'll tell your domina that she confided in my slave she carries your friend, the Brit's, child. Either she'll be submitted to the silvia which could kill her or I'll buy her. She's doomed at my disposal, unless you submit to me now and any other time I request it," she said, her threat clearly heard and felt as she roughly squeezed and pushed his cock.

Why did she hate him so? In his position as slave, even as gladiator and champion, he had no say in defense against her, a free Roman woman. He weighed his options as she bent and sucked on his erection. He felt her teeth graze him. Damnation, he had no choice, at least, not one available now.

He plucked her off his cock, threw her onto the pallet and pushed her legs open. Staring at her as hate filled him, Marcus rammed into her, not caring if he hurt her, and knowing by this act he betrayed Gustina. But damn it, he would get his vengeance on this cunt beneath him. She would not touch Gustina. He'd swear his life on that.

CHAPTER TWENTY-TWO

Iduma knew the Roman was mad. Fury drove every swing. The practice swords they used for training supposedly would not cause injury, but the blow of the wooden gladius hurt down to his bones. The only defense the Brit had was to counter and anticipate every swing, yet doing so also brought doctore's whip snapping at him for not pressing attack. When did he have time to attack a demon-driven man?

In the last five days since his surprise fight in the Colosseum, Marcus drove himself hard on the practice sands. Ludo switched his sparring partners frequently as his lust for vengeance wore everyone down. Marcus had been assigned to the palus this morning, but even the wooden man, the free-standing post, wobbled under the attack.

Snap! Ludo's whip sounded loudly. "Gladiators, rest."

Iduma stayed crouched, sword and wooden shield steady, waiting for Marcus to lower his weapons. He saw the fire in the Roman's eyes, a wildness, untamed and angry. *Shit.* Though he'd said nothing to him, Iduma figured Gustina must have told him. What defense did he have if the champion of Aulus' house accused him of fucking his woman? *She was sent to pleasure me* wasn't a defense or an excuse. It was a pathetic attempt to keep from cowering, and the Brit had advanced too far to do that. Besides, the man took her back. She'd been with him the last five nights. It irked him to no end that she slept with the Roman savage, his friend, again. But he swallowed his tongue and said nothing.

Slowly, Marcus lowered his gladius. Iduma eyed him carefully, but the man gave him a crooked grin and offered his hand to get him off the sands. Iduma realized he'd fallen and hadn't registered it. Maybe he was becoming obsessed. As he grabbed Marcus' hand, he knew it wasn't a demon who held him, but a man on the brink of explosion. *Fuck the gods.*

"Tired yet?" He'd gauge the man's temper first, his own riling under the thudding of his heart.

The gladiator snorted. "You're still breathing, no?" He slapped the Brit's shoulder. "The gods must love you."

Iduma thought otherwise. "Doubtful but...."

"Marcus."

Iduma heard the guard to their side call. Marcus tensed and, in his brown eyes, the flame of madness turned to a dull gaze of hard resignation. "What in the name of Jupiter?" Iduma asked.

The champion's nostrils flared as his lips thinned. "Nothing. Just more requirements of a champion."

"Are you fucking serious?" Iduma's voice dropped and he took a step closer, as if there were no rift between them caused by a woman. "After a win, I can see, but now?"

"'Tis nothing more than a drop of blood."

"Or seed." He spat and looked into the man's eyes. Still shuttered. "Marcus."

With a quick shake of his head, the demon Roman dropped his practice weapons, turned and followed the guard. Iduma's gut twisted. He'd never seen Marcus truly beaten on the sands until now. The champion walked away, as if the gates of the Afterlife would have been a better alternative.

※

Marcus felt the snake slither over him, and he longed to rip its head off. The serpents' feminine hiss purred in his ear.

"Remember the times you took me, regardless of the circumstance?"

He shut his eyes. Oh, he remembered. When he'd been young and stupid, believing the gods had blessed him with her. Arrogant fool. Anger flared through his veins. His hands grabbed her hips and lifted her naked body off him. He could tell she was aroused, and he was hard and it made him sick. She refused to leave him be until he emptied into her. He glowered, flipping her onto her stomach.

"Yes," she groaned.

Her sound made him angrier. He lifted her hips, driving her face into the pallet and slamming hard into her. Every move spurred his hatred at himself and at her. Deep down, he knew Gustina would hate him if she knew, and for that reason alone, he couldn't remain angry about her spreading her thighs for Iduma. Nor could he be angry with the Brit—as much as he wanted to be. No, he had no right, being ordered to fuck the whore who stole his life.

He stopped, still hard inside her. Her muscles convulsed around him, begging his cock to release inside her, but his self-hatred made his erection shrivel in disgust. He was a whore of the worst sort. His hands shoved her ass away from him, and he leapt off the pallet, grabbing his subligaculum and tying it around his waist.

"I'm through for today." He could taste the vomit in his mouth as he spoke, bastard that he was. She lay there, smiling at him. Bitch. He threw her clothes at her. "Guards! The lady is finished."

Methodically fluid, she rose from the pallet, like a cobra raising its head to attack, only this snake smiled seductively, satiated, carrying his seed. A flow he couldn't halt in time.

He wanted to puke and drink three jugs of wine at the same time. The scampering of sandals outside the door heralded the guards' fumbling for their keys. Jupiter's ass, if he wasn't chained, he'd kick the thick wood door open to free himself of this spawn.

She sauntered up to him, knowing he couldn't hide. Her hand cradled his cheek. Her palm burned his skin like poison.

"'Til next time, my darling," she said huskily. For love of the gods, he could see her hardened nipples through the tunic. Savagely yanking the stola over her, he pushed her away.

"If they fuck you, I won't say a word," he snarled.

"They won't, for I have too much coin and power for them to violate me," she replied, flipping her long blond locks and turning to the door.

The gods truly hated him.

❦

Gustina waited, fidgeting on her last task of fetching more wine, hoping for Marcus and the others' return from the Colosseum. She'd be in trouble soon if they didn't hurry.

"Gustina," a voice whispered.

She wanted to jump and almost dropped the container until she saw Farina. "Why are you trying to scare me?"

Her friend smiled. "I wasn't. I was sent to see where you were."

She frowned. "I've got a jug and I'm coming."

Farina laughed. "Let me take that. From the sound of your voice, you'll drop it. They'll be back soon." She pried the container from her hands.

"Farina, please," she begged, trying to take it back. "If that bitch sees me without it, she'll tell the Domina...."

"That bitch isn't there." Farina smiled broadly. "The cunt's too worn out from taking care of Domina in her condition." She leaned in, as if conspiring. "Both conditions. Domina is carrying and the effects of the bitch being made to lose hers."

As much as she hated the woman, Gustina still shuddered. "I understand that is painful."

"So is childbirth," Farina countered. "Or so I've heard."

She couldn't shake the fear that snaked down her spine. She knew she wasn't, but if she continued with Marcus, there was the possibility. She clamped her eyes shut, closing off the thought and then opened them, forcing a smile on her lips. "I'll keep that in mind."

Farina eyed her speculatively. With a sigh, she handed Gustina the jug and reached for another. "Dominus wants to celebrate. But I do believe he'll soon be in search of a replacement for Verenia to warm his bed."

Gustina noticed her friend's blush. "You want to lay with him? But what of Iduma?"

Placing the jug on the floor, she glanced at her friend. "If I am in Dominus' bed I would be given position. And besides," her voice turned a touch sharp, "Iduma wants you. You know that, right?"

She gulped. That night would haunt her for an eternity. Submitting to another wasn't what she wanted. But denial was never available for a slave, especially a female slave. Thankfully, she had rarely been forced on many for actual fucking. Her former Dominus favored her only for himself, as disgusting as it was. If he liked it that way, why hadn't he turned to a boy? The answer always made her retch—she hated it so. He'd ripped her the first few times, chained her once to submit, yanked on her hair, and broke her to his way. And afterward, whispered in her ear she should thank him for she'd not be with child this way. Then he'd bit her, low, marking her, like a wild beast conquering his prey.

Marcus showed her gentleness. Even the other night, when he took her savagely, it still wasn't hurtful. No, he claimed her, his marking deep inside her womb, the memory radiated throughout her body even at the thought of him entering her.

And the Brit... she shook her head.

"So," she breathed deep, trying to clear her head. "You'd give up on Iduma for Aulus?"

"Wouldn't you give up Marcus and Iduma?" Her friend giggled.

"No." But the fact Farina said both names made her shiver uncontrollably. Calling every last bit of strength she had, she forced herself to stop trembling.

Her heart belonged to Marcus. She swallowed hard. The vision of Iduma's smiling face not out of the background in her mind. Her heart plummeted. No better than a whore....

Farina continued prattling on when the gates to the Villa opened. Both turned. The gladiators were back. Her friend squealed.

"Gustina, we must go bathe," she tugged her arm. "We need to go take these. Come on."

Her feet felt like lead. The men roared their victories, demanding wine and whores. And she found both Marcus and Iduma, not next to each other, but both staring at her.

∞

The gladiators sunk into the pits of the ludus, seeking the baths and their reward. Iduma scraped the sands off him with the strigil, watching the area with a hooded gaze. Marcus was across the baths, not talking to anyone. Not that unusual for him, but he'd bathed at the Colosseum. A woman had requested him, but whoever she was, the experience must have been bad. The man continued to scrape until his bronzed skin turned red by the oil lamps. The Brit's eyes narrowed. The champion paid a high price for his wins, apparently. Anger glowed around him as the others moved further away.

The doors to the Villa section opened and the cart carrying the wine, women trailing it, entered. The brotherhood all yelled in approval and descended on the whores and drink. Iduma noticed Farina was missing, but Gustina was there. She hung in the back of the lot, a frantic look in her eyes. He glanced back at Marcus. The man didn't even acknowledge their arrival.

Iduma stood and walked over to the cart, his intention to speak to her, even if only a moment. The closer he got, the more frightened she looked. That bothered him. She shouldn't be scared of him.

He stood before her, not touching her. She poured him a cup of wine as she had the others and shoved it into his hands. He'd misjudged her look. Anger and determination met his gaze.

"Gustina," he began.

"You're a fool to be before me, here," she interrupted, standing straight, shoulders back, almost daring him to step closer. But there was also a veil of defiance, as if warning him to stay back.

He ignored her and came a step closer. "Why? You're handing a victor a cup of wine." Another step. He felt her breath as she exhaled sharply. "Nothing amiss in that," he added, his voice dropping.

Her eyes darted past him. No doubt looking for Marcus. Iduma shook his head. Jupiter's ass, the champion's fuck before leaving the Colosseum must have been horrendous for he'd never seen Marcus so obsessed in cleaning, like that demon who possessed him wanted pain to remove the filth off of him.

"Gustina," he murmured again. The noise of the others around them drowned their voices and he knew he hid her.

"Farina isn't here."

He snorted and reached to touch her cheek. "I wasn't looking for her. I came to see you."

She gulped. He heard the sound and watched her elegant neck as she swallowed. He remembered that neck, kissing it, laving it with his tongue....

"Don't," she whispered.

"It wasn't a bad thing we did," he said. His thumb caressed her skin. So soft....

Her eyes filled with sadness. "Iduma, please, it wasn't that."

"He took you back," he said softly, but his tone was tainted with a sneer.

"You shouldn't want me." She stated it so quietly he strained to hear her.

"My wants, my desires are not always my choice."

"Nor was my presence in your bed," she added.

Ah, yes, the command to please him. He'd hoped.... "Did you regret what we did?"

"Iduma, I can't," she begged, stepping back.

"What is going on here?" Marcus' voice boomed loudly just behind him. *Shit.* He even saw Gustina jump.

"Just inquiring where Farina was, brother," he slapped the Roman on the shoulder with a smile pasted on his face.

Marcus glared at him. Iduma saw the fire there, deep embers burning. Tension oozed out of his pores and the Brit wondered if he caught a glimpse of the demon inside him. And how much the Roman heard. To his own mind, Iduma knew Gustina would deny being happy in his bed but he saw her eyes flicker at her lie. He gritted his teeth. Now was not the time to push her.

But the Champion's eyes roved the room. "Isn't she here?"

"No," Gustina replied, moving closer to Marcus. "Dominus called for her."

The two men frowned. "He called for her?" Iduma couldn't believe she'd be with the man by her own choice. A strange sensation twisted in his gut.

"Yes," she said. Her hand touched Iduma on his bare chest. "I'm sorry."

A rumble, deep, dark, dangerous, sounded loudly. Marcus' arm snaked around her waist, pulling her off Iduma. The Brit stiffened but didn't move.

"Gladiators," another voice echoed. Ludo. "We have issue?"

Gustina snuggled into Marcus' arm and Iduma banked the flare of rage within him. She wasn't his. Schooling his features, he noticed the Roman's fiery gaze shifted.

"No, Doctore," Marcus muttered.

"No," Iduma said. "Just inquiring about Farina."

Ludo's eyes swept over both men and Gustina. Iduma knew the man was not an idiot. But there would be no fights tonight over her. Not yet. The doctore gave a nod and walked away. Iduma tilted his head at the Roman.

"I'm sure there's another here you can fuck," the champion stated, grabbing a jug of wine and taking Gustina's hand. "Brother," he nodded and strode off with her to his cell.

Gustina shot him a look. He couldn't read it well in the dark, oil lit room, but was it an apologetic look? Regret?

He watched them walk across the training ground to Marcus' cell and disappear behind the door. Furious, he stood, trying to control his anger. She was his. After that night, he craved her like a dying man did water. Marcus was his friend, old and true, and he was dangerous when roused. But Iduma didn't care. He wanted Gustina back. Even if it cost him his life.

CHAPTER TWENTY-THREE

Aulus walked into his wife's chambers and heard her humming. The sound was melodic and surprised him by its beauty. He missed knowing she had a voice. Well, he knew the one she enthusiastically used as he made love to her. It was a wild cry, primal and he thrived on it. None of the slaves he'd bedded matched her, not even darling Farina. The girl was naïve and offered him the rare opportunity to teach her how to please a man. But for the moment, his ears picked up his wife and he gave her his full attention.

Especially in her condition. He'd made an offering that morning to Jupiter himself for blessing him so. With an heir, Aulus' house was complete. He sighed.

The humming stopped. Shit, she'd heard him. He rounded the corner to her sitting on a cushioned bench, combing her long dark brown hair. When she saw him, she smiled radiantly.

"I thought you were at temple."

He nodded as he reached her and kissed her neck lightly. "Made an offering to Jupiter for our blessing. A hundred ram."

She glanced at him, her face showing her amazement. "A hundred? Wasn't that overmuch?"

He laughed. "I'd have given a hundred bulls but they are a bit hard to come by at the moment, with the games."

"You jest," she prodded him with her brush but he liked the fact her smile remained.

His hand caressed her cheek. "No, I do not." His eyes zeroed on her lower stomach. "And today, you feel better?"

Naturally, her hand went to her lower stomach but her

curled lips didn't falter. "Medicus said that was natural and I was fine."

Aulus growled. He didn't like the idea another man had touched her.

"Darling," she murmured, touching his cheek.

He snorted but returned her grin. "I don't wish you to exert yourself."

Her grin disappeared. "I can and will do what I want. Carrying a child will not interrupt my life."

Inwardly, he grimaced. At times, Cernia was so self-centered....Setting his path forward, he changed the subject.

"Thirty days until any of our men will be in the Colosseum."

Cernia's eyes narrowed. "And you're not coddling any of them, are you? Sacrifices must be made but a whore's death is hardly noticed."

Aulus frowned. "Whore?"

"Gustina." When he started, she quickly added. "Marcus always gets lax if he's with her too much. And now you allowed that British gladiator to fall under her spell."

Spell? He played with the idea. The girl was nothing from what he could gather, but he knew his champion was under her influence. The man had lost his winning edge and when he took her from him, he rallied and returned to winning. As dominus, he'd rewarded his champion with her presence in his bed again. But the end games were coming. Was Cernia suggesting he take her away again? The man could explode.

"You have little knowledge of the man's affections," he said. "To take her again, he'll accuse the Brit of this and then this house will be divided."

She sauntered up to him, her voice low and seductive. His wife, the enchantress, the one woman he'd succumb to. When her thumb rubbed his lips softly, he barely heard her.

"I know someone who'd hold her, out of this Villa. We could sell her or at least lease her out, with a promise of her return on his victory." She smiled at him and stood on her toes to whisper in his ear. "With him understanding she'd never return without his wins and the advancement of this house."

His heart quickened with her so close. The moon would be hers for the asking. He sought her gaze, noticed the determination. Gods, impending motherhood suited her well.

He nodded to her proposal and drank in the sound of her sigh, wanting to devour her now.

She placed her hands on his toga. "Aulus?"

So caught in the web of her seduction, it took him a moment to realize she wanted his verbal confirmation of what she said. His lips curved into a one-sided grin. "Yes, may the gods strike me down if I don't do as you suggest." He pulled her in for a kiss.

She giggled. "Good. Then I say, we will win."

He decided he already had, claiming her lips as his.

∞

Marcus wheeled, gladius primed, ready to block Iduma's swing and counter it with his own. The clash of the wooden swords and shield reverberated across the training ground. The Brit gave him a sneering grin, thrusting his shield up against Marcus' attack and twisting his sword hand, aiming for another blow. The Roman blocked it with ease, holding both his weapons against the Brit's. They stood, facing each other for a couple of seconds before laughter erupted and they both stepped back.

Lowering his gladius, Marcus spat onto the ground. It was dry enough that all the practicing gladiators kicked up dirt, ladening the air with a thick coat of dust. With the heat of the rising sun, he was slick with sweat and grime, his eyes gritty and his mouth as dry as the sands. His glance at his fellow gladiator showed the Brit also in the same state. The dry and hot summer had descended and little could change it without the gods being pleased. Just let him into the arena and he'd kill them all to appease them.

"You're quite the form," the Brit spat, a slow grin on his face.

Marcus snorted. He hadn't killed him—yet. If he found the man close to Gustina again.... Of course, he hadn't seen her in a week. Training. Training for the final games. Aulus wanted, no, *needed,* them to win. All politics and rewards. The demon thrived on the practice, aiming to perfect his skills and dancing to grasp the real weapons.

"Just trying to help you keep your skills up, brother," he returned.

Iduma laughed but Marcus noticed the man's eyes, leery of

his motivation. Good. That would actually help him on the sands. Though that wasn't exactly Marcus' motivation for driving hard against him. No, the thoughts of him between Gustina's thighs made him border the lines of insanity. The demon prowled close to the surface. Doctore's instruction was hard this week, exhausting the lot of them. Marcus collapsed every night—alone. And no doubt everyone else had too, or that was the lie the Roman told himself as he lay on his pallet, his memories of her at the corners of his mind.

"Gladiators," Ludo cried, his whip snapping in the air. "Time for noonday meal. Rest, and after the sun is past its height, we'll resume."

The field broke, men dropped their tools to the ground and walked to the covered chamber and food. Marcus tipped his head at Iduma, who still held his weapon. The Brit didn't trust him fully. He smirked. He shouldn't, not if Marcus found him within reach of her.

Iduma lowered his weapon. "I didn't ask for it."

Marcus' eyes narrowed. Neither had talked about that night. He wasn't sure now was any better than before. He still wanted to kill him at just the thought of it. He opened his mouth and promptly closed it as Ludo walked up to them.

"Marcus, you are summoned."

Jupiter's balls! The only times he'd been summoned was by that bitch of a wife. His mouth tightened, and he felt his body tense. Hands clenched hard around the handles of the wooden gladius.

Ludo cocked his head, staring into his eyes, daring him to try. Marcus knew the man's victories and continued strength made him the strong doctore he was. The position required he know his men and how to subdue them, with or without the whip. With a large exhalation of the breath he'd been holding, he handed the wooden blades to his instructor and headed to the water barrels. Quenching his thirst, he took to the stairs, grumbling. The demon growled.

The guard brought him up the stairs, down a hallway to a chamber in the back. He heard the fountain running, the coolness of the shaded rooms, memories of a previous life struggling to surface. The filth from training made him squirm. If this was to see that bitch, just as well he was caked in sweat and dirt. She deserved no better, wanting him to fuck her just for a seed she'd destroyed years ago. Rage built with every step. Strangling her was such a better idea...except they'd kill him and leave Gustina prey to everyone. *Damnation!*

The door to the closed chamber opened and the guard pushed him in, slamming the door shut behind him.

"Lucilla, I swear..." he seethed.

"Shhh...," her low feminine purr softly interrupted. Her fingers touched his chest and slowly traced the contours of his pecs, down his abdomen, along the lines of his cloth.

"I'm soiled." In this tight space, a small room with only a slit window, the air stilled and his stench filled it, even blocking hers. Gods willing, he might get out of this. Except his cock twitched. Damn thing. His primal senses picked up on her arousal. She'd been playing with herself, to be ready for him. Like she did years ago, when they were one, and she remembered how he had no resistance to her in that state. He'd pray to any god who would listen to break this carnal hold she had over him. None, apparently, cared to listen.

She sniffed. Her fingers still followed his muscles, now on his back. "I know. It's so exciting this way," she whispered.

He heard a whoosh and felt the whisps of her stola hitting the backside of his legs as it fell to the floor. His eyes shut, trying to close the idea. Despite all his hatred of her, she still had an amazing body. Hands clenched, he stood still.

The tuck of his subligaculum came out. He felt the cloth move. Did she do it or did his own damned fingers? The piece fell off him and he heard her sigh. The demon stomped but his cock hardened as her fingertips traced his buttocks and came to the front. Her hand wrapped around his arousal.

"Yes, I remember, you love to be the animal at times. Like a mad bull," she said but he caught the carnal edge to her voice. "You know you want it."

"No, Lucilla."

"Yes, I think you should. You've been without, so I know you're hard with need."

The woman knew too much. For the love of the gods, maybe if he just got it over with, she'd leave him alone.

"You can't quench my wants or needs, Lucilla," he retorted, stilling his desires. Unfortunately, her stroking his erection worked the opposite. Her thumb rubbed over the slit on his head and she spread the leakage over him.

Anger rose to a blinding height inside him. He turned, grabbed her hips, her ass against him. With one hand, he pushed her over and he shoved himself inside her—hard. She made a guttural noise. It registered with him as he ground into her, over and over again.

Deep inside him, the demon rumbled. The boiling grew and Marcus roared, pulling out of her, spilling over her back, her ass and down her legs. Nothing in her cunt.

She turned, eyes aflame. "What in the name of Hades are you doing?"

"You may force me to fuck you, you little bitch. You know how to get me going and for that, I want to kill you. Be thankful to the gods I haven't," he yelled, pulling his garment up and tucking the ends in.

Eyes still on fire, she breathed heavily, making her breasts heave, her tightened nipples swell and bob. "That is the second time you've stolen from me."

He sputtered a laugh. "Stolen? My seed? I gave it to you." He certainly enjoyed watching her realize she couldn't control him totally.

She stood and her eyes turned to granite. "Listen to me well. The gods have ordained your victorious stream to me. I am willing to do whatever it takes to contain it inside me. Push me again and see it done."

"I'm already a slave. My death will not get you another child from me. To beat me will work against my cock's ability to harden. You've no other tricks."

The moment he said the words, he regretted it. He saw the flicker in her eyes.

"We shall see, champion," she said smoothly, tying her stola into place. "Guards."

The door opened and light streamed into the room, blinding him as they drug him out. But in that split second of sun, he saw the malicious twist of her lips and knew he was damned.

※

Gustina walked down the side of the atrium, carrying a basket full of lemons for her domina. The woman's request for them at noon seemed strange but then again, a woman in her condition might crave the oddest of things. Almonds and pears dipped in gamur was just one demand in what Gustina was sure to be many more. The smell of the sweet nuts and fruit in that fish sauce nearly made Gustina her stomach upheave.

She almost didn't hear the voices. Later, she wished she hadn't. A muffled sound, like a wounded animal crying in pain. Two guards stood next to a door of one of the cubiculum, a strange place for two guards to be. Since when did a bedchamber need guards? Last she knew, no one used that room. Puzzled, she stopped.

One of the guards opened the door. Gustina caught a glimpse and gasp. The guard grabbed Marcus' arm, pulling him out. Inside, a tall blonde finished tying her stola, her hair mussed, the bed behind her rumpled. The woman smiled triumphantly at the retreating gladiator. And Marcus had a blank stare.

Inside, her stomach twisted. She remembered that woman. She was a proper Roman lady, here on previous occasions, like the night Gustina was ordered to suck Verus' cock. For love of the gods, now she was here again and the evidence was too clear to ignore. He fucked that Roman woman. And he didn't look regretful.

Marcus didn't see her, but the woman did. A slow, devious smile curved her mouth as she stared at her. Gustina bit her lower lip, the basket shaking in her hands.

He had been angry at her being sent to Iduma and she'd been afraid he'd reject her as a whore but how could he? For wasn't that the role he had just played? She'd heard of women wanting the favors of a champion. But she'd no clue that meant the woman came here to slake her desires.

Furious at him, sickened by the thought of him thrusting into another woman, Gustina turned, almost gagging on the fruit. Her feet quickly carried her away from the Roman woman who was now openly laughing in the Atrium.

The days passed, another week by Marcus' counting. The days driving hard on the ground, sweating, swinging, attacking, over and over again were the only way to pass the time and drive the beast of loneliness from him. Gustina was still not allowed down—neither was any woman. The pent up energy of the gladiators was keenly felt on every swing, grunt and moan. The final contests were close, but he thought he might expire long before then if he didn't see her.

Thankfully, Lucilla had only been here twice since that day. Gods, he hated himself but the only way to endure it was to think of Gustina's thighs before him. Despite his hatred of his former wife, he knew his position. Slave. She could easily follow through with her threat to Gustina so he had no choice. The demon snarled throughout.

Two weeks. Then victory. And he'd have her back in his arms—forever.

Snap! "Gladiators!"

They all stopped in a unified motion.

"Baths then food. Tomorrow will come early."

They drudged to the boy near the storage chest. The wooden instruments were locked up like the real iron ones because, fashioned as weapons, they could be used as such. Even if blunt and dulled, damage could be done with them.

The young teen took the various instruments and laid them in the box quickly. Marcus saw he avoided some of the gladiators' eyes, others he met dead on. He knew the boy's glance to him would be indifferent. Marcus had no longing for cock, only women. So did Iduma. Anger flared briefly, unexpectedly, over that. A quiet voice in the back of his head prodded him, wondering if the Brit longed for Gustina again, too.

Many of the men jested over the baths, but Marcus was quiet. Something felt wrong. He couldn't pinpoint what, but it was like the gods whispered to him that there was change coming. It rubbed him wrong. The hair on the back of his neck bristled and the demon growled low, deep, menacingly.

Iduma sat only feet away from him, laughing with some Gaul whose name escaped Marcus. That unnerved him. He'd been here two years and knew everyone. Even the novices.. Whatever lurked ahead was dark, like death, but not welcoming like the Afterlife. Fate kept its head covered but was he the only one to see it in the shadows?

The Brit glanced at him, his eyebrows knitted, the look questioning. With a shake of his head, Marcus continued scraping the oil off him. He must be going mad in this place. A given considering his life, but he'd hoped with Gustina, he might have escaped it—or death.

He stood and tied the clean linen cloth around his middle and strode off to the dining area. Without a word to anyone, he grabbed a chunk of bread, dipped it in the barley stew, picked up a jug of wine he found along the back wall—one not opened for consumption but he didn't care. Frankly, he hoped someone would stop him. The desire for vengeance, a chance to lash out, out of line, out of context, out of the Arena, danced on the edges of his sanity. None of his brothers deserved his desire for blood, except maybe Iduma. His friend. The thought stopped his feet as a chill ran up his spine. An omen. He looked around him. No one else here but his gladiatorial brothers. He shook it off and left for his cell, yanking the cork out of the jug, spitting it across the field and tipping the contents down his parched throat.

The guard at his door watched but did nothing. Odd thing about these men who served Aulus. Many were big, some of them legionnaires released from service, but they found no value in normal jobs. Some were gladiators, freed but also unfit for normal labor. Half of them, together as one, could stop him from seeking vengeance. But out of sympathy, they'd remain uninvolved until coin—or blade—convinced them otherwise. The one before him stared blankly, uncaring about his sparse meal or thievery of the wine.

Marcus snorted, nodding to the guard as he pulled the door open for him. He bit off a chunk of the bread, downing it with a healthy gulp of wine as he walked in. *Sleep. Finish the wine and let sleep take control.*

A low level of light emanated from the oil lamp hanging above. Not much, but enough to let him know he wasn't alone. He stopped, letting his eyes adjust to the light. Finally, he focused.

Standing before him, slowly turning to see him was Gustina. She smiled. Her hair for once was entirely undone, hanging loosely over her shoulders, gleaming in the dim light, like bronze. Her simple tunic clung to her curves. Its neckline was low, allowing the swell of her breasts to be seen. The sides were split, exposing the side of her thighs.

Hunger grew at his appraisal of her. Like the better part of the slaves, she stood barefooted, her toes curling on the dirt-packed floor. Her pale blue eyes glistened in the light. Had she been crying? They weren't red nor were her cheeks stained.

She took a step toward him, then another. He stood like a statue, convinced if he blinked she'd be gone. When her hand wrapped around his and the jug neck, a devious grin came to her face.

"Share drink?"

Her voice sounded sultry, and he craved more. He tipped the bottle to her and she flipped it up to her lips, bending her head back. Her gulps of the liquid stabilized his mind. She was here, to be with him. The demon leapt and began dancing.

She lowered the jug, her eyes locked on his. He saw into her soul—the longing, the desire and something else. Sadness? Regret? It didn't matter. Not now. He pulled her into his arms, his lips sealing over hers as he kissed her hard, his tongue begging for an entrance. She opened to him and he invaded her. Her hands went around his neck, holding him tight as he lifted her off the ground, growling in her mouth.

He took her to his pallet and gently placed her down. His one hand cradled her head, fingers threading through her hair. The silken spun strands were soft, enticing. She gained strength to kiss him back just as hard, like a starving bird taking food from a parent's mouth. He vaguely heard the whimper in the back of her throat and his demon glowed. His free hand traced her neckline and found the pull to her tunic tie. An easy yank and it fell open. Quickly, he undid her leather belt straps and it thudded to the ground as her gown fell over it at her feet.

He felt her hands at his waist and smiled, pulling off her lips. Her hands searched for the tuck in his linen subligaculum. Finding the fold, she undid it and the piece fell. He put his fingers under her chin and tilted her head up to him. Those blue eyes swallowed him and her tug strong and fierce. Never taking his gaze off her, his hand wandered lower, following her neck, down her chest to a breast. He cupped it, his fingers at the hardened tip, and he squeezed it. She gasped.

When he bent to suckle, she arched her back, her nipple at his lips. He covered her rosy point and as he inhaled, he bit her lightly and felt her tense but his tongue was there, quickly laving the injured bundle of nerves. Her sigh, the relaxation of her in his arms almost undid him. He scooped her up into his arms and laid her on the blankets. His hand parted her legs and he eyed his jewel. Her nether lips were red, swollen and glistening wet with a primal need. She gave him an expectant look, but he kept his throbbing member back, even though it hurt him to do so.

With a lazy smile, he placed a finger at her slit and slid it in. She moaned, her eyes halfway closed, and her hips moved. Continuing to watch her, he fucked her with his finger. She was so wet and the scent of her arousal was killing him. But not yet. Bending between her knees, he kissed her slit with his tongue and delved deep inside.

Her juices were thick and sweet. Intoxicating. He lapped them up, swallowing each bit of her he could. Her hips buckled under his lavishing. When his fingers went further than his tongue, he bent them and touched her wall. She screamed as his fingers brought her to ecstasy. And as her walls pumped more fluid, his fingers left, replaced by his tongue, trying to capture it all.

He was between her legs and she crashed around his fingers and tongue. This was taboo in Roman society, for a man to devour a woman. Marcus had been a Roman, but not now. He brought her to climax but her movements told him she wanted him there with her. Her hand skimmed down him and found the head of his cock, sticky wet at the slit. She tried to maneuver him so she could accommodate him, but never came close. He took her hand, placed it around him and had her place him at her opening.

He stopped and gazed into her eyes. The fire that still burned was deep. A look he'd always remember. And he shoved his cock fully into her, tilting her hips off the pallet with his thrusts. She grabbed his arms as he rode her hard, breeding her. Their eyes locked, never wavering as he pushed and she held her spot. His own need became overwhelming as she shattered again around him, her own channel tightening, clutching at his cock. He thrust once more, with a large groan as he hit critical point and shot his seed into her deep, thick as fog.

Collapsing on top of her, they both gasped for air. He rolled off her, pulling her into his arms. Despite the heat, she trembled.

"Shhh...." He murmured and kissed her ear.

Not another word was said. They took each other two more

times that night. He knew she cried and he wanted to know why but she wouldn't let him talk. Finally, after the third time, they slept. His last thought was that he'd ask her in the morning why she was in tears.

But there would be no questioning. When he woke, she was gone from his chamber. Quickly, he dressed and was on the practice field, searching.

Tevia saw him and tried to dart away but he overwhelmed the house slave, his hand clutched at the slave's throat.

"Where is Gustina?"

The man on the ground eyed him frightfully, barely able to squeak out, "she's gone."

"I know. I woke and she wasn't there. Go get her for me." He dropped his hold.

Tevia sucked in air, shuffling his feet. "She's not here."

"What? You know where she is?"

"Marcus, she was sold this morning." Tevia shrugged. "Gone from the Villa."

The Roman stared, disbelieving. But the tingle running the length of his spine listened. It was then the whole of yesterday, the foreboding feeling, returned in full force. And her tears from last night.

She knew it was their last night together. Today, she was to leave.

Sold.

His demon howled in pain.

CHAPTER TWENTY-FOUR

Gustina sat in the barred cart, her legs bent and her arms wrapped around them. The sky was cloudy this morning, only adding to her dismal mood. As the cart rambled out of the Villa to Rome, her heart sank with each turn of the wheels. The pit in her stomach threatened to burn like lava.

She knew she was to be sold. Her domina told her yesterday, after noonday sun passed. She tried to keep a stoic face at the news but even she felt the color drain from her cheeks and the buzzing in her ears as the room began to spin. Farina caught her before she fell. Cernia gave her a snort of disgust and waved her away.

Thankfully, the woman had no further use for her that day and Gustina steered clear of her. Farina helped her get past the guards to spend one last night with Marcus. When he walked into his cell, it took every effort not to race into his arms, frantic, and burst into tears. The reflection in his eyes told her plainly he was on the verge of madness, either because of the training, Iduma, the games or the demon within. Or maybe because of her. Maybe she should not have come to him, but she had to. Her soul drove her to his arms one last night. She gave him the only thing that she possessed—herself, as pitiful as she was, a used slave. But the memory of his embrace, of him filling her, she had to have. It was the last bit of sanity in the cruel and heartless world of Rome.

This morning, when she slipped from his arms, trying not to wake him, she had to bite her lip to keep from crying as she snuck out the door. She refused to bathe before she left, wanting to carry his scent and feel his touch still lingering on her with his seed planted within. It was madness but a demand as calm as she could allow herself.

Even now, her eyes filled with tears, so she shut them, trying to stop the flow. It would do her no good to succumb to sorrow. She swallowed and buried her head in her knees and forced her mind to clear.

The other slaves in the vehicle joined her in solitude. Only Sefa also came from the house of Aulus but she barely knew the girl. Kept with the cook, Sefa didn't mingle with the rest of the house slaves. But she was young and somewhat pretty though her dark hair was dulled and she was as pale as the moon. Too much time spent in the overheated kitchen. And yet, Gustina found herself wondering if she, too, had slept with the gladiators, presented as a "prize" for winning like she had been. Had the girl wrapped her legs around Marcus? Iduma? She grit her teeth. What did it matter? Especially if it was Iduma? She cringed. She didn't hate him for taking her. It was her purpose that night and he was inebriated. She'd simply turned her emotions off. Otherwise, she would have collapsed. Her sentence was to please the Brit while that bitch got her Marcus.

Once more, her stomach flipped. With her gone, now nothing could stop Verenia from taking Marcus, wrapping her thighs around him. Her groan echoed inside the wagon's walls. Some of the others glared at her, the rest gave her a sympathetic eye. Nothing could halt the slow destruction of her heart.

And the sobs took control.

∞

Lucius glanced up at the sound of the rambling cart slowing in front of his Villa and frowned. He hadn't ordered any new slaves. It must be another attempt of Lucilla's to while away the time and his coin. If only she desired to use it on a child…. He wasn't ignorant of her expenses. She claimed to have consulted a priestess about conceiving and perhaps she had, but her other interests leaned away from future children and more toward playing. He knew that about her before he took her to wife but thought, under his guidance, she'd change. With a sigh of resignation, he left his desk to see to the cart.

The rambling contraption was a simple piece with timber stakes on the sides and rods on top. A rolling cage. And one about to fall to pieces judging by the creaks and moans of its wooden wheels. Lucius' lips pursed in disgust. The slaves inside looked no better. Younger than the vehicle, all carried the look of doom.

"Ah, Senator Vibenius," the driver stammered, jumping off his seat. "Arrived, just as promised."

The old cripple must be daft, Lucius decided. He didn't order any slaves. "Now look here."

"Oh! Darling, please," Lucilla called sweetly from the door as she hurried down the front steps. "Kapys, don't worry. I knew you'd come," she glanced at Lucius, touching his arm but still addressing the slaver. "As promised." She bestowed on him one of her radiant smiles, making her husband eye her carefully.

Half the cart disembarked. The two older men leapt off with ease. The young brown-haired woman didn't seem to hear the order to get out. Lucius noticed her cringing, sitting on the floor, as if impossibly alone in the small space. The slaver yelled, raising his whip to strike her when Lucius could take it no more. He grabbed the slaver's arm.

"No, no beatings. Can't you see her fear?"

He watched Kapys' puzzled gaze turn to the girl he was going to whip. "She's a miscreant. Heard she's a murderer too. Maybe a few whippings will cure her of her madness." He turned to Lucius, a look of concern in his eye, one that made the senator almost laugh at the audacity of it. "To protect your wife."

He'd laugh if he thought the man truly believed Lucilla in any danger. Lucius learned very quickly that his wife was not the innocent waif she presented herself to be. She blushed at the man's remark, amazing him to no end. Still smiling, she turned to him and leaned in.

"Lucius, please."

As if he could refuse her. But why slaves now? He had more than enough. With a sign, he frowned. "Lucilla, it is coin not needed to be spent now."

Her face contorted, like a child being denied a honeyed fig. When he didn't budge, she dropped the expression for a mild one and whispered in his ear. "'Tis but a favor. And one to add to our advantage."

She could sway even Apollo from war, Lucius decided, with her ability to turn anything into a profit, and no one could refuse her. He often wondered if that's how he became so entangled with her. A shake of his head dispelled the thought as ludicrous. When he met her at the baths, and later in the Forum during her late husband's trial, he fell in love with her. Who wouldn't? She was young and beautiful with a body to tempt the gods—even the Emperor if given the chance. At her smile, anything was possible.

He laughed. "And tell me of this new fortune."

Her face softened as she laced her arm through his. "The girl is on loan to us, from Aulus Valgus himself."

Lucius looked back at the slave. She was off the cart, shaking, but her shoulders were back. There was an odd look about her. She'd been crying as her eyes were red and puffy and cheeks stained with dried tears, but she stood straight with hands clenched, almost defiant. He tilted his head. Who was she?

His wife pulled him away from the group as his assistant paid the slaver and took the slaves off. Lucilla continued, "She is the slave Valgus' champion desires but his fill of her is interfering with his abilities on the sands. Did you know only a month ago, he claimed *missio* at the Arena?"

Lucius heard the tale but shook his head. He wasn't there.

"Quite the sight," she said, stroking his arm.

He felt her touch and the vibrations reached into him, down to his groin. His shaft hardened. It'd been too long without her. Oh, he wanted an heir from her. Letting her think he'd dissolve the marriage was a futile attempt to keep her legs crossed but for him. He couldn't pin her to a lover, but with her looks and talent, he had no doubt she spread her thighs for another. Damn Senate kept him from her bed way too often. His only requirement was the child had to be his or he would eject her. But could he really? A doubt....

"So," she hadn't stopped for a minute. "They hope the fact that she's gone will give him the incentive to win. It is a payout for both houses, since she'd be his reward and for her stay here...." she shrugged.

Only his wife would dally with a gladiator's emotions. Especially her former husband. Which actually aggravated him. "So you do this for your former husband's affairs?"

She stopped suddenly and gave him a waspish look. "Never. The bastard got what he deserved," she snapped. Then her façade changed back to Lucius' loving wife. "We do this to help my friends Aulus and Cernia. He wins, they give up a third of the winnings."

He glanced back over his shoulder at the pawn in this game, Gustina. Despite her lioness demeanor, he knew she couldn't fight back against Lucilla. But she wasn't theirs to dispose of. He pinched his nose, feeling his headache return.

If he didn't keep an eye out for the girl, and the girl ended up solely under Lucilla, it wouldn't matter what happened during the games. She'd be dead...or praying to be carried to the Afterlife.

∞

Marcus felt nothing but the anger and the loss. No one answered his questions. Jupiter, even Iduma looked lost.

His demon prowled, seething below, the taste for blood escalating. *Kill them! All!* It was the same chant inside his head and his heart. And it showed.

He destroyed the palus yesterday with the wooden gladius. The demon even smiled as what had been a sturdy pillar, made for steadfast beatings, splintered and broke. The entire training field silenced at the sound. Ludo's watchful gaze questioned him and he voiced no reply.

Marcus was gladiator. A slave. Nothing more. Except the pleasure of killing, and that he'd relish in soon. If he could just calm the voice in the back of his head. No, it was his heart. *Gustina.* What little good he had done for her. The void inside him grew.

"Marcus."

He stopped the swing of the sword against his current sparring mate, Ahaz. The Syrian was breathing hard, arm raised to the attack but Ludo's voice froze both of them. In a single moment, both dropped their blades and Ahaz his shield.

As Ludo approached, Marcus inhaled deeply. To be stopped like this meant only one thing. Lucilla. *Fucking bitch.*

"You are summoned."

He glared at the doctore, threw his gladius to the ground, spat and stormed off to the guards that waited. Following one up the stairs with another behind him, Marcus shook with anger. The demon prowled, snarling, teeth gnashing. Oh yes, he'd let the creature loose on that bitch. Wanted him to fuck her, did she? Hysterical laughter rumbled below the surface, his mind conjuring the bedroom with her neck between his hands, her face contorting, turning an odd shade of blue as she suffocated. His fingers ached.

The guards took him into the atrium and stopped. Marcus frowned. Not a bed chamber. Not that cunt of a wife. What in the name of the gods?

"For the champion of this house, you storm like Jupiter before hurling the thunderbolts down from the heavens." Aulus glanced up from the scrolls before him. With a snort, he stood and rounded the desk. "Steam actually escapes your ears even now. What has you boaring around my Villa?"

He dropped his head. Damn he hated subservience, but he ate his pride before the man. Aulus stood there, staring at him. Marcus could feel the heat of his gaze.

"I am usually summoned for another cause," he stated flatly.

Aulus raised his brows. "Yes, so I understand. The price of a champion. She is a pretty thing, is she not?"

Marcus' puzzled mind flipped. Lucilla? Were they talking about the same woman? His feet stuck to the floor but he wanted to run—an irrational thought as a slave inside a ludus. Especially with the two guards at the door. Granted, they'd be easy to plunder through. It was just the twenty or so outside of here that the odds stacked against a man as skilled as him.

The sound of laughter filled the air. Marcus turned. Aulus took the cup of wine from a slave off to the side and sipped, his eyes glued on the gladiator.

"You thought I meant that whore of a wife you once held dear," he nodded, walking to the settee and falling onto the cushions. "Dear Juno, never. I meant that slave, Gustina. Quite the piece that one."

Tension grabbed hold of his spine as Marcus struggled to not move. Why would this man strike the chord inside him that would raise Hades to consume them all?

Aulus shook his head. "You waste your anger on your brothers. Save it for the Arena. Win the crowd, and see her returned."

A red cloud covered his gaze and his blood roared through his veins making it difficult to hear the man, but Marcus struggled to fight through it. Had he said Gustina would return? The demon growled.

Aulus snorted and returned to his papers. "See tempers fall. Her absence was caused by entanglements beyond your control. Do what is required in all aspects."

Marcus heard his dominus' tone sharpen on the end. "What other duties are required of me outside the Arena?" Tension strung through him, knowing the inevitable.

Shuffling through the scrolls before him, Aulus didn't even glance in the gladiator's direction. "You know what else is required of a champion." His eyes looked up and he focused hard. "And there will be no issues brought forth by it. Do as you are commanded and see your desire fulfilled."

Marcus' temper flared. As if the man knew what his desire was....

"In fact, you've been called upon now," Aulus stated flatly, as if it was no greater than selling swine to market. He waved the gladiator off and the guards stepped closer.

Gritting his teeth, the gladiator tilted his head. "Dominus."

He turned, falling between the guards, regretting every step. They led him to the path he thought he'd been called to in the first place. At the entrance to a bedchamber, they motioned him in and closed the door.

The room was dark but the air hung thick with vanilla and honey.

"Marcus."

That voice, dark, seductive, feminine. Gods, he'd really married her. Fucked her because he wanted to. Memories of the past he hoped would fade, but she refused to let them.

"No." Frank, to the point. He wouldn't. Couldn't, actually. "Go fuck Terpio. You wanted to before. He's good enough to give you a child."

"Yes," she murmured. "But the gods said it must be the champion, not his brother. You are a champion."

His jaw tensed. "You did prove he was no brother of mine. Fuck him till his bollocks drop off but leave me be."

She avoided any remark. Instead, her finger touched his bare chest and lightly traced down over his muscles, causing a ripple in his nerves. Damn, his body betrayed him while his mind twisted with evil thoughts. Break her neck or her back, throw her, fuck her. Inside, he skidded to a halt. Rage ran through him. He turned, his hand around her neck, slamming her against the wall. The impact resounded but no one came and for that, the demon rejoiced. His hands tightened.

Lucilla glared at him, her breathing constricted, small inward gasps between his fingers. To his amazement, the look she gave him didn't show fear but grew deep and dark with desire. It appalled him, yet fueled his anger. Personal hatred even shied the demon within. That evil creature gasped and withdrew from driving him. His hands clutched harder.

But her eyes hardened as she strengthened under his hold.

"Let me go," she broke, between gasps.

With a certain amount of abhorrence that he meant to strangle a woman, the fact she had succumbed, her eyes not scared but actually enjoying the threat of death at his hands, forced him to tighten for another moment. He was so close to killing her before he threw her back, her head hitting the wall. A momentary gratitude hit him before a wave of unadulterated hate racked him and made him release her.

She liked rough foreplay. The bitch liked his violence.

Nausea washed over him. The thought that he started to strangle her sickened him, made worse with her enjoyment. The grin on her face confirmed she knew his thoughts. She laughed.

"Yes, memories linger," she calmly said. "How wild we were, and the games we played. We have a new game now," her voice turned husky. "I've acquired a new slave. Fine young girl, brown hair, pale blue eyes."

He shut his eyes. *Dear Jupiter, no!*

"Yes, I know exactly what she means to you. For the moment, she lives," she told him, her voice firm, not shaking from having been on the verge of suffocation. "Her safety relies on your hands. Giving me your cock will not harm you, but denial marks her as dead."

He turned around, unable to control himself. Desire to finish her grew...as did the twitching in his groin. Oh yes, he might hate her but she knew the key to his bestial need. The memories of the past begged to return from the dark recesses of his mind. The violence that reigned at times during intercourse, of their wild and animalistic acceptance of their base desires. An instinctive drive, one that continued into his damnation as gladiator. All so radically different with Gustina. With her, the need, the drive and desire remained but never so base, like a mad man run amuck. No, a hunger that only she could satisfy grew intensely, but never the brutality.

"Yes, you remember how it was," she whispered. "I am pleased." Her hand traced down his back, around his hip to his hardened cock.

He hated every fiber of his being. And where in the name of the gods, was that demon? Spiteful creature, to leave him when he needed him most. He needed that cold vacancy that filled him when he gave in to the darkness. The overwhelming desire to kill and return the world to balance fled.

Her fingers worked his linens and removed them. The warmth of her touch on him sent his world rocking. He'd refuse the bitch. Easy. But his cock didn't respond—*the bloody body!*

Her hand wrapped around his arousal, her body, now without stola, pressed against his. Her warmth penetrated his skin, invaded every pore.

"Fill me with your seed," she whispered firmly into his ear, like a woman on top of the world, everyone bending to her needs. She rounded his shoulders, never releasing the rigid hard-on, in fact her grip tightened, more demanding. "Give me your cock and she lives another day."

Breathing hard, hatred became a powerful incentive. To fuck her saved Gustina, but for how long? Aulus promised he'd get her back if Marcus remained champion. But he had also insisted the gladiator do as required to see his reward in the girl. The blonde before him smiled. She'd won. Despite his anger, his disgust, the woman made him hard. Her hand knew the right touch.

Groaning with hate, he grabbed her and impaled her with his cock.

CHAPTER TWENTY-FIVE

Terpio arrived at Lucilla's Villa, his mission two-fold. He'd found that bitch who killed his wife and he ached to see Lucilla again. An overwhelming need to forget her, or at least make her come to him out of desire, made him spend the better part of three weeks working at the Forum and searching for the wicked cunt who escaped execution.

He found the slave.

And Lucilla hadn't come. Had she tired of him, after all these years? The thought turned rancid in his mind. They hadn't consumed that much passion to be vacant of the desire now. His, if not hers, burned with an intensity that brought him close to madness. None of the female slaves he had gave him close to the satisfaction he got with Lucilla. The drive forced him to come seek her, despite the risk, despite the damage to his pride. Self-preservation, the need to bury himself in her, hear her coo his name, made his feet set the path to her door.

A slave brought him into the atrium, supplying him with a cup of wine as another left to find her. He sipped the drink, trying to calm irrational nerves. No, to cool desire before it overtook him. A scan of the greenery and water fountain before him was a pathetic maneuver to distract him, but it did help to slow the beating of his heart to a sane tempo.

Senator Vibenius' house had many slaves. They flittered before Terpio's gaze. His eyes picked up on their movements but none gathered his attention until he caught a glimpse of one. Short, brownish hair, slim, and she walked differently than the rest. Upright, regal in a way, her shoulders back, she carried a look of a warrior, of a slave beaten but not forgotten. The sway of her hips, the steel back nagged at his mind but he couldn't place the thought. He frowned and took another sip.

That's when he saw her. Lucilla. Arriving through the front door, taking her stola off her head, Lucilla smiled boldly, like the cat who'd killed not only the mouse but found its home, too. Her eyes sparkled but her glance was away from him, so the smile wasn't for him. *Damn.* What made her smile? Another lover? His stomach churned.

Her footsteps came to a sudden stop as her eyes found him. The curve of her lips vanished.

"Terpio," she said, her voice on the verge of lowering deep, as if a secret. "To whatever do I owe your presence?"

He gave her his lopsided grin as he walked to her, taking her hand and bending to kiss it. "A desire for you, my love."

She stiffened in his grasp. "Away," she ordered the slaves attending on her. The two women left. Taking the cup from his hands, she drank, her eyes narrowed. "Being here is a danger, Terpio."

"Well worth the risk," he answered. He didn't like her attitude right now. She had been happy. "I saw the smile you carried. Returning from another cock?"

She spun, glaring at him. He watched with fascination. Lucilla was very much like a feline, schooling her expression, a flash in her blue eyes. An animalistic grin returned to her lips. "You do not own me. But I do enjoy your cock." Her voice turned husky as she stepped closer to him, a finger tracing his jaw. "I do miss you between my thighs, yet for this cycle the priestess refuses me to have anyone outside my husband."

He snorted. "And you believe that drivel? Of a dried up old prune, who hasn't had a fuck in Jupiter only knows when?"

"She has Juno's voice. Of course, I will listen."

Terpio gritted his teeth. Something wasn't right but he couldn't figure it out. She was hiding something. He grabbed her free hand and placed it at his hardened cock.

"And what about me?"

He heard her gasp, saw her lick her lips as she stared down at the bulge held in her palm. She didn't try to move her hand. No, she actually pressed into him, her fingers tightening. As much as it pained him, to know he'd have to release her hand and deny his desire, he had to. She had to know he still wanted her.

She stood still, in her own house, hand at his arousal. A very blatant act of infidelity, especially if Lucius walked in. Terpio let go of her hand. Her head tilted up, her eyes meeting his, dark in lust.

"Terpio, you know I want you," she whispered, her voice low and strained. He watched her swallow hard, his insides twisting on a need for her, wishing it was his cum she had a hard time forcing down her throat. But then, she turned away from him, wiggling her hips, as if her tunic had stuck to her crotch. "I can't, though. The priestess told me not to," her mouth opened as if to say more, but she quickly shut it.

He groaned. Closing his eyes, Terpio struggled for control before he said a word. What else was there to say? Thoughts inside his head scrambled, confused, by the desire.

"How long will you make me wait?"

She smiled. "See all worries removed. Three weeks."

He sighed. Three long weeks. "I may have found the slave."

She paused. He noticed the hitch in her step but decided that came from surprise that he had changed the subject.

"Truly? Where?"

Terpio leaned back, resting against the stand of the statue of Diana. "Apparently, my brother bought her before her execution. She resides at the Villa he fights for."

She gave him one of her devious smiles, the type that enticed him. But this time, the hair on the back of his neck bristled.

"Yes, in fact, I hadn't the cause to tell you yet," she sat on the lounge, grabbing a honeyed fig out of a bowl on the table. "I saw her there myself."

"Not good enough. You know I looked. Why not tell me upon discovery?" His anger flared. Secrets. With her, secrets oozed out of her pores. No wonder she had problems with bearing a child. The gods didn't favor those who tried to outwit them. At her shrug, he picked up another fig and sat next to her. "It is of no matter. I will acquire her from Aulus." He fed her the fig and she purred, sucking it into her mouth. Those luscious lips—how he'd love to lick the honey off them.

"No need," she replied. "I have the girl now."

"What?"

"Yes, as a loan, so to speak, from Cernia and Aulus. Your brother craves her cunt. But it is affecting his abilities in the Arena. He actually forfeited a match, declaring *missio*," she shook her head and stood. "So I suggested she stay with me until the games have concluded."

He leapt, heart in his throat. Gustina here? He longed to have her back. She might have killed his wife or not. At this point, he didn't care. But if Lucilla denied him, the thought of the girl here drove him mad. His erection throbbed at the thought of her ass. So sweet and tight and her mouth, he'd trained her just how to suck him dry. He shifted uncomfortably.

Lucilla's mouth pursed. "She is under my care, and so far has done nothing requiring punishment."

"Lucilla, you deny me but this...."

"Will not come to fruition this time." She kissed his cheek. "Go, now, before Lucius returns. He might think you're here for more base reasons."

He was. With a snort, he bent his head to her. "Take care of her. And we will see her to justice next time." And he left. His desire for Lucilla still burned deep, but the idea of taking Gustina again placated him. He smiled.

∞

The new Villa had many slaves. No gladiators, none of the grunting of men honing their skills for the next round of spectacles. Nothing here but house slaves for a Senator. The house was quiet, a harmonious blend of work and silence. Gustina found the quiet made her jumpy.

She'd found at first the solitude fit her mood. But that lasted only a day. A week had passed since she arrived, though to her it was more like a month. A day without Marcus was bad. Now her heart lay at her feet, beaten, battered, cast away... He had no voice in her sale, according to her last domina. Cernia mentioned something about how he needed freedom from her to win again, or something like that. Hard to remember as she fought her own need to cry out or scream at the words the woman said about selling her. She'd bitten her lip to stop the tears that pooled in her eyes from falling.

In her entire life, however long that was for she'd no knowledge of her true age, she'd known nothing outside the yoke of slavery. Mostly long, tedious tasks to appease a Roman, whether by bathing, food, cleaning or fucking. To always live in fear of what would happen next, whether food would come, if there'd be enough or a blanket to lie on, that had been her existence. Life with her first domina had been good. The woman seemed to care for her. But the dominus ruined her in ways that still made her tense.

Marcus was the only man who'd given her any hope. He saved her. Showed her pleasure. And how had she repaid him? Her gut twisted painfully. She spread her legs for his friend. That she was ordered to do so by her domina wasn't a defense. Iduma wasn't mean. Actually, he was very kind, in a way. The fact he told her no, that he'd let her leave didn't convince her as she knew he was hard. She was a slave and knew repercussions would rise from not doing as told. Bile rose up her throat and she dropped her scrub brush, her hand over her mouth.

"Gustina."

Faintly, she heard the slave next to her, Dora, call to her. She swallowed and picked up the brush, dipped it in the bucket and resumed scrubbing the tile floor.

"I'm fine," she muttered.

Dora wasn't moving. "You've had that look three times past noon hour. Memories of him?"

With a quick nod, Gustina kept scrubbing. "I can't forget him."

Dora nodded. "Give it time. You won't truly forget, but the pain will lessen."

"You're right," her voice cracked.

She'd done everything required. Tried to keep her profile low and unnoticed. Her new domina, that bitch she remembered with Marcus at Aulus' Villa, had so many slaves attending her, Gustina could hang back, praying to the gods not to be noticed. The woman's eyes, searing bright blue, always seemed to laugh at Gustina, as if this was a joke with a cruel ending. Her skin prickled at the thought that Lucilla knew Gustina's love of Marcus.

Her stomach flipped again.

"Are you well?"

She nodded, pushing her brush harder.

Laughter came from just down the hallway. Scrubbing the tile in the walkway outside the atrium, Gustina looked up.

Walking only a stone's throw from her, too close for her comfort, was her domina with her last dominus. Terpio. Her heart dropped into her stomach. She felt faint, light-headed, buzzing in her ears. The man's arm supported Lucilla's and they talked, murmured actually, smiling as if nothing in the world was wrong. But for Gustina, her world, any safety she might have felt, crashed. If the man saw her....

"Gustina, what now?" Dora's voice was barely audible, but she grasped Gustina's wrist and the connection made her hear the words.

She was shaking. Oh yes, she remembered him. Terpio still looked young and handsome. Not as big as Marcus, but he had strength. His walk showed his confidence in his ability to have whatever he wanted. And last time he saw her, those same brown eyes that now danced in merriment with her new domina, shot daggers at her as she knelt above his wife's body, holding the dead woman's head in her lap, the wine cup in her hand.

"That Roman," she whispered.

"The one with our domina? Yes, he is here often. What of him?"

Here? Often? Dear Jupiter, no!

Then his head turn in a jest from Lucilla and his gaze fell right on Gustina. Fear snaked down her spine—a spine that straightened, forcing her shoulders back. She turned her fear into her only defense. A look of complete control, a dare for him to push her. Her only offense was to mask herself in indifference.

He smiled, gave a slight nod in her direction, and returned to give Lucilla his whole attention.

She saw him round the corner and heard their voices fade.

"You know him?" Dora asked.

Gustina never answered. Instead, as the nausea came and flooded her mouth, she ran to the nearest potted plant and retched.

"First position!"

The gladiators stood on the training grounds, paired except for a few that practiced against the newly-acquired palus. Every man raised his weapon and shield to start.

"Begin!" Ludo instructed, his whip snapping in the air.

Iduma lunged at Marcus. His arm swung down, the attack strong, and he felt the champion's gladius quiver against his. After the hit, he backed away, breathing deeply.

His partner glared. Marcus looked like fire bound tightly in a bag that ripped at the seams. Anger seeped from every orifice the man had. Steam from his ears, fire in his eyes, flames with every groan. It was a mutual feeling. Iduma's own madness threatened to overwhelm him.

Gustina's absence was sorely felt.

Though she denied him, claimed their night together was one soon to be forgotten, Iduma couldn't. Every time he lay on that pallet, he felt her presence. Memories refused to fade. They haunted his dreams.

Her tears that night stained his floor. With a gentleness that surprised him, he'd wiped them away, soothing her nerves with his low voice and light touch. She was beautiful. A gift from the gods. Wrong to take, but his own conscience lost to the throbbing arousal. Slowly, he undressed her without pulling her closer. His fingers traced her contours—the swell of her breasts, the curve at her waist, the round hips. Her nipples pearled, no doubt from being exposed or perhaps because of him. He never asked, he just leaned forward and took a lick.

She quivered but didn't step away.

He was lost.

He remembered her soft skin. How he coaxed her wetness. The feeling of sliding inside her. The quiet gasp from her lips.

Marcus' two gladius broke his memory by slamming into him. A blow made the weapon's handle collide with his jaw. It knocked his balance and when his shield and weapon tried to block the Roman's attack, he fell to the sands, right on his knees. Pain shot up his thighs and radiated from his right jaw. The bitter taste of blood was on his lips. He welcomed the discomfort. Needed it. He took what he should have left alone. He shook his head.

The Brit glanced up and saw the flames engulfing the

champion's eyes. He laughed.

"Where are your senses, Brit?" The Roman offered his hand.

If he only knew, he'd kill me now.

"Lost in a dream, brother," Iduma answered, taking the hand.

"Wake or find yourself in Elysium," Marcus returned.

Iduma snorted. Yes, the Afterlife would be easier. He studied the Roman. The man's eyes looked troubled, but retained an odd flare. A demon, perhaps?

"We fight in a week," the Brit threw out. He needed to know if the man counted the days as he did. Oh, he knew of Gustina's return if they won. Aulus had called for him, told him to watch the champion, remind him if needed. Right. His dominus knew that Iduma wanted her back for himself. The thought should unnerve him, but it didn't.

Marcus took a sip from the gourd the child slave gave him out of the water bucket. He dropped it back into the water, laughing. "Climbing the walls for real iron, are you?"

Iduma snorted. "A desire I'm not alone with. Let us go kill and be rewarded with drink again."

They both laughed as the water boy left them and they resumed position.

"Marcus!"

Iduma saw the flash of hate in the gladiator's eyes before the shield of dullness fell into place.

Doctore motioned the Roman to follow the soldiers. With a spit in the sands, Marcus dropped his wooden weapons and left.

Iduma watched. The man left with a resignation that wasn't hidden in his step. The Brit sighed. The Roman woman's brazenness to come here for the gladiator's cock was a surprise but in a way, it made Iduma's guilt lessen.

He might have fucked Gustina, relished in it and felt the sting of guilt. Yet, he knew she met his thrust with her own. Her hands on his back, their touch burned a mark not easily forgotten. But no longer did Jupiter punish him for his desire—not if the champion's own cock serviced many, like it would do so now. No, for if Marcus couldn't stay true to Gustina, then Iduma had no qualms over wanting her back in his bed. His argument to the demon roving inside the champion was very simple—stay away from her for only he, Iduma, could protect her.

CHAPTER TWENTY-SIX

Marcus followed the guards up the stairs to the Villa in greater Rome, his chains clanking between his wrists. It always irked him. The champion of Aulus' house, vaulted in followers and women wanting to get close to him, a few who paid to be with him, sexually and for his blood, seen as dangerous and sexual—in the Arena. Outside the fights, his position was reduced to slave, still dangerous but not a god of the Arena. Just a man capable of killing. And he knew the rumor of his demon circulated widely.

So, now, five days before the end of the spectacles began, he was forced to go service some woman. He'd laugh at this if it wasn't so pathetic because he knew whose house he stood before. Senator Lucius Vibenius's Villa. Jupiter's cock, she wanted him to fuck her here? Madness fought with the urge to laugh openly. Gods, she was worthless refuse and made him nothing more than a whore. The demon snarled.

The guards took him to the side entrance, the slaves' door. Drug inside the building, they took him to a chamber off the Peristylium, the garden of the house. The smell of jasmine and herbs filled the air, a sweet, enticing aroma he would have relished if he wasn't chained, brought to fuck the domina. His blood boiled as he entered the chamber.

The room was large, sheer sheets of silk hung, beautiful, expensive and caustic. Like a spider's web, he decided. On a raised dais in the center of the room, cushioned with pillows and silks, lay Lucilla with a rose-colored gauze wrap draped over her shoulders. The material clung to her curves, displaying her nipples, hard and erect, through the fabric. It parted, so her ivory stomach and bare mound were displayed for his view. This room reeked of incense, honey, vanilla and her.

He eyed her carefully, like she was a snake, coiled and ready to hiss.

"You risk too much," he stated as the guard unlocked his manacles and retreated from the room.

She stood, not as a snake rising but as a feline, long and silky, sauntering to him, her nails raking down his arm. "Risk always brings advantage." She grinned.

He turned, looking around her room. The bright plush pillows and cream-colored hanging scarves showed the riches of the senator. Tables scattered across the room held bowls of pears and honeyed figs—her favorite, as he recalled. Incense filled the air. He also noticed the slaves in the shadows, another favorite of hers. Have her help ready and waiting to serve her, but she had them stand to the side, in the dim light. He recognized the dull blue tunics, a way to blend them into the walls.

No, she hadn't changed, just reinvented herself in wealthier standings. Always the center of attention. Lucilla wanted to be the one in command, the one everyone answered to, and she enjoyed her pets with a bit of fear mixed in with their servitude. He snorted. She'd relished in his bed because he answered her needs when they were husband and wife. A touch of danger, of carnal desires, with a touch of pain mixed in. Fear of her denying him, of bringing him to the edge of bliss only to remove her touch. Just as now, she enjoyed his displeasure of being here, of having to service her. He could think of only one way to get a measure of comfort, a reprieve from her sinister laugh at his position.

His hand swept across the room before him. "I see you have done well as the senator's wife. He's denied you nothing."

She frowned, a look of confusion flitted across her face. "He likes for me to be happy."

Marcus stepped closer, snaking his arm around her waist to pull her to him. Her scent was overwhelming, a mixture of honey, vanilla, and arousal. His fingers flexed against her body, knowing her skin was soft. Against his chest, she had nowhere to go so he bent his head, his mouth taking hers, his tongue forcing her lips to part and he tasted the figs on her breath. He kissed her hard and deep before he pulled away.

Her eyes widened. He got an adverse sort of pleasure as surprise engulfed those blue gems he'd fallen crazy over years ago. Short, hot pants came from her, the heat burning the surface of his skin. His hands gripped her waist and she trembled. It took a lot to get this stone queen, the ruler, to admit she was taken. She hadn't relinquished yet but he knew she was close. This time he'd win. He'd take her, claim her, mark her with his seed. Urgency soared through his veins. The pressure from his hardened cock already pulsed madly.

"Happy? The man has no idea how to make you weep in joy." He slammed her body into his as his mouth sealed her lips, tilting her head back in his assault.

Her hands rose tentatively up his chest and around his neck. Inside he moaned. She was losing control. She wiggled her hips against his rigid shaft, begging for him. Without releasing her mouth, one of his hands lowered and ripped the subligaculum off, freeing his cock. Her hand reached down and caressed it with her nails before wrapping her hand around it. He smiled against her mouth. Memories of her flooded his mind. As much as he hated her and Terpio, she did have a body and knew how to use it.

A few strokes with her hand and he could no longer take it. In a swift move, he tucked his fingers in the neck of her wrap and pulled the light gauze, the few fragile threads that held the fabric together. Rent, it separated, pooling on the floor. Her hard nipples grazed his chest. He growled loudly, not caring about the female slaves in the room, grasped Lucilla's hips to raise her off her feet and lowered her to the cushions. He knelt between her legs, saw the desire darkening her eyes. And the surprise. She'd forgotten what it was like to be taken—truly taken, no longer in control. He gritted his teeth to suppress his grin. With his hand, he guided his cock into her willing flesh and they both moaned as he filled her.

Off to the side of the room, as one of the many slaves kept close but distant, Gustina stood. In the shadows like the rest, she knew her features were hidden from her domina's view. And from Marcus.

She barely felt them at first—the stream of tears on her cheeks. To stand idly by and watch her gladiator, her lover, fuck another woman so vigorously made her heart shatter. She'd seen him arrive, his wrists in chains. The look he gave to this place ranged from indifference to disgust. When his eyes swept the room just minutes ago, she fought the urge to step forward, to let him know she was here. Something held her back. One of the gods, perhaps.

When he grabbed her mistress, slamming her against him, the first sting of tears threatened to fall. But at that deep kiss, when he virtually lifted her in his arms, her gut twisted. Even now, bile rose uncontrollably. At his first thrust into Lucilla, Gustina couldn't see anymore, her eyes blurred. It took all the energy she had to keep from sniffling. His second drive into Lucilla made Gustina's gaze quickly scan the room for the closest door. She was to stay put, but pain ripped up the inside of her. At the next meeting of their hips, and Lucilla's moan, Gustina turned and, as fast as she could, slipped from the room.

In the hallway, she ran to the closest urn and retched. Her throat hurt with the acid and she was sure her heart came up with the little bit of food she'd eaten. Hollowness filled her where her heart used to be.

"Gustina," Dora's low voice whispered, her hand on Gustina's back.

Wiping her mouth with the back of her hand, she stood. Everything before her swayed but she managed to stay upright. Dora helped steady her, but the look on her face made Gustina think she must have turned green.

"How long have you been ill?"

The bile wanted to rise again. She forced it back down. "A couple of days, maybe."

Dora snorted. "And the last time you bled?"

Gustina frowned. "I'm not sure." In her mind, she plotted the days. The week after laying with Iduma. She remembered now, pleased she'd not have to face Marcus carrying another's child. Her thoughts stumbled as panic seized her. That was weeks ago, though how many she couldn't recall. She'd lost track of everything once taken to this place.

"It's his, isn't it?" Dora prodded. "The champion's heir."

The magnitude broadsided her. This time, when the vomit

came, she turned and spewed bile into the urn. Wicked how it expelled any food in her. Brushing any evidence from her mouth, she turned to her friend.

"I can't be," she moaned, but deep inside, she knew it. She carried Marcus' child. Her hand went instinctively to her lower abdomen. It was still flat.

Dora grabbed her hand, pulled it away from her body and gave Gustina a weak smile. "You know, you'll have to rid yourself of this."

She swallowed hard. Pain wrenched her insides. She nodded vaguely as the idea settled. "No."

"Gustina," her friend whispered. "Why do you think he's here?"

"She paid for his cock."

The slave guffawed. "For more than that." She stepped closer, her soft voice dropping lower. "She needs his seed."

Gustina didn't think she heard her correctly. But the sympathetic look in Dora's eyes only confirmed it. Their domina wanted Marcus to get her with child. Gustina closed her eyes, everything inside her plummeted and she fell to the floor.

Dora took her arm and helped her up. The air shifted, turned fuzzy and her ears began to ring as Dora added, "If she finds out you are with child...."

It wasn't *if* she found out, Gustina knew. And the verdict would be the same—she'd be forced to rid herself of the child. Her whole world went black.

∞

Marcus plunged into Lucilla over and over, driving but it wasn't with passion of caring. No, his lust only acted as the tool to his anger. Each move was harder, more demanding, bordering close to violence. She had wanted him once, as her husband, as her lover. At one point, she'd carried his child, but he found her desires unleashed, wanting his brother's cock as well. Then the walls of his world fell with her love when she and Terpio threw accusations at him of betrayal and theft. Was he a cast off babe? Had he wrongfully taken the family fortune in a game of dominance? She had contorted every word he'd ever said into vile, evil, power-hungry scheming.

She'd thrown him aside after she'd rid her body of its

encumbrance. Inside, he turned cold and violent, filled with a demon that sought blood and vengeance.

He stared down at her, watching her beautiful body take his thrusts and shoves, wrapping her legs around him, her voice husky with every groan. Even worse, he heard himself growl. It was as if his mind and body were separate. Her slick channel convulsed around his shaft, coaxing it to release and he couldn't stop it any longer. One final push and he buried deep, only consciously aware that she'd won. His seed spilled inside her. She purred, edging his anger higher.

He was a gladiator, a champion, but Lucilla made him a whore.

Untangling her legs, he shoved her body away from him. "That is it. No more."

She remained reclined on the cushions, but looked at him with a wicked smile. "Unless I need...."

"No, not now," he tucked the tail of his subligaculum around his waist. "I fight in five days. I do not have the time to waste my energy on this shit." When she opened her mouth, he quickly added, "You can't threaten me over this, Lucilla, you have no more hold. Gustina was sold." He turned and went to the door.

She laughed. It was evil. "Yes, darling. They sold her to me."

The last word stopped him. His hands clenched as the demon snarled. He shut his eyes, fighting back the roar, the overpowering need to kill.

"You wouldn't boast of having her without taunting me before now," he gritted.

She stood, pulling the remains of the wrap around her shoulders, and sauntered up to him. He heard the soft sound of her bare feet getting closer and tensed.

"I didn't have to show her to you. You've been on display," she murmured with glee. "And quite a beauty to watch, your muscled body pleasuring me, taking me, as it were." She was at his side, smiling. "You know, I keep several slaves with me at all times."

His insides wrenched. *The slaves along the walls. Gustina.*

"Gustina," she called. But no one moved. "Gustina, come."

Another girl hurried over to Lucilla. "She's gone, domina."

"And where did she go? I did not give her permission to

leave."

The slave whispered into her ear. He couldn't hear anything more than the faint tones. Lucilla's laughter rang loudly. "Marcus, darling, you did quite well, for a common whore. Poor Gustina, I'm afraid she ran when she saw you take charge and love me so...enthusiastically." Her lyrical rumbles grew.

Fire burned deep inside him. The demon hissed and growled, stalking. The taste for blood grew stronger. Her blood.

Hatred at his former wife and at himself flamed inside him. Darkness fell across his vision and his blood boiled out of control. His hands clenched. The demon roared *kill her!*

with each second To see her boiled in oil, scalding, screaming to die, rolled through his thoughts which turned murkier as time sped by. A sacrifice to Jupiter, he'd relish the slaughter of the bitch.Her eyes turned evil, like a serpent. A sound blasted through the chamber. A demand for vengeance. His hands around her neck.

The vision vanished as two Roman guards grasped his arms, pulling him off her. His gaze narrowed. Her neck had red marks but she still stood. *Cunt.*

The guards bound his wrists in chains as well as his ankles before he calmed enough to connect the sounds of metal in his head. He lunged forward against the iron fetters, choking himself into submission. A guard kicked his side, another smashed the flat of a gladius against his cheek. A trickle of blood fell, hot against his face. He collapsed to his knees in front of her, gasping for air.

She'd won...again.

Because of him slaking himself on her, because of Lucilla's burning need to see him suffer, she refused the guards' desire to stake him. No, instead, she'd gutted the meager remains of his heart and soul. Gustina's life forfeited because he was the bastard who loved her.

a deafening howl.

The guards dragged him from Lucilla's chamber. He twisted and heard a deep roar, his voice, reaching out to choke the demon, battling the air, straining against...nothing.

Unfortunately, one noise above his own rantings was clear. The laughter of Lucilla.

CHAPTER TWENTY-SEVEN

Iduma ducked as the Syrian, Ahaz, swung again. He looked at the man and laughed. Kneeling on the ground, his gaze lifted to find his brother gladiator also smiling in jest.

Ludo's whip snapped in the late afternoon sun. "Break. Seize weapons and repair to baths."

Ahaz extended his hand to the Brit. Grabbing it, Iduma rose. "Swing like that in the arena, and all will take worth."

The Syrian laughed and let go Iduma's hand.

The gates to the ludas opened and three Roman guards entered, a chained Roman gladiator imprisoned in their circle. Marcus.

Iduma's gazed narrowed. The champion's face was battered, jaw swollen, a bruised and bloody lip, but his demeanor was like Mount Vesuvius, smoke billowing from his ears, fire in his eyes. The man's afternoon distraction was not of the usual sort, the Brit determined. It was as if he'd been at a fight, leaving another fire burned. *Was it Gustina?*

"Ah, the all important Champion returns," Ahaz jested. "Still in chains and worse for wear. His ability to thrust outside the arena fades like the day sun."

Marcus turned his head, his searing gaze locking in on the Syrian. Iduma could sense the rising hostility, seeing the Roman's shoulders tense, his biceps flexed and his hands tightened into fists. The guards came to a halt, stopping him as well, and with a dull, solitary look as if they were dealing with a disobedient child, unlocked the fetters around Marcus' ankles and wrists. Collecting the chain and cuffs, the guard took the other soldiers and left.

LOVE & VENGEANCE

When the gate to the ludas shut and the latch fell into place, Marcus walked over to Iduma and Ahaz. The fire burned brightly in his eyes, despite the swelling that reached up his cheek. The Syrian continued to chuckle until the Roman got to them. With lightning speed, he struck the man's face, between the eyes. Off guard, Ahaz's head flipped back, the sound of bones and cartilage breaking filled the air. Blood poured out the Syrian's nostrils and torn lip. His eyes rolled back as he fell onto the ground with a thud. Marcus stood over the prostrate man, his chest heaving, his eyes still filled with anger. Planted firmly above Ahaz, Marcus dared the man to rise, but he didn't.

Iduma stood tensely. He expected the next fist would land his ass on the ground. He probably deserved it, but the champion didn't even look at him. He just spat at the ground near the Syrian's head and stormed off to the baths.

Iduma saw Ludo out of the corner of his eye. The doctore's mouth twisted and he shook his head. Calling to two other gladiators to take Ahaz to the medicus, he ordered the rest to the baths. The Brit hoped the Roman's anger tempered in the pools, though he suspected it wouldn't. No, the man wanted vengeance and his demon now ruled. The medicus might find himself very busy tonight.

❦

Aulus plucked another grape from the wooden bowl. Hunger dominated him, so being interrupted from an afternoon taste of grape and cunt, he sighed. Ludo would not leave without saying his piece. But the man's tongue wasn't moving. Shit. Standing up from the chaise where he reclined for Farina to stroke him, he grew angry that his cock had to wait for some fucking gladiator tale.

"Do come on," he prodded, gesturing with his hand for Ludo to start talking.

The gladiator trainer's voice sounded stern, paternal. "What seized your thinking, to send Marcus to that cunt, at her Villa, so close to the games? Did you wish to be minus your champion?"

Aulus turned. His doctore appeared to be sneering at him, like a wayward child caught with his hand in the fig jar. It irritated him. "The coin was sufficient in him rendering his services...."

"To a woman who destroyed him."

With a roll of his eyes, he plopped the grape into his mouth. "He has returned, in one pieced."

Ludo laughed. "Yes, indeed he has, despite a battering of his own received there. He instantly took Ahaz out, with enough fire to take down several more if the gods hadn't intervened."

The gods, Aulus snorted. He'd heard. The gladiator stormed to the baths and then left for his cell, a bottle of wine close at hand. "How is the Syrian?"

"He'll live. Able to fight."

With a broken nose. The medicus had made his report. Many times, doctore had sent men into the spectacle already damaged. This was nothing new.

"He was close to removing the Brit from the games, had he the chance."

Outwardly, he sighed loud. Inside, he twinged. The Brit progressed rapidly in the training ground, his last two fights a marked improvement. Though the rift between him and Marcus had also grown to a dangerous level. He thought it wasn't so bad, but it changed. Lucilla's request for yesterday had been unusual. Women often sought favors after a win, but not before. When the gladiator returned, not only did he attack one of his brothers, he also returned bloody. Something was amiss, terribly wrong. Why exactly did a senator's wife buy the privilege to lay with a gladiator, particularly one she'd called husband once and threw aside for Lucius?

"And how is he now?"

Ludo studied him, as if trying to find the words. "He is an angry man. That demon in him threatens to consume his body and then no one will be safe. I can keep him busy on the sands, but it will not work if you throw him to that she-wolf again."

"I will keep him here and her away from him—for now," Aulus glared at his doctore, the only man he trusted with his gladiators. "But afterwards, at his win, I can't...."

"Yes, dominus," the man bowed and exited.

※

Cernia lay on the lounger sipping lemon juice as Farina

fanned her. The heat of the day climbed to unbearable heights, making her lightheaded and irritable. Even the grape she'd just eaten seemed hot and unsavory. She sighed. If she had anticipated the next nine months feeling this miserable, she'd have avoided it. Aulus never pushed her for children, never threatened dissolution of marriage without one. Unlike poor Lucilla.

The woman continued to rant, pacing back and forth before her. Senator Vibenius' wife appeared at her door, demanding entrance. Her pounding at the door had scared the poor slaves and, as much as Cernia wanted to send her home, the look on her friend's face prompted her to let the woman in. She appeared infuriated, but there was something new—fear.

Cernia prepared for her friend to demand another meeting with the champion. It'd been three days. The games for him and this ludas were in two. She knew Aulus would deny it so she'd have to turn her away. Pity. The man's escapades were rampant in the training sands below. The only gladiator he hadn't tried to hack to death was the Brit. That thought intrigued her, since Iduma had the champion's slave that night. She figured he'd be high on the list. Or maybe it was that demon. It had possessed him. Hushed tones made it to her ears implying the man was mad.

She shook the thoughts and tried to focus on her friend. But the heat was overwhelming.

"So it came this morning?" she asked, trying to sort out the truth from her friend's ramblings. Perhaps if her own thoughts remained focused, she might have heard Lucilla correctly from the start.

Lucilla stopped and faced her, rage clearly on her face. "A month of having him fuck me and nothing! Nothing! The gods hate me!"

Cernia raised her eyebrows. Somehow, she didn't think the gods just arbitrarily despised her. "Perhaps he was not the right champion."

Lucilla threw her arms up. "I'd think you'd sympathize with me." She paced again. "And that slave I'm holding. Whatever her name is."

She knows the girl's name, Cernia thought nastily. "Has she done something wrong? Parted her legs for Lucius?"

Lucilla stopped dead, just stood for a moment like a statue.

She inhaled deeply, still staring at the wall when she spoke. "She's carrying a child."

Cernia frowned. No wonder Lucilla was so mad.

"I have to deal with that mess of getting her to rid it."

"She should know that would happen."

Lucilla laughed. It sounded sinister. "No, she's tried to ignore her condition but she's ill at everything. Every blasted urn I swear must be cleaned daily from her retching." She shuddered. "Are you plagued with this?"

Cernia smirked. She'd been lucky so far. "No, mostly tired. And hungry." She motioned to the slave to fan faster. "And hot."

With a snort, Lucilla continued pacing. "Claims it's Marcus' so you should be happy you placed her with me."

The fan passes faltered. Cernia looked up, irritated, and noticed Farina there. The girl's face was passive but if memory served, she and Gustina had known each other. "Leave," she sternly waved the slave away. When the girl was gone, Cernia leaned back. "Perhaps the gods have favored you. You find his seed has planted and grows under your care. Tell Lucius that the gods have spoken to you, that a child is expected. And then claim Gustina's child as yours."

Her lips twisted. "He would not believe a slave he knows of is the vessel for his heir."

Cernia's lips curved up one side. For a woman so driven to sleep with her former husband to get with child, she now missed the obvious solution. "Gustina is young, and as I recall, fair to the eye. Have her lay with your husband and tell him later that the child is his. That the gods have granted your prayers without all the illness and risk of dying to deliver his heir."

Lucilla tapped her finger on the table nearby, obviously thinking.

"Lucius will not do it. Neither will that girl. She's too ill to finish any task assigned, let alone spread her thighs."

"She is a slave, Lucilla. She will do as commanded. Give her tartar and salt. It will settle her long enough to complete the task. If it will aid matters, tell her by doing this, she will not have to take the tonic to rid herself of the child. It is a nasty procedure, one that will lay her up for days, bleeding and miserable." Inside, Cernia winced. She'd forced the same

LOVE & VENGEANCE 227

concoction down Verenia's throat just two weeks ago. Vile mess....

Lucilla tilted her head. "And what of our agreement? To return her if, I mean when, Marcus wins?"

Cernia smiled. It was an opportunity to rid herself of that murderer. She didn't care that she ever came back, regardless of the fights and her condition. But she schooled her thoughts and leveled her gaze at Lucilla. "Your need comes first. I'm sure I can persuade Aulus to postpone their reuniting." She grinned.

Lucilla smiled back, looking confident her problems were solved. Cernia relaxed, knowing her fears that girl would kill her, too, dissipated.

~

Farina stood outside the room, breathing hard. Did she hear correctly? Gustina was pregnant? Her mind stumbled. Whose child? Marcus? Iduma? Or another? She strongly doubted it was another man's. She'd been gone for over two weeks and the child was almost certainly conceived here. Her own stomach flipped. She'd seen Verenia in the last few weeks. The bitch was pale, weak and useless. Even now, she was assigned to lighter tasks, away from Cernia. Hopefully the domina was remorseful, considering her own condition. No, on second thought, she couldn't be. Aulus' wife had odd flavorings, the fact she had a husband, one as virile as him, amazed Farina. Gods knew, she appreciated the situation but...poor Gustina.

She tried to be quiet and listen. Lucilla ranted like a crazed woman. Although she was barely able to hear them, what became evident made her blood race and pound in her ears. Gustina's child would be taken from her by this wild woman. The weight of this turned heavy. Her heart twisted.

Either Iduma or Marcus was father to a child they'd never know.

Poor Gustina. To take her child no doubt meant death.

Gulping her own fear and sadness, she inched away from the wall quietly. She needed to let them know, though this news to a madman like Marcus made her flinch.

Despite the odds, someone had to help Gustina. Somehow, someway. And she prayed the gods would protect her.

Marcus sat at the table, the bowl of stew before him, partially eaten. The lump of bread next to it, crumbling. Only the jug of wine moved, tipped to his lips as he slugged. He prayed to feel nothing. The bitter liquid flowed down his throat, burning slightly, but he ignored the pain. It was nothing compared to the rip in his soul. The tattered remains of it and his heart floated inside him. At this point, he only wanted them gone. Let the pain consume him.

His life was worthless, meaningless. Visions of Gustina floated at the corners of his mind. Her beauty. Her trust. His betrayal. Worse than hers, as far as he was concerned. Both ordered to fuck another but he twisted it, by trying to beat Lucilla at her own game and losing. At the cost of Gustina's life and his eternal soul. As if the gods would allow him in the Afterlife.

The rest of the gladiators, his brothers, sat away from him. At first, they'd stared at him, wary of him after the bashing of his wooden gladius in the field. He didn't care. The demon drove him and he gladly gave it life. Even now, it stalked beneath the surface, looking for an opening. Blood. Death. *Kill them all!* The chant repeated over and over.

More wine. He needed more.

The murmuring voices around him stirred, enough to cause him to notice. His vision was blurred but he looked up anyway, saw the various men moving because someone else entered. A woman. He squinted. Farina.

She looked nervous, her eyes darting about the room. They landed on him but not for long. She'd seen him and paled. The demon pranced proudly.

Then she found Iduma. His gaze narrowed. Was that a timid smile on her face over the Brit? Damn. He grabbed the near-empty bottle and drank.

He saw her lean to Iduma, telling him something in his ear. She still looked frightened. Perhaps she should, being the only woman in the room full of thirsty and sex-starved gladiators. He shook his head. No, she kept staring at him and at the doorway to the upper Villa. Then the Brit looked at him, his face dead-pan straight.

Something inside him clenched. He didn't know what or

why but he needed another bottle of wine and the fuck with them. Violently he stood, knocking the bench beneath him over. The clattering noise silenced the room, all eyes on him. Bastards, the whole lot. He slammed the empty clay jug against the wall. His leg jabbed the edge of the table but he didn't feel the stab. No one stopped him from walking to the side, to a cart that held wine jugs for storage, ones they were not to get, but he did anyway. As champion, he did and would. He grabbed one, glared back at the rest of them, yanked the cork out with his teeth and spat it across the room. With a grunt, he left the room and stumbled to his cell.

There, perhaps the wine would fill the hole in his chest and stable the violent force within him. That demon. A force that grew stronger daily. The last remnants of humanity slowly disintegrated.

He slumped along the wall in his cell, downing half the jug in one swallow.

Gustina's life was at stake because of him. Because he loved her. It was the reason she was forced to sleep with Iduma. His thoughts wrapped around that. The wine and demon fought for control. Memories of her talking to the Brit that night after the fights. Visions of her wrapping her legs around him distorted into her doing so with Iduma. Both denied it happened and yet not enough. He knew they did.

Lucilla invaded him. Her sultry walk, swing of her hips, ample breasts and sweet cunt. Her body always got his. Always. He was no better than the evil beast inside him.

He'd hurt Gustina by fucking Lucilla. As much as he hated the bitch, he'd plunged into her, willingly, even if it was to prove he could and Gustina watched his betrayal, blatant, undeniable.

Iduma deserved her. He could take care of her. Not Marcus, not slave nor free.

He swallowed more wine. Only one thing remained. He'd win the games, be the champion at one cost and he knew it was one Aulus wouldn't deny. He'd win, and remain a gladiator for the house of Aulus—his reward not money, not wine, not whores. Actually, it was simple. He'd remain a slave, a gladiator, for Gustina to be set free.

CHAPTER TWENTY-EIGHT

Terpio shifted the papyrus again. *Where did it go?* A simple sheet, one trivial piece among hundreds and he'd go claim his prize again. If Lucilla was too busy going to priestesses about her barren state and ignoring him, he'd find out about her new slave himself. His slave, Gustina. She should have been executed. Finding her at Lucilla's was a revelation. The girl tempted him so. If Lucilla held him off, he'd take her instead. A smile crept over his lips at the thought.

He ran his fingers through his dark hair. But where was that parchment? Searching for this again was futile. He should have known it was worthless. She had to have it. Why, though? Uttering a sigh in disbelief, he turned and stalked out the door to Lucilla's, stirring at the thought of causing her excruciating pain over the lost document.

∽

Gustina pushed the brush one more time across the tile floor, the hard surface a discomfort to her knees. Forward and back. Coming back, she swayed for a second, the bile inching up her throat. Warm and muggy in the early afternoon hours, she rocked back to rest against her heels, willing the vile stuff down with a swallow. It took a minute for her to regain control but the illness retreated. She sighed, leaving the bitter taste ever presnt. Dora had given her dried flat bread to eat this morning. The idea that dried, stale bread could calm her stomach was a pleasant surprise. What a terrible aspect of childbearing. But she hadn't vomited yet, so maybe that and the barley gruel worked. It amazed her that the only time she didn't feel like retching was when she ate.

If she could just find a cure for the fatigue. She slept hard and it was never enough.

Plunging the brush into the bucket, she dropped it before her, leaning onto it as she pressed out. Her movements were slow and sluggish but she continued at her task. Having her domina angry with her would be perilous. The conceited, unforgiving and vindictive domina hardly noticed her. For that, she thanked the gods. After that afternoon when she explicitly called Gustina into her chambers and let her watch Marcus fuck her domina, she always smiled at the slave, the grin sadistic and vengeful.

When Lucilla discovered she was carrying, the woman exploded. She ordered silva procured and even now, Gustina awaited her return, fearing she'd force the abortive cocktail down her throat and make her lose Marcus' babe. Her eyes flooded again. Regardless of what she'd seen, of how he'd taken the bitch over and over, harshly, demanding and enjoying it, Gustina's heart couldn't lash out against him. So this was what love was? She shook her head. She'd have no more of it. Her insides twisted now. What would she do next time he arrived? She knew she'd be forced to witness, to endure the champion pleasing the Roman whore. Last time she ran from the chambers, unable to bear the sight. If she fled again, domina would surely physically punish her.

The thought of him coming here again and doing that made her ill. Shoving the brush forward across the tile, she took her anger out on the floor. So intent on her task, she didn't hear the footsteps until the sandaled feet were in front of her. She glanced up. Her dominus, Lucius, looked down at her, a concerned look on his face.

"Child, they are simply tiles, not Hannibal and his troops."

She bit the inside of her cheek. What a fool she must look like. "Yes, dominus."

The man bent before her, tilting her chin up with his fingers. "Gustina?"

"Yes, dominus."

"I know your domina can be," he paused, as if trying to find the appropriate word. "Cruel, at times, but you are safe here." He smiled at her.

Gustina swallowed. She'd rarely seen this man, her new

dominus, but he looked like a gentle man. He made her feel secure, which surprised her. She nodded. "Yes, dominus."

He chuckled. "Go on about your work." And he walked on.

She stared after him, Dora's words haunting the back of her mind.

"Go and lay with our dominus. Let him believe the child is his. He needs an heir. Domina cannot conceive. He would protect you and your child."

To do so made her a whore no different from her domina, or Marcus. To not, meant the death of her babe. Her hand fell absently to her stomach. It still remained flat, but inside she knew the babe lay there. Marcus' child. She closed her eyes. Yes, she'd give her life to secure a life for her child. Even if that meant submitting to another. In the recesses of her mind, she heard a hiss. "Whore...."

∽

Lucius walked down the corridor, eyebrows furrowed. That slave, Gustina, concerned him. She looked deathly pale. A pretty little thing as far as slave girls go, but there was something else about her. He couldn't place it and that irked him to no end. He was supposed to be good at figuring others out. Her eyes looked—what was the word—troubled? No, *haunted.* Whatever had happened to her to bring such misery?

He sighed. Obviously she had had a bad time while at Aulus' house. Odd, for the man ran that Villa and ludas with such precision...oh well, he'd discover it later if need be.

Pushing the girl from his mind, he turned the corner to his desk and found Terpio.

The man stood as soon as Lucius saw him. The senator didn't trust him. Terpio spent way too much time at the pubs, the races, and with his wife. If Lucilla wasn't trying so hard to be blessed with their child, he'd suspect she might fall prey to the young man. He shook his head. No, the young man was a contradiction in terms. Either he was immeasurably smart or a complete imbecile.

One aspect of Terpio never escaped—he was the supposed brother to Marcus, the champion gladiator, slave to Aulus. And he had also been Lucilla's brother-in-law. A fact that Lucius could never forget, as much as he wanted to. Inhaling deeply, he tensed.

"Senator Vibenius," Terpio hailed, stepping forward.

Pasting his political smile on his face as he turned, Lucius answered, "Terpio, to what do I owe your attention?"

Terpio's cheek twitched. "I'm looking for your wife, Lucilla."

Lucius exhaled. The man's attempt was bold. Something wasn't right. "She's out, as you have found."

"Yes, and I'd hoped you knew of her return."

He frowned. "And what is it you would have of her?"

Terpio's head dropped, the insipid look of friendly demeanor gone. "I'm in search of family record. A scroll is missing. I don't know if Marcus had hold of it or not but if he did, perhaps Lucilla has hinted where it might lay if not fortuitously possessing it."

Lucius' lips curved up in disgust. *Little prick, accusing Lucilla of stealing.* He snorted. "Perhaps if you tell me of the contents, I'll see if by chance she has it, by happen-stance, of course."

Terpio shifted. The senator eyed him cautiously. The man was younger than he, not that Lucius considered himself old at forty, but Terpio was closer to Lucilla's age by appearance. Her former brother-in-law held all the markings of a proper Roman—dark hair, brown eyes, aquiline nose—and he wore the mantle of governmental position well. Maybe too well…there was a tale of Terpio's wife being murdered by a slave. It happened not long after his marriage to Lucilla. They'd been in the northern provinces, on a trip for the Senate and he'd taken her along to amuse her with the outer reaches of the Empire. If memory served to purpose, she had begged to accompany him. It hadn't seemed important at the time but perhaps there was more to it, a voice in the back of his head prompted.

Terpio and Lucilla's previous involvement involved the dissolution of her marriage to Marcus, Terpio's brother. Lucius was not in Rome then either. But he returned after his duties to the Senate were completed, to meet this beautiful woman, almost as if the gods had placed her before him to be his wife. Lucius' widowhood grated on his nerves and he didn't care for whores. A young Roman woman like her, doting on him, was too good to ignore. He cared not of her previous husband. The issue had been resolved in court by the man's betrayal. She appeared before him as a blessing of the gods. He never pushed for details.

Now, he wondered if he should have.

"It is of a personal matter, Senator. I will not bore you with unfortunate family affairs." Terpio's voice broke his musings.

"Understood. But without any signifying mark, it will be difficult to tell a slave what to look for."

Terpio's step away from him hitched at that remark. "It is a written text. One I fear no slave could discern the meaning of beyond mere slashes."

With a half smile, Lucius did his best to mask his growing distaste of the man. Granted, most slaves had no knowledge of the written word, as neither did many lower Romans outside a phrase or two. But his body slave knew script. He taught the man well, for there were times it came into use.

"Very well then, I shall tell her of your visit and need for such discussions."

He watched Terpio swallow nervously.

"Gratitude," the man bowed and turned to leave.

Lucius shook his head. *What was Lucilla up to now?*

Terpio walked to the door, furious. Lucilla had to have it. The woman was going to drive him mad unless she released it. The price of his world lay wrapped in that document.

His path he knew by heart from previous times to the Villa, and with his mind distracted by the turn of events, he walked without paying attention until his foot hit something solid. He grunted as pain stabbed his toe. His sandal became wet as filthy water sloshed out of the bucket he'd run right into.

Looking down, he found a slave girl, brown-haired, for all he saw was the back of her head as she bent over to hold the container from tipping over.

"Stupid girl," he hissed. The fault was clearly his for not paying attention, but it irked him more that she didn't even glance up. "Look at me," he ordered.

She didn't move. He saw her bare shoulders tense under his gaze. She was slight of build, but the exposed back was smooth ivory skin and made Terpio tighten. The slave tattoo on her shoulder was halfway covered by her hair. He caught a glimpse of the curved ink and a shiver passed through him. That mark looked too familiar.

"I said, look at me," he hissed, reaching forward and grabbing a fistful of hair.

Slowly, her head tipped up as she rose to her feet. Her hands at her sides clenched for a second. Shoulders straight, she looked up into his face, with a defiantly set jaw, narrow lips, and pale blue eyes glaring at him.

He smiled slowly. "Gustina."

Her eyes were hard, icy even. Not his beautiful Gustina. *Damn how he'd missed her so*. He reached forward and touched her cheek with his fingers, tracing down. It was like touching silk. The memories flooded back. He'd been cruel to her, but nothing more than any other dominus. She was beauty in a world of deceit and darkness…one he had helped create.

Absorbed in feeling her again, at first he didn't notice her breathing harder, a tremble actually. But her eyes never fluttered. Perhaps their reflection hardened further, to hate? No, not him. He never taught her hate. Distaste, maybe, but pleasure could be found in pain. Her glare faltered, anguish flashed before anger returned. He'd show her ecstasy in a sea of pain. Yes, he would do that.

But she stood before him, like a statue in the void. They'd killed her emotionally.

"My darling Gustina," he cooed. "I will take you from here. Show you the world you belong in," he muttered. "But not now. Not now. Soon, I promise you."

Her piercing stare broke. He saw it. Her eyes glistened, the only reaction he'd get. No, he wouldn't leave until he got more. His hand snaked around her lithe waist, pulling her to him. He heard her grunt and relished the noise. Hard against him, she had to relent. Giving her no choice, his mouth descended on hers, sealing her lips with his as his tongue prodded for entrance. When she relented, he delved in and sighed.

∽

Gustina's world tilted from abysmal to horror. Terpio. Her old dominus. The man who blamed her, made her a scapegoat for his wife's death when he was the murderer. He'd made sure she was convicted to die. Marcus saved her. Now that he found her, he'd no doubt have her sentence carried out at his own hands. And in taking her life, he'd kill the babe inside her. She'd do anything to stop him, even if that meant...she shuddered.

She knew he frequented this Villa, prayed to the gods he'd never see her. They ignored her pleas.

The moment he grabbed her, all her defenses fell. Old habits locked into place. She was a slave and he a Roman. There wasn't a way to deny him, even if he didn't own her any more. The fate of the gods put him here, once more demanding her body. His lips on hers, though, were not expected. He'd never been one to kiss her when he took her. It surprised her. When his tongue invaded her mouth, her stomach twisted. But he was caressing the inside of her slowly, like a lover not a master.

Gustina stood, afraid and angry. This was not his Villa. He was not her dominus. Part of her wanted to scream, the other half acquiesced to him as expected of a slave. When his hand smoothed down her back, over her behind, she stiffened. He lifted the end of her tunic. Fear whipped through her and she clenched her rear cheeks tight, refusing his prodding. He pulled from her mouth but not far as he laughed.

"You know you liked it," he murmured, his other arm around her waist locking her against him.

She squirmed. His arousal pushed against her. Not this time, no. She'd refused to let him defile her. But he did the unexpected. His hand skirted over her naked hip to her front and dipped to her mound, cupping it. At her gasp, his finger slid into her.

"Ah, Gustina's missed my cock," he growled, another finger entered her and he fucked her with two digits rapidly.

Damn. Even she heard her juices as he entered her. Bile fought its way up her throat and she wanted to retch. Her body was out of sorts, carrying a child. She always felt wet and wanting which disturbed her in many ways, as well as the desire to vomit, sleep and her bladder was always full. Of all the Romans to discover her body's tormented state, though, she then prayed the gods struck her dead. The last thing she missed was this prick's cock.

The anger took hold and gave her the strength to beat her

submission to him. Her hands pushed hard against his chest, shoving him away from her.

"Why, Gustina, fighting the inevitable?" He gave her a wicked smile as he stepped closer.

She'd fight him as long as she could, knowing it wouldn't work but the last thing she wanted was for him to fuck her.

"Terpio, darling." A voice echoed far behind Gustina. Lucilla.

Gustina watch the wretched man's demeanor change. He straightened and muttered softly to her, "I will see you again." Stepping around her, his voice changed to jovial. "Lucilla."

Gustina stood, trembling, no longer hearing their words drifting down the hallway disappearing around the corner away from her. She collapsed to the floor. Her skin prickled, like pins scattering all over her, everywhere his hands touched her, even inside her. Anger and fear clenched her and made her nauseous. Quickly she covered her mouth with her hand, swallowing the vile contents before she lost it on her clean tiles.

Too late. The vomit spewed past her lips, onto the floor she'd meticulously scrubbed for hours. Lucilla and Terpio looked at her, laughing.

"Stupid cunt," her domina said harshly. The woman fingered a small bottle from the medicus, certain for Gustina to see its presence. "I'll deal with your insolence later. Perhaps dear Terpio could use his beautiful Roman cock to teach you a few things. Is that what ails you? Missing a good fucking?" They cackled like a pair of hyenas at her, pausing to whisper to one another.

Gustina stood frozen, remnants of her retching clinging to her hands and tunic. The smell of it, the feel of its acid on her tongue, made her begin to swoon. She bit her lip until it bled, determined not to pass out. If she did, she might wake and find herself at his mercy, or worse.

I will see you again. His words repeated in her mind. She knew next time there'd be no escape. He'd fuck her. And then he'd kill her.

CHAPTER TWENTY-NINE

Lucilla hooked her arm in Terpio's as she led him into the Atrium. Her breath caught when she found him in her Villa and Lucius home. What she hadn't expected was the flash of jealous rage through her when she saw him holding that slave. But didn't she drive him to that by refusing him in her bed? She'd never felt that emotion before and didn't like it. No man owned her, not even her husband. Control sat in her hands, not anywhere else. Swallowing the petty feeling, she smiled and greeted him as warmly as she could. She needed his help but for the first time, fear tried to take hold in her. She shook it off. Her plan would work.

"Lucius told me you came in search of me?"

He smiled his charming grin, his eyes sparkling like it was a game. "Yes." He pulled her closer.

She gritted her teeth. If Lucius saw this, only with the help of Jupiter could she explain it. She tried to step away from him. "Terpio, please."

But he wouldn't release her. "You didn't tell me you had her." His tone was menacing.

She furrowed her brows for a second before she caught herself. Control. Schooling her face into a ready, seductive smile, she laughed. "She arrived but shortly ago. I thought you'd be pleased." Now if she could twist his thinking into forgetting the whore. "Let us not ponder this. You came for something else."

He squinted as he veered ahead. "I can't find that sheath of my father's," his voice dropped low. It sounded distraught. Now he wanted it?

"Darling, it is safe," she began, but he cut her off.

"Do you have it?"

They stopped in the middle of the Atrium. She waved the slaves away and walked to the table, pouring them cups of wine. Turning, she held his out to him. "No, you know that." She stepped toward him, her own voice lowering. "You came here for that? And inquired about it from Lucius?"

Terpio rolled his eyes as he paced. "Everything involves that piece. It is not in my Villa. It was to remain there, so why did you take it?"

Sitting on the lounge, she smoothed her stola. He was like a child in so many ways but one, and she so enjoyed his cock. If her plan worked, she'd have him back in her bed shortly. "For times like this, when you act as if the gods were storming after you. It is safe. No one has privy to it. This is an honorable house, the slaves even are tame...."

Hysterical laughter rolled from his lips. "Really? You have a murderer under your roof and you claim them to be honorable?"

"She is necessary."

Within a second, he stood before her, his face red with anger. "Pray tell, how? I should take her and...."

"Ah, but therein lies the problem," she sighed. *Men.* "You wish her dead. I need her alive, at least for eight more months."

"Why?"

She grunted with aggravation and tried to hide her disgust as she took a sip of wine.

"Are you with child?" His question she should have expected. Anger rolled inside her. Apparently no one else had problems getting with child. The gods must despise her....

"No, not yet."

"But I thought you said—"

"I have found my solution," she interrupted him. "I need you to take your little whore and murderer and keep her for a bit."

He smiled as he sat next to her. "Wonderful, I'll arrange it."

"I want you to arrange nothing," she interjected. Gods, the last thing she wanted was for that slave to be killed. "I've need of her to live for now, dear heart."

"But I don't understand."

"I am not with child…again. Lucius will move quickly to see this marriage dissolved. And as you are so close to me, he'll arrange for your position to die as well."

His mouth twisted before it curled. "But then we can be together."

She tilted her head sadly, her hand cradling his cheek. "No, love, not that way. The girl is with child. I shall claim it is my child, a gift from the gods, so as not to ruin my beautiful body."

He frowned as he backed out of her touch. An unusual tactic on his part, she decided. He was angry. *Interesting.*

"You would present a fucking slave's child as your own? From the gods? Have you gone mad?"

She laughed quietly. "No, I have elevated myself. What I require of you is a place for her to rest for a month and then return her to me as worthless because she is with child."

His face turned hard as stone. "You want me to house the woman who killed my wife for your little intrigue?"

"Yes, and not to abuse her." She smiled.

The look in his eyes told her he was considering what advantage he'd gain from this.

"I'll pay you for her keep even," she added.

"And you'd present as heir a bastard, not even of his own line?"

"He will have lain with her. It is all right and just."

Terpio's face paled. Perhaps she'd been wrong to include him but he needed Marcus gone as well. From what Cernia said, the man wouldn't last in the Arena, so wrapped in fury of Gustina being gone. With the gladiator beaten, his position secured as slave if he lived, no one could stop her plan.

"Just keep her as a slave? She'll try to kill me," he muttered.

"No, give her menial tasks. We'll need her well and able to carry that child. Remember that. And when it is born, I shall take it as a sign of the gods to raise it, then you may do as you must with the girl."

Terpio's eyes were glazed, as if he wasn't really there, but he nodded.

She smiled broadly as she sipped her wine. Now, she had to get Lucius in on this without his knowledge. He needed to fuck Gustina tonight. Yes. Lucilla could barely contain her excitement.

∞

Aulus couldn't believe what he just heard. His champion requested the unbelievable. "The spectacles begin tomorrow. You are to fight in the primus and now, before you win, you make this request?"

The Roman gladiator stood defiantly before him. He looked raw. The past couple of weeks, he'd pushed himself in the practice fields hard, destroying any of his brothers who fought with him. Aulus also heard how he drank to excess every night, rarely ate, was surly to any and everyone. Ludo claimed the demon had him. Perhaps. But would the demon make these demands?

"I will win." His words showed his confidence. If he took that resolve and his actions prior to the games, it should be a show of the ages, one fitting for a triumphant Emperor.

"And if the crowd demands your freedom?" Aulus didn't want to consider it, but it was a possibility. He'd seen it happen before. And after a hundred days of games, and being driven harder now that Trajan had returned and sat, watching, the power of the mob only grew.

Marcus didn't flinch. In fact, he seemed more determined as he shifted his weight and his shoulders squared. But he never looked his dominus in the eye. He fixed his stare on the wall behind the man. "I do not want whores or wine or money. I want Gustina found and freed." He swallowed. "And Iduma freed to care for her."

Aulus stood from his perched seat behind the table. "I don't understand. I thought you gave the world for the girl."

Marcus remained quiet but there was a tick in his cheek. Telltale sign. *Damn, the stupid gladiator was in love with her.*

"Getting her back, paying for her freedom is nothing. She is a worthless slave," he rounded the table, watching his jab reflect off the gladiator. The man knew he wasn't lying. Gustina's value was next to naught, especially after her sentence to death. But still. "But to release Iduma. I think you have stayed on the sands, in the blinding sun and heat, for too long. The Brit is worth coin I'm not willing to part with." He spoke the truth. "The man's value has increased. His training and wins are an added value to this house."

"Free him to care for her," Marcus paused for a second. "And I will remain here, your champion, till I am called to the Afterlife."

Aulus stood before him, still not believing. "You'd give up your freedom and the woman you love," he saw the flash in the man's eyes and knew he broke past his stoic walls. "Oh yes, it is very plain. But you'd give her to the Brit? The man you've tried to annihilate on the fields these past days?"

Ludo reported to Aulus daily on the training of the men— and to report on the champion. He'd practiced with the Brit and won decidedly every time, with Iduma on his back or kneeling, obviously well beaten and the wooden gladius at his neck or heart. The doctore said Marcus looked possessed every time. Anger and fury reflected in his actions, his breathing, and his attack.

Even now, the pain showed in the champion's eyes. Briefly, but Aulus caught it.

"Yes."

The reply was solid, hard. Aulus pursed his lips, contemplating. He could lose the Brit but he'd have Marcus. A high gamble. Though the champion was a prime specimen, if the demon truly took him, the fury could destroy him and anyone else nearby. But then again, he won thousands for Aulus. His skill on the sands was not matched yet, outside of the one incident. All was wrapped up in the girl. The one who drove the man to this. He shook his head.

"You win the primus, and the crowd, and I will grant your wish."

The Roman gladiator's tension drained before Aulus' eyes. *Utterly disgusting.*

"Go to the ludas, finish today's training. Tomorrow is up to you."

Marcus bent his head. "Dominus." He turned and left, the two guards on his flanks.

Aulus continued to shake his head. *Jupiter's balls.*

༄

Iduma spun fast, his sword in the air. He swung the gladius only to have it clash with Marcus' again. The vibration resonated through the wood, an interesting feeling considering the dull instruments. The strength of the champion's defense forced the Brit backward, landing hard on the ground. Dust from the training field filled the air like a cloud. He tasted the grit in his mouth, inhaling it through his nose, and his eyes burned.

The Roman stood above him. His eyes glazed red. *The demon*. For love of the gods, the man wasn't even worn out by the day of training in the heat. *Shit.*

Ludo kept them training hard, even up to the day before the spectacles. He argued they needed to be able to fight in the grueling heat of the summer day since they were scheduled for the afternoon rounds. His reasoning sounded sane until moments like this. Iduma attempted to spit the dirt from his dry mouth.

Marcus held both his gladius in one hand and gave his free one to the Brit to help him up. Warily, he took it. He noticed the Roman's anger and rage drove him the last two weeks but today, something was off. The man wasn't calm, but neither did he have the look to kill everyone. Well, maybe it was just not today.

Iduma watched him as they walked to the water barrel. Did he tell the man what Farina reported to him? That Gustina was carrying a child? The problem was, he didn't know how Marcus would take it. Today, he was borderline civil. Not that he was talking or laughing, but news like this could drive the man over the edge. The question was, which way? Make him fight to win to get her back and claim the child? Or drive him to kill them all, believing it was Iduma's. Oh, he wasn't stupid. He knew, though he'd tried denying it, that the Roman figured he had bedded her.

No, the problem was quite plain—Iduma wanted her for himself. He hoped the child was his, but even that was a precarious situation. Most female slaves were forced to abort their child. But from what Farina claimed to overhear, Gustina would have the babe, only to have it taken from her. Anger raced up his spine, jolting Iduma to want to kill. So this was how the Roman acted out of love for her? The Brit feared he wasn't the only one. He'd kill anyone who'd harm her.

Snap! The sharp sound of the doctore's whip brought every man to a halt.

"Gladiators," Ludo began. "Head to the baths. Tevia will

have positions for tomorrow and present them there. Sup and sleep. Tomorrow will be upon us quickly."

Marcus' eyebrows raised as he glanced at Iduma. A look of indifference. Inside, the Brit snarled. The Roman always got the primus. He could only hope his was close to it, to get the respect his skills now earned him.

Should he tell him? No, he decided. It was possible, though unlikely, that the gods might favor him over the champion and his showing in the arena would gain him his freedom. Domina had promised if that was the case, she'd make sure Gustina would return for him and him alone. Satisfaction yet betrayal slithered through him. Though Marcus would no doubt kill him in the long run, both of them knew that Iduma was the better man for her. He wasn't possessed like Marcus with an evil being, threatening death and destruction to all.

And if Iduma got his freedom, he'd get hers and take her with him. The gods had spoken to him. He was the one designated to take her as his and protect her. And they also told him the Roman knew.

At that moment, Marcus looked right into Iduma's eyes as they handed another slave their wooden swords. The Roman had a strange glare, not mad, not possessed, but a combination of regret and agreement. He nodded at Iduma and strolled past him.

Why did the Brit feel a wave of doom and glory wash over him? As if the champion of Aulus' house knew Gustina would be Iduma's and to that, the champion agreed?

◇

Gustina gulped. She stood in the doorway to Lucius' bedchamber. Lucilla gave her no opportunity out of this. The task was easy. Go to her dominus and submit to him.

She was made to drink a vile tasting concoction but it did settle her stomach of nausea. Bathed in luxury for a slave of lemon-scented oil, she sat as Dora brushed her hair until it shone brilliantly. Lucilla gave her a sheer white wrap to wear and told her regardless of his state of mind, to disrobe and crawl on the bed next to him. An odd order, but she nodded.

Dressed and bathed like this, Gustina shuddered as she looked into the chamber. Lucius was in bed, propped against pillows, bare-chested. If his eyes were open, she'd believe maybe he did want her. But he didn't move.

"Dominus?"

No reaction.

Lowering her head, she smiled and hoped if he was awake, he didn't see it. Slowly she walked to the bed and removed the wrap. Still he didn't seem to notice. Her hand fell to her stomach. Only a minor bulge was there, not enough for anyone to notice but her. She slid under the cotton sheet. Snuggling up next to him, Gustina touched his bare skin. He was naked. She swallowed and let her hand fall to his cock.

The senator responded to her, becoming hard in her hands, and a minor groan escaped his lips. Otherwise, he did nothing. She was puzzled while she stroked him. Was he asleep? Drugged?

He stirred, his eyes slightly opened. He glanced down at his arousal and her moving hand. His head turned and found her. It was a sluggish move. He'd been drugged.

Inside, she relaxed. He'd not follow through with this but she needed him to. Dora was correct and Lucilla confirmed it. If he fucked her, she'd be able to keep the babe. But Lucilla made the point perfectly clear. To fail meant aborting the child. No, she'd protect Marcus' babe, even if it meant doing this. Bile wanted to creep up her throat but the potion she drank fought it.

Suddenly, Lucius growled. He grabbed her and swung her onto the pallet. Quickly, he parted her legs and entered her. She gasped, unprepared. His cock plunged in, out and in one more time. With a moan, he collapsed, falling to her right, his erection depleting as he fell into a deep slumber.

She closed her eyes tight. It was enough. The man was naked, his body half draping hers. She couldn't move. Wasn't supposed to. Domina wanted her to spend the night here, so he saw her nude and next to him the next morning.

One hand was pinned under his body but her free one rested over her abdomen. Her babe was safe. The child of a slave, one who'd do anything to protect its life. Including whoring herself to another man. Normally, she'd retreat inside herself, knowing that it was only her body that was used by another for base means. But this time, she couldn't. Why her domina wanted this she didn't know. But she feared she'd never see the Roman gladiator again or show him his child. The sting in her eyes hit hard as her vision distorted. And the tears dripped down her cheeks.

CHAPTER THIRTY

Lucius dreamt the oddest of dreams. He stood in the Forum, his fellow senators oblivious to his presence. The buzz of their voices droned on but he couldn't understand them. No, all he saw was a young woman. Slight of build with light brown hair, her skin glowed in the sunlight, the same light that lit up her pale blue eyes. An interesting woman. One moment, she appeared frightened, like a lamb taken from its mother. She wasn't Roman. When she turned to look behind her, her shoulder bore the mark of a slave. Most slaves looked bored with their position in life, some looked terrified if called upon for services rendered. But as she turned back to him, her eyes turned dark, sultry as she motioned to him.

The dignified tone of the Forum faded to the raucous sounds of a brothel. Whores practiced their trade everywhere and in any fashion. He'd been in these places before when he was younger. As a senator and married Roman, he devoted his time to Rome and his wife, a woman whose name escaped him. Soon, everyone around him faded but the girl. He watched her stand, in the middle of the crowded main room, her gaze always on him as she slowly undid her tunic and it fell to the floor. Her nude body in all its glory, stood before him, begging him. Blood surged through him and pooled in his loins. Tightening, he clenched his hands. It was wrong to take a whore yet his arousal demanded otherwise.

In one swift move, he was before her. Her hands grabbed his robes and lifted them as she licked her lips. When she clasped his erection, he knew he was doomed and he took her there, in the filth of the house of whores.

Strange dream. His mouth was dry and his head pounded. He lay on his stomach in an awkward position. As if he was on pillows or something. A cool breeze brushed his back and he realized he was naked. He never slumbered nude. Prying his eyes open, he gazed around him. It wasn't pillows he was on top of, but a woman. Not Lucilla. No, it was that slave, Gustina. She slept, though how he had no idea with his weight on her. He moved off her, hoping she didn't wake.

The girl's eyes looked puffed and her lips swollen. Dear Jupiter, had he taken her abruptly? Or had she cried afterward and been unable to escape him? He closed his eyes tight but it only made his head hurt more with all the movement. And since when did he decide to fuck a slave when he had a beautiful wife?

Perhaps since Lucilla wandered from their bed. The thought zipped through his mind. He tried to deny it, but she must have because he wasn't attentive enough to her. The Senate took so much of his time. Hence the gods refused him a child for being a negligent husband. Oh, he had loved her, embedding his seed inside on many occasions recently, but the nagging fear it wasn't enough remained.

The curtains to the chamber opened and his wife entered, followed by a handful of servants. She breezed into the room but stopped short of the bed.

"Lucius." Her face paled before him. "I, I didn't," her voice faded.

The senator for once couldn't find his voice to save his life. He watched as if he were at a play as she stormed to the side of the bed where the sleeping slave lay and whipped the sheet back.

"Get up, slave!" Lucilla fumed, her eyes murderous.

Gustina stirred, so deep in sleep she struggled to open her eyes. In an instant, the awareness of her domina glaring at her brought her awake. She flew off the cushions, reaching for her clothes. "Domina," she answered, her head lowered as she tried to cover her body.

"Leave."

"Yes, Domina." And the girl fled the room.

Lucilla turned to Lucius. He couldn't read her expression. It appeared a mixture of relief and minor irritation, carefully school to docile. "Darling, did you have to?"

LOVE & VENGEANCE

He sat on the side of the bed, his head in his hands. The sun streamed into the room as the slave moved the curtain. The light seared into his head. The pain needed to stop. He had to get up and attend the spectacles today.

"Here, drink this tonic." A cup was forced into his hand. He glanced to his left. Lucilla sat next to him. "I have a bath drawn for you," her eyes went down and up him. "You apparently need it this morning."

"Lucilla, I didn't—" he began, but she cut him off.

"The gods came to me last night and told me of your visitor," her tongue twisted. "I believe for now, it is prudent to loan her to someone else to watch, until you can control your cock. Yes, that's the answer." She spun to leave, adding over her shoulder, "get ready dear. We must leave for the Colesseum by the fourth hour."

He groaned. The games. *Shit*.

※

Marcus bent over and pulled the leather ties tight, his anger flaring. *Exhibition*. Since when did he ever do exhibition? He guffawed. *Kill*. Blood racing, his ears filled with the pounding of it as the madness began.

Early that morning, Aulus had the guts to tell him that in honor of the Emperor, before the executions and the main fights after noonday sun, there would be a simple match to display talent. Marcus couldn't believe the words. His elevation to primus kept him out of these petty matches. But not now, not on the last day of celebrations. He spat on the dirt floor of the Colosseum caverns.

His demon prowled beneath the surface, vying for death. He'd give it to the creature soon.

Iduma wandered over to him, ready for the festivities. He shrugged. "All for the emperor."

Marcus snorted. "I remember Trajan. Man's too busy counting his accolades to give a damn about us."

"We are his accolades here," the Brit offered.

He laughed. "Oppius Gallus Lucro's gladiators rank close to Aulus' house. This is more a match warranting an afternoon hour than prior."

"Yes, but we are to simply go through the motions, not defeat them now."

Marcus' gaze narrowed as he looked beyond the Brit, onto the sands. A man, condemned to die by a lion, brought the crowd to their feet, attempting to flee the starved creature. That lion was like the thing inside him that stirred even now, hungry for blood and death. He could feel its vibrations throughout his body, pushing for the kill, but he had to contain it, store its anger until the primus.

Oh, he knew the emperor. Had been privy to his box on occasion. One thing about family and Lucilla. Connections and a seductive body got them through the guards. The emperor was young then, before the latest war. A titan among men, Trajan was intelligent, calculating and also his own favorite admirer.

The vision of the past turned red as the inner beast rose its head. The crowd outside applauded and yelled loudly as the lion tore its human meal to shreds. Their turn was next. Still gazing through the iron bars, he said to Iduma, "Watch yourself out there. I do not trust Lucro's men to be happy either at simple play."

The Brit guffawed. "May the same be said of you. You're to have top position later, to reap reward soon after."

Marcus heard the words but ignored the tone. A distant thought threaded through his mind that the Brit wasn't warning as a brother, but more with regret. No, the Brit would soon find he'd have more to celebrate. Freedom and Gustina.

The demon's growl silenced for a moment before it deafened him.

Slaves hurried on the arena floor, scurrying the lion back to its cage. Screeching as the door slammed on the creature, the floor underneath lowered, taking the cat away as an ensemble of men cleared the sands of blood and bones.

Inside, Marcus heard the hysterical laughter of evil rolling but he clamped his mouth shut. A young man handed him his two gladius and Iduma his helmet, shield and sword. He eyed the Brit as the gladiator tugged on his leather arm wrap, making sure it was in place. *Nervous habit of a gladiator.* Marcus shrugged. They all had them. His was simple—close his eyes and let the fumes of death seep into him deep, waking the killing monster inside him, a beast relishing the clank of metal and the sound of flesh ripping apart.

The Syrian, Ahaz, and another brother gladiator appeared

at their sides. Ahaz as another murmillo like Iduma and the other, a retiarius with his trident and net. Marcus snorted. Retiarius, or net-men, were a nuisance, flinging that net, and what good could a trident really do against true blade? But they had been the rage for years and so every house had one.

The gates opened and Marcus with his brothers walked on to the sands to the roar of the crowd. Detestable lot in the stands, cheering on murderers, he thought. Romans standing and stomping for the demonstration made the mob of Rome. The strength of their influence could be keenly felt. He flipped his gladius in his hands and raised them above his head, bellowing back to the crowd. And the noise level raised.

Across the sands, another gate opened and four of Lucro's gladiators came out. A big, bulky set, one was a hoplomachus or hoplite fighter with a thrusting spear, short sword and round shield, concealing a dragger beneath. Another was a murmillo and a secutor, a chaser with a large shield, dagger and short sword. The last gladiator of the bunch was the biggest of them yet, all limbs clad in padding and greaves, holding a small shield and the short curved blade of a Thracian. All had their specific helmets hiding their faces.

Let them hide. Death does not care.

Marcus, the only gladiator not wearing a helmet, inhaled deep the gritted smell of the sands and the layer of death and blood that filtered through the air. A familiar fragrance, sweet and spicy. It got his blood boiling. Muscles tensed, readying for the coming victory, Marcus led his group of brothers to the center of the sands to meet Lucro's men and they all turned toward the Emperor's box.

The editor prattled on about the Lucro's and Aulus' houses and their victories on the sands. Marcus wished the idiot would simply give the signal to begin. The demon prowled, chanting *kill them all!* But he needed to calm the beast. Death will come, but not now.

A couple of boxes to the left and one row up, Marcus found his dominus and domina sitting. Farina stood with them, but even from this distance the girl who never cared for the games or paid much attention, had her eyes riveted on them. She looked mad with fright. *Odd.*

Below, a box next to the Emperor's, the Senator's box, caught the champion's attention. As usual, he caught Lucilla saunter into her husband's box. She glanced to Marcus and gave him a sultry smile. Even from this distance, he knew she did. Behind her, he saw the sunlight flash off light brown hair....she wouldn't have brought Gustina here?

The thought made him remember when he was summoned to Lucilla's Villa to fuck her and Gustina had to watch. His heart sunk.

The editor yelled for the games to continue but Marcus didn't hear him. He faltered in his step right as the secutor challenged him, knocking him off his balance as the large shield slammed into his side. The layered leather greave protected him but the move infuriated him. Challenge with the weapon was more expected, not a simpering fools way with a shield.

Kill them all!

No, he dampened the desire. This was display only. To get his win at the primus, he needed to curtail that blood-craving creature inside him. But that didn't mean he had to simply play nice. Not at all...he turned, raising his right arm high and swinging downward, hitting the shield fast. He spun and his left arm's weapon stung the gladiator's greave forearm. The man's weapon fell as he winced in pain.

Marcus grinned.

⁂

Lucilla entered the box, flush with excitement. Everything was falling into place so nicely for her. Lucius never mentioned last night. Not that she'd expect he would. That tonic she gave him in his wine made him sleepy, dosed with a drug that'd let him drift in and out of a euphoric sleep—enough for that slave to climb in next to him, arouse him and get the desired results. Oh, she was grateful this morning. Of course, the little cunt did her part as well. In fact, she was so asleep, it was hard to get her ass out of the room. She inhaled deeply, calming her agitation at the girl. After all, wasn't she carrying Lucilla's babe? And she remembered Cernia complaining of being tired.

She shook the tremor that swept through her and reformed her smile. "Lucius," she called, walking up to her husband.

He gazed up and rose to greet her. She noticed his eyes were not warm but wary. Had she been too quick to absolve his "indiscretion"? Or did he suspect he hadn't over-drunk the wine? But his lips curled slightly as he pulled her close.

"Lucilla, how nice of you to come today."

As if he'd thought she'd miss it? She had way too much involved in today. But she managed to appear flustered and pleased at his attention. "I couldn't wait. The Emperor and the spectacles. What a day!" She turned her head down somewhat, trying to assume that demure look many wives and daughters projected but she doubt she ever possessed. "I brought a guest today, darling. I hope you do not mind."

Terpio stepped up. "Senator Vibenius, I'm so honored."

Lucius smiled but it didn't quite reach his eyes. "Terpio Flavus, what a pleasant surprise."

Terpio bent his head slightly in deference. Oh yes, her husband looked pleased over it. Good, she thought.

Lucilla ruffled her stola as an excuse to turn to the sands and scan for Marcus. Her main reason for making such a fuss in arriving, besides checking on her husband, was her scene for the gladiator. The champion's popularity had risen since his last showing—as if it had any higher it could go—and if the crowd pushed for him…the only flaw in her plan was if he won and was rewarded with freedom. Another reason to shuffle that bitch of a slave to Terpio.

She found him, staring straight at her. With a smirk, she raised her chin to show her domination in this game, her lips curving in a lopsided grin. *Oh yes, victory was hers.*

⁓

Marcus couldn't believe that bitch had the audacity to grin at him. The fire inside him was stoked to flames at the thought. After he beat the secutor down, Marcus turned on the rest. But the demonstration was over. Only his opponent had blood. An overly heavy swing of the champion's sword, but he didn't kill the bastard like his demon wanted.

They cleared the sands to a clapping crowd. Once inside their respective gates, a guard stood watch as they turned their blades, shields and helmets over to a servant to take back to the locked vault.

"What in the name of Jupiter were you about out there?" Iduma fumed. "That bitch that you called wife? Certainly Gustina wouldn't have riled you into being a gladiator who broke the simple rules of show."

Marcus snarled quietly when her name rolled off his tongue. While he knew the Brit was better for her than he was, the core of him demanded he kill the bastard and take her for himself, damn the consequences.

"All I saw was that insect," he muttered.

Iduma squinted. "You didn't see her? I'd figured after all this time...I saw her. She looks tired, by chance, but well, in case you wondered."

Marcus glared at him. "Gustina? She's here?" He'd never seen her at the games but then again, Cernia only brought that whore of a slave with her, Verenia. He shuddered.

Laughter filled the antechamber as Iduma left for the resting cell. "Yes."

At the bars, he scanned the boxes. He found Lucilla's, though his view was distorted by dust and the afternoon sunrays. But he did find her, standing behind...he flew to the gated door, gripping the bars. She stood near Terpio. He saw her flinch, even from this distance, as his ex brother stared at her. His blood boiled.

"I've heard," the low voice of Ahaz began. "That the slave formerly of our Villa has a secret." The Syrian laughed. "By chance, I might care to tell you."

Marcus turned to him, anger branching throughout his body, tensing at the sensation. The man knew something about her? "What, Syrian? Speak it now and you may make it through the games."

Ahaz laughed louder. "Dominus sold a slave carrying a child. Amazing, isn't it? Wasn't she involved with you? Or Iduma?" The Syrian's eyes turned hard. "A surprise, really, to learn the Champion can't even keep his woman from spreading her legs for any—"

The last word he might have said was never heard. Marcus' demon took total control. His fist landed squarely on the man's chin and the Syrian struck the ground hard.

No, no more fighting for the boisterous slave. Marcus' would take his life, but then Aulus would withdraw his support and not find the girl to free her. *Damn! Jupiter's balls!*

A child? He tried to focus again through the gating but couldn't see. Had to be Iduma's. Regardless, the Brit's position still boded better than his after the games. It was then he noticed his hand was wet. Strange, it was the middle of the day and he was nowhere near where the crowd might have dropped water or wine.

Another drop. He began to shake irrationally. It suddenly leaked through his troubled mind that the wetness wasn't from rain on a cloudless day or wine from the stadium. No, they were his tears. He lost her in more ways than one. With a hard swallow, he kept his fears and sorrow at bay. The time for that was later, after he won and Aulus fulfilled his wish. Then, the ground could split open and devour him into the Afterlife.

CHAPTER THIRTY-ONE

The noise was deafening. Gustina's blood curdled at it. Clear, loud, enthusiastic, it sounded so different than the last and only time she'd ever been here. The day of her execution. The day Marcus saved her. To this day, she still knew not why he placed her above the rest. Fear kept her questions silent when they lay as lovers. She knew she loved him, despite her own apprehension. Slave relationships were shaky to start with. They had no foundation on solid ground. To be in love with a gladiator only took the dread to a higher level, because many saw the Afterlife so easily by a quick flick of a wrist, a single slice of the blade and all was done. And despite her attempts to hold her heart at bay, she fell for the Roman-turned-gladiator.

Nausea crept up her throat but she swallowed hard. The roar of the Romans all around her made her want to cringe at the very least, when her true desire was to run away. What if they turned on her? And why had her domina, who acted as if Gustina was no better than a whore for doing as she was commanded and sleeping with her dominus, act as if nothing happened and drag her to this? Lucius' eyes flicked at seeing her, only for a second, one she should have missed if she'd been obedient and fixed her gaze low. *Did he remember?* Her skin prickled at the thought of his touch. She'd do anything to save Marcus' child, but spreading her thighs almost undid her.

She did her best to ignore Terpio. Oh, his eyes slid to her often. *Lying bastard wanted her again.* She bit her bottom lip for a second before she caught herself. All the Romans before her cared nothing about her. She was simply a pawn. Well, pawns were necessary to play the game. So she just needed to figure out how.

The crowd silenced as a man's voice boomed across the arena from a perch above one of the massive gates. Dressed in a garish toga of shiny gold and ivory design, his words were loud and deep. She overheard Terpio suggest Lucilla sit as the Editor spoke. Puzzled, she watched the man as impassively as she could. The gilded man spoke of a demonstration between vying houses and their gladiators. His announcement brought the crowd to a cheering ovation, one that sent tremors down Gustina's spine. *For love of the gods, now was not the time to faint!*

Loud, creaking sounds of metal and wood broke through the voices surrounding her. Looking down discreetly, Gustina saw one set of massive iron gates open. In marched four gladiators. She recognized them instantly. From Aulus' Villa, she saw Iduma first. Tall, blond hair escaping the edges of his helmet, he strode confidently out carrying a sword and shield. Her mind stumbled at seeing him. He was a good man, the Brit. She never blamed him for their indiscretion. And she did have feelings for him but he never stirred her heart as deeply as Marcus did. Would she fight so hard to keep the babe if it was his? She knew the answer before the question popped into her head. Of course she would. But he wasn't her Roman, her savior, the man she loved.

Iduma and the other two helmeted gladiators tipped their heads up to the crowd. But the next fighter didn't. She recognized him instantly. Marcus. He stormed across the sands as the crowd's volume rose. When he glanced up, his swords raised to the standing ovation, her mouth dropped open. Her heart skipped a beat, wondering if he saw her. She both hoped he did as well as prayed he didn't. Instinctively her hand strayed to her stomach. Stopping it from doing so took every ounce of strength she had. It fell to her side and she clenched both fists in anxiety over what he would do, if he knew. And the sudden fear, that he'd reject her.

Another gate swung wide and the other set of gladiators entered. Meeting Marcus and the rest, they saluted the emperor, waiting for the orator to give them the start before all fell into chaos. Gustina had never witnessed the fights. Her chance views of watching them practice had been limited at best and she'd remained in the Villa when games occurred. Now, here, her eyes were riveted to the scene below. The sound of swords clashing, men grunting, bellowing fierce growls at attacks and the sound of sand crunching beneath bare feet.

Marcus, though, scared her. He roared like the demon he supposedly possessed had taken charge. Lunging at his opponent, his blade sliced into the man's leather and it seeped red. Blood. She gasped and quickly covered her mouth. Slaves were to remain silent. But it was too late. Lucilla glanced back at her. Though Gustina did take satisfaction at her domina's expression, for her smug smile of moments ago fled. She quickly dropped her gaze, struggling to don the submissive stance of slave. Within a flash, as another wave of clanking emanated from below, she peered through her lashes to watch.

Men, battering, and blood. Not much but enough, mixed with the applause of the people around her, it chilled her blood. She'd heard the word *demonstration* uttered from the man in the raised platform, but the smell of death surrounded her. It was a hungry creature, salivating for more blood, more carnage. She could hear it gnashing its teeth, snarling like the lion had just before.

Closing her eyes, she tried to relax, to block out the noise and keep her fear away. Marcus and Iduma were trained for this. Her love was a champion, winning repeatedly for the crowd. But she needed him to continue living, his child needed him living. It was an abstract thought, since he'd never know of her condition, but for some reason her womb vibrated deeply, and she prayed to the gods for him to live.

She'd give up anything she had left for him and his child to live.

⁂

Lucilla downed another cup of wine and thrust the empty container back at Gustina to fill again. But the girl didn't respond. Glancing back, she saw the girl pale under the sunlight during the demonstration. Her lips curled in satisfaction. She pushed it again and the slave took it, filling it.

"Lucilla," her husband whispered to her. "You switched body slaves today?"

Lucilla inhaled the taste of Lucius shaky behavior. Nothing

like rubbing it farther in about last night. The man, though her husband by law, loved her and she did care for him as much as she could, but his controlling attempts needed to cease. The gods gave her the answer to her barrenness and she'd use every available chance to show him she was in charge in their marriage, not him.

"Yes. Considering her penchant for disturbing the peace, I'd rather have her under watch than loose in a house without my presence."

Lucius raised his brows but said nothing. The magistrate to his side called for his attention and he turned, too quickly Lucilla thought, to talk to the man. She snorted.

"Is your new slave a worry?" Terpio asked.

She relaxed. His voice was strong enough it carried and she caught the tick in Lucius cheek, knowing he heard him. "Why, nothing that a good lashing wouldn't correct."

Gustina bit her lower lip. Truly a wonderful day, Lucilla thought.

"I know her type," he continued. "Perhaps, I may be of assistance...."

The heat bore down on the Colosseum as the afternoon progressed. The awnings were extended from the moorings, covering part of the seating. The best seats closest to the sands and the arena itself did not fall under the shade of the stretched canvas. Only the boxes that held the Vestal Virgins, the Senators and the Emperor had their own tenting blocking partial viewing to those sitting directly above them—the boxes that held the next level of spectators like the magistrates, the wealthy landowners and the well-positioned lanistas.

Aulus knew the routine well and made sure to get an invitation to Lucro's section. Granted, the lanista was one of his biggest rivals but comfort on a day like today, especially with Cernia's condition, warranted complimenting the prick to get an invitation. Of course, that also entailed putting up with the man's arrogance and lack of good breeding.

"Aulus, truly, we may return to our section," Cernia said softly to her husband's ear.

He took her hand and squeezed. "No, you are in need of shade. I will not have you fall under the heat." He kissed the top of her head as he glanced back at Farina and gave a nod. With Verenia still ill, he insisted she bring this slave to attend on her. The girl was familiar with the games and knew her position well. Right now, it was with his wife and, later, in his bed.

The game's primus was next and anticipation filled the stands. Aulus scanned the seats, trying to gauge the crowd. The main fight was to involve four, not two, gladiators. His two prime men, Marcus and Iduma, against Lucro's top two. It rubbed Aulus wrong for the change in proceedings. But Trajan enjoyed the demonstration tremendously and had become bored as the afternoon dragged on. No doubt the heat played its part in the emperor's yawning but several of the senators and lanistas witnessed it. A quick decision was made and the primus turned into a gathering of the top two fighters from the highest-ranking houses.

Lucro made some remark that had the others around Aulus laughing but he'd missed it. His gaze narrowed, but he joined the jovial spirit even though he didn't want to. Given his choice, he would have stayed in his normal seats, but his wife and heir demanded he swallow his pride to pursue seats in a better box.

The trumpets sounded above the deafening noise of the mob sitting in the stands. The primus was next. The gates opened and his champion and the Brit entered the sands together.

Aulus' mind replayed the champion's request. He wanted Gustina found and freed and Iduma freed as well to care for the snippet. The return for such a gesture meant having his champion forever. He'd thrown a stone into the river and watched the currents when he reminded Marcus' that the Brit may win the crowd and his freedom, then what of the promise? But the man wasn't a complete idiot. He insisted Gustina be found and freed as well. Thinking gladiators—who would have guessed? But would this crowd be turned so? Only the outcome would tell.

⁂

Marcus stood, watching from the dark alcove behind the barred doors. She stood in the back of the senator's box, her features shaded, but he knew the figure. His woman. Gustina.

He feared he'd never see her again. Doubted she wanted to see him after the last encounter when he bedded that cunt. His own stupidity taunted him, thinking he could take control and show the evil creature not all the world was hers for the asking. But the gods showed him who was in charge. And it wasn't him. The bitch's satisfaction, her laugh, he still could hear.

No, he understood he held nothing for his love. He was a traitor, a murderer and a whore.

She would bear a child. His? Not likely. The gods would never grant him any form of relief in this life or the next. No, it had to be Iduma's. It *would* be the Brit's, regardless of who the true father was.

Once he wanted to kill the man for fucking her. But now, it was reversed. He wanted to die. To ever believe she could save his tattered soul, mend it, and make him alive had been a fool's dream. No, the gods would deny him even that. He was damned. Better to leave her with the Brit.

Prepared to face the primus, to win, selling his soul to Hades so she could be free, Marcus breathed deep. The change in the games wasn't good. To put him and Iduma up to fight Lucro's men left the chance, though obscure, neither made it out alive. He gave Tevia a request to pay tribute to Jupiter that regardless of the outcome, she'd be set free. Aulus' body slave nodded, and before he left, Marcus got what he really wanted. The knowledge his dominus knew his dying desire and that he wouldn't die without it.

The crowd stomped their feet, their clapping hands joining as one massive noise to bring on the primus. The cleaning crew on the sands worked as hard as they could but the last bout had been bloody.

Marcus stood and closed his eyes, breathing the smell of the blood and dirt deeply. A truly intoxicating scent, blood. It filled his nose and he could hear his heart pounding faster and faster. Sweet, tangy, mixed with dirt and torn flesh, it drove his longing, his *need,* to feel it. Nothing felt the same as sinking his blade into another man, the red river spurting and pouring from the slash. The gulping of the victim when he found purchase in the right spot, the fear in the eyes as he became coated in blood. Death swirled around them and he relished it, longing to sacrifice to it, elevating him to the status of a god in the Colosseum.

A slave boy shoved two gladius before him, his tools for the spectacle. Iduma was at his side. He hadn't heard the Brit arrive and under normal circumstances, would have said nothing. But this time, it was different.

"Watch yourself, Brit." He considered adding more, but decided this was sufficient. To add her to the mix might ruin the man's concentration.

Iduma laughed. "Speak for yourself brother. She waits for you."

No, she does not. She is for you.

The fop in the gold and ivory robes, the editor, once more began his oration of the event. Marcus drowned his voice out as he gripped the handles of his swords.

With the trumpets and the yells, the screeching of the doors opening seemed silent. Marcus walked out on the field, letting his mental self disappear as he concentrated on the men walking toward them. The tall one was there, cocky in his walk, over confident of the outcome. *Ass.* His cohort not any less. Arrogant assholes, bother them.

The editor from above silenced the mob and sectioned the gladiators off in pairs. Marcus got the big brute. He smirked. Nothing new. He flipped his swords in his hands and swung them up as the crowd roared.

Planting his feet in first position, Marcus stood, toes embedded in the sand, ready. The gladiator in front of him grunted. Marcus couldn't help but grin.

"Begin!"

He swung at the titan in front of him. The man blocked his blow. Cocking his chest to the right, he swung again, high and low. His blade impacted the greaves but nothing more than a groan was uttered. Anger inflamed him as he spun and struck again, but the blades did no damage. Stunned, Marcus squinted. Something was off.

His demon wasn't there.

No snarling, no demanding of blood and death. No *kill them all!*

He blinked again, his insides searching for the beast. For the first time in ages, he stood on the sands and didn't know what to do.

The gladiator in front of him yelled his attack, his blade in the air and his shield covering him.

Out of total habit, Marcus parried the attack, blocking the giant's advance one swing at a time as he tried to figure his bearings. No drive for the kill left him bereft of attack plans. He suddenly found himself faced with another man in the arena to amuse the mob with blood.

Lost, fighting to regain balance, he blocked every blow and found his strength ebbing. Out of the corner of his eye, he found Iduma one on one with his man. Good, if he kept with the attack, he'd win. Then Marcus would release his soul at the mercy of this man's sword.

But it didn't work that way. Iduma roared, blaring across the sands, sword in front as his armed hand came to the man's side. His opponent leapt back, out of reach of the sword as the Brit lost his footing and fell the floor, his blade underneath. A cry of pain echoed in the air as the Brit rolled on the sands, pulling his small knife out and shoved it into the foot of his attacker. The man tried to move his foot only to express a rearing pain. Iduma twisted the blade, bringing the man to his knees and then to the ground, blood pooling around his feet.

Marcus saw this and yelled, racing to his man, swords high. The Lucro man stood, half-bent and defensive. He swung as Marcus began to fall, but missed. Within a second, the champion's blade fell, its sharp edge hitting a hard substance at the skull of the man. Pressing further, Marcus drove the blade harder, breaking the man's head open as he collapsed. No sound came from his lips as Marcus pushed. The usual euphoric feeling of his muscles driving him to a place of victory as death descended over them was absent. Odd. The win failed to register with him. No, he raced to the Brit.

Marcus stared at Iduma, holding his brother in his arms, arms now drenched in blood.

The Brit laughed shakily. "Go, brother. Claim your victory." He coughed, blood spewing across him. More blood filled the Brit's mouth and he spat it out, his body racked as the wounds took their toll. Another gag and the man stopped, mouth open, bloody and his eyes rolled back, dull and vacant of life.

Marcus opened his mouth and a roar of indignation resounded off the walls as the man before him descended to the Afterlife.

Iduma's man staggered to his feet, bloody, the wound across his chest open but not complete. Blade in arc, he swung at the champion. The gladiator ducked, rolled and stopped behind the man.

Coming to his feet, weapons poised, Marcus still silently called for the demon but the vacancy continued. *Had it ever existed?*

Nothing jolted the creature or Marcus' killing need. The other gladiator sliced at him and the sting etched along his chest but nothing more. When the blood trickled in his hand, he first noticed the cut. And that he'd dropped one of his swords.

Hatred pushed him where the demon hadn't and he yelled. The attack on Lucro's gladiator came fast and hard but Marcus' opponent didn't stop. Struggling to stand, Marcus' injured hand refused to cooperate and the man sliced into his flesh. He swallowed the pain that rolled through him as he tried to manage the remaining sword with one hand. The other gladiator, though bloody himself, laughed.

The sound riveted Marcus into action. Pain or not, he faced the man who killed Iduma. Killed the man Marcus was sure Gustina would be safe with. And he was the Roman's only friend. Anger and mourning engulfed him. He pounced on the gladiator, his sword piercing the gladiator's exposed middle abdomens, the sound of flesh ripping radiant to the champion's torn soul. His victim fell, the blade deep in him as blood poured out. Marcus twisted the blade and the well of red intoxicating blood increased.

Within a minute, Marcus stood above him, inhaling gulps of grime and sweet, tangy blood, pleased. But as he turned to leave, he saw the Brit's body on the sands, lying in a pool of blood, eyes wide open, as if watching him from the Afterlife.

Marcus stood, unable to move away. His plans were ruined. He must see to Gustina's safety. He, a killing machine, to protect another life or two. *Two.* She carried Iduma's babe. How could she want him, especially now that he allowed the Brit to die?

Emotionless, fighting to retain control, he vaguely heard the mob around him. Did they want him free? To see him kill more?

The result out there wasn't what he believed would happen. Aulus promised to free

Gustina and Iduma. Iduma was dead. Was the bargain dead as well?

And where in Jupiter's name was that demon?

CHAPTER THIRTY-TWO

The tears wouldn't stop. She tried to make them stop, but it was impossible. Shutting her eyes did little good. Tears seeped out anyway. At least she managed to hold in the sounds of her sobs. But the afternoon played over and over in her mind.

Iduma slain.

Marcus looked as if his life ended as well. She heard the anguished howl from his lips despite the raucous cheering of the crowds that filled the Colosseum.

Her stomach twisted and her ears buzzed. Leaning against the wall, she tried to gulp in air before she collapsed.

"Gustina, are you all right?"

She opened her eyes and found her dominus staring at her in concern. A Roman worried about his slave? Publicly? With a hard swallow, she nodded. "Yes, dominus. I just, just," and the tears started again.

Everyone in their section stood, talking animatedly about the last match. Her domina and Terpio spoke to another man, though Terpio looked her way periodically, a sly look in his eye. *Dear Juno, she was going to faint.*

Lucius took her arm and helped her sit on the marbled bench. "Can't have you falling. You'd be trampled." He smiled at her.

Lost, Gustina didn't know what to do. Slaves don't sit in the presence of their owners. And his attention confused her. She'd forced herself on his drugged body last night. Surely he knew that. Instead, he kept her from fainting and now shoved a cup into her hands.

"Drink this. It will help."

She nodded and took a sip. The red wine was warm and tart as it slid down her throat. It heated her insides, settling her stomach which surprised her.

"I know you came from Aulus' house. You knew the slain gladiator?" His voice was calm, soothing even. She hated her domina for last night. Her husband was a good man. But she said nothing, only nodding her head to his question.

Without thinking, her hand went to her stomach. He noticed and his gaze came back to her.

Jupiter, help!

∞

Lucius thought the last match was the best he'd seen in a long time. Not a huge fan of the gladiatorial fights, with Trajan here, he could not refuse. Lucilla here was not a surprise. Anywhere Roman Society sat, she was present. Her companion, Terpio, shouldn't have been a surprise but it was. For his wife to arrive with another man boded ill. Especially as the vermin pawed her in the presence of her husband and she didn't even object. Lucius supposed it was her way of letting him know she wasn't happy he lay with a slave. He shook his head.

Bringing said slave was also unusual for her. Her justification might work for other men but he didn't believe the girl had the strength to cause a ruckus. In fact, she looked pale and ill.

No matter how hard he tried, his mind was still murky about last night. And he nursed a headache still, which was so unlike him. He vaguely remembered his rigid cock entering her, then he'd awakened next to the girl, neither of them with clothes on. But he wasn't the sort to mess with the help, not since he was a young man. Lucilla was beautiful and alluring so why would he bed a slave?

The puzzle had too many missing pieces and that irked him.

The last match had been quite spectacular to see. It took his thoughts off his aching head and his cock's adventure. But when he heard the slave squeal, he turned. She looked as white as the marble he sat on and a wave of compassion swept over him. Helping her sit down, he gave a better look. Her color was returning after he'd given her the spiced wine.

He wasn't surprised she knew the slain gladiator. But when her hand rested on her lower stomach, it made his mind flip. They'd only had last night. Wasn't it a bit early to know if she carried a child of his?

The slave in front of him began to shake. He squinted. Her eyes were fixated on the people behind him. "What frightens you?"

She looked at him and her voice dropped. "My former dominus."

Lucius paused. Aulus wasn't here. He glanced behind him. A couple of senators in deep conversation stood two benches away and Lucilla with Terpio. For a brief second, Terpio's gaze slid to the girl but turned away when he saw Lucius.

That swift dart of the Roman's eyes made the senator frown. "Terpio Flavus?"

She nodded. "He condemned me for killing my domina. But I'm not the one who tainted her wine."

The frightened wounded look of the slave before him set his mind to recall the tale. He vaguely remembered the stories of how Terpio lost his position in government. It occurred when he had taken Lucilla with him on senate business ,so they weren't in Rome. If he remembered correctly, Terpio not only lost his position but his mistress and his wife. What was the story on his wife? Wasn't it the woman had been poisoned? And the blame was placed on her body slave? *Gustina?*

The girl had been in his Villa now for a couple of weeks. He'd seen no signs of foul-play by her. In fact, hadn't he seduced her last night? And she remained in his bed afterward? Yes. And he sat here, fine and healthy, despite a nagging headache.

"Do you know how she came upon such an end?" he prodded.

Her head bobbed quickly. "By drinking wine newly arrived that day."

"From Terpio?"

Her eyes looked troubled. "I know they had disputed everything of late. I assumed he ordered her gone since they fought. She could be very cruel to him." Her head bent down, again. "She wasn't pleased he took me every night." A shudder racked her shoulders.

Terpio? An intriguing twist on the man who condemned his brother to slavery for being a traitor. The same individual who hung on Lucius' wife and hoped her husband would endorse his return to position.

What was the man up to?

Lucilla worked hard to keep her smile. Lucius' comforting that slave in a way should have consoled her. It worked well into her plan but ire still filled her. What was it about this girl? Terpio had an absurd fascination with her, blaming her for his wife's death—a death she knew he wanted. Marcus also held her in high regard. Lucilla snorted. The slave was a whore, like him. And a condemned killer.

Now, Lucius too. Her back teeth gritted as she forced her lips up in a smile, speaking to Terpio.

"As we leave, you will take her," she continued, the noise of the mob loud enough to drown her words.

"Yes, as we agreed," he replied. His smile was genuine. Another stab at her. Jupiter, she'd kill the cunt if she didn't need her baby.

Lucilla tilted her head, hiding her hate. "The gods bless us." She smiled. An arm slid under hers. Lucius. Good. "And I must go celebrate their blessings with Cernia and Aulus, for having a victory today and in the future."

Her husband gave her a quizzical look. The gods couldn't have blessed her better by laying this gift at her feet. "Darling, Terpio will take your problem away."

He frowned. "Gustina?"

Damn, when had Lucius become so familiar with the cunt's name? Definitely time for the whore to go.

"Yes." She reached up on her toes to his ear. "It is for the best. I need you all for me."

Her husband nodded.

Over his shoulder, she glared at the crying girl. Tears for the gladiators. Lucilla chuckled inside. The slave hadn't seen a good reason to really get upset...yet.

Cernia walked into her Villa and sighed. Her back hurt and she was tired. A day at the Colosseum wore her out. She wanted a bath and food, not necessarily in that order.

Verenia appeared before her. "Your bath, domina."

She nodded. It pleased her the slave recovered. Nasty procedure, aborting a babe, but necessary. The fact that her friend intended to steal that murderer's babe and pass off the child as her husband's to raise still rubbed her wrong. The senator didn't deserve that deceit. It was up to the gods to decide, though. Right now, she had her own blessing to thank them for. If she could just get past the exhaustion, hunger pains and feeling sick with hardly a bulge showing. She sighed.

Verenia helped her but Cernia did notice her wince and her eyes glistening from the after-effects of the drug aborting her child. She ignored the girl's discomfort.

After her bath, she did feel better except for the hunger. As she settled on the lounge near the Atrium, she sent the girl to get her food.

"Domina, Lucilla Vibenia."

Cernia looked up and found Lucilla walking toward her. "Lucilla?"

The senator's wife laughed, her face animated with a grin that sparkled. "Cernia, I had to come and help you celebrate your victory today!" She reached her and kissed Cernia on the mouth.

Cernia smiled at her guest. "Yes, it was a momentous day, even at the loss."

"Ah, but your champion remains the top in Rome," Lucilla added, sitting down on the next lounge. "Truly worthy at any price."

Truly? She doubted Aulus felt the same at this moment. Her stomach wanted to collapse, empty of nourishment. But she nodded in agreement.

"Ah, and," Lucilla waved to her slave to come closer. Dora came carrying a wine pitcher. "I brought a wine to celebrate." She took the jug and pulled the cork from the lip to pour into waiting cups. Handing the jug back to Dora, she waved the slave back.

Cernia took the proffered cup from her friend, though she did see a panicked flash in the slave's eyes that vanished quickly.

"Yes," she said. "But as he is still reigning champion, I take it you will…."

"For the love of the gods, no, not today," Lucilla laughed.

"Ah, then you know, we'll need that Gustina returned," Cernia stated, taking a grape from the bowl that Farina held before her.

Lucilla gazed at her. "Alas, I do not have her." She popped a fruit into her mouth.

"Truly? She was in your hands to keep until this day."

Her friend didn't look at her. In fact, she avoided her gaze, taking more grapes.

Cernia's stomach roiled. Aggravated, she downed another grape and took a sip of the wine.

"I found her in Lucius' embrace," Lucilla reported, as if she was mad which Cernia knew was a farce. All the woman cared for was her husband's money and position, but having him in her bed? "I can't have that whore taking his seed when it is mine."

"Granted, it could be planted in her."

"No, she still carries your champion's babe. I told you I have need of that seedling."

Her tone actually made Cernia cringe. "You will carry this plot further? That babe will bear no resemblance to your husband."

Lucilla's laugh made a chill wrap around Cernia's spine. It sounded evil to the core. Her belly ached and instinctively, she placed her hand on her mini bulge. A jolt of pain riveted her stomach. Hunger as an expectant mother turned odd. Ignoring the pain, she glanced at her friend again. Lucilla's eyes glowed eerily in the sunlight as she returned the stare.

"Few know of this deception," she muttered softly as she walked closer to Cernia, her hand holding her wine cup, whirling it. It was then Cernia noticed it remained mostly full. She frowned.

Lucilla waved the slaves away and stood before her, placing her cup on the table before them. Her stare hadn't broken, but her expression went from excitement over the babe she'd steal from the slave to quizzical. How strange....

That's when another twist in her stomach hit. Stronger, harder than the other. She gasped.

Lucilla bit her lip. Trying to stop a smile? Why would a grin form at her pain? But before Cernia asked, it subsided.

Her guest came to her side, the hint of curved lips gone.

"Oh, dear, it must be the heat and hunger, don't you think? Here, drink this." She pressed the wine cup to Cernia's lips.

The spicy wine slid into her mouth and down her throat. It tasted so sweet, only a tang remained afterward. She took another sip and pulled back. Lucilla put the cup down, a tick in her cheek making Cernia's gaze narrow. Why hadn't her friend drunk any of the wine? She brought it.

As the last thought came to her, so did another wrenching pain, bad enough to cause her to double over. She reached for Lucilla, grabbing hard as the pain engulfed her. "What is happening to me? To my baby?" A glance at her friend made her panic. Lucilla had a sadistic gleam in her eyes, her head tilted, watching her like she would a flower withering under the hot sun.

"Lucilla!"

But the woman wheedled her way out of Cernia's reach. "No need to worry. I hear the pain won't last long."

Cernia widened her eyes, horrified. "What have you done?"

Her lips curled as she stepped back. "Evened the playing field. Eliminating any possible interference."

Daggers drove inside her, slicing her abdomen. They were inside her, ripping her to pieces. "Lucilla!" She reached for her and fell to the tile floor, her hand snagging the hem of Lucilla's stola.

The woman's hand grabbed the fabric and yanked it out of Cernia's weakening hold. "Good bye, Cernia." And she turned her back to her.

Cernia tried again but the pain stabbed at her. It was then she realized she was wet between her legs. She twisted and saw her yellow stola turning blood red. She screamed.

Marcus sat in the baths, numb. The others had come and gone only for him to still be here. Somehow, he'd taken the Colosseum's dirt off his body, but the blood and grime remained. No amount of scraping with the strigil could remove it. Slowly, he pulled himself out of the oil, grazing his skin again with the instrument. Nothing worked. All he heard was the crowd's applause as Iduma fell, bleeding as his life ebbed away. He shut his eyes, trying to will the scene and noise to leave him. But there he found Gustina, standing behind Terpio. A chilly scenario, just like this bathing chamber.

She is waiting for you.

He frowned. Iduma's voice. Rapidly he rubbed his eyes. He must be going mad.

You're not mad yet. This time, the voice was right next to him, as if Iduma sat there. *Go and save her.*

Marcus snorted. "I am a slave. I cannot leave here because a spirit comes to haunt me."

Jupiter, that was it. The demon deserted him so ghosts could come.

Listen for the wail.

"A wail? From the ludas?" He laughed. Even to him, he sounded possessed. "There's wine and whores. Wailing all night for cocks and cunts."

Listen. She needs you more than ever now.

He tried to shake off the voice. Angry, he rose. He scraped his abdomen again one last stroke. The edge hit the slice in his side and he winced at the sting. Without looking, he knew it bled again. He grabbed his subligaculum, wrapping it around his waist. Fuck. He'd go get wine and drink himself to sleep.

Go.

Fuck, he was going. Straight to the wine stacks near the gates to the Villa. He remained champion. For that, he deserved a better jug than the shit his brothers were downing.

At the gate, the guard opened it, lowering his head in honor of Marcus' win. *Cock's blood, he probably won a month's wage today.* It only stirred his self pity. The win brought him fame and that was all. It took more than he gained. He'd lost his friend and his woman. And the protection of her baby. He downed a hefty swallow.

Then he heard it. It wasn't a wail but a bloody scream. From the Villa.

He dropped the wine jug and bolted past the guard up the stairs.

∞

Aulus barely made it into his own house when he heard it. A woman's scream. It ripped through the Villa like a lightning bolt. Cernia! He took off at a run to find her.

It took but a minute to find her. On the tiles in the Atrium, curled up, clutching her stomach. Blood pooled around her legs. Her face was twisted in pain and she doubled again as another ear-piercing sound flooded his ears.

"Cernia, darling." He was at her side, kneeling, his knees in the blood. After years of gladiatorial games, one would think he'd be immune to the mess but this time, it was different. Amongst the floral scent from the garden of the Atrium was the tangy odor of iron and spice. His hand stroked her face as she calmed but her skin was pale, like the marble of the columns in his house.

Farina knelt at his side, a blanket in her arms. He grabbed it from her and bent to cover his wife and pick her up. Thankfully, her screaming stopped but her skin was cool to his touch.

"What happened?" He didn't look at the slave, concentrating too hard on Cernia.

"Senator Vibenius' wife arrived, bearing gift for the win." The girl's voice was shaky.

"And?"

"They talked and sent us away, but we heard anyway." Farina leaned closer. "The domina's gift was a jug of tainted wine the woman brought. Verenia noticed the smell later. Silva."

Silva? The drug to rid a woman of child? From Lucilla? He shook violently. "Call the medicus."

"Yes, dominus."

Aulus sat next to his wife. At least she was breathing, but she still bled. The child was no doubt gone. The gods were angry at him but for what? He needed to know and correct it so, hopefully, they'd leave her with him. But his mind drew a blank until the answer came to a screeching halt before him.

Marcus.

The gladiator's eyes were on fire as he stood, breathing heavily from his jaunt to the Atrium. Skin glistening still from the baths. Yes, there was the problem. Aulus promised to free the man's woman. He'd failed to do so. An oversight to be rectified...with another price.

"I heard the screams. A woman in pain."

Aulus nodded and realized his vision of the champion blurred. The thought of losing Cernia was undoing him.

"She's been poisoned."

Marcus frowned. "Who would hate you so like this?"

He lifted pained eyes to the gladiator. "It wasn't for me. It was for you." He clutched his wife's hand tighter. "Lucilla."

Verenia had been standing off behind the decorative screen, but Aulus knew she was there. Tentatively, she approached. "I know why, dominus. The woman is incapable of getting seed to lay." She swallowed and glanced at Marcus. "Gustina carries a babe and she plans to steal it and call it her own."

Aulus looked at his wife. She had passed out. It left him with only the slave girl. "Why attack my wife?" His voice was harsh with determination to find out the truth.

"Because she knew what the woman wanted." Verenia ducked her head. "She wants to destroy those who know."

Aulus' heart plummeted. She tried to kill his wife, her friend, to protect her deceit. Then she'd have no worries....

His thought never finished as a soul-wretching cry filled the air. A war cry. A demonic yell for vengeance. From the one man who demanded his freedom now.

Marcus.

Without a sound, he nodded. Knew the man understood.

In a split second, the gladiator was gone—on the prowl for love and vengeance.

CHAPTER THIRTY-THREE

She stood again in Terpio's Villa. Her legs shook and she forced them to be still. Clenching her hands at her sides, she still couldn't believe this had happened. Returned to him, her former dominus. A murderer. She feared now he intended to kill her.

Gustina's gaze roved over the interior of the building, noticing no changes since she'd been dragged from here months ago. A shiver raced over her skin. Memories flooded her mind. The night her domina lay dead, and he grinning at her for holding the woman. An eerie cast on his reflection. As if he knew something she didn't. *Or was it regret?*

She shut her eyes, forcing the vision from her mind. Her stomach roiled. Hunger. She was simply starving. It overwhelmed her at times. Dora told her it was a sign of the gods that all was well with the child. His hunger—yes, the babe was a gladiator's son, her instinct told her, and he was ravenous. She licked her lips and bit her lower lip. Patience. She needed to remain calm.

That was one thing she remembered so well about Terpio. To be impatient, or afraid, in his presence usually brought the whip or worse. To protect her child, she'd appear docile until she could find a way out of here.

Buzzing started in her ears and the room turned hazy. She put her hand against the column to steady herself. Thoughts rushed into her mind, visions of Marcus on the sands, bloody and enraged, like a bull. He'd sliced after the other man, possessed like a demon. A man she barely recognized. She'd cheered for her champion, silently of course, and prayed to the gods he'd win.

The shadowy images of Iduma clouded her mind. He too had swung, attacking his opponent, but he fell beneath his opponent's blows. Never to rise again. Her vision blurred. Was she wrong to have shunned him so? Had her denial of his passion for her been wrong? Maybe, if she'd given in, she wouldn't have been sold to the deceitful woman, the one who turned her over to Terpio. No, no, she couldn't. Her heart belonged to the champion. But still, the Brit's death tore at her heart. She did care for him, but she didn't love him like she did Marcus.

"Gustina!"

Startled, she turned and saw Neleus setting down the basket he carried. In an instant, he crushed her in his arms.

"We thought you went to the Afterlife," he murmured, his face at her neck, buried in her hair.

She had missed him. Her only friend in a household of submissive, silent slaves. Terpio's affection for variation left no one safe, or so she assumed. Neleus, though, broke through her wall of withdrawal after the first time she was assaulted. Close to her age, he'd assured her that she'd survive. He taught her the way to shut off the emotions, to distance herself even if her body was abused. A method she'd become used to, wearing it as armor, as most slaves did. It was comfortable, safe…until she met Marcus. She closed her mind at the thought and smiled back at him.

"No, the gods weren't finished with me yet."

He grinned. "I'm pleased. I know this is not the place you wanted to be but it eases the heart to see you again." Taking a step back, he eyed her carefully. She fought to keep her hand from going to her stomach. No need to disclose her condition yet. But it was as if he knew. He frowned at her. She bit her lower lip, her insides fluttering. "You stood there, looking as if Jupiter had rejected you."

Gustina swallowed hard and tried to return his smile. It didn't work. "I prayed to the gods to never return here." She lifted her eyes to him. "Apparently, they refused my prayers. Terpio will kill me, now that he has me again."

"Tsk," Neleus snorted. Taking her arm in his, he guided her to his basket of fruit. "Hardly. If nothing else, he's been unbearable since that Roman cunt stopped using his cock."

Gustina tensed, puzzled. Neleus normally ignored the exploits of Terpio outside the Villa, so whom was he talking about?

He must have picked up on her thoughts as he continued. "Yes, that overpriced whore of his, Lucilla, denied him her bed for another cock."

It was good he grasped her arm. She stumbled at his statement. Yes, she saw the cock that replaced Terpio's. But why would she choose a slave? Why Marcus? For the love of the gods, no doubt he'd take his anger on this out on her...the "killer" of his wife. She shuddered at the thought.

"Oh, Gustina," Neleus said softly. "I think it isn't as you fear. I truly think he has missed you."

She stopped, her legs no longer moving. Heart racing, her ears buzzed again and the edges of blackness surrounded her. If he missed her, she was in bigger danger. "Oh, Neleus," she whimpered, her hand falling to her stomach as she collapsed to the floor.

∞

Lucius walked into the bathing chamber, wanting to jump into the waters and cleanse away the filth of the day at the Colesseum. A day of blood and dirt, most of the *dirt* coming in the form of politics and Lucilla. Sitting with his fellow senators always made the day better because he wasn't a man who was thrilled by the games. The day grew tiresome with her there with that toad, Terpio. And his wife had brought that slave Gustina. The poor girl. The games were too much for her. At the primus, he heard her wail, muffled but still audible to the discerning ear. The champion and another from Aulus' house. She must have known them.

Lucilla heard her too. He saw the quick smile on her face before she realized he saw it. *Whatever was the woman up to?*

He rubbed his eyes. And last night, he bedded the girl. Damn, he just couldn't recall it. She was pretty enough but he wasn't the type to fuck slaves or join with others who visited the whores. No, those days had been short and brief, in his youth. The Senate and his beautiful wife commanded his full attention. So why last night? If he could only remember....

"Dominus."

He opened his eyes. Lost in thought, he'd barely noticed

the slave removing his clothing, but free of the cloth, he walked to the stone pool and sank in. The soothing waters calmed him instantly.

"Yes, Sisera?" He looked at his body slave who stood near the doorway. "Did you find it?" This slave was more attentive that any man he knew. And, better yet, he knew how to read. He sent him to rifle through Lucilla's belongings, in search of a document she might have taken that concerned Terpio's family. He hoped it was found and then he could kick the man out of his house and away from his wife forever.

Sisera was slight in build. Quiet but also bold when sent on a task. He stepped closer. The slave held a thick scroll. Pleased, the senator motioned to the other slave to get him his robes. He rose from the waters, waiting.

"You may not like what you find, dominus," Sisera stated flatly.

Lucius frowned. He saw the flicker of a smile in the slave's schooled features, which threw him. *Now what had the bitch gotten herself into?*

∽

Marcus strode down the streets to Lucilla's house, anger in every step, but not over his domina's poisoning. The cunt maneuvered her position to take Gustina and to steal her babe. He seethed. There was little doubt in his mind she'd kill Gustina after the child was born. Though Aulus set him free, Lucilla had placed him on this path—to kill his former wife. But first, Gustina must be safe.

The demon growled as Marcus' hand gripped the handle of the sword he stuck in his balteus. He figured he must be an odd sight. A gladiator storming down the streets on the outer edges of the city. It was late afternoon, and most Romans were bathing or eating. Gladiators armed and walking freely would frighten people because no one forgot the days of slave uprisings. The memories of the wars against Spartacus and his renegades still lingered even after a hundred years. He'd expect the praetorians to arrive soon. He'd kill them all if they stood in his path.

Kill them all!

Yes, he heard the evil inside him. The snarling became louder with every step, drawing him closer to her. It was time for Lucilla to meet his dark companion, the creature she and Terpio let loose when they condemned him a traitor, stripping him of all humanity. Gustina made his madness retreat so they took her away. No more. It was time they paid for their crimes.

As he got to the backside of the Villa, he saw a slave girl exit a door with a basket of colorful cloth. Laundry. Her eyes widened when she saw him and she dropped her load.

"Marcus," she whispered loudly as she raced to him. "You must go and save Gustina."

His gaze narrowed, not recognizing her. "I'm here to do that. Then I'm going to kill your domina."

She gulped and stepped back. "But Gustina isn't here. She's in more danger where they sent her. She is with child and...."

He couldn't help but shudder. To keep being reminded she carried Iduma's babe ate at him, regardless of his feelings for her or the loss of his gladiatorial brother. He beat the impulse to crush the girl for bringing it up. "I thought Lucilla owned her."

"She doesn't, not but in face only," the slave stuttered.

This made no sense. "Explain yourself. Who are you in this house?"

"I'm Dora, Lucilla's body slave." She glanced down, her voice turning bitter. "Not a position I desired. But I do hear many things. Gustina was to be here until you won today and hence returned to your Villa. When domina discovered the girl carried, she concocted her plan to keep the child as hers," Dora stopped. A sob escaped her mouth. "She forced her to lay with our dominus so he would think the child is his and the gods want domina to raise the child, since seed is denied growth in her."

Marcus couldn't quite quell the minor pleasure of knowing the gods hated Lucilla. If she couldn't conceive, then she'd steal another's babe. And his domina knew the plan. What a truly evil creature his wife had turned into.

"Gustina was sent to another, until proper time to announce her condition."

Fury flashed through him. To another? "Where?" he snarled.

"Terpio Flavus. The man who accused Gustina of

poisoning his wife and sentenced her to die."

His demon roared and his vision turned blood red. If he touched her, Marcus would rip his heart out.

Kill him!

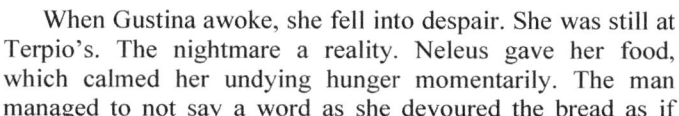

∞

When Gustina awoke, she fell into despair. She was still at Terpio's. The nightmare a reality. Neleus gave her food, which calmed her undying hunger momentarily. The man managed to not say a word as she devoured the bread as if she'd been starving for days. But there was his knowing look, tinged with sadness. Could he tell she was carrying? Or did he dread turning her over to Terpio? Perhaps both?

Instinctively, her hand strayed to her stomach. And every time, she stopped it before it got there. Such a minor sign, especially when her stomach still appeared flat. But she knew beneath her tunic, a small hard bulge formed. She'd protect her babe.

Now, though, an hour later, she followed Neleus to Terpio's bedchambers. She remembered this route well. Fear snaked up her spine. No wonder her fellow slave had had that look earlier. How many times he comforted her after she returned from here, soothing away her pain and tears, teaching her how to forget? Her skin prickled as the memories flooded her mind and wrapped around her, closing in tight, strangling her.

Her lower stomach and its hidden secret suddenly turned heavy, like a lead weight. She breathed in deep, trying to settle her nerves.

Before her, seated on a lounge, was Terpio. Upon seeing her, he smiled and got up.

"Gustina, the gods have blessed me."

And cursed me. She stopped. He stood not much taller than her. Fine black hair, brown eyes, he was the epitome of Roman breeding. Barefoot and wearing a long flowing robe, he went to the table nearby. He picked up a pear and knife, slicing a bite off. She watched, the knife drawing her attention. A weapon. Small but lethal.

As he ate his piece of fruit, he stared at her hungrily. "Oh, how I have missed you," he cooed, walking to her. He sliced another piece off and offered it to her mouth.

A favorite game of his, being the giver of pleasure. Repulsive, considering the farce disappeared when his cock rammed into her. Her body steeled against him. The babe nestled in her womb needed protection. Slowly, her mouth opened and he slid the fruit inside. The brush of his fingers and the edge of the blade against her lips almost made her recoil.

His grin broadened. "It will be good to see you." His gaze lowered, "again."

Her hands clenched at her sides. *Never*.

Another piece of pear pressed against her lips. She opened her mouth, her teeth grabbed the fruit and tugged it from his grip. Terpio laughed and waved Neleus away.

"I understand you've been with my brother," he stated, setting the knife on the table.

His brother?

"Ah, he didn't tell you. Interesting." He sat on the cushioned lounge and motioned for her to come. "Marcus wasn't always a gladiator. He is my brother."

Her feet stumbled for a second. Visions of her champion came to mind. His dark hair and warm dark brown eyes, broad shoulders, muscled body. He was a Roman. She knew that. But related to this beast before her?

"He is a traitor, nothing more," Terpio added, as if he'd said too much. The stern look cracked and he laughed nervously. "But enough of him." His hands grabbed her arms and crushed her against him.

She gasped, the wind knocked out of her at the impact. His body wasn't hard like marble as Marcus' was. Her hands automatically came up against his chest, flattening, trying to gain her balance. But his arm snaked around her waist and he buried his head in her neck, his stiff arousal against her abdomen.

Fear in her swelled as he pushed his staff against the bulge of her babe. Anger fought for control. He would not do vile things to her again. Her body tensed. When he nipped at her neck, she gritted her teeth. No. Not. Again.

His hands lowered and caressed her buttocks' swell, cupping underneath, pressing her against him. "Oh, Gustina," he sighed against her mouth.

Wine. His breath reeked of it. A rancid smell, making her

stomach ache and bile threaten to rise. His hand wandered under her tunic, his fingers traced the slit between her legs, and slipped inside her. She winced.

"And you've missed me, I feel," he whispered.

Hate flared through her. Her body betrayed her and him. She didn't miss him but this wetness was a constant issue with her condition. *How dare he use it as a favor to him!* Tense, she let her anger grow as she heard his fingers fucking her, the sloppy noise of her own juices irritating her. She could hear him panting.

"Oh, yes," he muttered and spun her around, her backside against him. "And I hear you're with child," he continued, his hand under her from the back, fingers in her cunt again. "I'm not happy you let another fill you but that does mean I can now." He shoved her over.

No! Her hands gripped the table. She heard him say her name again and the rustling of fabric. Her tunic flipped up, exposing her ass, the silk of his robe against her legs parting. His hardened cock resting in between her cheeks. He withdrew his fingers and sighed, placing the head of his cock at her slit.

"Gustina, how perfect," he slithered into her.

She wanted to scream, to move, but couldn't. His hands held her hips as he began to stroke in and out. Frantically, she looked for something to use and that's when she saw it. The bowl of fruit and the small knife next to it, its handle barely visible. He moaned behind her and thrust deep into her again.

Her hand strayed to the table. His moans grew and she turned slightly to see his head up. She grabbed the knife right as he chanted, "Oh, yes, yes," and moved his hips faster, bruising the babe with every obscene thrust. No, his seed would not fill her if she had a say. Gripping the weapon, she swung back and hit him. He howled. She pushed further, to the hilt, and her hand hit flesh. Quickly, she yanked it back and stabbed again, this time turning the blade.

The silk robe, a cream colored fabric, turned crimson. Blood poured from the wounds in his side, his hand clasped over the cut.

"You bitch," he snarled and came for her.

With a shriek, she swung again, giving in to her anger, her own demon. There were no longer consequences, no more fear. She'd protect Marcus' unborn child, keep the babe safe from this hideous creature, no matter what. The blade missed him as he bent over and then came again. Furious, she raised her hand and plunged down, hitting his shoulder. The razor-sharp blade sliced into his flesh, like the other two cuts had. But this time, she watched with a morbid fascination as it disappeared into his upper chest.

In anger, he tried to grab her but she sidestepped him. His hand pressing against his side was coated in blood. He spat. "Give me that knife, you stupid cunt."

As he stepped toward her, rage flooded her. For all the times he fucked her. For fucking her now, as if she was nothing. And if he was Marcus' brother, it wasn't Marcus who was the traitor. No. Her body vibrated with madness. No, Terpio was the traitor. With a yell, she swung again. And again. She vaguely heard him groan with pain. "You killed my domina!" she screamed and buried the knife. "You betrayed Marcus!"

Blood. It was everywhere. He was covered in it, groaning. The floor. Her hands and arms. She looked down, her blue tunic was streaked with crimson.

"Gustina!"

Her hand was caught in mid-swing. The voice was familiar. Warm. It took a moment to penetrate her reddened sight. Steady hands pulled her away from Terpio, into an embrace. Strong arms surrounded her as she buried her face in a wall of muscle.

"Shhh," he coaxed, his hand stroking her hair. "Gustina, you're safe."

Marcus. His warmth heated her cold, murderous thoughts and actions. She wanted to get inside him. She hadn't seen him in so long, she feared letting go. He continued to calm her, his hands rubbing her back.

"How did you know?" she asked, her mouth against his chest, her voice muffled.

He chuckled. "Dora."

She nodded. Thank Jupiter for her! But how did he get free, to be able to rescue her?

∞

Marcus couldn't believe the sight before him. Murderous

ravings streamed through him, more than willing to tear Terpio to shreds anyway. If he touched Gustina, he was dead. To enter his brother's room and find her stabbing him, attacking him straight on, stopped him in his tracks. Jupiter, she was covered in blood. The whole room and Terpio looked worse than the Colosseum did after the games.

He could let her finish him. But he decided she'd never be able to live with the grief. She'd been accused of murdering her domina. He doubted that, but killing Terpio was real and they'd both know it.

Within his arms, she was safe. He'd protect her. Prying the knife from her grasp, he glanced down at his brother. The man lay in a heap on the floor but his eyes watched them, warily. Suddenly, he laughed, the sound tinged with madness before he started to cough. Blood seeped from his mouth.

"What a sight, brother," Terpio said. "Both of us fucking the same whore." Another blood-filled laugh. "Not the first time for that either."

Marcus' mouth tightened. Lucilla.

The demon purred as Marcus' fingers wrapped around the knife hilt. *Kill him!*

He pushed Gustina aside and knelt next to Terpio. The gazed look of impending death filled the man's eyes. Perhaps he would indulge and send the ass on to the Afterlife. He pressed the blade to Terpio's neck.

Terpio flinched. "Go on. Do it. But you're wasting time on killing me."

"You killed her, not me!" Gustina yelled.

He laughed again. More blood, only now it came from his ears as well. "I didn't. Found out later it was Lucilla. She used her favorite weapon, poison." He looked at her. "I've wanted you from the start. Loved even," he told Gustina. The gaze turned to Marcus had the look of a madman as he put his own hand on the hilt, over Marcus'. "She lied. Lucilla. The document, everything." His voice faltered, going faint. "You are the son of our father."

The news hit Marcus hard. He wasn't a cast-off then. It took a moment to register the meaning. He wasn't a traitor, a thief. He was an innocent condemned by a conniving whore. But what would Lucilla have gained? He opened his mouth to ask, but as he did, Terpio took the last of his strength and pushed his brother's hand, driving the blade into his neck. Eyes locked on Marcus, he gurgled, more blood spilling from his neck and mouth before he stopped moving. The light in his gaze faded as he left for the Afterlife.

CHAPTER THIRTY-FOUR

Lucilla huffed in indignation. That priestess didn't have any type of connection to the gods. Lucilla knew perfectly well that her machinations would succeed. The fact that the imbecile at Juno's temple eyed her, Senator Lucius Vibenius' wife, as if she were rabble, or worse, a whore, was an insult of the highest level. She'd see the woman boiled in oil over it.

Harrumph! Virgins. What did that woman know? Probably never been fucked a day in her life!

"Tamera," she called, removing the end of her stola from around her head. "Tamera!"

The slave appeared. She approached Lucilla gingerly. "Apologies, domina."

Stupid girl. Lucilla seethed as the girl began to help her unravel the layer and reconnect the bindings for inside use. Frankly, she wanted to slap her but that would not accomplish anything. Still so much to do.

"Wine," she ordered, parting the curtained area near the atrium. She looked up and stopped.

Across the space, leaning against one of the pillars, arms crossed, head cocked, stood Marcus. He was a surprise. No one was with him, not even a guard. How did he get in here? *Surely Aulus hadn't freed him.* But the champion of Rome stood before her, dressed as a gladiator—barechested, subligaculum, and tooled leather and metal balteus around his waist. Greaves and batting on his forearms and legs. All he needed was his gladius. She squinted. He didn't have one, she decided. He wore too little clothes to hide a sword in. His muscles and strength displayed his overpowering might.

Perhaps he was more than a man. What had she heard about him? That he could crush a man's skull between his hands....

Pulling herself upright, she smiled. "Marcus. What a surprise."

He said nothing but a tick in his cheek worked furiously. His gaze was hard with death.

A chill raced down her spine. "To what do I owe the honor of Rome's champion?" She'd act as if he were nothing more than a merchant. His angry glare burned with revenge.

"Why?" he asked.

She frowned. "Whatever do you mean? Why?" The man was a slave, a gladiator no less. Not on his domina's level. And most definitely not a Roman of her high position.

"What did you hope to gain from this venture?" His voice was steady, level even though tinged with authority. She studied him for a moment. This gladiator, who had been her husband once, had changed as a slave. More defined, muscular, hard planes sculpted by hours on the sands. His face, once a soft, Roman patrician façade, erased by the sun, by endurance and tension. Still a handsome man, in a manner of speaking, except his eyes. Once a golden brown, warm and endearing, they now bore an edge of madness. She'd heard of his possession, most of Rome had. And from his appearance now, the rumors were true.

But Lucilla herself knew who held the power, equated the balance between them. She laughed. "Position. I gained position. Something you would never do, even if it arrived at your feet carried by the gods." She stared back at him. He was nothing more than an insect, to be squashed by those far superior.

Unfortunately, he didn't flinch at her cold appraisal. Too bad. She was so going to enjoy torturing him. Taking a grape from the bowl before her, she popped it into her mouth and hummed, her gaze never leaving his.

"If you've come for the cunt, she's gone. I sold her to another, whose fondness for willing and skilled bed slaves will fit her."

Like a predator, his gaze was fixed on her as he pushed himself off the pillar, taking a step toward her. "I doubt your intent was for her to be a whore. Not when she carries the answer to your prayers."

"Ah, I have no desire for females."

"You know that is not what I mean," he seethed as he reached her. He ran his eyes down her body and back to her face. "No, the gods deny you another chance at a child suckling from your breasts. So you plot and plan to steal another's for your deceit."

Her back stiffened. "The gods deny me nothing. They gave me a means to an end without the possible destruction of my body." She shifted on her feet, her finger touching his chest. It was hard, like granite. She traced the planes of his muscles with it, marveling at the feel. Heat formed deep inside her. Despite how much she despised him, she still craved his cock. "Besides, your child would be raised in one of the highest houses in Rome. Surely that is the best option, versus being condemned to slavery, do you not agree?"

༄

Marcus' blood raged. Surely the gods would never allow this. But the end of her argument finally registered in his head. She referred to the child as his. His brow furrowed. No, he dreamt it was Iduma's. As much as he refused to accept it, he was well aware the Brit wanted Gustina again. Jupiter's cock, he saw the man embrace her at the ludas that night of celebration. The man had done well at the games and had been amply rewarded. Marcus figured that included Gustina as well. But she spent her evenings with him, so when? The question tortured his thoughts. A small voice inside, cool and calm, not demonic, insisted that her babe was his afterall.

And this whore before him, the cunt he called wife years before, now meant to take one more thing from him. Gustina's child. He'd kill the witch first.

Kill her!

His demon thudded loudly inside him, humming at the thought of her blood.

It took every amount of energy to stand and keep from outwardly reacting to her jibes. Oh yes, he remembered her well. Control. Lucilla liked control, demanded it. He had fallen under her spell—and so had his brother and Lucius. To fall prey to it again could very well bring Gustina death, but he was no longer that fool.

Her eyes darted about the area and he caught the uneasy

twitch to her mouth.

"I have no need of your services," she stated, eyes narrowed. "I did not send for you. Guards!"

He took a step closer. "I came because you have commanded it." A simple statement, truth seeping at the edges. In the past, she called for his cock after every win. Now, her deceitful actions became her summons.

A hurried laugh escaped her rouged lips. "Ignorance doesn't become you. I just stated I no longer need your seed in me. I have it in that vessel of a slave. Guards!"

One corner of his mouth curved into a cruel smile. "I came alone."

She squinted. "I see no wooden gladius on you. The mob didn't demand your freedom."

He took another step, he could smell fear rising above her scent of vanilla and honey. She stumbled back but caught herself.

"There is no one to call, Lucilla."

"You are nothing but a slave," she gritted. "I will have you removed."

When she opened her mouth to call again, he chuckled. Even to his own ears, the sound was filled with the promise of retribution.

"Your position has been eliminated." He took another step. "Your guards are gone…"

He heard her sudden intake of breath. Pleased, he continued. "Your slaves abandoned you to the champion of Rome." Standing before her, he shook his head. "All those years, all those people you've destroyed to gain your position…all for naught now."

Lucilla's jaw tightened as she glared. "Your bitch is one of them. Terpio desires her death."

Anger threatened to overtake him. Controlling it, he stepped into her space. She backed away from his advance till she hit the marble pillar. "Yes, my dear brother. You've done your job well," he snarled.

Breathing hard, she frowned, lost by his comment.

Behind him, he heard Gustina enter the area from the entrance he did. Lucilla's mouth fell agape and his demon danced. Despite her own turmoil, Gustina had followed him to Lucilla's from Terpio's. She was still covered in his blood.

Lucilla's horrified look gave Marcus intense pleasure.

"She is fine." He watched Lucilla's face drain to ash white. "My brother revealed an interesting bit of information about me. Would you care to hear it?"

Her mouth tightened and her gaze narrowed, centering on him. "Terpio is a liar."

"Interesting words," he pressed her against the marble without touching her. "He claimed you were one, before he took his life."

Shock flickered across her eyes. "He's dead by his own accord?"

He ignored her question. "There was more delivered. Why? Why did you do it? What did you hope to gain?"

She trembled, fighting for control over her emotions.

No, he refused her that wall to hide behind. Reaching up, he grasped her neck. "Why?" He squeezed tight. The throat beneath his hand vibrated as she struggled to breathe.

"You are nothing," she shuddered in gasps. "Not you. Not that slug brother."

Marcus' vision of the woman before him turned blood red, blackness at the edges as he pressed into her skin. Her lips turned a fascinating shade of pink as her skin turned whiter, gasping for air.

Kill her!

"Marcus," a soft voice called, the light touch of a feminine hand on his bare back. Gustina. Her warmth seeped into him, calming his killing edge—the anger that pumped viciously as he closed his hand around Lucilla's throat. He glared at his former wife. Eyes large, mouth wide open, struggling to breathe. Fear and panic reflected in her eyes and her face was ashen. Gone was the haute beauty. The monstrousness of her revealed at last. He reveled in it. But the pressure on his back brought him back from madness.

With a final squeeze and a slam of her skull against the marble, he released her, quickly stepping out of her path as she fell to the floor.

"You don't deserve an easy way out," he sneered at her. The tickle of hair teased at his arm and he snaked his arm around Gustina, hugging her tightly, her presence steadying him. For a moment, he'd forget about the whore and hold the woman he loved.

The one who carried his child.

A strangled laughter came from the floor. Lucilla rubbed her neck, still red from his hand. "I'll see you dead for this. A runaway slave? Trying to kill a Roman senator's wife? I'll see both of you crucified."

"I think not," a voice from across the room stated boldly.

Marcus and Gustina turned. Lucius stood there, the look on his face stern, as if he was in the senate debating strongly over an issue. His eyes, though, held a murderous gleam. The sound of a scroll crunching in his palm, echoed in the silence. Marcus frowned. Terpio had mentioned documents. Now the senator held a set as he stormed into the room.

Lucius stopped before Marcus and Gustina. Handing the scroll forward, he said, "Marcus Flavus, I believe you'll want these. It is your father's correct will and the one forged by Lucilla. In it, you will also discover your true lineage, absolving any charges held against you. It is your freedom." He smiled at Gustina as his fingers lifted her chin and his thumb wiped at her wet cheek. "Poor Gustina. I am sorry to have allowed you to suffer the abuse of my wife. I grant you your freedom as well. You two are citizens of a Republic that in itself is right and just." He glared at Lucilla. "And corrects its errors created by devious creatures."

Gustina's sob registered in Marcus' ears. Holding her tight, he tried to calm her tremors. She'd been through so much, he needed to get her out of here. With a nod to Lucius, he took the scroll and Gustina and walked away.

Behind them, he heard Lucius tell Lucilla, "As for you, I absolve my marriage to you. You will leave here with only your clothes that you brought with you. No slaves. No coin. And understand my intentions well—Rome will hear of your devious attempts to deceive us all."

"Lucius!"

"Get out." The senator passed them before they reached the curtains.

"Lucius! No!" she wailed loudly in anger until the praetorian guard came in. They passed Marcus and Gustina as if they were statues. They closed in on Lucilla, grabbed her, and pulled her to her feet. She screamed.

Terror filled Lucilla. How had this happened? Terpio's treachery worked against him. He was dead, according to Marcus. Under normal circumstances, she would have laughed at his stupidity but now she trembled, his rage slashing at her from the Afterlife. He must have told Lucius about the papers. Damn it all! She'd hidden them so well, she thought no one would find them. Except a slave.... He must have sent that one he trusted. Sisera. And it was true, the man could read.

Numbness encased her as the guard dragged her down the streets. She felt nothing, just an occasional sharp poke from a stone or, perhaps, a sword piercing her insides from the gods. Her cleverness was supposed to have elevated her position in society. And now everything was taken from her. Lucius dissolved their marriage. His protection. She cringed.

Suddenly, she fell to the hard pavement from a shove. It woke her from her confused thoughts and she looked around. The guards had dropped her in the middle of town where all the whores were housed. Horrified, she glanced about. Several men heard the commotion and her cry as they let go of her. The drunkards leered and staggered closer, filthy, disgusting, reeking of stale wine and sweat. They encircled her. When the first one reached out, laughing, and grabbed her stola, ripping it off her, another's hand clasped her breast. Her terror screeched through the air loudly.

※

Marcus took Gustina far away from Lucius and the direction he knew they'd take Lucilla. The cunt deserved the ongoing sentence of being fucked by anyone of the lower ranks, the type that visited whores of her nature.

He headed to his father's villa, several blocks away from the city proper. It was a home Terpio had not used, nor gotten rid of. Strange, but Marcus was glad. Inside the darkened building, he stopped, allowing his eyes to adjust. A smile came to him. Terpio had simply shut the doors. Furniture remained as it had always been. He set Gustina on a lounge and turned to light a lamp but her hand stopped him.

"Don't leave me." It sounded like a whimper.

"We need light," he said.

"No, stay. I can see. I need to feel you."

He sat and pulled her into his arms. With her head tucked

under his chin, he sighed. *His woman.*

"Marcus," she said, freeing herself. "There's something I must tell you."

"Shhh," he murmured. "Later."

"No." She pushed at his chest. Even in the dark, he saw the dried blood on her neck and chest. He'd bathe her and then...she interrupted his thoughts. "I am with child. Your child."

He blinked. Lucilla indicated it. Terpio said it. But since both of them were born liars, he didn't believe it. He saved Gustina. Did she feel the need to try to convince him Iduma's babe was his? His own mind refused to recognize the possibility it was his. "It's fine. I'll raise Iduma's as if the babe's mine."

The sound of a slap echoed in the quiet chamber as her hand made contact with his chest. "The babe is yours. Iduma was once, long ago. I know, as a woman would, that it isn't his." She moved to his side, grabbed his hand and placed it over her babe. "Yours." A small grin quavered at her lips.

The hardened bulge beneath his fingers intrigued him. A child. Lucilla never liked being laden with his child. Rid herself of it as soon as possible. But Gustina sounded proud, happy. Could he believe her? Did it matter?

"May the gods strike me dead if I'm wrong." She tried again to smile.

He snorted. "I believe you. And this makes you happy?"

She snuggled next to him, her fingers dancing on his chest, her leg wrapped over him. "Yes. Because I love you."

His heart swelled. Inside, the demon that lurked for years, prodding him, cajoling him to kill, went mute. A wave of contentment washed over him. The gods appeared to give him a gift. Her. He tipped her chin up so he could look into her eyes. Those blue gems were dark, beckoning.

"Gustina, I love you. I will love you forever," he promised softly and bent to kiss her. As he pressed against her lips, his tongue traced the seam, parting them. He heard her sigh as she opened her mouth, surrendering to him. Her love poured into him and he embraced her tightly. He'd never let her go.

The demon inside him faded away, its mission done. Marcus' heart began to beat again. They found what all had sought, their love was forged under the Roman sun, polished by blood and sand.

Gustina pulled back, took Marcus' hand and pressed it against her stomach. He stilled, as if afraid to touch her. She pressed his hand tighter, watching his look of surprise turn to wonder, a smile spreading across his face. And deep inside, she shivered as her child fluttered at his father's touch.

Author's Notes on **Love & Vengeance** in the world of Ancient Rome

The Roman Empire existed for centuries, existing as a republic and an empire during the late BCE to roughly 300 CE when Rome fell and the now Christianized Emperor Constantine moved his people to Byzantium, today's Istanbul. Rome itself is a fascinating place during this time. Considered the head of the civilized world, it held a large population, over a million souls, by the time of Emperor Trajan. To live in Rome was to be part of a dynamic that still resonates today.

I've always been fascinated by Rome. My father's family from Sicily originally sprang from Italy itself so no doubt family leaned me toward my interest in it. Then the movie *Gladiator* splashed across the screen and made the past more real. Starz took it a step further with its series *Spartacus*. These two made me yearn to write of the period and its people, leading to *Love & Vengeance*.

As a historian, it wasn't enough to just tell the story but to try to make 108 CE spring to life around the reader. For the city itself, Alberto Angela's book, *A day in the Life of Ancient Rome* gave an in-depth feel for the city, how it was arranged, how people lived and worked. As to the gladiatorial games, Konstantin Nossov's *Gladiator, Rome's Bloody Spectacle*, Fix Meijer's *The Gladiators* and Philip Matyszak *Gladiator, The Roman Fighter's Unofficial Manual* brought the games and their participants to life. The execution Marcus witnessed, the condemned subjected to beasts, is an actual execution and its outcome in the Colosseum.

During this time, the language used in *Love & Vengeance* is as close as possible to the real thing. What we consider "cuss words" were not necessarily considered such then. The baths, particularly Trajan's Bathhouse is portrayed as the real one was, the bikini outfit Lucilla wore is exactly how Roman women dressed for the public baths. Physical activity was also part of the daily routine for Romans. Researching the Roman gods is a whirlwind of numerous deities that the Romans adopted from other culture added to their own. They felt they were the rightful owners of the Greek Empire, hence they adopted Greek gods, sometimes giving them Roman names (Zeus now Jupiter) plus they 'rescued' many Greek statues, inserting them into Rome to be appreciated and admired as Rome's own.

Trajan's period was considered one of the most enlightened times of the Empire, with an expanding economy, more lands conquered and more praising Rome. Unfortunately, Rome's darker side did include rituals like gladiatorial games, babies abandoned outside the city and left to die because of their illegitimacy or other reasons, and fanhood of gladiator champions—including the women who followed their favorites by buying trinkets of theirs or even sleeping with them or taking their blood to cure the ill. Some of the books to explore life then include:

As the Romans Did by Jo-Ann Shelton
The Caesars by Suetonius
Roman Sex by John C. Clarke
Roman Housing by Simon P. Ellis
Peoples of the Roman World by Mary T. Boatwright
Everyday Life in Ancient Rome by Lionel Casson
The Gods of Ancient Rome by Robert Turcan
Handbook to Life in Ancient Rome by Lesley Adkins & Roy A. Adkins
Plus many more.

For more on Rome and other stories, please visit ginadanna.com

Gratitude. *Gina*

ABOUT GINA DANNA

Born in St. Louis, Missouri, Gina Danna has spent the better part of her life reading. History has been her love and she spent numerous hours devouring historical romance stories, dreaming of writing one of her own. Years later, after receiving undergraduate and graduate degrees in History, writing academic research papers and writing for museum programs and events, she finally found the time to write her own stories of historical romantic fiction.

Now, under the supervision of her three dogs and three cats, she writes amid a library of research books, and her only true break away is to spend time with her other lifelong dream—her Arabian horse. With him, her muse can play. Please visit her at ginadanna.com

If you enjoyed Gina Danna's *Love & Vengeance,*
please consider telling others and writing a review.

Made in the USA
Las Vegas, NV
25 October 2021